'Martin is not only one of the finest crime writers of his generation. He is the heir to Julian Symons and H.R.F. Keating as the leading authority on our genre, fostering and promoting it with unflagging enthusiasm, to the benefit of us all. I'm delighted that our community can show its gratitude by honouring him in this way.'

Peter Lovesey

'Martin Edwards is a wonderful choice to receive the Diamond Dagger. He's a very fine writer but has also devoted huge energy to both the CWA and Detection Club – all done quietly and companionably, which is a rare thing. I love a man who takes care of archives. I am delighted for him, but as we always say: it's for lifetime achievement – but please don't stop what you do so well!'

Lindsey Davis

'Martin Edwards is not only a fine writer but he is also ridiculously knowledgeable about the field of crime and suspense fiction. He wears his learning lightly and is always the most congenial company. He is also a great champion of crime writing and crime writers. His novels feature an acute sense of place as well as deep psychological insights. As a solicitor, he knows the legal world more intimately than most of his fellow novelists. He is a fitting winner of the Diamond Dagger.'

Ian Rankin

BY MARTIN EDWARDS

The Lake District Mysteries

The Coffin Trail
The Cipher Garden
The Arsenic Labyrinth
The Serpent Pool
The Hanging Wood
The Frozen Shroud
The Dungeon House
The Crooked Shore

The Harry Devlin Series

All the Lonely People
Suspicious Minds
I Remember You
Yesterday's Papers
Eve of Destruction
The Devil in Disguise
First Cut is the Deepest
Waterloo Sunset

The Rachel Savernake Series

Gallows Court
Mortmain Hall
Blackstone Fell

Fiction

Take My Breath Away
Dancing for the Hangman

Non-Fiction

Catching Killers
Truly Criminal
The Golden Age of Murder
The Story of Classic Crime in 100 Books
The Life of Crime

BF

BLACKSTONE FELL

MARTIN EDWARDS

HEAD of ZEUS

An Aries Book

First published in the UK in 2022 by Head of Zeus
This paperback edition first published in 2023 by Head of Zeus,
part of Bloomsbury Publishing Plc

9 7 5 3 1 2 4 6 8

A catalogue record for this book is available from the British Library.

ISBN (PB): 9781801100229
ISBN (E): 9781801100236

Cover design: Edward Bettison

Printed and bound in Great Britain by
CPI Group (UK) Ltd, Croydon CR0 4YY

MIX
Paper | Supporting
responsible forestry
FSC® C171272
FSC
www.fsc.org

Head of Zeus Ltd
5–8 Hardwick Street
London EC1R 4RG

WWW.HEADOFZEUS.COM

Dedicated to Dea Parkin, my partner in 'Crafting Crime'

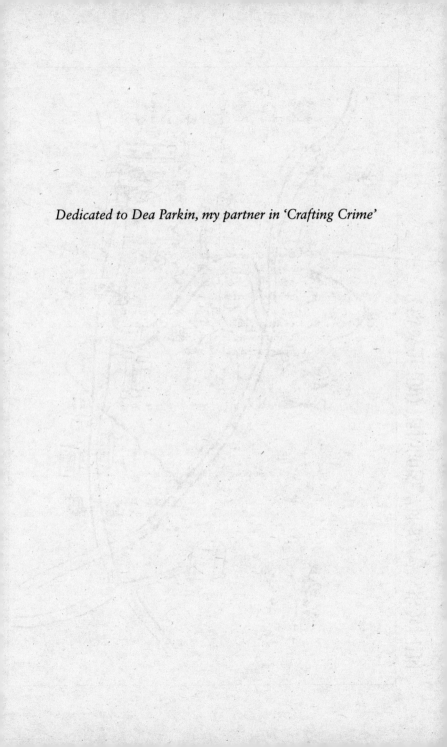

NELL FAGAN'S MAP OF BLACKSTONE FELL (NOT TO SCALE)

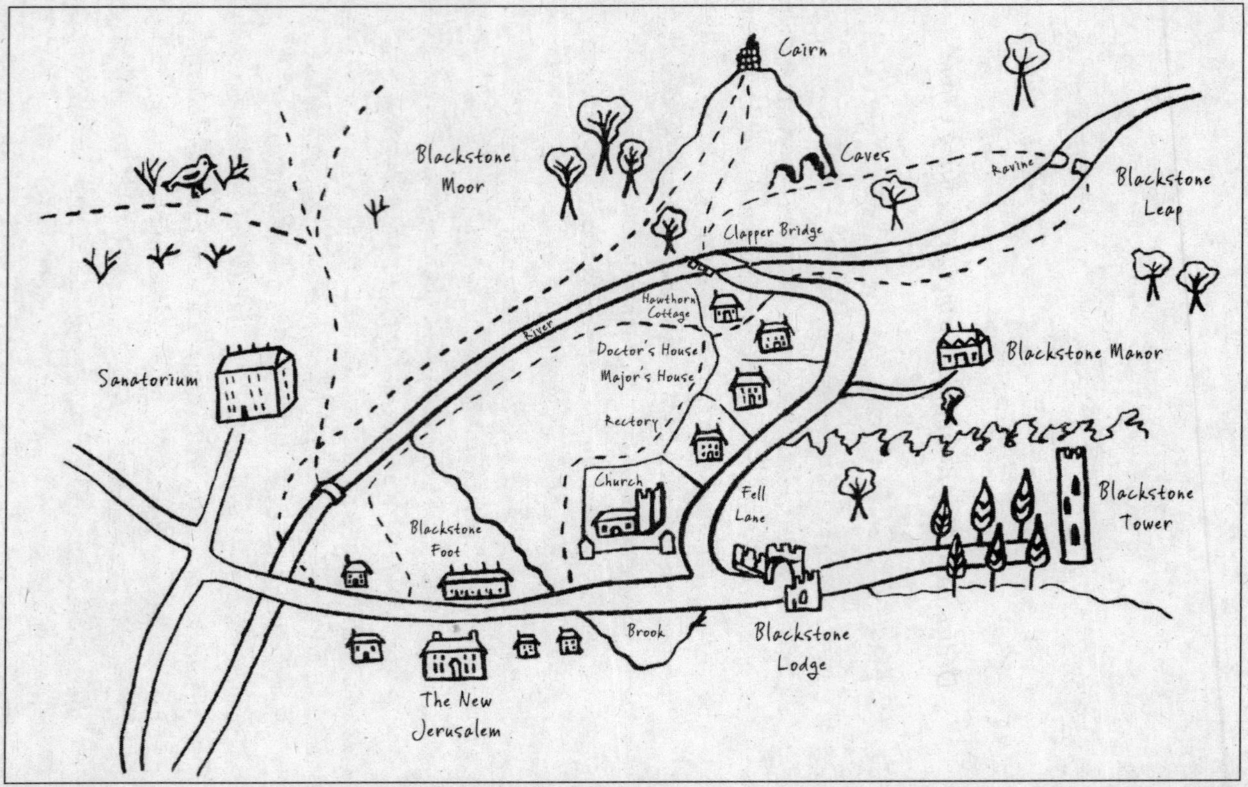

I

'Seeing isn't always believing.'

Nell Fagan was talking to herself. She stood on a wide ledge of rock, a natural platform jutting out from Blackstone Fell. Under a low autumn sun, this remote corner of the Pennines masqueraded as a green and pleasant land. Beech leaves gleamed golden in the ravine below. A river rushed from the gorge past the village which shared its name with the Fell. Mellow light bathed the grey stone of manor house, rectory, church, and graveyard. Beyond the church, a tall round tower cast long shadows.

Her mind whirled. Could she believe the evidence of her own eyes, or was her vivid imagination playing a cruel trick? She'd hoped the peace and quiet up here would help to straighten out her thoughts, but she lacked Rachel Savernake's cool head. If only she had someone to confide in, to help her make sense of the apparently impossible; but she'd misjudged her approach to Rachel and made an enemy of her. In any case Rachel was in London, and so was Peggy, her oldest and closest friend. Nell was on her own, two hundred miles from home. The Smoke and the Slump belonged to a different world.

Nobody in Blackstone Fell knew who she was or how she earned a living. Far less that murder had brought her here. She'd adopted a false name and was pretending to be an ardent photographer. It gave her a good excuse to poke around, snapping pictures of people and places at every opportunity.

Last night she'd walked down to the lower village to wet her whistle at The New Jerusalem. The public bar was a stronghold of taciturn masculinity, but she'd made her way in a man's world, and the old curmudgeons weren't going to intimidate her. Even if she was no diplomat, nobody could accuse her of lacking courage or self-belief. Announcing herself as the new tenant of Blackstone Lodge, she insisted on standing everyone a round of drinks.

She was bursting with curiosity about her new home, she explained. What was this story about its strange past? Why had nobody ever lived there until now? Had people really disappeared without trace? Should she be afraid? The regulars responded with shrugs and vague mutterings and turned their attention back to the dartboard. If an outsider was stupid enough to rent a place with such wretched history, that was her lookout.

The rector's wife was right, Nell thought. Judith Royle maintained that the villagers gave nothing away to strangers. Certainly not to an ungainly Londoner who reeked of tobacco and gin and could talk the hind legs off a donkey. When she wondered aloud about what went on inside Blackstone Sanatorium, nobody paid any attention. If the R101 had crashed on Blackstone Moor the other day, rather than a French field, they'd barely have spared the airship a glance before getting back to their dominoes and shove ha'penny.

She felt an unexpected chill. The sunshine was deceptive, like Blackstone Fell. A gust of wind rattled the tripod on which her camera perched precariously. It was a Vest Pocket Kodak in a vivid shade known as Redbreast. To be on the safe side, she unscrewed the camera from the tripod.

A sudden cacophony shattered the silence, deafening enough to make her bones rattle. She glanced up. A huge lump of rock was thundering down the jagged slope, heading straight for her. Throwing herself backwards, she lost her balance. She collapsed in a heap and the camera slipped from her hand. The boulder missed her head by inches and smashed the tripod to smithereens.

The shock dazed her. Her ears were ringing and her ankle hurt. She'd grazed her cheek and bruised her elbow. The taste of blood was on her lips. Heart pounding, she wondered if she'd be buried in an avalanche. She dared not move an inch.

Craning her neck, she stared at the rocky outcrop above her head. Not a soul to be seen. Birds sang in the distance. The breeze ruffled her hair. Nothing else happened.

As the minutes passed, her confidence rose. Gingerly, she shifted her leg. The movement made her wince, but she'd not broken a bone. She was still in one piece.

'Better to be born lucky than rich,' she told herself.

Was the falling boulder a chance event, an act of God? The face of the crag was unstable, loosened by recent storms. When she'd mentioned coming to the Fell to take photographs, the rector's wife had warned of the risks and urged her to keep away. Nell took no notice. Over the years, more than one villain had tried to cause her harm. For an investigative journalist, jeopardy came with the job.

Struggling to her feet, she dusted herself down. The pain in her ankle was easing. Shame about the tripod, but thank goodness her camera was undamaged, even if its red sheen was scarred. At least she'd not lost her precious photographs.

A long soak in her tub would set her right. The descent from the ledge wasn't challenging and she put her best foot forward, only to halt in mid-stride. Placing weight on the damaged leg brought tears to her eyes.

For a good five minutes, she massaged her ankle. Her scuffed satchel had escaped the boulder. She groped inside for her flask and swallowed a mouthful of brandy.

That was better. Fortifying.

She closed her eyes and tried to persuade herself that she was a victim of freakish misfortune. The fall of the boulder was pure bad luck.

In her head she heard Peggy's brisk voice, reproaching her long ago for a childish fib.

'You're not so good at lying as you think. I can see straight through you.'

Stern words. Peggy had become her governess when she was five years old and she never stood for any nonsense, but she didn't mean to be unkind.

Nell couldn't say the same for Rachel Savernake. There was a menacing edge to Rachel's cool disdain. Nell itched to find out more about her. Why was she so fascinated by crime? Nell knew in her bones that a story lurked behind that lovely, enigmatic facade, begging to be told. Unfortunately Rachel guarded her privacy with a ruthless zeal. Their one and only meeting had ended in disaster. She'd felt the lash of Rachel's scorn as the young woman echoed Peggy's old rebuke.

'Did you really imagine that I'd fall for such a tissue of lies? You're only deceiving yourself.'

Nell breathed out. Any journalist worth her salt played games with the truth, but this was no time for wishful thinking. Peggy and Rachel were right. She must be honest, if only with herself. The boulder hadn't crashed down of its own accord.

Someone wanted her dead.

She expelled a long, low sigh. No hope of catching her assailant. This side of the Fell was steep; the climb above the ledge was best left to mountain goats. Out of sight, a gentler ascent from the lower village wound up the far side of the crag to the summit. Yesterday, Nell had lumbered up that way, intent on getting her bearings. At the top, in the teeth of a fierce north wind, she'd steadied herself against a cairn. The boulder was poised on the edge. To shift it wouldn't require great strength. Now that lump of rock had almost killed her.

This ledge was visible to anyone standing close to the cairn. Perhaps someone had climbed Blackstone Fell with murder in mind, or perhaps they merely wanted to spy on her. Nell imagined an enemy catching sight of her as she bent over the bright red camera. Kodak's advertising boasted of its gloriously colourful appearance and urged girl graduates, brides, and debutantes to take up photography. A would-be assassin had found Nell an irresistible target and come close to committing the perfect crime. When her body was found, everyone would presume she'd suffered a tragic misfortune and that the boulder had tumbled of its own accord.

Already, the culprit might be anywhere. Crossing

Blackstone Moor or strolling along the river bank back to the upper village, with no one any the wiser.

Nell took another gulp from the flask.

The brandy burned her throat, a sensation she adored. Alcohol fuelled her self-belief. Squaring her shoulders, she breathed out. Now she knew what she was up against. The attempt on her life proved she was on the right track. Blackstone Fell was home to a killer. Perhaps more than one.

A couple of Woodbines and a dog-eared copy of *The Amateur Photographer* had slipped out of the satchel. She retrieved them and put the camera in its case. If she'd made a false move, she wasn't alone. Her arrival in Blackstone Fell had panicked someone into attempted murder. But she'd lived to tell the tale.

A muddy path forked close to the base of Blackstone Fell. One route zigzagged down to the river. The other led to the mouth of a cave before looping back to re-join the main track at the riverbank, close to the stepping stones at Blackstone Leap.

Nell strode in the opposite direction, away from the ravine. She followed the path along a shelf of land which jutted out above the water and then descended towards the clapper bridge. On the other side of the bridge was a pebbled lane that meandered through the upper village. The river flowed down the sloping land towards the lower village, known as Blackstone Foot. The main path followed the course of the river, while a track branched off and wound back up the incline to meet the lane close to the churchyard. Whoever pushed the boulder had a choice of routes from any part of the village to the far side of the Fell and back again.

Halfway across the bridge, she heard a rifle shot.

She froze. There was nowhere to hide. And nobody in sight. She didn't dare to breathe.

A second shot rang out a few moments later. A distant squealing filled the air.

Looking up, she saw a flurry of birds flying off towards the Tower.

She waited.

Nothing. The tension seeped out of her. She realised where the shooting came from. Yesterday afternoon, the rector's wife had invited her to tea. Judith Royle had mentioned that her husband owned an old rifle, and enjoyed taking pot shots at birds in the rectory orchard or the open countryside.

That must be it. The Reverend Quintus Royle was a man of God. He didn't want to kill her, just a harmless bird or two.

Nell exhaled. Her prejudices about rural England were confirmed. She'd always regarded Wordsworth and Thomas Hardy as overrated. As for the season of mists and mellow fruitfulness…

'Welcome to Blackstone Fell,' she muttered to herself. 'I'd sooner take my chances in Soho.'

Nell headed down the lane. On her right was an empty stone cottage. The land agent had offered her a tenancy, but she'd chosen to rent the tower gatehouse. The cost was a pittance, thanks to Blackstone Lodge's dark history.

Imposing wrought-iron gates on the left marked the entrance to the manor house, home to Professor Sambrook and his two adult children, Denzil and Daphne. At the turn of the century, the professor was renowned as Britain's leading alienist, a rival to Freud, Adler, and Jung. Shortly after building Blackstone Sanatorium to treat his patients and conduct research, his wife had been killed in a car accident. For the past twenty-five years he'd shunned the outside world.

Nell was itching to discover what went on inside Blackstone Sanatorium. She had a prejudice against psychiatry – witchcraft for the intellectual classes – but she'd come here to follow up a curious lead. Was something sinister going on behind those high stone walls out on the windswept moor?

Now something else had happened, something that—

A dark blue car roared out of a gateway, swinging past her nose and into the lane. The shock made her stagger and the driver gave a belated fanfare on his horn.

'Hey!' she bellowed. 'You could have killed me!'

He screeched to a halt. The car had shot out from the grounds of a house opposite Blackstone Manor. Its sleek appearance and acceleration were worthy of Le Mans. Turning in his seat, the driver pulled off his goggles and waved at Nell.

'Awfully sorry!' he called. 'She really is a fast lady. Keeps taking me by surprise.'

'Me too,' Nell growled.

'A thousand apologies.' The man's grin was undeniably engaging. 'We met yesterday afternoon when I called at the rectory. Mrs Royle introduced us.'

'Of course I remember, Dr Carrodus.'

As she approached the car, she was conscious of his scrutiny. 'That's quite a limp. Surely I didn't wing you? I'd never forgive myself. I'm supposed to heal people, not hurt them.'

'Don't worry, you're not to blame.'

'You've not been hopping over Blackstone Leap? Those stepping stones are lethal.'

'Tripped as I was making my way down the Fell.' The untruth rolled off her tongue with the ease of long practice. 'Wrecked my tripod, but I'm still in one piece.'

If Carrodus had missed her with the boulder and then failed to run her over, he seemed remarkably sanguine about her survival. He was a bachelor on the right side of thirty whose good humour and faint Welsh lilt contributed to his charm. He lacked the professional gravitas of an elderly physician, but Nell was willing to bet he had an admirable bedside manner. The rector's wife certainly seemed taken with him.

'With any luck, you've nothing to worry about. Tweaked muscle rather than a sprain. Apply a cold compress and for heaven's sake, rest up. As for that graze on your cheek, give it a good wash and a touch of iodine, and you'll be right as rain. I'd offer to take a look-see in the surgery, but I'm late for my weekly clinic at the sanatorium and after that I've got a long drive.'

'Thank you, Doctor, but I'm a quick healer. I'll be running around in no time.' She assumed a serious expression. 'Not like those poor souls cooped up in the sanatorium.'

'Don't you worry, they are in the best possible hands. Professor Sambrook is a leader in his field.'

'So I hear.'

'Brilliant mind, but his academic papers go over my head. Frankly, I'm flattered that he allows a humble village GP to darken his doors.' He guffawed. 'Between you and me, I feel like a Jung pretender.'

He was so delighted with his pun that Nell felt obliged to laugh. 'I wonder…'

'Sorry, must dash!' He waved. 'And watch your step in future. Cheerio!'

His eyes vanished behind the goggles and he sped off in a cloud of fumes.

Watch your step.

Many a true word, Nell thought. Rounding a bend, she spotted Major Huckerby in his shirt sleeves. He was up on a ladder, trimming the holly hedge that separated his garden from the rectory. They'd chatted earlier, as she wandered around on a reconnaissance of the village, taking photographs at every opportunity. He was a widower and she diagnosed loneliness; his pleasantries had an undertow of melancholy. Perhaps she was reading too much into a single conversation. Peggy always said she let herself get carried away too often for her own good.

The major waved his shears in greeting.

'You're hobbling,' he called.

'Nothing serious.'

'Young Carrodus didn't send you flying with that flashy new Lagonda of his?'

She smiled. 'Turned my ankle on the Fell. My own stupid fault.'

Major Huckerby's dark hair was liberally flecked with grey. Twenty years the doctor's senior, he remained a fine figure of a man despite an incipient paunch. Nell had a romantic vision of him striding across a parade ground, immaculate in military uniform, medals gleaming in the sunlight.

'Glad to hear it. Carrodus is a decent cove, but the way he tears around the country is a damned menace. Anyone would think his name was Henry Segrave.'

'And look what happened to poor Sir Henry,' Nell said. 'Such a shocking waste. There was simply no need to kill himself. Why on earth do people throw away their lives for no good reason?'

The major's brow furrowed. He lifted the shears as if to shoo her away before resuming his onslaught on the hedge. As she limped past the lychgate of St Agnes Church, Nell wondered if somehow she'd offended him.

Blackstone Tower reared up ahead of her, above an avenue of ancient black poplars. Even on a lovely afternoon, it seemed to brood over the village, menacing and malign. The man who owned the Tower had a demeanour to match. Nell had encountered him that morning. Powerfully built with thinning grey hair and a grizzled beard, he'd strode down the lane as she demonstrated to the major how her camera worked. The major's friendly greeting was met with a long, hard stare at the pair of them. Nell felt as if she were being hypnotised. Finally, she and the major were dismissed with a brusque nod.

'Curmudgeonly fellow, Harold Lejeune,' Major Huckerby had murmured. 'I suppose one must make allowances. Believe me, grief hits a man hard.'

And not only men, Nell thought grimly.

'Miss Grace!'

Nell was lost in thought. Once she got back to London, should she swallow her pride and try to enlist Rachel Savernake's aid?

'Miss Grace!' The voice became shrill. 'Did you hear me?'

Nell swore. She'd thought she'd heard *disgrace*. That was the trouble with using an alias. It was so easy to forget who you were pretending to be.

Looking over her shoulder, she saw the rector's wife rushing towards her. Nell switched on a smile to compensate for her rudeness.

'Hello, there! Sorry about that, Mrs Royle.' The woman glared at her. 'Daydreaming, don't you know?'

Judith Royle's golden curls were tucked out of sight beneath a brown hat as shapeless as her coat. She was as demure as a Madonna, but dressed dowdily, as if to apologise for her svelte figure. Stuck-in-the-mud parishioners no doubt disapproved of her on principle. Nell had pigeonholed Judith as a church mouse, cowering in the angular shadow of the Reverend Quintus Royle, permanently anxious and pathetically eager to please.

Not this afternoon. The delicate features were crimson with anger.

'Didn't you recognise your own name?'

Nell took a step back. This combative response was as alarming as it was unexpected.

'I'm sorry,' she repeated. 'I didn't hear—'

'It must be a peculiar experience,' Judith Royle said through gritted teeth, 'to accustom oneself to a false identity.'

It wasn't in Nell's nature to remain on the defensive. Over the years, she'd faced down foes much more formidable than a rector's wife.

'You must excuse me, Mrs Royle. I haven't the faintest idea what you're talking about.'

'It's quite simple. You are not Cornelia Grace, are you?'

Nell frowned. 'Indeed I am. Cornelia is my baptismal name. Though when I'm at home in London, everyone calls me Nell.'

Judith Royle's mouth set in a stubborn line. In a low voice, she said, 'I'm not a fool.'

'Perish the thought. A simple enough mistake for anyone to—'

'Please, don't make this any more difficult. You're not the person you claim to be.'

'Why do you say that?' Nell adopted a self-righteous tone. 'I can only presume you're labouring under a misapprehension.'

Judith Royle shook her head. Nell was perplexed. This woman wasn't the sort to say boo to a goose. What was going on? Better find out before matters got out of hand.

'Listen, it's chilly now the sun has gone in. Why don't you come to the Lodge? I'd love to repay the hospitality you showed me yesterday. We can have a natter over a nice cup of tea.'

The rector's wife wavered. 'I don't...'

'Please. Let me set your mind at rest.'

'Oh, all right.' Marriage to the rector, a joyless puritan twice her age, must have accustomed her to giving in. 'But I can't be out long.'

'Then we'd better get a move on.'

Beyond the church, the lane turned and began its descent to the lower village. Nell and Judith Royle crossed over to an unmade track leading to an arched stone gateway. To the left of the arch was a high stone wall, on the right was the gatehouse. Blackstone Lodge was in the Gothic style, irregular in construction and adorned with battlements. The effect was lopsided and disconcerting, as if the architect had indulged in a private joke.

'I always wondered what it's like inside,' Judith Royle said.

Her voice was trembling and so was she. As Nell fumbled in her bag for her door key, she glanced at her companion. Sometimes seeing *was* believing. The expression on that pale Madonna's face spoke for itself.

Judith Royle was scared to death.

2

Blackstone Lodge was draughty and smelled of damp. Nell lit the fire in the cramped sitting room before putting the kettle on. The ceiling was low, the floor uneven, the windows so small that even on a fine day they let in very little light. The furniture was cheap, the rough walls whitewashed. In this spartan setting, the only decorative touch was a carved design on the ancient wooden fireplace surround: *aabaaabbaabaaababaaaabbbb*.

Nell tossed another log onto the blaze. 'Sorry I can't offer as much comfort as the rectory. Strange to think, this little place is so old, yet I'm the first person who has ever actually lived here.'

Judith Royle didn't reply. She'd shrunk into the shabby armchair, as if drained by the effort of confrontation. Her own home was far from cosy, all dark panels and flickering candles, its gloom matching the rector's austere manner. Judith had called to invite Nell for afternoon tea as soon as she'd arrived. Nell had jumped at the opportunity to quiz the rector's wife about Blackstone Fell and its inhabitants.

Nell settled down opposite her guest, glad to take the weight off her sore ankle, and stirred plenty of sugar into her tea. She had a sweet tooth, and often reflected that if she didn't give in to it so readily, she wouldn't be so heavy and unfit. Her trouble was that self-awareness always came more easily than self-improvement.

'Now then,' she said. 'We don't want any crossed wires, do we? Not after you've been so welcoming. Please let me put your mind at rest.'

She gave a beatific smile. Before setting foot in Blackstone Fell, she'd armed herself with a cover story in case anyone questioned her credentials. While making the tea, she'd rehearsed the familiar lines in her head. They sounded plausible enough to her.

Judith Royle cleared her throat. 'Your name isn't Cornelia Grace. And you're not a photographer, either.'

'Who told you that?'

'Please don't prevaricate.'

'I take a great many pictures,' Nell said.

'Not a professional photographer, anyway.'

Nell sighed. 'Did I give you that impression? Perhaps I was carried away with enthusiasm. I'm just a keen amateur.'

'Who are you, really? And what are you doing in Blackstone Fell?'

'I'll tell you the truth,' Nell lied. 'Though I'd be grateful if you didn't mention this conversation to… anyone else in the village.'

Judith's expression gave nothing away. 'This is strictly between ourselves.'

Is it really? Nell asked herself as she took a sip of tea. She didn't believe she was the only fibber in the room.

'As it happens, my full name is Cornelia Grace Fagan. I'm a journalist. Over the years I've written for several daily newspapers.'

The rector's wife leaned closer, allowing Nell to breathe in her lavender perfume. 'What brings a reporter from London to Blackstone Fell?'

'I'm happy to share my secret with you,' Nell said. 'First, though, I'd like to know why you ask. All these questions have come… rather out of the blue.'

Judith pursed her lips. 'I suppose you're entitled to know.'

Nell drank some more tea as she waited for the younger woman to compose her thoughts.

'You see, I received a letter.'

Nell blinked. 'About me?'

'Yes, one of those horrid anonymous things. A crude message made out of words and letters cut from a newspaper and stuck on a blank sheet.'

For once in her life, Nell was at a loss for words.

'You mean… a poison pen letter?'

'That's right.'

'May I see it?'

'I told you what the message said.'

'I think,' Nell said, 'it's the least you can do. If someone's besmirching my good name, I'm entitled to be given chapter and verse.'

Judith hesitated. 'I suppose there's no harm in showing you.'

'No,' Nell said piously. 'The damage is already done.'

Judith fumbled in her handbag. She fished out a piece of paper and held it up for Nell to read. Printed letters and words were pasted erratically on the sheet.

'*Cornelia Grace is not her real name. She is an impostor and up to no good.*'

Nell sniffed the document, as if to discern the foul stench of libel. Judith Royle raised her eyebrows and stuffed the paper back into her handbag.

'Why would anyone send this to you?' Nell asked.

A touch of colour appeared in Judith's cheeks. 'It wasn't addressed to me specifically. Our maid found it on the doormat and brought it in to me while Quintus was out of the house, visiting a sick parishioner in Blackstone Foot.'

'Why bother the rector and his wife with something so distasteful and defamatory?'

'Blackstone Fell is a small place,' Judith said. 'The church is at the heart of the community. Word gets around fast. Everyone will know you visited the rectory.'

'Was your husband's name on the envelope?'

'There... there wasn't an envelope. The sheet was folded; you saw the crease.'

'Then the maid may have read it?'

'I can't imagine for a single moment that Myrtle would do something like that.' Judith sounded as shocked as if Nell had growled an obscenity. 'She's frightened... no, in awe of Quintus. I'm sure she wouldn't dare.'

'So you read the message and decided to have it out with me?'

'Well, yes. I mean, it's an unpleasant business, but you know what they say. No smoke without fire. Nobody would invent such an accusation.'

'What does your husband have to say about it?'

'I haven't discussed it with him.' As Judith lifted her cup, her hand shook. Some of the tea splashed into the saucer. 'Or anyone else.'

Nell gave her a hard stare. 'Glad to hear it. The laws about disseminating a libel apply in the backwaters of northern England, just as they do in Fleet Street.'

'I thought it best...' Judith's voice faltered. 'I decided to speak to you first and find out what you are up to.'

'I'm beginning to understand.'

Beginning, yes, but that was all. Nell was sure that Judith Royle had written the anonymous note herself. The real question was: why?

Dr Carrodus put the stethoscope back in his black bag. 'Nothing to worry about, sir.'

Professor Wilfred Sambrook buttoned up his twill shirt. He was a tall, thin man in his mid-sixties, with a high, furrowed brow and a goatee beard. Both his eyes were pale blue, but one of them was made of glass. He would have seemed even taller but for a stoop. Scoliosis, Carrodus reckoned, though the old fellow would have none of it. A lifetime devoted to studying disorders of the mind had left him with minimal interest in matters of physical health, even his own.

'The headaches and breathlessness I've experienced are not significant, in your judgement?'

'Not in the least, sir. You simply need to remember that you're not as young as you were. Take it easy, make sure you get plenty of rest, and you'll outlive us all.'

The professor snorted. They were in his oak-panelled room on the first floor of Blackstone Sanatorium. Framed scrolls and certificates from Oxford, Paris, Berlin, and Vienna covered the wall behind his vast mahogany desk, testaments to his international renown. They dated back upwards of a quarter of a century. Learned tomes crammed floor-to-ceiling bookshelves. A bronze bust of the great man in his younger days occupied pride of place on the top of a large bureau.

'Better safe than sorry,' the doctor said. 'By all means seek a second opinion if you're anxious. It won't offend me in the slightest.'

The older man's good eye wandered around the room, as if he was bored. 'I'm not in the least anxious. I merely thought that as you were here in any event…'

'Quite, quite.' Carrodus picked up his bag. 'No trouble at all, sir. I'll get on my way and let you get back to your work.'

The professor's gaze settled on the leather-bound volume on his desk. Carrodus gave a small bow and said goodbye, but received no answer.

In the corridor he bumped into Denzil Sambrook. He was a doctor of philosophy rather than of medicine, and even taller and thinner than his father, with the same domed forehead and a receding hairline.

'How did you get on?' he asked.

'He'll see us all out if he takes proper care of himself,' Carrodus said cheerfully.

'The one thing he never does,' Denzil murmured.

'Overwork, that's my diagnosis.' Carrodus sighed. 'Don't want to speak out of turn, old chap, but why does he bother? From what you've told me, he hasn't published anything for decades, and hasn't given a lecture in donkey's years.'

Denzil nodded. 'He's obsessed with his researches, but they seem to go around in ever-decreasing circles.'

'Why doesn't he put his feet up? With all due respect, it's not as if the sanatorium is overflowing with patients. He could leave everything in your capable hands.'

'Nothing would please me more. We need fresh thinking. Not just in the sanatorium, but everywhere. Society is in a mess. We could…' Denzil shook his head. 'Better not get on my soapbox or I'll keep you here for hours. Between you and me, my father simply isn't the man he was. This past few weeks, he's gone rapidly downhill.'

Carrodus frowned. 'You think so?'

'Yes, it isn't so much these headaches and breathing difficulties. It's his state of mind. He's convinced he's on the verge of some mythical breakthrough in his work. Utter delusion. I've begged him to hand over the reins to me, but he's dug in his heels. He won't let go.'

A door opened down the corridor and a woman moved briskly towards them. Daphne Sambrook was a foot shorter than her brother. Small eyes peered from behind tortoiseshell spectacles. At close quarters, Carrodus glimpsed the jagged scar on her forehead that thick, curly hair, mousy brown in colour, did not quite conceal.

'Well, Dr Carrodus?' she demanded.

'Hello, Daphne,' the doctor said. 'Your father works too hard, that's the top and bottom of it.'

'Don't tell me,' she said ironically. 'You've prescribed plenty of rest.'

'You may mock,' he said in genial reproof, 'but the simple cures are the most effective. Mother Nature knows a thing or two.'

She made a derisive noise. 'I suppose you'll be wanting to pick up your cheque for your expert services, Doctor. I'll be in my office when you're finished gossiping.'

As she hurried away, Denzil Sambrook coughed. 'Sorry about that, old boy. My sister simply can't help being rude and sarcastic.'

Carrodus waved away his apology. 'Think nothing of it. Can't be easy for Daphne. Brilliant father. Intellectual brother. And she's a frustrated artist. Thank goodness you've been able to give her a decent job.'

'Deputy matron?' Denzil's eyebrows rose. 'Glorified bookkeeper would be closer to the mark. Takes after our mother, God rest her soul. Not the faintest interest in science or medicine or politics.'

'She's a capable businesswoman. Quite apart from her artistic talents.'

'Which she squandered on painting squiggles in all the colours of the rainbow. Absolute rubbish.'

'*Chacun à son goût*,' Carrodus said in a passable French accent.

'Ever the diplomat, eh? Fact is, nobody was ever going to buy her daubs, except possibly to hide a damp patch on a wall. As you well know, she'd have starved to death if she'd stayed down in London.'

'Just as well you came to the rescue,' the doctor said with a teasing grin.

'At least she's gainfully occupied, balancing the books of the sanatorium and our family trust. I don't mind telling you, at one time I did wonder if you and she…'

Carrodus shook his head. 'I'm afraid she finds me too shallow.'

'More fool her. She's well on her way to becoming a dried-up spinster.'

The doctor grimaced. 'Don't tell me you'd describe her as a superfluous woman?'

Denzil Sambrook yawned. 'You're teasing me, old boy. It's not simply about women left on the shelf, with so many young men killed in the war. Fact is, the world is full of superfluous people.'

3

'Let me be frank,' Nell said.

Judith Royle hunched up in her chair, as if trying to make herself invisible. Nell wondered if, within the past hour, the rector's wife had tried to crush her to death. It wasn't impossible, although Nell baulked at the idea of this petite, nervous woman putting her shoulder to the rock and shoving it over the brink. If Judith wanted to commit murder, her method would be less crude. Nell conjured up a vision of the rector's wife as a poisoner, glancing around to make sure she was unobserved before dropping arsenic into a bowl of soup or lacing scones with strychnine.

At the very least, she had concocted a poison pen letter. Nell had spotted copies of the *Times* and the *Daily Mail* lying on the sideboard in the rectory. She always liked to discover what newspapers people read, believing that they yielded clues to a person's disposition and habits. A journal of record for solemn Quintus Royle, a popular rag for his wife. The typeface of the letters and words on the anonymous note amounted to a journalistic fingerprint; Nell recognised it at once. The message was composed of clippings taken from the *Daily Mail*.

A passing remark of Judith's clinched the deduction. Over tea yesterday, she'd mentioned her enthusiasm for paper-making and for mixing herbs or flower petals in the pulp. The sheet was unquestionably handmade. When Nell had sniffed it, she'd detected a fragrance of rose. Judith had given herself away stupidly, a hapless amateur in deceit.

The rector's wife drummed her fingers on the side of the armchair.

'Sorry,' Nell said. 'Wool-gathering.'

'I told you, I need to get back home. Quintus will wonder where I have got to.'

Quintus Royle was a man of few words, most of them sarcastic. He treated Judith like a servant. No doubt he expected her to account for her movements, as well as for every last penny she spent. Small wonder that she seemed so downtrodden.

'I understand.' Nell adopted a confidential, woman-to-woman tone. 'You know, all my life I've wanted to write. My ambition was to work in Fleet Street, but even in this day and age, female reporters aren't taken seriously.'

Judith shifted in her chair, patience and good manners wearing thin.

'You see, Mrs Royle, I was determined not to be condemned to a life of writing about fashion or cookery. Goodness knows, my dress sense is rotten and I can't bake a cake to save my life.'

'There are worse things to write about.'

Appealing to female solidarity was clearly hopeless. 'The truth is that I want to write stories that capture my fancy, illustrating them with my own photographs. I love a mysterious murder; the more intriguing, the better.'

Judith shuddered. 'I find that sort of thing extremely unpleasant.'

'My speciality,' Nell said, provoked into exaggeration, 'is strange disappearances. That's why I've come to Blackstone Fell.'

'I don't follow.'

'Remember what happened here?'

Nell threw her guest a conspiratorial glance. She was in her element now; the main risk was her besetting sin of overconfidence.

'Here?'

'You know this Lodge has a mysterious history.'

'I'm vaguely aware of some ridiculous legend, if that's what you mean. Childish nonsense, I never paid any attention. Mr Lejeune has never mentioned it, and if anyone should know whether there's any substance in the story, it's the person who owns Blackstone Tower.'

'Curious fellow, isn't he, Harold Lejeune? One of his ancestors built the Tower, and the family has lived there for centuries. Yet recently he sold this gatehouse to Professor Sambrook and his son.'

'Sad, but not surprising,' Judith Royle said quickly. 'Mr Lejeune isn't a rich man, and the upkeep of the Tower must be crippling.'

'To judge from the crumbling brickwork and the overgrown grounds, he doesn't spend a penny on it.'

'Surely that is his business, not yours or mine?'

Nell was unabashed. 'He might at least have popped round to introduce himself. I'd love to see inside the Tower; it looks so extraordinary. I saw him on the lane this morning, when I was taking photographs. The major said hello, but he didn't even speak. Extraordinarily rude.'

'His privacy is very precious to him.' Judith Royle seemed flustered. 'Ever since he inherited the Tower, he's kept himself to himself. Since he lost his wife...'

'His wife?' Nell was taken aback. 'Isn't he a bachelor?'

'Oh no, he was married to a beautiful Italian woman.'

Nell leaned forward. This made sense of the major's cryptic reference to grief. 'And she is dead?'

'I'm afraid so. They were a devoted couple. Her name was Chiara. She ran a guest house and they met when he stayed there before the war. Years later he inherited the Tower and brought her back to England.'

'What happened to her?'

'Fifteen months ago she succumbed to the ravages of cancer. Such a tragedy. They only ever had eyes for each other. They didn't have much to do with the rest of the village, and spent a lot of time abroad. I'm afraid that didn't make them popular, but I found it rather romantic. My heart went out to both of them. She battled bravely, but lost the fight.'

'Ah, I see.' Nell experienced a sense of anticlimax. For a moment, she'd speculated wildly about wife-murder.

'Her death broke poor Mr Lejeune's heart,' Judith said. 'Since then, he has... withdrawn even further into himself. It's very sad. I'm afraid your curiosity about the Tower will go unsatisfied.'

'What about the men who disappeared from this Lodge?'

'My husband was rector at the time of the second... incident. He doesn't believe there's a shred of truth in the story. Poppycock was the word he used.'

'I simply can't ignore it.' Nell cupped her chin in her hand. 'My readers will be thrilled it if I can solve the mystery.'

Judith stared at her. 'You came to Blackstone Fell under false pretences simply to research an old wives' tale dating back three hundred years?'

'Why not?' Nell was spinning a line, but that didn't stop her from sounding indignant. 'People talk less freely if they know they are speaking to a journalist. And this is such a remarkable puzzle. The first occasion in particular. Think of it! A man is witnessed entering a building, and locks the door behind him. When the door is opened, there is no sign of him inside.' Nell paused. 'Edmund Mellor vanished from this very spot!' With a melodramatic gesture, she indicated their surroundings.

It was getting dark outside, and although the fire burned brightly, Judith Royle's face was in shadow. 'I'm sure there was some perfectly straightforward explanation.'

'I want to discover it,' Nell said. 'This story will make a wonderful feature. It might even stretch to a book. Especially if it was a criminal case. If Edmund Mellor was murdered.'

'Murdered?' Judith was startled. 'If you ask me, it's a lot of fuss about nothing. The so-called witnesses were mistaken. Or else they simply didn't see the man leave the Lodge.'

'That doesn't explain why Mellor was never seen again after coming to Blackstone Fell.'

'The tale became embroidered over the years. That's what happens, call it human nature. A rector's wife sees it in the raw. People love to spread tittle-tattle, and it's all too easy to take advantage of the credulous. I can't imagine any newspaper printing hearsay and wild speculation.'

Nell could name half a dozen newspapers which did

nothing but. She struggled to stifle her amusement. 'Readers love a riddle. Anyway, there is more, isn't there?'

'What do you mean?'

'The previous owner of Blackstone Tower vanished too, didn't he?'

'That was entirely different. My husband saw Alfred Lejeune that day.'

'Is that so?' Nell knew the story already, but was interested to hear Judith Royle's account.

'Yes, Quintus has been rector for a quarter of a century. His belief is that the wretched fellow left the Lodge unobserved and went for a walk on Blackstone Moor. He must have lost his bearings. The mist descends quickly over the low ground, even when the sun is shining everywhere else. It's easy to stumble off the safe path and be swallowed up in the mire. There are treacherous bogs and hollows that you can't see until it's too late.'

'Dangerous place, Blackstone Fell,' Nell said.

'Don't believe everything you're told.'

'You believed an anonymous accusation about me, didn't you?'

Judith Royle jumped to her feet. 'With good reason. The author wasn't mistaken; you admitted that yourself. Now you'll have to excuse me. I've outstayed my welcome.'

Her voice was muffled. Nell thought she was on the verge of tears. 'Please, don't be upset. We're only just getting to know each other.'

'I don't know you at all! You deceived people about your identity, as well as your reason for renting the Lodge. I invited you to tea in good faith. A modest act of Christian charity. You repaid me with dishonesty.'

'Sorry to vex you, but it was a perfectly harmless subterfuge. I insist on doing my research first-hand. It's hard for a woman to earn a crust in journalism. A little white lie is neither here nor there.'

Judith Royle took a deep breath. She was making a visible effort to control her emotions.

'Please, Miss Fagan. I implore you to abandon this charade. No good can come of it. Blackstone Fell is a small community. Inward-looking. And there is – yes, I admit it – darkness here. Quintus would be the first to agree. Your interfering, poking your nose into other people's lives, can't do any good.'

'Darkness?' Nell asked.

'Surely a woman of your experience can smell it in the air? The brooding moors, the deadly marsh, Blackstone Leap.'

'Not to mention the sanatorium,' Nell said. 'From what I can gather, the name is a euphemism for a private asylum. I'd like to talk to Professor Sambrook, as well as his son and daughter.'

The rector's wife shook her head. 'Please reconsider, Miss Fagan. Go back to your friends in London. That's where you belong.'

'As it happens,' Nell said, 'I'm catching the train to King's Cross this evening.'

'You are?' There was no mistaking the note of hope in the question.

'Yes, there are people I need to see. But I won't be away for long. This story begs to be written, and I intend to write it.'

Judith Royle moved to the door. 'If that's your final word.'

'I hope I can rely on your discretion,' Nell said softly. 'Rest assured, you can rely on mine.'

Even in poor light, the distress on the younger woman's face was vivid. For an instant she stood motionless, as if paralysed by dread. Finally, she flung the door open and rushed outside.

'Miserable night.'

The taxi driver resembled an elderly undertaker, his mournful voice a perfect match for his haggard appearance. His black cab probably doubled as a hearse. Threads of mist were gathering as he heaved Nell's case into the back, but his remark sounded like a standard greeting rather than a weather forecast.

'It was lovely in the sun this afternoon.'

Nell had never managed to break her habit of contrariness. Sometimes this provoked people into telling her more than they wished to reveal. Occasionally it led to her getting the sack.

The driver grunted. 'Nowt lovely about Blackstone Fell.'

'You're not from these parts?'

He exhaled noisily by way of denial. 'Nah, Heptonstall.'

'That isn't far away, is it?' He'd made it sound like Timbuktu.

'Far enough. Folk say Blackstone Fell is the last place God made.'

'Is that right?'

'Not blooming likely. If you ask me, it's the work of old Nick.'

He wheezed with laughter at his own jest. The ancient jalopy groaned in sympathy as it bumped along the rutted lane. Nell felt her bones shaking. What were their chances of making it to the station in one piece? At this rate it would be touch and go whether she caught the last train.

'I must admit, it's eerie.'

'Don't blame you for getting out.'

'I'll be coming back.'

He gave an on-your-head-be-it grunt. 'Takes all sorts.'

'What's wrong with Blackstone Fell?'

They were rattling down the slope past the cottages of the lower village, which huddled together as if for comfort.

'Middle of nowhere, isn't it?'

'Isn't the isolation part of its charm?'

'Charm?' He grunted. 'They don't like outsiders round here.'

After an attempt on her life, an anonymous accusation, and a warning to leave the village within the space of a few hours, Nell could vouch for that. 'I suppose outsiders don't care too much for them?'

'Right enough.' He gave a catarrhal laugh. 'All the other cabbies give these parts a wide berth.'

Hence his extortionate fare. 'What makes Blackstone Fell so unpopular?'

'They're a law to themselves hereabouts, always have been. Cut off. Inbred. Nobody knows what goes on behind them closed doors. Mebbe it's best not to know.'

Beyond the houses, the lane threaded through the moorland. In the desolate open country, the mist was thickening. Her thoughts drifted to London. Absence made the heart grow fonder. This place made her nostalgic for good old urban murk.

A sudden noise disturbed her reverie.

'What's that?'

'Dogs barking.'

His tone implied that her question was idiotic.

'Yes, but which dogs? What's causing them to make such a racket?'

'Asylum dogs, aren't they?'

She peered through the window, but in the murk the dogs were invisible.

'You mean they come from Professor Sambrook's sanatorium?'

'Asylum,' he insisted. 'Call a spade a spade. Those dogs are there to round up any poor devil that escapes.'

'You mean they set dogs on patients?'

'No, the dogs are there to stop 'em climbing the fence and getting lost in the marshland. Many a man's died in that dirty swamp. Some folk who perished there never had a Christian burial.' He added judiciously, 'Better to be nipped by a hound than suffocate in the slime.'

The narrow road bent away from moors and the barking grew fainter. As the car jolted forward, Nell made up her mind.

If she didn't look out, she'd sink up to her eyes in the mysteries of Blackstone Fell. She couldn't manage this on her own. She needed to bury the hatchet with Rachel Savernake and seek the help of that mysterious, formidable young woman.

4

Jacob Flint leaned against the market bar counter of the Exmouth Arms, making quick work of a pint of mild. He was in dire need of alcohol after hours spent in court, listening to bewigged lawyers sparring over papier-mâché spirit guides and bogus ectoplasm. It was enough to make anyone want to drink themselves into a stupor.

A distinctive aroma filled his nostrils. A peculiar compound of gin, tobacco, and musty tweed known in Fleet Street as *eau de Nell*.

At that moment, a hand clamped on his shoulder and a familiar voice hissed in his ear. 'Penny for 'em.'

Looking up, he saw Nell Fagan's florid cheeks reflected in the glass. The mirrors adorning the ornately carved bar-back enabled the landlord to keep a sharp eye out for trouble. The 'guv'nor', a burly fellow in collar and tie, cast a wary glance at Nell. Nine out of ten of his customers were men, and some female patrons were on the lookout for clients of their own.

'Evening, Nell. If you really want to know, I was thinking about fraudsters exploiting the vulnerable. The *Clarion* is running a crusade to expose fake spiritualists.'

'Your editor detests them, doesn't he?'

'Today he had me covering Dinah Sugrue's trial. She was lucky to get off with a fine and a slap on the wrist.'

'Ah, Dinah Sugrue. My Aunt Eunice mentioned her name only this morning. A third-rate medium by the sound of her.'

'How desperate must you be,' he mused, 'to fall for someone who pretends to put you in touch with the dead?'

'Don't say that to my Aunt Eunice. She's a devout believer.' Nell dug a shagreen cigar case out of her handbag. 'Smoke?'

Jacob shook his head hurriedly. He'd once made the mistake of sampling Nell's cheap cheroots. The acrid smell had haunted his sinuses for days.

'The vapour that oozes out of Dinah Sugrue when she's supposedly in a trance turned out to be nothing more exotic than sheets of old newsprint.'

'Don't tell me.' Nell lit her cigar. 'Editorials from the *Witness*?'

He laughed. The *Witness* was the *Clarion*'s deadliest rival. 'Long time no see. Brixton's your stamping ground, isn't it?'

'I like to get about. Catch up with my chums.' Nell studied the spirits arrayed on the bar-back with a practised eye before waving to the barmaid. 'Gin and tonic for me, and the same again for my handsome friend.'

The barmaid giggled. Jacob had taken a liking to her.

'Obviously you've forgotten,' Jacob murmured. 'Flattery doesn't get you everywhere.'

'Such cynicism in someone so young,' Nell said sadly. 'I'm just glad to see an old pal.'

They were simply professional acquaintances, but exaggeration came easily to Nell. She always pushed things to the limit. Jacob had last seen her being carried out of a pub in Chancery Lane by two hefty journalists after excessive celebrations of a scoop about a razor gang.

'What brings you to Clerkenwell?' he asked.

'I popped into your office and was told that you'd probably roll up here after filing your story. Isn't the Sugrue trial a come-down after your recent murder melodramas?'

'As you say, my editor loathes these so-called psychics.'

'Yes, when Gomersall gets the bit between his teeth, there's no stopping him. Researching for an all-guns-blazing exposé?'

Jacob's eyes narrowed. No reporter liked his competitors to get wind of work in progress. 'I don't…'

'Take that look off your face, I'm not out to pinch your ideas. Quite the opposite. I'd be glad to help.'

'Help?'

She leered at him. 'You scratch my back, young man, and I'll scratch yours.'

'Sounds like a Faustian pact.'

'The best kind, in our trade.'

The barmaid arrived with the drinks. Nell pressed coins into her small hand and told her to have one herself.

'Cheers,' Jacob said.

'Bottoms up.' They clinked glasses. 'Hardly set eyes on you since you were catapulted to greatness. I'm afraid you'll become too grand for the hoi-polloi like me. Chief crime correspondent of the *Clarion* at such a tender age.'

Jacob stared into his pint. Perhaps she'd hit the nail on the head. Had promotion come too soon? He was under no illusion about how much he needed to learn. His promotion owed a great deal to good fortune. As well as to Rachel Savernake.

'What are you up to these days?' he asked.

She stubbed her cheroot out on an ash tray. 'You heard on the grapevine that I parted company with the *Globe*?'

'Yes, sorry about that.'

Sorry, but not surprised. Nell changed jobs the way other women changed their hats. Sometimes she jumped, often she was pushed. Her flair for scenting a story was matched by a knack of antagonising people, not least her superiors.

'Ungrateful beggars! That's the Street of Shame for you, dear. Build you up one minute, knock you sideways the next. Ah well, *c'est la vie*. Down the hatch!'

She polished off her gin and tonic and signalled to the barmaid for another round.

'That's better. Anyway, to answer your question, I've gone freelance. More money, if you play your cards right. More freedom, too. I'm sick of writing recipes; they make me want to drown myself in semolina. You can't beat a good murder.'

'Unless you're the victim?'

'Ha! Don't I know it? Believe it or not, someone tried to finish me off yesterday. Only by the grace of God am I standing here, calming my nerves with a little drinkie.'

'Upset another editor, did you?'

'Cheeky monkey! This was in darkest Yorkshire. Your home turf.' She paused. 'Blackstone Fell.'

He felt her eyes raking across him like sharp fingernails. 'Never heard of it.'

'Blackstone Fell, Blackstone Leap, Blackstone this, that, and the other?'

He shook his head. 'Yorkshire's a huge county. More acres than there are letters in the Bible.'

'Goodness, you're a mine of useless information.' She

arched her bushy eyebrows. 'So you've never traipsed around Blackstone Fell?'

'Am I missing much?'

She ticked items off on stubby fingers. 'An abandoned cave dwelling, a dangerous stretch of river, a sinister tower, an asylum on the moors, and deadly marshland. Not to mention a history of mysterious vanishings from a Jacobean gatehouse.'

'Blimey, I'll catch the next train. Remind me, where exactly is Blackstone Fell?'

'Ten miles from where the Brontës hung out. Makes Wuthering Heights look like Blackpool beach.'

'On second thoughts,' he said, 'I'll save the treat for another day.'

The next round arrived. Today was Thursday and Jacob had toyed with the idea of asking the barmaid if she fancied going to the flicks over the weekend. Nell Fagan's presence was cramping his style. Better find out what she was playing at.

'Why did someone try to kill you?'

Nell hesitated. 'A huge rock tumbled down from the top of a cliff and only missed me by a whisker. I didn't see another soul, so maybe it was an accident. But it gave me the heebie-jeebies, I can tell you.'

Jacob took a swig of beer. Heebie-jeebies? This dumpy woman didn't have a nerve in her body. Gomersall, the hard-bitten editor of the *Clarion*, reckoned that Nell Fagan could have become Britain's finest woman reporter. She was her own worst enemy, though there was a lot of competition. Even by the flexible standards of Fleet Street ethics, she played fast and loose with the facts when it suited. Jacob wasn't convinced by her attempt to brush away the rock incident. Not that it mattered. Experienced reporters kept their cards close to their chest, especially if they lacked the security of a regular income. If she'd dug up another scoop, good luck to her.

'I did want to ask a small favour,' she said.

'You can always ask.'

She glanced around. The market bar was packed to the rafters as postal workers from the cavernous Mount Pleasant Letter Office gathered after a day's work to wet their whistles. Their supervisors congregated in the adjoining saloon bar, paying a penny or two more for their drinks in return for carpet rather than sawdust on the floor and the luxury of tables and chairs instead of bone-hard benches.

'Better if we're not overheard.'

No risk of that, he thought, given the noise people made with a few drinks inside them. Not to mention the racket from the old Joanna next door in the market bar, where the pianist was banging out 'It's a Long Way to Tipperary' as if his life depended on it. But she was insistent.

'Come on, let's go next door.'

He followed as she limped through into the saloon bar. A gaudily dressed woman wearing a ludicrous amount of mascara stood up and seized the hand of a hopeful-looking little man in a brown mackintosh. As they staggered out into the night, Nell plonked herself down at the vacated table and beckoned Jacob to join her.

'That's the ticket,' she said, gulping down the rest of her gin. 'I got back to Brixton in the small hours and I've been rushing around all day.'

'What've you been up to?'

'Social calls, you might say. With Aunt Eunice, for instance, the lady I mentioned. There's someone else I need to see and that's where you can help.'

Even through the dividing wall, there was no escaping the tuneless roar of 'Goodbye Piccadilly, Farewell Leicester Square'. Jacob shut his ears to the din.

Nell said, 'You've made quite a splash this year, young fellow-me-lad. I remember saying as much to that other whippersnapper. Our mutual friend, Inspector Oakes.'

'Did you now?'

Philip Oakes was the youngest and brightest detective inspector at Scotland Yard. Jacob guessed that Nell's attempts at soft-soaping him had met with little joy.

'I asked him if the rumours are true,' she said.

'What rumours?'

Nell beamed. 'That you work hand in glove with Miss Rachel Savernake.'

'What did he tell you about her?'

'Nothing I hadn't picked up already,' she admitted. 'Her late father was a hanging judge. Never saw him in court, but I hear he put on his black cap with the glee of a man donning his best trilby. Lost his marbles and retired from the bench to moulder away on an island in the Irish Sea. Not much of a life for his daughter, but when the old devil finally kicked the bucket, young Rachel inherited a fortune. He wasn't cold in the grave before she hot-footed it down to London and started poking her nose into bizarre crimes. The Chorus Girl Murder, wasn't that how it began?'

'I'll take your word for it.'

'Don't be coy, Jacob. We're on the same side.'

'Keep talking,' he muttered.

'Rachel Savernake has a reputation for solving

extraordinary puzzles. Take that strange business up on the east coast in summer. The deaths at Mortmain Hall. You were Johnny on the spot, lucky lad. But I heard a rumour that she was there at the same time.'

Jacob folded his arms and said nothing.

'All right, I don't blame you for keeping mum, but she's put noses out of joint at the Yard. They loathe anyone who plays the amateur detective, especially a woman who is as sharp as a stiletto.'

'Did Inspector Oakes say so?'

'That tight-lipped beggar lets nothing slip unless it suits him, but he's smart enough not to be jealous. I'm sure he respects her, but he's curious too. She keeps a very low profile. No gay parties, no society balls. Her name never features in the gossip columns. A journalist's nightmare.'

'You've summed her up perfectly.'

'I've never even seen a published photograph. Why would such an attractive young woman be camera-shy?'

Jacob rubbed his chin. 'I suppose she is quite pretty.'

'Aha!' Nell sniggered and lit another cheroot. 'I bet you carry a torch for her.'

'Absolutely not.' To his dismay, he felt his cheeks burning. 'Our acquaintance is purely professional.'

'Methinks he doth protest too much. Don't fret, dear, your secret is safe with me. I'll wager all Lombard Street to a China orange that you've not dared to try your luck with the lovely Rachel. Afraid of boxing out of your league, eh? Faint heart never won fair lady. When I walked in here, I saw you ogling the barmaid. Plucking up the courage to ask her out? Too late. She's flirting with that fat grocer now.'

Jacob refused to demean himself by looking round, but out

of the corner of his eye he spotted the girl's reflection in the mirror on the bar-back. She was tittering at a compliment paid by an oleaginous, over-fed man twice her age.

He made a show of consulting his watch, and said, 'Lord, is that the time?'

'You don't fool me. A conscientious young chap like you will have written his report about Dinah Sugrue's monkey business before coming here to get sozzled.'

He glared. Nell loved to provoke. Her ability to see through pretence only made things worse.

'All right,' she said. 'I'll cut to the chase. This favour concerns your friend Rachel. I need to see her urgently, before I go back to Blackstone Fell tomorrow night. I wondered if you'd give me an introduction?'

'I don't mean to be rude,' Jacob said, 'but when did you ever wait to be introduced? Why not barge in unannounced, as usual?'

'Look, Jacob, I don't make a habit of asking other people to do my dirty work. Snag is, I blotted my copybook. Rachel regards me as persona non grata.'

'She does?'

'Hard to believe, I know. It all goes back to when a little bird told me that she was mixed up with that death at the Inanity. The conjuring illusion that went wrong, remember?'

He closed his eyes. That was a night he'd never forget.

'Obviously there was more to that than met the eye. The only reports worth reading were yours, and even they seemed… reticent. I heard whispers that she was in cahoots with the police, but nobody would say a word. Anyone would think people are scared to talk about her.'

'I'm not sure I follow.'

She gave him an old-fashioned look. 'Don't prevaricate. I spent ages ferreting around for scraps of information about the woman. Thin pickings, let me tell you. I decided to go to the horse's mouth. I asked her for an interview.'

'Rachel hates people intruding on her privacy.'

'You're telling me. She only has a handful of servants, but they guard her as if their lives depend on it. I pleaded with the housekeeper on the telephone, but she refused to let me speak to her mistress. But you know me. I never take no for an answer.'

'True,' he sighed. It was Nell's greatest strength and also her greatest weakness.

Nell puffed smoke into his face. 'I went round to that mansion of hers, Gaunt House. Her right-hand man, that hulking brute Trueman, was about to chuck me out into the street. I had no choice but to tell a few porkie pies.'

He winced. 'You lied to Rachel Savernake?'

'For goodness sake, it's not like fibbing in the confessional. She can't damn me for eternity.'

Don't be so sure were words that sprang to mind.

'Tell me what you said to her.'

Nell became shifty. 'I may have given the impression that you and I had become... well, very close. Thrown together one night after a Fleet Street knees-up.'

He groaned. 'You didn't...?'

'Not to worry, I took the blame. Said you'd had too much to drink, whereas I've got hollow legs. I told her you're a perfect gentleman, even in your cups.'

'Thanks for nothing.'

'Don't look so horrified! Honestly, there was a time when half the hacks in Fleet Street had designs on my virtue. I had to beat them off, let me tell you. Anyhow, I said you were full of admiration and respect for her. Though I did hint that you'd let something slip. Pillow talk, so to speak.'

He cringed. Nell took no notice.

'You mumbled in your sleep. Something about Rachel's own past, the reason why murder obsesses her. I wanted to sing her praises in print. A wonderful human interest story, the sort *Globe* readers love. Young woman, lots of money, baffling murder mysteries. The enigmatic beauty who keeps one step ahead of the Yard. I can see the headlines now. I promised she'd come out of it smelling of roses, and looking better than Norma Talmadge. On the back of the publicity, she could set up her stall as a top private detective.'

Jacob was ashen-faced. 'In other words, you told her I can't hold my liquor, I jump into bed with women twice my age, then in an alcoholic daze I blabber other people's secrets to my latest conquest? And to put the tin lid on it, you threaten to put the face of this reclusive young woman on every breakfast table in the country?'

For the first time in their acquaintance, Nell's expression was contrite.

'I suppose when you put it that way...'

'How could you?' he demanded.

'Sorry, dear, but nothing excites me like an exclusive. I was having a rotten time at the *Globe*. The editor loathes the idea of a woman covering a murder case. He'd prefer me to wax lyrical about a new species of begonia at the Chelsea Flower Show. Or the latest bread-toasting gadget from the Ideal Home Exhibition. This story was my chance to prove I'd not lost my touch. Anyway, I didn't threaten your precious Miss Savernake. I thought she'd be thrilled. Remember, the only thing worse than being talked about is not being talked about. Oscar Wilde said that.'

'Yes, and he went to jail and finished up in an early grave.' Jacob puffed out his cheeks. 'How did Rachel take this?'

'Badly,' she admitted. 'She didn't believe a word I said.'

'Thank the Lord for small mercies.'

'An ice queen, that's what she is. I've never met anyone like her. I'd put nothing past Rachel Savernake. Softly spoken she may be, but those eyes! They gaze into your very soul.'

A phrase taken, no doubt, from Nell's proposed exclusive. 'She sent you off with a flea in your ear?'

'That doesn't do it justice!' Nell gave a melodramatic shiver. 'No beating around the bush with that one. She said I was a rotten liar. For all your faults, she said, you had better taste.'

Jacob breathed an unchivalrous sigh of relief.

'Downright offensive, even if I'm no spring chicken. She told me in words of one syllable that she'd tolerate no publicity of any kind. I wasn't to write about her, with or without her co-operation. Or even mention her name in print.'

'And you agreed?'

'Of course not. What do you take me for? I reminded her it was a free country. We fought a war to preserve a free press.'

This wasn't the moment to question Nell's grasp of history. 'What did she say?'

'She told me the *Globe* wouldn't touch my story. And they wouldn't touch me if I persisted in harassing a respectable private citizen. Before I could say another word, she called in that big fellow, Trueman. He manhandled me out of the house.'

'What then?'

'I had a snifter or two to calm my nerves. I don't mind admitting, the woman got under my skin. It's that cold intensity. She seems utterly remorseless. Silly as it seems, she scared me more than any East End villain.'

It wasn't silly. If someone crossed Rachel, she was capable of making them pay a terrible price. Jacob kept his mouth shut.

Nell finished her gin. 'Next day, the editor summoned me to his office. Query over expenses. Between you and me, I'd gilded the lily with one or two claims. I said I'd lined up a fascinating story, but he told me not to touch crime again. We had a set-to, and he gave me my marching orders from the *Globe*. I wasn't heartbroken, you know me, a cat with nine lives. But when I sounded out a couple of old chums I'd worked for in the past, they didn't want to know. It was as if the word had gone out. Nobody wants to touch me with a barge pole.'

'You blame Rachel?'

'She's obscenely rich and as ruthless as her father. I don't think she plays by any rules but her own. I'm sure she pulled strings. I feel like Billy Bones after Blind Pew handed him the black spot.'

'And you expect me to persuade her to meet you? After what you told her about the two of us?'

'Water under the bridge, Jacob. To err is human. Please don't force me to beg. I'd rather offer you an incentive.' A theatrical pause. 'How about attending a séance conducted by the Pythoness of Primrose Hill?'

Jacob stared. 'You mean Ottilie Curle?'

Nell grinned. 'If you wish to be prosaic.'

Ottilie Curle was London's most renowned medium. As far

as the *Clarion* was concerned, she was also a fraud with an eye for the main chance.

'How on earth can you fix that?'

Nell beamed. 'Aunt Eunice has invested in her services as a go-between with the dear departed. She's so excited, you'd think she'd bought a ticket in this new Irish Sweep. I can persuade her to invite you as an honoured guest.'

'Ottilie Curle never has any truck with journalists. Let alone crime reporters.'

'Quite. So why not become the nephew of a friend of mine, visiting from Scotland, and an ardent spiritualist?'

Despite himself, he laughed. 'Are you serious?'

'Never more so, Jacob.'

'It won't work.'

'Och, laddie, don't tell me you can't manage a Scottish accent, I won't hear of it. You know all the supernatural mumbo-jumbo after sitting through the Sugrue trial. Trust me, it's a piece of cake. You need to have more confidence in yourself.'

'I'm not…'

'This is the least I can do in return for your help with Rachel Savernake,' Nell wore the smug expression of one who has played a trump card. 'I won't be there for the séance. Probably just as well, I'd most likely laugh my head off. The séance is on Sunday, and by then I'll be back at Blackstone Fell. Not that it matters. Auntie Eunice is a dear old soul, and she's bound to take a shine to you. I bet Ottilie Curle does, too.'

He groaned inwardly. The offer of a chance to spy on an unsuspecting Ottilie Curle was too good to miss. He was desperate to investigate the woman at close quarters, but so far all his efforts had drawn a blank. She claimed to encourage searching scrutiny of her methods, but only allowed examination by the credulous or the converted. Sceptics were never allowed near.

'Rachel doesn't blow with the wind. Why would she give you the time of day?'

'Last time I wanted to write a story about her. This time I'm asking her to help solve a mystery. Different kettle of fish, isn't it?'

'I suppose so,' he said.

'Don't look so glum. I'll swear on a stack of Bibles never to put a word in print about the woman. All you need do is lay on the charm. She'll be putty in your hands.'

'What do I say?'

'Tell her I've stumbled across a puzzle that's right up her street. Inexplicable disappearances. Sealed-room mysteries. Not to mention a killer on the loose in Blackstone Fell.'

5

Jacob rang Rachel Savernake's home from a kiosk close to the pub. Nell had told him what to say, ignoring his insistence that the call was the longest of long shots.

Martha Trueman answered the telephone. She was much the same age as Rachel and Jacob and called herself the housemaid. Rachel's closest confidante was closer to the mark. Despite the size and grandeur of Gaunt House, only two other people worked there: Martha's brother Clifford and his wife Hetty, the cook and housekeeper. Jacob wasn't on visiting terms with the rich and famous or the landed gentry, but he was sure the bond between Rachel and the three Truemans was unique. They were not so much a mistress and her servants as a tight-knit cabal.

'Nell Fagan?' Martha said. 'Yes, I remember. That woman ought to write novelettes rather than newspaper columns. She claimed you'd succumbed to her seductive wiles, and then been extremely indiscreet in your sleep.'

She was barely able to conceal her amusement. He ground his teeth. 'Is it true that Rachel persuaded the *Globe* to give her the sack?'

'Any misfortunes Nell Fagan suffered,' Martha said, 'she brought on herself.'

'Believe me, she knows she was in the wrong. She asked me to apologise on her behalf and say she's desperate to make amends.'

'Tell her to stick to writing harmless drivel.'

'Nell is no fool. She was following capital cases at the Old Bailey when I was still in short pants. Crime has fascinated her ever since she sat in on Crippen's trial. She's not ready to be put out to grass.'

'You'll be telling me next that she's Rachel's soulmate.'

'The two of them have more in common than you might think.'

Martha laughed, a musical sound. 'Is that so?'

'Yes, she's uncovered a mystery which is tailor-made for Rachel. Two men in Yorkshire disappeared from a locked gatehouse, three hundred years apart. If I could just explain…'

'It's no good telling me. Rachel's the one you need to charm.'

'Can I speak to her?'

'I'll ask her to come to the telephone.' Martha sounded like a resigned mother watching a child get into yet another scrape. 'Good luck, Jacob; you'll need it.'

'Is she in a good humour?' He couldn't quite keep the anxiety out of his voice.

'Oh yes.' Martha giggled. 'At this very moment, she's looking forward to some Hanky-Panky.'

'Told you so,' Nell said.

Jacob had re-joined her in the Exmouth Arms, the bearer

of unexpectedly good news. A fresh foaming pint awaited him. From the woozy gleam in Nell's eyes, he deduced that she'd not stinted on the gin in his absence.

'I'm amazed.' He treated himself to a generous swig. 'Rachel rarely gives anyone a second chance.'

'Loves a touch of mystery, doesn't she?' Nell brimmed with complacent glee as well as booze. 'A locked-room puzzle? I was sure she wouldn't be able to resist once you tickled her fancy.'

'There's a strict condition. You must be entirely frank. She was adamant that she wants to know everything that you know. No holding back, no keeping secrets.'

'One law for her, one for the rest of us, eh?'

'I'm serious. Try to hoodwink Rachel, and you'll live to regret it.'

'*La belle dame sans merci.*' Nell grunted. 'Don't forget, I've got first-hand experience that her bite is worse than her bark.'

'Will you promise?'

'Cross my heart and hope to die.' Nell peered at him. 'She scares you, doesn't she?'

'I wouldn't say that.'

Nell patted his knee. 'Don't take offence, Jacob. I had complete confidence in your silver tongue. I bet that on the quiet, the glamorous Miss Savernake has a very soft spot for you.'

'Don't be ridiculous.'

'You're blushing. Touched a nerve, have I?'

He said quickly, 'These men who disappeared – do you think they were actually murdered?'

'What else? One person might vanish into thin air – but two, from the very same spot?'

'And you're the new tenant?'

'Faint heart never won front-page story.'

'Alright, when can I meet your Aunt Eunice?'

'Tomorrow. Let's have lunch with her in Kentish Town. Gird our loins for our date with La Savernake.' She belched. 'Plenty of time before last orders. Let me buy you another pint to celebrate.'

He drained his tankard. 'I've had enough, thanks.'

'Spoilsport. The night is young.'

Shaking his head, he got to his feet. The last thing he wanted was for Nell to be hungover when she met Rachel. Things could easily get out of hand.

'Come on, let me pour you into a taxi so you get home in one piece. I need to practise my Scottish accent.'

'If you ask me,' Hetty Trueman said, 'you're making a big mistake.'

'The reason I didn't ask your opinion,' Rachel Savernake said pleasantly, 'was because it was entirely predictable. You make Nostradamus look like a cheery optimist.'

Hetty scowled. 'Tease me if you want. My hide is as thick as a rhino's. That Fagan woman is trouble. I'm surprised at young Jacob, letting her use him as her mouthpiece. He should have learned more sense.'

'Jacob sees himself as an artful negotiator.' Almost absent-mindedly, Rachel filled in the last blank spaces in one of Torquemada's crosswords in rhyme before pushing the book to one side. 'Journalists trade in their own currency. She'll have tipped him off about a story in return.'

'She's not to be trusted.'

'Agreed, but forewarned is forearmed.'

They were in the sitting room of the vast house on the square, each woman with a glass at her elbow. Clifford Trueman had recently taken up mixing cocktails and was experimenting with different recipes.

Rachel sipped her Hanky-Panky. 'Delicious.'

Hetty wasn't so easily distracted. 'The last time that woman came here, she caused a real kerfuffle.'

'It would have been awkward if she'd actually stumbled across some information that could… embarrass me. Obviously she was drawing a bow at a venture. Our cosy little *ménage* baffles her, that's all there is to it. The truth is, she doesn't know a thing about us. She's not short of courage, but she's rash. Look how easy it was to discredit her.'

'You couldn't be certain that she was on the fiddle.'

'How likely was it that she'd resist temptation when it came to expenses? A journalist who drinks so much?' Rachel was amused. 'It's a wonder the jails aren't full of them.'

Hetty gave a reminiscent sniff. 'She reeks of gin. I smelled it the moment she stepped through the door. I daren't imagine the state of her liver.'

'She's a born risk-taker. Cirrhosis won't kill her. Carelessness will be the death of her.'

'You make her sound like Jacob Flint.'

'Jacob is impetuous, but his survival instinct is formidable. Nell Fagan is heading for an early grave. When she called on us, those transparent inventions about poor Jacob made me angry. On reflection I should have pitied her.'

'She's a threat.'

'She's not a wicked woman.'

'She's brash and she has too much to say for herself. That sort can be dangerous.'

'Jacob is right. She hasn't lost her eye for a story.'

'This taradiddle about people vanishing from an old gatehouse?'

'In 1606 and 1914. An astonishingly large span of time.'

'It was so long ago. Even the last incident was before the war. The world was very different then. Sounds like she's clutching at straws. Why waste any more time on old news?'

Rachel took another taste of her cocktail. 'My compliments to the bartender. His skills would add lustre to any speakeasy. The taste is deep, dark, and bitter. Just the way I like it. The flavour is complex, with a hint of mischief. Perfect.'

Hetty sighed. 'There's no dealing with you when you're in this mood.'

'All those years stuck on Gaunt with Judge Savernake, I was a prisoner in all but name,' Rachel said. 'I yearned to escape from the island. With a fat fortune and the freedom to do whatever I please.'

'Your dreams came true.'

Rachel yawned. 'So they did.'

'The world's your oyster. Make the most of it.'

'Don't you see? I hate the social whirl. Everyday amusements bore me stiff.'

'You can travel, go wherever you please.'

'We came to London. A big change, after being cooped up on the island. At present, my wanderlust is satisfied.'

'You have this house. A magnificent art collection. And one of the finest libraries in private hands.'

Rachel put down her glass. 'They aren't enough.'

'You have us.'

'Yes, thank God.' Rachel squeezed the older woman's hand. 'I'd be nothing without you. Remember, we all grew up living with danger. It's in our blood. Without it, we're half-asleep.'

'Speak for yourself. Why get mixed up with another murder? You can have anything you want. If you need a challenge, those puzzles in the *Observer* are tricky enough. Let alone the chess problems you love to solve. No need to play with fire. Why take the risk?'

Rachel smiled. 'Taking calculated risks makes life worthwhile. Even if you won't admit it, deep down you know it's true for all of us.'

'Cliff's a law unto himself,' Hetty said. 'As for Martha, she's young. Headstrong. Of course she craves excitement.'

'So do I.'

'You're as bad as that Fagan woman. If you don't mind your step, one day your luck will run out.'

'Walking a tightrope has a special thrill. As for Miss Cornelia Fagan, with any luck, she's learned her lesson. She's astute enough to pique my interest, but I'm sure there's more to her story than she's told Jacob. The only question is whether she'll reveal everything to me. She's the type who loves to keep things up her sleeve.'

'More fool her.'

'Exactly.'

'Why do you think she's so anxious to see you?'

Rachel shrugged. 'Tomorrow we'll find out.'

'You're excited,' Hetty said. 'I recognise the signs. You'll do as you want, of course, same as ever. When you get an idea in your head, there's no stopping you. That's what bothers me. You're...'

'Say it.'

Hetty folded her arms. 'You're addicted to murder.'

'The more outlandish, the better.'

'It's downright unhealthy.'

'You think so?' Rachel savoured her Hanky-Panky. 'Put it down to my flawed character. I'm equally enslaved by your husband's cocktails.'

'The Pythoness of Primrose Hill?' demanded Gomersall at the *Clarion*'s morning conference the following day. 'The woman's as slippery as the so-called ectoplasm Dinah Sugrue spews out.'

'True,' Jacob said.

'How strong is this new lead?'

'Curle is conducting a séance on Sunday, and I've wangled an invitation. Her services have been hired by a friend of a friend.'

Nell Fagan's name would not pass his lips. Some things it was better for an editor not to know.

Gomersall raised bushy eyebrows. 'Good work. It's about time Curle was nailed. She's craftier than Sugrue; that's why she's never been prosecuted. The woman is a downright menace to society.'

'There's no serious harm in what these people do, is there?' The question was put by Barrett, a sandy-haired young man newly recruited to the political desk. 'I mean, isn't it almost a public service if she's keeping a few old dears happy, pandering to their fantasies?'

Gomersall put his hands on his hips. 'Spiritualists thrive on poverty and misfortune, lad, and don't you forget it. In my book, they are crueller than ragamuffins who lure the greedy and the gullible with the prospect of easy money in a game of Find the Lady. These mediums exploit the weak and credulous. The sooner you get that into your skull, the better.'

Barrett gaped. He'd never been on the receiving end of one of Gomersall's tirades before. 'I only meant—'

'Never mind what you meant, if you want to make anything of yourself on this newspaper, you need to smarten up your ideas. You wouldn't give quarter to a lying politician, would you? Let me tell you, these fakers are a blight on society, worse than the rottenest member of parliament.'

Barrett began to jabber an apology, only for George Poyser, the news editor, to silence him with a sharp jab in the ribs. At least the fellow had the sense not to argue, Jacob thought. Gomersall's mission to unmask dishonest mediums was inspired by a personal tragedy. In his native Lancashire, his grandmother had been fleeced of her savings by a man who pretended that Gomersall's cousin, drowned in the Battle of Jutland, was trying to get in touch with her from the Other Side. A Mancunian psychic researcher had exposed the medium as a charlatan, only for the old lady to suffer a fatal stroke within hours of learning that she'd been played for a fool.

Plenderleith, the dour city editor, turned to Jacob. 'Take care at your séance, laddie, once they turn the lights off. These mediums can be very seductive, I hear. Holding hands with strange women may give you a thrill, but you never know where it may lead.'

'Bonnie Scotland!' Eunice Bell cried. 'I once holidayed in the Trossachs. Such delightful countryside!'

'Hamish comes from the far north,' Nell said. 'Off the beaten track.'

'Aye, a wee hamlet,' Jacob confirmed. 'Invergibbet.'

For the purpose of his introduction to Ottilie Curle, he'd metamorphosed into Hamish Parlane, a well-to-do young man from the Scottish Highlands.

'I must apologise,' Eunice said. 'I'm afraid I've never heard of the place.'

This was unsurprising, as Jacob had made it up. 'So you're Nell's auntie?'

'She'll always be Cornelia to me.' Eunice touched Nell's hand. 'We're not blood relations. I often tell people, we're closer than that.'

Eunice was a small woman of seventy with thinning hair and a wistful look in her watery eyes. Her skin was pale, almost translucent. Nell had told Jacob that Eunice had an aneurysm. According to the doctors, she didn't have long to live. She'd always had a mild curiosity about spiritualism, but since she'd received the diagnosis it had developed into an obsession.

An elderly maid served a lunch of chicken salad. A water jug stood on the table and Jacob guessed that Eunice kept no alcohol in the house. Her dining room was a haven of aspidistras and antimacassars. A faint whiff of mothballs hung in the air. On the top of a sideboard stood a picture of Herne Bay framed with seashells, together with a dozen photographs of assorted children. In two of the pictures, Jacob recognised a young and sturdy Nell Fagan. That determined jawline was as unmistakeable as the bent nose and thick tangle of hair.

'My father was an author,' Nell said. 'Writing runs in the

blood, you see. His shilling shockers sold by the bucketload. See them on that shelf?'

Jacob studied the long line of books bearing Randolph Fagan's name. The first title was *The Clue of the Cobweb*, the last *The Mystery of Hannah Tart*. Perhaps his favourite was *The Dead Octopus Riddle*.

'Rattling good yarns, eh?'

'Believe me. He was always so full of life, and then one day he just dropped down dead. I was seven years old. Mamma was a semi-invalid who never got over her loss. She passed away when I was fifteen. Luckily I wasn't a destitute orphan. Father left me well provided for, and I was brought up by a devoted governess. Peggy arrived when I was five and from that moment on, she acted *in loco parentis*. In some ways, she still does.'

'How is Peggy?' Eunice asked.

'In formidable form. She sends her love.'

'Oh, I'm glad they didn't find anything wrong with her.' Eunice turned to Jacob. 'Peggy got back home last night. She'd been for a check-up.'

Nell nodded. 'Peggy is Eunice's cousin. As a girl, I spent more time in this house than I did in my own home. Eunice became my honorary aunt. She and her own mother, Ada, brought up several children who had lost their parents or suffered similar misfortunes. The two of them were saints.'

Eunice's pale face lit up. 'It was a pleasure, dear, you know that.'

'About the séance,' Jacob said, trying to curb his impatience.

'Oh yes, I'm coming to that. One of the children we raised was a very special boy. Darling little fellow, with the most wonderful golden curls.' Eunice pointed to a photograph of an infant in a sailor suit. Another image showed the same child on a swing pushed by a youthful Nell Fagan. 'Nathan was a babe in arms when we took him in. Not long afterwards, Cornelia's father died. She became like a sister to Nathan.'

In a flat voice, Nell said, 'Aunt Eunice wants to make contact with Nathan.'

Eunice shook her head. 'Cornelia doesn't approve of spiritualists, Mr Parlane, I'm sorry to say. Peggy is a sceptic too.'

'At least Hamish is a fellow believer.'

Nell gave Jacob a pointed stare, and he said hurriedly, 'Aye, aye. I am that.'

Hamish Parlane's true love, a lass called Flora Kilbride, had succumbed to a virulent strain of polio at the age of seventeen. He pined for Flora and longed to hear from her now that she'd gone to a Better Place.

'We both understand the pain of bereavement, Mr Parlane,' Eunice said. 'I pray the séance will bring comfort, for you as well as for me. Nothing would give me greater joy than to have one last conversation with Nathan in this earthly realm. Soon I'll be joining him on the Other Side.'

'What happened to Nathan?'

'It was such a tragedy. He had all his life ahead of him. He was so handsome and bright. We almost burst with pride because of his achievements. When he was still quite a tender age, he rose to giddy heights in the world of finance. He became chief accountant of Weaver's Bank.'

Nell glanced at Jacob. The name rang a faint bell in his memory.

'The bank collapsed on New Year's Eve, almost seventeen

years ago,' she muttered. 'Nathan was made a scapegoat. It was horribly unfair.'

Eunice dabbed her eyes with a tiny lace handkerchief. 'As far as we are concerned, Mr Parlane, Nathan was murdered.'

'Murdered?'

Startled, Jacob forgot his Scottish accent. Nell shot him a fierce glance.

'As surely as if Ormond Weaver thrust a dagger into his heart.' Eunice turned to Nell. 'You'd better explain, dear. I can't bear to think about it.'

'Weaver was a crook,' Nell said tersely. 'A handsome rogue who lived the life of Riley on other people's money. From the moment he set up the bank, he was milking its funds.'

'What happened?' Jacob asked.

'When the balloon went up, Weaver was charged with fraud. He wouldn't say a word to the police, but in the dock at the Old Bailey he put all the blame onto Nathan. He was a plausible devil and the jury lapped up his evidence. I watched him lying through his teeth. Making a scapegoat of a young man whose only crime was to trust his employer.'

'Nathan simply did what he was told,' Eunice said. 'He had no idea the documents he signed were false. Weaver exploited his good nature. But the shame was more than the poor boy could bear. He... no, I can't even bear to say it...'

'He put his head in a gas oven,' Nell said shortly.

'How dreadful,' Jacob said.

'Such a sensitive young man,' Eunice said. 'It broke our hearts. Especially...'

'Weaver's trial turned into a farce. His counsel was brutal.' Nell mimicked the pompous tones of a veteran barrister. '*By committing suicide, Nathan Hart effectively confessed his guilt. He perpetrated one crime to conceal another.*'

'Shameful,' Eunice said. 'Wicked.'

'The prosecution case collapsed. They couldn't call Nathan to tell his side of the story, so the villain of the piece walked free. The jury wasn't even asked to bring in a verdict.'

Jacob winced. 'So much for British justice.'

'God moves in mysterious ways,' Eunice said grimly.

'The bank's creditors sued Weaver for every penny he had,' Nell said. 'He fled across the Channel with a suitcase full of banknotes.'

'His luck ran out when he reached Austria,' Eunice said. 'There was an outbreak of diphtheria. Within a few days he was dead.'

'So he got his just deserts?' Jacob said.

'And the creditors recovered their funds.'

'Except,' Nell muttered, 'for the thousands he'd already spent.'

'All that mattered to us,' Eunice said, 'was the official enquiry into the bank's activities. It took a long time, but eventually poor Nathan's name was cleared.'

'Too late to save him,' Nell murmured.

'I dread to think of that wretched boy suffering some kind of eternal torment,' Eunice said. 'Simply because a rogue took advantage of his good nature and besmirched an innocent man's reputation to save his own skin.'

'I understand,' Jacob said. 'Ottilie Curle has promised to put you in contact with Nathan?'

Eunice blushed. 'Cornelia is cross with me, Mr Parlane. She thinks I'm deceiving myself and throwing away my money. But every penny I spend on the séance will be worth its weight in gold if I hear from Nathan. I need to make sure he knows the truth. His good name wasn't tarnished, and Weaver didn't get away with his crime. There was a happy ending.'

'Aye,' Jacob murmured, for want of anything better to say. 'We all like happy endings.'

'A kilt would suit you.' Nell gave Jacob a measuring gaze as he joined her in the back of the Hackney cab.

'No,' Jacob said. 'Absolutely not.'

'If you want to be a Scotsman, why not go the whole hog?'

'Not for all the tea in Invergibbet.'

'Nervous about what happens when the lights are low, and the Pythoness tickles your thigh?' There was a sour tinge to Nell's amusement. 'No need to panic. You're perfectly capable of looking after yourself.'

'Yes, I am.' He added ruefully, 'Not that Rachel would agree. When I'm in her company, it feels like being at school again.'

Nell sighed. 'I wonder if I'm doing the right thing?'

Jacob was startled. When had a moral dilemma ever given Nell Fagan pause?

'What do you mean?'

'I feel as if I'm wasting her time with a funny little mystery about an old legend. I'm sure she has better things to do.'

'Don't tell me you're getting cold feet. Not after taking so much trouble to see her again?'

She shook her head. 'Rachel Savernake fascinates me, I don't mind admitting. Between you and me, I reckon that she and I would make a formidable crime-solving team.'

'Are you serious?'

'On second thoughts, better leave that sort of thing to the two of you. I'm too old to change my ways. Besides, La Savernake and I are chalk and cheese. The woman's a virago. We'd only get on each other's nerves and end up tearing each other to shreds.'

Jacob was puzzled by this uncharacteristic bout of introspection. He also felt driven by an obscure desire to defend Rachel.

'I'm the first to admit, I don't fully understand her. Cold as she seems, beneath the surface there's plenty of charm. And a mischievous sense of humour when she's in the mood.'

'She's bewitched you, all right,' Nell said. 'Oh well, I suppose the worst she can do is throw me out of the house again.'

'Play straight with her and you've nothing to fear.'

Nell bridled. 'Oh, I'm not afraid of her. Poor Aunt Eunice is the one I lose sleep about. She's an old sweetie, but nowhere near as robust as Peggy. I hate to see her falling for a confidence trick. I'm glad you're determined to expose Ottilie Curle.'

Despite himself, Jacob felt a twinge of uncertainty. Was Gomersall wrong and Barrett right? Everybody needed hope to cling to. Wasn't it better to clutch at straws than plunge into an abyss?

'The prospect of the séance is keeping the old lady alive.'

'That's what is so rotten about the whole damnable nonsense. I can't find it in my heart to talk her out of it.'

She stared out of the window. Her mood had changed overnight, Jacob thought. The *joie de vivre* of the Exmouth Arms had vanished. Was she nervous of Rachel Savernake? Or simply missing her usual lunchtime gin?

He remembered the tragedy of Gomersall's grandmother. 'You don't think the publicity will harm Eunice?'

A sigh of resignation. 'These days she reads nothing but *The Lady* and spiritualist tracts. The *Clarion* never darkens her doorstep. So you can damn Ottilie Curle with a clear conscience.'

'Just as well.'

'I'll miss Eunice terribly when she's gone.' Nell managed a bleak smile. 'I can't even console myself with the prospect of talking to her on the Other Side.'

6

'How brave of you to take a tenancy of Blackstone Lodge,' Rachel Savernake said.

She switched off her shiny new radiogram as Nell and Jacob took their seats. The housekeeper had showed them into the sitting room to the accompaniment of 'Walk Right In'.

'Such a dark history,' she continued. 'Two men vanished from the gatehouse, never to be seen again.'

'As you can see, I'm still in one piece,' Nell said. 'It takes more than a mysterious legend to scare me.'

Hetty Trueman returned with a silver tray. She set down a teapot and cups, made from flawless Spode china. They were worth more than Jacob earned in a year, as Hetty had once pointed out, when a cup slipped from his fingers. Mercifully the carpet was so soft and thick that the china wasn't even chipped.

Rachel lifted the tongs. 'Sugar?'

'Two lumps, please.' Nell beamed. 'My sweet tooth will be the death of me.'

Afternoon tea in the palatial surroundings of Gaunt House. What could be more civilised? Jacob surrendered to his armchair's voluptuous embrace. Rachel looked demure, with dark hair newly bobbed and not a trace of make-up on her pale skin. At twenty-six, she could pass for seventeen. Just as long as Nell didn't underestimate her. When Rachel exerted her charm, you needed to be on guard. Beneath the velvet dress was an iron woman.

Martha came into the room, moving as always with unconscious grace, her tray laden with food. Cucumber sandwiches with the crusts cut off, scones with clotted cream and jam, tempting slabs of Victoria sponge and chocolate cake.

'You've excelled yourself,' Rachel said. 'This looks delicious, Martha.'

Nell failed to suppress a sharp intake of breath at the sight of the girl's damaged cheek. Cold slugs of embarrassment crawled down Jacob's spine, but as Martha followed her sister-in-law out of the room, she treated him to a saucy wink. Shocked glances meant nothing to her. Years ago, a man had thrown acid in her face. The scars failed to disguise her natural beauty or subdue her impish sense of humour.

'I read a few lines about Blackstone Fell in a gazetteer,' Rachel said. 'Lonely spot, by the sound of it.'

Nell nodded. 'The landscape is bleak and the weather often wretched. People only go there if they have a very good reason.'

'I'm curious as to why you visited Yorkshire.' Rachel sounded pensive. 'Sixteen years have passed since the last disappearance. The story has whiskers. There must be something else.'

'You're absolutely right,' Nell said unexpectedly.

'Ah.'

'But let me tell you first about the men who vanished.'

Rachel shrugged. 'The floor is yours.'

Nell dug a cheroot out of her handbag. 'Mind if I smoke?'

'Yes,' Rachel said.

Nell opened her mouth, as if about to protest. To Jacob's relief, she thought better of it and stuffed the cigar back into her bag.

'I came across the story in the newspaper archive at the British Museum. I wanted to learn about Blackstone Fell, for reasons I'll explain later. You see, Miss Savernake, I pride myself on thorough research.'

'Glad to hear it.' Rachel gave Jacob a sidelong glance. 'So many journalists make things up as they go along.'

'There's no better source of background detail about a place than the local press. I trawled through years of back issues. In 1914, the *Sowerby Bridge Chronicle* carried a contemporary report of the vanishing of Alfred Lejeune, with passing reference to the earlier incident, which was described as an interesting coincidence.'

'Jacob said the first case occurred in 1606?'

'Yes, shortly after the Tower was built. Work on the gatehouse now known as the Lodge had just been completed. Robert Lejeune's first guest at Blackstone Tower was Edmund Mellor. His family came from York, like the Lejeunes. Robert and Edmund were both thirty-five. They'd known each other as children.'

'What do you know about them?'

'Mellor senior was a church lawyer who fell out of favour with the authorities and died when his son was fifteen. Edmund had seemed destined for the law, but after developing a yen for travel, he spent years in the Iberian Peninsula.'

'Was he married?'

Nell shook her head. 'He returned to England shortly before he vanished. He and Robert Lejeune hadn't met for years, but Robert tracked Edmund down in London and proposed a reunion in Yorkshire.'

'Did Edmund Mellor pursue his interest in the law after returning to this country?'

'Not as far as I know. His mother was dead and he'd fallen on hard times. I suppose he found it difficult to settle down again. All the indications are that he was a hothead and a malcontent. The invitation to Blackstone Fell seems to have been an act of kindness, all the more welcome because it came out of the blue.'

'Congratulations,' Rachel said. 'Your powers of recall are formidable.'

Nell smeared a thick layer of butter over a scone. 'I'm blessed with a good memory. I don't need to take copious notes, even if I spend a whole day immersed in dusty files. What's more, I never forget a face. A godsend in my line of work, Miss Savernake. When a story is moving fast, you don't have time to flick through a notebook to check your facts.'

'Admirable,' Rachel murmured. 'Now, what do we know about Robert Lejeune?'

Nell hesitated. 'He sounds like a typical Lejeune. Odd and unpredictable, despite his generosity towards Mellor. The family aren't venerated as local benefactors. In fact, they have a reputation for misanthropy.'

'Was Robert's father a lawyer, like Mellor's?'

'No, old Lejeune was a former member of parliament. Once upon a time he'd been Queen Elizabeth's most trusted lieutenant in the north of England. As a young man, Robert dabbled first in engineering, then in architecture. His father persuaded him to enter government service in London, and gave him an *entrée* into high society. He mixed with the likes of Bacon and Cecil, but then his father died, and he returned to Yorkshire. He bought five hundred acres at Blackstone Fell and set about building a new home. Not an ordinary home, but a peculiar tower with no particular purpose.'

'A folly?'

'In appearance, yes, but the family has lived there since the seventeenth century. Robert designed the Tower himself. He was an architect *manqué*. Not that he was a second Vanbrugh or an Inigo Jones. Most people regard the Tower as a blot on the landscape. Carrodus, the village doctor, finds it amusing, and the Reverend Royle calls it an abomination.'

'What happened when Edmund Mellor arrived at Blackstone Fell? Was he accompanied by servants?'

'No, he was on his own and desperately short of money. One afternoon, he was spotted by a man named Furniss, the rector, who was outside in the garden of the rectory, tending to his collection of herbs.'

'Furniss and Lejeune were friends?'

'I believe not. Until Lejeune came to Blackstone Fell, Furniss ruled the roost in the neighbourhood. He regarded Lejeune as a usurper and hated the Tower. It ruined the view from his rectory.'

'Had Furniss met Mellor?'

'No. He only learned Mellor's identity afterwards, but the description he gave was crystal clear. Unquestionably, Mellor was the man he saw, hurrying down the drive from the Tower. The door to the Lodge is beneath the archway and faces the stone wall on the other side of the drive. Mellor took a key from his pocket and unlocked the door. His movements seemed furtive, and he threw a quick glance over his shoulder, but Furniss was standing in the shade of an old oak tree. He didn't think Mellor had seen him.'

'And then?'

'Mellor went inside the Lodge and – it seems – locked the door behind him. Not a living soul ever clapped eyes on him again.'

Jacob, having eaten a scone and drunk his tea, never found it easy to keep out of a conversation. 'Perhaps he simply came out of the Lodge again, ambled off for a walk over the moors, and sank into a bog. Mellor didn't know the area. Sounds like a place where it's easy to stray off the beaten track.'

'The rector was adamant that he never budged from the spot,' Nell said. 'Moments after seeing Mellor, he was joined by a chap from the lower village who helped with the garden and other odd jobs. The two men stood talking and they had an uninterrupted view of the Lodge. The gatehouse is one hundred yards away. If you're looking in that direction and anyone comes out of the door, you can't miss them.'

'The men weren't keeping watch on the Lodge,' Jacob said. 'Chances are, they were distracted.'

Nell brushed away his objection. 'I can only tell you the story as it was handed down. Twenty minutes later, Robert Lejeune strolled down the drive from the direction of the Tower. He looked around, as if he expected to see someone. Finally he knocked on the gatehouse door, but there was no answer. The men in the garden saw him peer through each of its windows in turn. Then he cupped his ear to the glass, as if to check whether he could hear something. It was a pantomime of bewilderment. After wandering around aimlessly for a few minutes, he walked over to the rectory and asked Furniss if he had seen his guest. When the rector told him what had happened, Lejeune didn't believe him. Cross words were exchanged and eventually Lejeune was persuaded to go back and knock again. He called Mellor's name, but there was no reply. The door was locked and there was only one key. A key Mellor had taken from its place in the hall of the Tower.'

'Why?' Rachel asked. 'For that matter, what made Mellor want to enter the gatehouse in the first place? And why do so in a furtive manner?'

'Robert Lejeune didn't know, but he admitted Mellor was rather nosey. Mellor had proposed that they go out for a breath of air. Lejeune had letters to write, but promised to meet him at the Lodge. Lejeune asked Furniss's companion, a strapping young fellow called Colbridge, to help him charge down the Lodge door. Mellor had a weak heart, and Lejeune was afraid his friend might have collapsed. When the two men broke into the Lodge, they found it empty. No trace of Mellor.'

'Describe the interior of the Lodge,' Rachel said.

'I can do better than that,' Nell boasted. 'I took a photograph of the interior. Yesterday, I went to my favourite chemist and gave him the film. He developed it into negatives and within an hour I had the prints in my hand. The wonders of modern science! And I sketched a map of the village to give you a rough idea. Take a look.'

Nell delved into her handbag and with a conjuror's flourish produced a crumpled sheet of paper and a photograph.

The picture was dark and grainy. Jacob screwed up his eyes. He could barely make out the details. 'Rather a hovel, isn't it?'

'It isn't exactly the Ritz. Not that I've ever been inside the Ritz. See, the external door opens straight into the main room.'

'Barely big enough to swing a cat.'

'I gather the original design presumed that a gardener would live there. Now there is a tiny kitchen plus a scruffy hole masquerading as a bathroom, with a cramped bedroom at the top of those narrow steps. The mullioned windows are far too tiny for a grown man – and Mellor was six feet tall – to squeeze through.'

'Unless he was a contortionist,' Jacob said.

'And as far as I know, Mellor never joined the circus. Or performed on the stage.'

Rachel studied the photograph. 'Is there an attic?'

'Upstairs there's a tiny lumber room as well as the bedroom, nothing else. And no cellar. The Lodge was built over a brook which meanders over and under ground and finally joins the river further down the hillside. As you can see, the fireplace is small. The chimney is too narrow for anyone bigger than a malnourished child. Even if anyone managed to shin up to the roof, where would he go? Lejeune got on Colbridge's shoulders, but Mellor wasn't hiding on the roof. The windows were all locked and so was that solitary door.'

'Surely enquiries were made in case Furniss and Colbridge were mistaken? What if Mellor left the gatehouse without their noticing?'

'Yes, that was the likeliest explanation. Lejeune went to great lengths to trace his friend. After questioning people in the village, he led a troop of them in a search of the moorland. To no avail. Edmund Mellor had vanished off the face of the earth.'

'And Lejeune?' Rachel asked.

'He lived in the Tower to the end of his life. In later years he married, and his wife gave birth to a son, so the line continued. But he abandoned any thought of building a second gatehouse on the other side of the arch. The Lodge was simply used for storage. Out of respect for his dead friend, he insisted that nobody should live there. And nobody ever has.' She gave a crooked smile. 'Until now.'

'Did Mellor have good reason to make himself scarce?'

'Possibly. Since coming back to England, he'd interested himself in politics. In some quarters, that may have made him unpopular. One thing is clear. When he went missing, few people shed a tear.'

'If he was tempted to flee the country,' Rachel mused, 'why do so in such a bizarre and elaborate fashion? Why make a mystery out of it?'

'Suppose Furniss and Colbridge conspired.' Jacob's brain was working overtime. 'What if the rector murdered Mellor and then asked Colbridge to bury the corpse in the garden? Or in the churchyard? What if the sexton and his men left a grave conveniently open? For all we know, he's been buried there from that day to this.'

Nell blinked. 'Full marks for imagination, Jacob. To the best of my knowledge, Furniss lived to a ripe old age with an unblemished character, even if he was more concerned about his own comfort than his ministry. Suppose he'd had the time to kill Mellor and bury him before Lejeune came looking, what was his motive? Why would a man of God kill a perfect stranger?'

'You never know,' Jacob said darkly. 'Nothing is impossible.'

'Except,' Nell said, 'for the vanishing of Edmund Mellor.'

'History repeated itself in the present century?' Rachel said.

'Yes,' Nell said, 'except that this time a member of the Lejeune family went missing, rather than an outsider. Alfred Lejeune was a bachelor of fifty. He inherited the Tower in 1913 after an elderly cousin succumbed to a stroke. The Lejeunes had a good innings, but by the early years of this century they were a dying breed. Alfred and his younger brother Harold were the last of the line. Both men lived up to the family tradition of eccentricity.'

'In what ways?'

'Alfred was a stick-in-the-mud antiquarian, Harold a globetrotting plant hunter. Obsessed with chasing down rare geraniums and suchlike. The brothers weren't close to each other, let alone to the cousin who owned the Tower. Alfred hadn't visited Blackstone Fell since he was a child, but after he moved into his new home, his interest in the past led him to research the story of Edmund Mellor. He was a corresponding member of the Halifax Literary and Philosophical Society and wrote a monograph about Mellor's disappearance. Along with bits and pieces I've picked up from the locals, it's my main source of information.'

'How useful,' Rachel said.

'It would be even more useful if he'd finished the monograph. His idea was to write it in two parts. The first told Mellor's story. The second was meant to explain the riddle, but he never wrote it. In view of the hoo-ha about his own disappearance, the society published the incomplete draft in a pamphlet. There's a copy in the British Museum.'

'Are there any clues in what he wrote?'

'No. His prose is dry and factual and gives no hint of his

thinking. As far as I can make out, he decided to replicate the circumstances of Mellor's disappearance as an experiment. Alfred wanted to lock himself inside the Lodge while he explored. He tried to persuade the Reverend Quintus Royle to act as a witness, watching from the grounds of the rectory.'

'As Furniss did,' Rachel said.

'Yes, but Royle is an old curmudgeon and he refused. As it happened, a man who lives in the upper village, Major Huckerby, was taking a constitutional when he noticed Alfred unlocking the gatehouse door. Alfred went inside the Lodge, but the major thought nothing of it. Some hours later, Alfred's manservant raised the hue and cry when his master couldn't be found. When Huckerby heard of this, he mentioned what he'd seen. The gatehouse was always kept locked, but this time there was a spare key. The manservant went inside, but Alfred was nowhere to be seen.'

'Nobody kept the gatehouse under surveillance,' Rachel said. 'Alfred might have come out again.'

'Just like Edmund Mellor,' Jacob said. 'I still think—'

Rachel interrupted. 'Carry on, please, Miss Fagan.'

'Alfred was a solitary individual who often went rambling in the neighbourhood. People assumed that he'd done just that. When it became clear that he wasn't around, there was an extensive search. There were several places where he might have come to grief.'

'Such as?'

'There's a small network of caves at the base of Blackstone Fell. Over the years, people used to live in them, although it was dangerous, because the rock is unstable. At the time, an old tramp called Nash had made his home there. He was questioned, but denied all knowledge of Alfred. There was nothing to prove that he had anything to do with the disappearance. Not long afterwards, the roof of the cave fell in, and Nash was buried alive. Nobody ever lived in the caves again.'

'The gazetteer mentions a narrow stretch of river which has claimed several lives.'

Nell pointed to her map. 'Blackstone Leap is as dangerous as anywhere in England. You can cross the river on stepping stones, but woe betide anyone who slips into the water. If Alfred stumbled on the stones and fell in, he'd have been swept away. There are underwater caverns where a body might be trapped forever.'

'So Alfred might have drowned?'

'Or perished in the marshland. The bogs are just as deadly for the unsuspecting walker. The authorities concluded that one way or another, Alfred had suffered a fatal accident.'

'No remains were ever found?'

'Nothing. Occasional sightings of Alfred were reported. It's only to be expected when a case receives some publicity. The authorities followed up every lead, but none came to anything. Then war broke out and Alfred Lejeune was forgotten.'

'Was he popular in the village?'

'He'd lived in Blackstone Fell for less than six months. Since he was something of a hermit, he made little impression on the local community. Quintus Royle disliked him, but that means nothing. The rector doesn't seem to like anybody, not even his wife. When I broached the subject with Major Huckerby, he confirmed his part in the story but couldn't add anything of value. He was bruised by idle gossip that he'd invented his story of witnessing Alfred's entry into the Lodge. As he said to me, he had no reason to lie.'

'So Alfred's brother inherited the Tower?'

Nell considered the question. 'If you think Harold Lejeune did away with Alfred,' she said slowly, 'you're mistaken. He had no opportunity. At the time, he was out of the country, and had been for a good twelve months. Rambling around the Dolomites, in search of rare plants.'

'When did he come back?'

Nell helped herself to a slice of Victoria sponge before giving her reply. 'Not for seven years. That's how long it took before Alfred could be presumed dead. It's a legal requirement.'

'And Harold remained abroad all that time? Throughout the war?'

'As far as I can gather, yes. What's more, he had no motive to kill Alfred. As far as I can make out, nobody gained financially from his demise.'

Rachel looked puzzled. 'What about the money he left?'

'Next to nothing, I believe, just like his cousin. The Lejeunes were otherworldly; they didn't care for material possessions. Alfred collected old books and manuscripts, but they are of no great value.'

'One of them might be a fabulous rarity,' Jacob said.

'Perhaps.' Nell's tone was dismissive. 'If so, nobody spotted it, certainly not the Lejeune family solicitors. The library was auctioned off, along with the rest of his effects. The estate was insolvent by the time he was officially declared to be deceased. The Tower was going to rack and ruin.'

'Seven years?' Jacob mused. 'So he wasn't declared dead until 1921?'

'Your mastery of arithmetic is dazzling.' Rachel's frosty tone implied that he had interrupted a meticulous line of cross-examination. 'Please continue, Miss Fagan.'

'The Tower is still in a dreadful state of repair. The stonework is crumbling and I'm told the roof leaks like a sieve. One of these days, the whole edifice will collapse in a heap of rubble, if the rector is to be believed. I don't think Quintus Royle will shed many tears.'

'Have you looked inside the Tower?'

'No. The present owner doesn't encourage visitors.'

Nell tucked into her Victoria sponge. Rachel scrutinised her, as if trying to read her mind. A waste of time, in Jacob's opinion. If he knew Nell, she was thinking about her stomach. And wondering how to spin out her yarn until cocktail time.

'How do you explain the disappearances?' Rachel asked.

'To be honest, Miss Savernake, I don't. They seem inexplicable. Perhaps both men got out of the Lodge and died somewhere else. How they managed, it, who knows? I doubt they were victims of foul play, if only because nobody gained by their deaths. It's a genuine puzzle. If you're willing, I'd like to harness your skills as an amateur detective.'

'I'm still curious as to why you want to speak to me,' Rachel said in an icy tone. 'You're not deterred by our last encounter?'

Nell shifted in her chair. 'I've already apologised for – um – fibbing about Jacob. Can we wipe the slate clean?'

'What took you to Yorkshire?'

Jacob threw a glance at Rachel. She was concentrating all her attention on Nell. The room was warmed by a fire, but he felt as if the temperature in the room had dropped by several degrees. As if Rachel had set a test for her visitor, and Nell had failed.

'I agreed to be honest with you,' Nell said.

'You did.'

'Very well. I went to Blackstone Fell to solve a murder.'

7

Nell stuffed a piece of chocolate into her mouth before washing it down with a gulp of tea. Building suspense, Jacob thought, as she did when holding court at Fleet Street's favourite watering hole. Female journalists were exiled by management decree to the back room of El Vino's, but that never bothered Nell. Her salacious yarns and saucy limericks commanded a gleeful audience. And because she was a woman, she was never allowed to buy a round.

'Two weeks ago,' she said, 'I was approached by a young man called Vernon Murray, a clerk at the British Museum. He wanted my help to catch whoever murdered his mother.'

She paused for dramatic effect. Rachel's expression didn't flicker.

'Five years ago, shortly after Vernon went up to Cambridge, his father died. Old man Murray was something in the City and left his widow very comfortably off. She was much younger than her late husband and had a passion for the theatre. Eighteen months after being widowed, she got into conversation with a handsome young fellow during the interval of a Noël Coward show. The chap told her he was a playwright. Not that any of his masterpieces have been published or performed.'

'His name?' Rachel asked.

'Thomas Baker.' Nell bared large teeth in a grin. 'No, none of the theatre critics have heard of him, either. He was only five years older than her son, but he swept Ursula Murray off her feet. Vernon loathed Baker, and accused him of taking advantage of Ursula's fragile temperament. Her response was to say that Vernon cared more about his inheritance than her happiness. When Baker proposed, she accepted without a moment's hesitation. After the wedding they waltzed off to the Riviera for a long and expensive honeymoon. Vernon left Cambridge with a pass degree. Apparently that's a badge of failure. His mother made him an allowance, but he blamed Baker for its lack of generosity. Ursula was determined to support her new husband in his writing.'

Rachel shrugged. 'A common tale. A spoiled brat's jealousy of a new stepfather, coupled with an unwillingness to stand on his own two feet.'

'Vernon is no angel.' Nell sounded defensive. 'He tried teaching at a prep school, but the boys made his life a misery and he resigned after a single term. He's extravagant, and although he took a clerking job, he sank into debt. At first his mother bailed him out, but he needed more help.'

'And she turned off the tap?'

'At Baker's behest,' Nell said. 'Even worse, she was taken ill. At least so Baker said. According to him, she'd suffered a nervous collapse, caused by anxiety about Vernon's irresponsibility.'

'What did Vernon do?'

'He didn't believe a word of it but he feared for his mother's wellbeing. In his opinion, Baker married her for money, nothing else. If she was sick, Vernon was determined to seek an independent opinion. Baker insisted that Ursula's only chance of recovery was to be cared for by a leading specialist. This summer he whisked her off to a sanatorium.'

'Let me guess,' Rachel said. 'At Blackstone Fell?'

Nell nodded. 'The sanatorium is run by Professor Wilfred Sambrook. Getting on in age, but supposedly a leader in his field.'

'Which is?'

'Psychiatric disorder.'

'If he is a recognised authority, then it's reasonable to presume that Ursula Baker was genuinely ill.'

'Baker may have exaggerated her symptoms,' Nell said.

'An expert would soon establish the truth.'

Nell made a face. 'Diagnose a complex, you mean. That explains everything, specially if you throw in a repression dating back to childhood.'

Rachel gave a faint smile. 'You said yourself that her temperament was fragile.'

'Baker said Ursula needed absolute peace and quiet. Nobody from outside was to disturb her. In particular not her selfish son.'

'What about her husband?'

'If Vernon is to be believed, Baker's method of coping with distress was to squander his wife's riches on actresses and roulette. Vernon was beside himself with worry. A few weeks ago, he headed to Blackstone Fell and took a room in The New Jerusalem, the local inn. But when he turned up at the sanatorium, he wasn't allowed to see his mother.'

'They were carrying out the professor's orders.'

'Yes,' Nell admitted. 'Vernon demanded to see the professor, but had to be content with the old man's son. Denzil Sambrook said Ursula was delirious and gravely ill. Any excitement or upset could finish her off.'

'Vernon didn't believe him?'

'He didn't know what to believe. If his mother was at death's door, then of course he wanted to see her. He kicked up a stink, but Dr Sambrook stood firm. He insisted that the patients' wellbeing was their sole concern and summoned reinforcements in the shape of a hulking attendant. There was nothing Vernon could do. He caught the next train back to London, intent on confronting Baker.'

'And did he catch up with him?'

'Yes, outside a casino club off Leicester Square. Baker emerged arm in arm with a pretty young woman. When he told Vernon to mind his own business, the poor sap took a wild swing and caught his stepfather a glancing blow on the cheek. No serious harm done, but he drew blood. The girl's scream brought a constable hurrying over, but Baker refused to make a complaint.'

'Magnanimous to a fault.'

'Absolutely. When Vernon begged the constable to make enquiries about his mother because her life was in jeopardy, he was told to thank his lucky stars he wasn't up on a charge of assault. Or facing an action for slander. The girl backed Baker to the hilt. She said Vernon was looking after number one. Baker was heartbroken about his wife's illness and had put her in the best possible hands.'

'The young lady was simply offering comfort at a difficult time?'

'Out of the kindness of her heart, making sure that in

his misery he didn't spend too much time and money at the Hermes,' Nell said grimly. 'Vernon slunk away with his tail between his legs. He's a weak character.'

'He takes after his mother?'

Nell shrugged. 'He was still agonising over what to do – and how to buy more time from his creditors – when he received a telegram from Blackstone Sanatorium. His mother had died.'

'What was the cause of death?'

'Heart failure. Vernon discovered that Ursula had made a new will a month earlier. This was drawn up by her London solicitor, before her nerves finally gave way.'

'Was she of sound mind at the time?'

'Oh yes, if Thomas Baker engineered the whole business, he made a good job of it. He'd told Ursula's solicitor that he was worried about her state of health, and arranged for her to have a thorough examination forty-eight hours before making the will. Under its terms, Vernon received a modest bequest, but the bulk of the estate went to her husband. In consideration of Ursula's natural love and affection for him, to use the lawyers' phrase.'

'A true romantic,' Rachel said.

'Unlike Baker. He insisted on the funeral being held at Blackstone Fell. She was buried in the village graveyard, much to Vernon's fury. He said her dearest wish was to be interred with his father in Kensal Green Cemetery. He convinced himself that his mother was the victim of foul play. Baker visited her the day before her death. It was the first time he'd seen his wife since her admission to the sanatorium.'

'How long did he stay at Blackstone Fell?'

'That's the difficulty. After leaving Ursula, he seems to have caught the train home. Not that Vernon believes that. He thinks Baker disposed of her somehow, so that he was free to enjoy himself with her money and a procession of stage-struck blondes.'

'A serious accusation. Did he have any evidence?'

Nell shook her head. 'None. Vernon lost his temper at the graveside. Picked a fight with Baker, and accused him of murdering Ursula. Once again he came off worst. The professor's son bundled him out of harm's way and urged him to go back to London. Everyone's sympathy was with the grieving widower. The blameless victim of an unprovoked attack.'

'Vernon Murray was humiliated and short of money,' Rachel said. 'So he turned to you?'

'First he went to Scotland Yard, but they wouldn't give him the time of day. He couldn't afford to hire an enquiry agent and he'd heard on the grapevine that I'm a terrier when I get my teeth into an investigation. The case was a lifeline, a chance to remind everyone in Fleet Street of what I can do. I even thought about trying to persuade you to collaborate. This story is right up your street, as well as mine.'

Rachel's face was a mask. Nell's bright smile faded.

'Anyway, I thought better of it.'

'So you visited Blackstone Fell?'

'Yes, but I didn't want to get sent off with a flea in my ear, like Vernon. I looked for somewhere to stay.'

'Why not book into the inn?'

'I didn't want anyone to associate me with Vernon. The Sambrooks live in an old manor house in the upper village, and two properties were to rent there. When I talked to the land agent, I discovered that they were owned by the

Sambrook family trust. One place is a cottage, opposite the manor. The other is Blackstone Lodge.'

'So they own the mysterious gatehouse? It no longer belongs to the Lejeune family?'

'It was sold recently. The word is that the owner of the Tower is short of money. I'm the very first tenant.'

'If the Lodge has never been occupied before, why did the Sambrooks buy it?'

Nell shrugged. 'The professor and his son are men of science. They aren't superstitious. My guess is that Denzil also has a good head for business. They must be buying up property in the village with an eye to the rental income. They certainly didn't break the bank on refurbishing the Lodge. Junk shop furniture and a bed that feels like it's made of nails.'

'Have you met your landlords?'

'Not yet. I decided to pretend to be an amateur photographer. An excuse to snoop around.'

'Have you brought any photographs?'

'Not with me. So far I've only met the village doctor, Major Huckerby, and the rector and his wife.'

'And Harold Lejeune?'

'The owner of Blackstone Tower?' She made a dismissive gesture. 'Only seen him in passing. We haven't spoken.'

'And what's the current state of your investigation?'

Nell exhaled. 'I'm not sure how it's happened, but my secret is out. Even the meek little rector's wife has warned me to leave. And someone tried to kill me on Blackstone Fell.'

With suitable melodrama, Nell described her near miss with the boulder and the strange episode of Judith Royle and her anonymous note. As she reached her peroration, she rewarded herself with another slice of cake.

'Naturally,' she mumbled with her mouth full, 'I shall continue with my enquiries. I wanted you to be in possession of the facts.'

'You've seen Vernon Murray since you came back to London?'

'Yesterday and this morning.'

'Twice?'

Nell said huffily, 'I feel it's my duty to keep him informed. And to keep a motherly eye on him. His spirits are very low.'

'What did you say?'

'I said I felt there was something fishy going on at Blackstone Fell, but I didn't have anything much to go on yet. And I didn't tell him about the attempt on my life. He's jumpy enough as it is.' She hesitated. 'I almost wonder if he regrets asking me to investigate.'

'Does he know you have come to see me?'

Nell chewed thoughtfully. 'I may not have mentioned it.'

'Despite seeing him on two separate occasions?'

'I don't want to bother his head with the details of what I get up to. But if anything should happen to me, I hope that you...'

'You regard me as a kind of insurance policy?' Rachel asked. 'An avenger, if your luck runs out and all else fails?'

Jacob detected a note of menace in her voice. His spine prickled.

'Not at all,' Nell said. 'I reckon the mystery of Blackstone Lodge is right up your street. If you can make sense of it for me, it would make an excellent article in one of the weeklies. I know you don't like your name to be bandied around in public, and I promise not to do that. In the meantime, I hope to find out what happened to Ursula Baker. So I return to Blackstone Fell tonight.'

'If you do,' Rachel said, 'you're risking your life.'

Jacob could contain himself no longer. 'Do you really think so? Perhaps the boulder toppled over by accident. As for the poison pen letter…'

'Don't be bashful, Jacob,' Rachel snapped. 'Share your wisdom with us.'

He turned to Nell. 'Before you moved to the *Globe*, you had a spell with the *Mail*, Mrs Royle's favourite paper. Perhaps your picture appeared next to your byline. If she recognised you, then she may have been aggrieved and perhaps even alarmed if she has secrets of her own to hide.'

'Secrets?'

'She's young and good-looking, and her husband doesn't understand her. My guess is that she's been rolling in the hay with one of the parishioners. No wonder she wants to scare you off. She's terrified that you'll print a story about her in a scandal sheet.'

Nell's eyebrows shot up. 'Ingenious.'

Jacob threw a nonchalant glance at Rachel.

She ignored him. 'What else would you like to tell me, Miss Fagan?'

Nell belched as she consumed the last morsel of cake. It seemed to help in arriving at a decision. 'I've taken up enough of your time. Thanks for listening, Miss Savernake, I'm relieved to have got it all off my chest. If you have any theories, I'd love to hear from you.'

'Curious,' Rachel said. 'I expected you to ask me to accompany you to Blackstone Fell.'

'Goodness me, no.' A startled look flitted across Nell's face. 'That wasn't why I came here. In any case, Blackstone Fell is no place for a young woman like you. I'm twice your age. I can afford to take a chance or two. Anyway, it takes more than a lump of rock to finish me off.'

'I hope so, Miss Fagan.' Rachel's voice became icy. 'When I agreed to this meeting, my condition was that you would be entirely candid with me. Correct, Jacob?'

'Yes.' Jacob's heart sank.

'Yet you are withholding significant items of information from me, aren't you?'

'Perish the—' Nell began in a tone of outrage.

'Please.' Rachel held up a hand to silence her. 'I'm not a child. You haven't lied in the same ridiculous way as last time, but you've failed to tell me the whole truth. Deceiving me is unwise. Now, if you'll excuse me.'

As she jumped to her feet, the door swung open. Martha stood there, holding Nell's scruffy coat. Beyond her, Jacob saw the bulky figure of Clifford Trueman in the hall. No bell had rung. It was as if the servants were telepathic.

Nell heaved herself up from the armchair. 'Miss Savernake, if you'll only be reasonable…'

'Goodbye,' Rachel said.

As Martha helped Nell on with her coat, Clifford Trueman advanced into the room.

'About the disappearances,' Nell said. 'Keep the map and the photograph. If you have any ideas…'

'Yes,' Rachel said softly. 'I have ideas, but I shall let you work out that little conundrum for yourself.'

Nell glowered. 'You complain about my keeping cards close to my chest. All right. But what about you? I never knew anyone so close. You have secrets of your own that you'd hate to come out. I'd stake my life on it.'

Wincing as she put weight on her damaged leg, she stomped out of the room with as much dignity as she could muster.

'Goodbye, Miss Fagan,' Rachel said softly. 'I doubt we'll meet again.'

'Martha must be a mind-reader,' Jacob said when he and Rachel were alone again. 'She can't have listened at the door. Didn't you tell me this room is soundproof?'

Rachel stretched lazily in her armchair. 'We've acquired the latest Dictograph from America. The Truemans can listen in to conversations in this room at the flick of a switch. I saw you admiring my new radiogram. A marvellous piece of equipment.'

'You turned the music off when we arrived.' Light was dawning in Jacob's mind. 'Did you activate the Dictograph at the same time?'

She patted the grille of the radiogram. 'An ingenious toy. Isn't it lovely? I asked Martha and Cliff to be ready to escort Nell Fagan from the premises. Your friend is so predictable. Dogged and resourceful, but muddle-headed. Her judgment is poor.'

'That's why she imagined that she and you might form a crime-solving partnership. Together, you'd make a good team.'

'Stealing your thunder, Jacob?' Rachel tutted. 'If she wanted my help, she should have realised that I'm not as gullible as her readers.'

'Weren't you rather harsh on her? Last night she swore to be entirely frank with you.'

'And today?'

'She told you a good deal. Not only about the two disappearances, but also concerning the case of Ursula Baker, and the fact that someone may have tried to crush her to death…'

'On several occasions Nell Fagan chose her words with peculiar care. You didn't notice?'

'Actually, no.' He bristled. 'Surely that is just your own suspicious mind? You don't trust Nell, so you anticipate the worst.'

She shrugged. Her unruffled assurance often got under his skin, but he knew her well enough to realise that it was a mistake to allow himself to be provoked.

'When we talked on the way here, I got the impression that her thinking had changed overnight.'

'I wonder if she was encouraged to change her tune. Did she speak to anyone after you parted yesterday evening?'

'I'm sure she went straight home. I heard her give the address to the cabbie. This morning she called at the British Museum and on her old governess before our lunch with Eunice Bell.' He considered. 'I suppose it's possible that Nell mentioned you to Vernon Murray. But why would Murray discourage her from taking you into her confidence? She said he was jumpy; was that the reason?'

'As usual, you ask good questions.' Rachel was at her most infuriatingly inscrutable. 'But are they the right questions?'

Nettled, he said, 'You poured cold water on my ideas about the disappearances, but obviously both men sneaked out of the gatehouse. I wonder if they escaped through some kind of tunnel that ends up elsewhere in the village. The churchyard, perhaps, or the rectory. If they were lured…'

Rachel smiled. 'You bragged to me once about your love of history. Top of your class at school, didn't you say?'

'You have a good memory,' he said cautiously.

'And yours is like blotting paper. Nell Fagan boasts about her visual memory, but your ability to recall detail is priceless.'

He was taken aback. Rachel Savernake didn't throw compliments around like confetti. 'Thank you.'

She waved at Nell's photograph of the Lodge interior. 'The past is like a photographer's dark room. As a picture develops, you never quite know how it will come out.'

He didn't bother to conceal his bafflement. 'Um…'

'Consider dates, Jacob,' she said briskly. 'When did Edmund Mellor go missing?'

'Is it significant?'

'Rack your brains.'

'1606?' His brow furrowed. 'I've got a vague recollection that *Macbeth* dates from then. My favourite play.'

'A murder story,' Rachel said dreamily. 'A drama about killing a king.'

'Am I getting warm?'

'I won't spoon-feed you. Let's say that you're not stone cold, but you need to think around the problem. Remember everything she told us. Test your imagination.'

'I don't quite…'

'Amuse yourself with the riddle when you have an idle moment.' She stood up. 'Now we have other work to do.'

'We do?'

She stood up. 'There's more going on at Blackstone Fell than Nell Fagan will admit. We need to speak to Vernon Murray.'

8

'Why should I talk to you?' Vernon Murray said.

Willowy and weak-chinned, he looked as petulant as he sounded. The bruise on his cheek made him easy to spot in the crowd spilling down the steps outside the British Museum. Jacob and Rachel had secured a description of their quarry from a helpful attendant before intercepting him on his way out at the end of his working day. They'd shepherded him to a quiet corner of the forecourt.

'Nell Fagan is a friend of mine,' Jacob said. 'Right now she's on her way back to Blackstone Fell.'

Vernon turned his coat collar up against the drizzle. 'What business is it of yours? Or mine, for that matter?'

'Nell asked for my help,' Jacob said.

'What sort of help?'

'You persuaded her that your mother was murdered,' Rachel said.

'And who are you?' Vernon snapped.

'Rachel Savernake.'

If the clerk recognised the name, his glare gave no hint of it. Jacob was puzzled. Was it wrong to assume that Vernon had discouraged Nell from calling on Rachel's assistance?

Or was this peevish young man a better actor than he seemed?

Vernon glanced over his shoulder. 'My private affairs are none of your concern.'

'I'm curious,' Rachel said. 'Nell Fagan saw you yesterday and then came back here again this morning. Why was that?'

'If she's really a friend, ask her yourself what she found so interesting,' Vernon snapped. 'I have a train to catch.'

Jacob gripped the other man's arm. 'We're on your side. We only want…'

'Get off me!'

With a loud, almost hysterical shriek, Vernon wriggled out of Jacob's grasp. From the corner of his eye, Jacob spotted a heavily built constable on Great Russell Street turn in their direction. The officer stroked his walrus moustache, his attention attracted by the squeal of panic. Vernon broke into a run and disappeared into the milling crowd. Jacob made as if to follow him, only to be restrained by Rachel's firm hand.

'Don't cause a scene,' she said. 'The policeman looks as though he'd enjoy arresting someone just to stave off boredom on a miserable autumn evening.'

'Sorry,' Jacob said. 'I didn't mean to overstep the mark. I never imagined he'd scamper off like a scared rabbit.'

He braced himself for a scathing retort. As so often, Rachel took him by surprise.

'Don't worry. We learned a good deal.'

'We did?'

'Certainly. For instance, you noticed his curious choice of words? *Ask her yourself what she found so interesting.*'

'Nell isn't here to ask.'

'You're missing the point.' Rachel betrayed her exasperation. 'Those are the words of a spoiled brat who always wants to be the centre of attention.'

Jacob wrinkled his nose. 'Possibly.'

'What else could he mean? If I'm right, the next question is this. Why did she come here at all? Given her enthusiasm for the newspaper archive, I wonder if she was looking up a back issue. And if so, which?'

'Even if you're right, does it matter?'

'Nell was due to call on her governess and then meet you for lunch with Eunice Bell. After seeing me, she meant to return to Yorkshire. A hectic schedule. She'd already reported to Vernon Murray. If she took the trouble to research in the newspaper library, she will have had good reason. She's a freelance without a reliable source of income. Living off her savings as she dreams of a scoop that will revive her career. Why fritter away precious time?'

'Put that way,' Jacob said in his best judicial manner, 'you may be on to something. But it doesn't tell us what Nell wanted to find.'

'The chief librarian responsible for newspapers should be able to give us a clue. Luckily, I've made his acquaintance.'

'You have?'

'Nell Fagan isn't the only person who finds the Museum an invaluable resource when investigating crime. My library is extensive, but it doesn't tell me everything I need to know. Thankfully, there are riches on my doorstep. If Mr Wagstaffe runs true to form, he'll still be at his desk. A man who loves his work.' She paused. 'Almost as much as he relishes the admiration of young women.'

'Ah.'

'Don't be offended,' she said, 'but this time, let me do all the talking.'

'What are you going to say?'

'I'll think of something. He enjoys playing the knight errant, coming to the rescue of a damsel in distress.'

She strode off towards the Museum entrance. Jacob thought that anyone less like a damsel in distress was hard to imagine.

'Really,' Horace Wagstaffe said, adjusting his pince-nez, 'this is a little irregular, Miss Savernake. I'll make no bones about it, I wouldn't do this for anyone else.'

A bird-like pedant in his fifties, he'd invited Rachel and Jacob into his inner sanctum, a cosy den reeking of old newspapers, calfskin-bound tomes, and mint humbugs. Jacob had accepted the offer of an enormous sweet. It guaranteed that he kept his mouth shut.

'You're so very generous.' Rachel had an uncanny ability to simper at will. 'I swear I wouldn't dream of placing you in an awkward position if this wasn't so crucial to Albert's future happiness.'

She'd introduced Jacob as Albert Cheetham, a distant cousin from Barnsley. As she explained in hushed tones, Albert was due to marry a debutante called Emily, but dreaded her learning of an incident from his past that threatened to blemish his spotless good name. In Yorkshire, he'd once been arrested in connection with a sordid business in a public park, involving a rich and brutish mill owner. The man had taken advantage of Albert's youth and poor head for alcohol, and local newspapers reported the charges in lurid terms. Thankfully, the case had never come to court. Rachel hinted that the mill owner had pulled strings through some dubious freemasonry. Nevertheless, if this unpleasant incident came to light, Emily – a highly principled Methodist whose father was a minister – was sure to break off the engagement.

Rachel said that Nell Fagan was planning to expose the mill owner's multiple misdemeanours in the *News of the World* and Albert feared she might reveal his own unfortunate involvement with the man. Two hearts would be broken, as Rachel told Wagstaffe with a little cry in her voice – and for what?

'To err is human,' Wagstaffe said with a horrid leer that, in his own mind, was probably a roguish smile.

'I knew you'd understand!' Rachel exclaimed. 'I hear Miss Fagan faces a tight deadline to deliver her copy in time for Sunday's edition. She came here this morning to research.'

Wagstaffe gave a disapproving sniff and Jacob deduced that he and Nell had crossed swords in the past.

'She is one of our regulars. Between you, me, and the gatepost, she isn't the easiest to deal with. Rather coarse, in my opinion. I'm not surprised she's working for a scandal sheet.'

'We cling to a sliver of hope,' Rachel said. 'The story never reached the national press. She may know nothing about it. On the other hand, if she examined Yorkshire newspapers from 1927, poor Albert will be forced to prepare for the worst. If not, the chances are that his secret is safe. Of course, we are placing our trust in you, but I've assured Albert that you'll never breathe a word outside these four walls.'

'The course of true love never runs smooth,' Wagstaffe said

sententiously. 'A young chap is bound to… um… sow a few wild oats. Let me make enquiries. Do help yourself to another sweet, Mr Cheetham. Miss Savernake…'

'Please do call me Rachel,' she cooed. 'Thank you, but no humbug for me.'

'I'm bound to say, Rachel, that you're already sweet enough.'

Rachel gave a tinkly laugh of delight and Wagstaffe smirked his way out of the office.

Swallowing the rest of his humbug, Jacob muttered, 'That's my reputation down the Swanee.'

'Given the – to coin a phrase – indecent haste, it was the best story I could come up with. I didn't want him to regard you as a rival for my affections.'

'Thanks.'

'Don't be petty, Jacob. If Waggy surrenders to the green-eyed monster, we won't find out what Nell Fagan was up to.'

Jacob rolled his eyes. 'Waggy?'

'Last time we met, he asked me to call him that.' She fluttered her eyelashes. 'But not, I think, in the presence of a third party.'

Jacob gave a snort of derision and shoved another humbug into his mouth. He was still brooding when Wagstaffe trotted back into the room.

'Success!' the little man trilled. 'That's the beauty of a meticulous system, Rachel. A place for everything and everything in its place.'

'How wonderful,' she breathed. 'You're so good at keeping on top of things.'

He glowed with bonhomie. 'Believe me, Rachel. Anyway, you'll be relieved to hear that this morning Miss Fagan requisitioned back numbers of the *Globe* and the *Clarion* from as long ago as 1914. In those days Mr Cheetham was an innocent young schoolboy.'

'A schoolboy, certainly,' Rachel said. 'Thank you for bringing such marvellous news. Miss Fagan must be on the trail of long-ago misdemeanours. We worried needlessly.'

'Good news, eh, Mr Cheetham?'

Jacob almost choked on his humbug. 'Champion.'

Wagstaffe chortled. 'Care to celebrate, Rachel? I'm sure Mr Cheetham wants to run along and enjoy his fiancée's company, but perhaps you and I could have a bite together? There's a jolly little restaurant near where I live in Notting Hill...'

Rachel rose. 'How wonderfully generous of you. Unfortunately, both of us must run. The engagement party is this evening. You've given the happy couple the perfect present.'

'Oh dear me, what a shame.' He paused. 'Although naturally I understand. I wonder if tomorrow evening...?'

They were out of the room before the little man completed his sentence.

'1914,' Jacob said as they went in search of a taxi. The drizzle had turned into a downpour. 'The year Alfred Lejeune vanished from Blackstone Lodge.'

'Yes.' Rachel sounded pensive.

'We're not much further forward.'

'I disagree.' She waved her umbrella at an approaching cab. 'Among other things, we've learned that Vernon Murray is frightened.'

'That bruise on his cheek. Do you suppose someone roughed him up? Has Baker intimidated him?'

'Who knows?' she said as the taxi pulled in beside them. 'Nell Fagan has woven a tangled web. Young Murray is trapped in it.'

'I don't understand.'

'If it's any consolation, neither do I.' She swivelled, pointing the tip of the umbrella at Jacob's heart. 'Come back to Gaunt House and have dinner with us.'

It was a command rather than an invitation, but he was happy to accept. They climbed into the back of the cab.

'You'll have to sing for your supper.'

'Surprise, surprise,' he said wryly.

'I need you to tell me everything you've learned since Nell Fagan first spoke to you about Blackstone Fell.'

'I'll do my best.'

'I have the utmost faith in your command of detail.' She smiled. 'Your reward will come after dinner with Trueman's latest masterpiece.'

'How can I resist? What's it called?'

'Blood and Sand.'

'What do you make of it?' Jacob asked.

It was nine o'clock and he and Rachel had adjourned from the dining room to the library. During a lavish meal of devilled sole and entrecôte, Jacob had regaled them with a reprise of his conversations with Nell Fagan and her aunt. After serving the cocktails, Trueman had departed to listen to the radio, a favourite pastime, while Hetty and Martha also made themselves scarce.

Rachel savoured her drink. 'At first I wasn't sure. Blood and Sand is recommended in Harry Craddock's book – but scotch whisky in a cocktail? It's not everyone's idea of a marriage made in heaven. On closer acquaintance, I rather like the hint of earthiness, the touch of acid. The hue of blood seeping into sand. Cherry Heering and freshly squeezed orange juice, if you prefer to be prosaic. Trueman shakes the ingredients with just the right combination of muscle and finesse.'

Jacob tried to contain his impatience. 'You'll have to watch that Craddock doesn't poach him for a job at the Savoy. Actually, I was wondering what you make of the Blackstone Fell mystery.'

'Nell Fagan is an unreliable storyteller,' she said, putting down her glass. 'I've no doubt she told us less than the whole truth. Vernon Murray is definitely scared. Beyond that, it's as murky as a London pea-souper.'

'Frustrating.'

'Exciting,' she said. 'I love strolling through the city streets on a foggy night. That moment when you finally see your way through the murk never fails to thrill.'

'What if the fog thickens?'

'Fog always clears in the end,' she said. 'You simply need to stay calm and not lose your way.'

'You weren't so calm when you told Nell you weren't prepared to see her again.'

'You're misquoting.' She took another sip of her cocktail. 'Her slipperiness is infuriating, but she was right to think that her story would intrigue me. I only wish she'd honoured her side of our bargain. Instead, she's rushing in where Vernon Murray fears to tread. There has already been one attempt to silence her.'

'The business with the falling boulder might have been an act of God.'

'God may move in mysterious ways, Jacob, but that incident sounds to me like clever opportunism.' There was a touch of admiration in her voice. 'Someone spotted a chance to kill her, and seized it. She only survived thanks to a stroke of fortune. There is such artistic satisfaction in committing the perfect crime. A murder that doesn't look like a murder.'

'It didn't work.'

'On that occasion, no.'

'You think her life is in danger?'

'If someone in the village wishes to kill her, another chance is sure to come their way. The landscape is dangerous. If all else fails, she wouldn't be the first to disappear without trace from Blackstone Lodge.'

'Vernon Murray is a coward. Letting Nell take all the risk.'

'Nell Fagan is a grown woman. She has made her choice. As for Murray, you saw the dread in his eyes.'

Rachel finished her cocktail as Trueman walked in without knocking.

'Immaculate timing. Blood and Sand is marvellous. My congratulations.' She stared at his expression. 'What's the matter?'

The big man loomed over her. 'A tragedy occurred on the London Underground earlier this evening. At the British Museum Station, to be exact. I heard the news on the radio. According to the BBC, a man slipped from the platform and went under a train.'

Jacob swore.

'I took the liberty of ringing the nearby hospitals, claiming to be a frantic brother. Finally I managed to persuade a young woman to reveal the name of the deceased.'

Rachel's voice frosted. 'Go on.'

'The dead man is Vernon Murray.'

'A dreadful accident?'

'Sheer bad luck, so the story goes. Wet night, damp platform, surging throng of commuters. Chance in a thousand.'

In the ensuing silence, Rachel's words echoed in Jacob's brain.

'The perfect crime. A murder that doesn't look like a murder.'

9

Nell Fagan's bed in Blackstone Lodge was lumpy and uncomfortable; even so, she overslept on Saturday morning. The previous night she'd sampled the bottle of Gordon's she'd brought from London and she awoke to find her head throbbing. A long, busy day had left her exhausted as well as hungover. When she finally crawled out of bed and set foot on the floor, the pain in her ankle made her yelp.

It took an age to bathe, dress, and munch a slice of buttered toast and an apple. The sheer quiet of the gatehouse was strangely oppressive. In London, there was always some kind of noise in the background. People, cars, buses. She'd never known a place like this, where she felt so isolated.

Glancing out through the window, she saw a man sauntering down the drive from the Tower. Carrodus, the village doctor, swinging his black bag.

She flung open the door and hurried outside, almost colliding with him.

'Miss Grace!'

Remembering her alias in the nick of time, she said, 'Sorry, Doctor.'

He grinned. 'Better be careful or you'll turn your other ankle. And be warned, my services don't come cheap.'

'I'll mind where I'm going in future,' she promised. 'What brings you to the Tower?'

'Harold Lejeune asked me to drop in.'

She peered at him. 'Nothing amiss, I hope?'

Carrodus shook his head. 'No cause for concern, I'm glad to say.'

Nell hoped this young chap wouldn't prove drearily scrupulous about medical confidentiality. 'I want to ask him about the Lodge's strange history.'

Carrodus laughed. 'Those tall tales about grown men vanishing in a puff of smoke? Tommyrot, if you ask me. No need to be frightened by the village folklore.'

'I'm simply curious. Alfred Lejeune went missing sixteen years ago, well within living memory.'

'The rector must know something about it. He's been here since the year dot. As for Lejeune, he won't be able to help you. He didn't set foot in the village until long after the war.'

'I'd still like to talk to him. So far we've only glimpsed each other in passing. I suppose that if he's unwell…'

Carrodus smiled. 'Let me set your mind at rest. I don't think I'm speaking out of turn if I say Harold Lejeune prefers his own company to that of others. I gather he was reclusive even before he lost his wife.'

'Ah yes, Mrs Royle mentioned that she died of… heart failure, was it?'

A frown. 'Stomach cancer, actually. Mrs Lejeune fell sick shortly before I arrived in Blackstone Fell. She bore her illness with courage, but it took a toll on her husband.'

'How very sad. I believe she was Italian?'

'And a proud one. Wonderful country, she told me.' Carrodus consulted his pocket watch. 'Now, if you'll excuse me.'

'So Mr Lejeune is quite all right?' She felt an obscure sense of anticlimax.

'Heart palpitations. Disconcerting, but no need to worry, he's certainly not at death's door. Frankly, a day in bed is all he needs to set him right.'

Carrodus exuded the confidence of the young and healthy. Nell supposed that his patients valued the medicine of reassurance as much as any pills or potions. She was conscious of his measuring gaze.

'That limp of yours isn't getting any better. Not been gallivanting around, I trust? In this cold wind, your ankle will stiffen up in no time. A bit of bed rest won't do you any harm, mark my words.'

Nell gathered that bed rest was Carrodus's customary prescription for ailments of all descriptions, but he was right about the weather. She could feel the cold seeping into her bones.

'I'm not...'

With a wave of the hand, he moved away. 'Good to see you again, Miss Grace. Forgive me, but I must dash. Remember what I said about resting up. Cheeribye!'

He escaped before she could insist that, limp or no limp, she felt as fit as a fiddle. In truth, the ankle was giving her hell. After going back indoors, she treated herself to a medicinal brandy before flopping back on the bed. Two minutes later she was fast asleep.

***

'I never knew you were a football fan,' Jacob said.

He and Detective Inspector Philip Oakes detached themselves from the raucous mob. Fifty thousand supporters were swarming out of Highbury stadium onto the streets of north London. They'd just seen the Gunners share the spoils in a hard-fought derby match against the Hammers. The raging passions of the contest were hardly captured by the prosaic score-line: Arsenal 1, West Ham United 1.

'I like to lose myself among the masses on the terraces. I find the anonymity intoxicating.'

Oakes was tall, thin, and in his thirties. A conveniently nondescript appearance enabled him to melt into any crowd. A passer-by who spared his malleable features a second glance would be hard pressed to recall anything other than a sharp chin and thoughtful brown eyes. Criminals frequently underestimated him, a mistake that had condemned more than one man to the gallows.

'Makes a change from being on duty, eh?'

'I'll say. Escape from superiors wanting me to solve cases with one wave of a magic wand.' Oakes tightened the knot in his red and white scarf. 'An afternoon of freedom. Ninety minutes to bellow about the players' mistakes, the opponents' skulduggery, and the referee's shameful parentage.'

'Honours even,' Jacob said. 'In the end it was a fair result.'

Oakes pointed to two groups of rival supporters berating each other on the opposite side of the road. Any minute now, they'd start a fight.

'True football fans are one-eyed. Forget the cant about play up, play up, and play the game. We want to win.'

'Let's get some beer. The drinks are on me.' Jacob grinned. 'Or strictly speaking, on the *Clarion*.'

'There's a spit-and-sawdust place on the next corner where they serve a good pint. It'll be packed to the rafters. Nobody will be able to listen to us. The regulars make such a racket, you can hardly hear yourself think.'

'Just as well I'm learning to lip-read. Comes in useful when I see folk whispering things they don't want me to know.'

Oakes shook his head in mock dismay. 'You gentlemen of the fourth estate; your cunning never ceases to amaze me.'

Jacob liked the inspector and hoped the feeling was mutual but Oakes was, in his understated way, almost as hard to fathom as Rachel Savernake. Shrewd judges tipped him as a future commissioner, and nobody climbed so far and so fast without possessing a core of steel. Why had he agreed so readily to enquire about Vernon Murray's death and meet up on his day off? Jacob's inner cynic refused to put it down to sheer good nature.

Once inside the pub, it took him an age to shove his way to the front of the queue at the bar. Everyone was arguing about the match. The only point beyond dispute was the brilliance of Boy Bastin, scorer of the Gunners' only goal. Fresh-faced and eighteen, he resembled a schoolboy, but already he was the finest outside-left in England. Watching him race down the wing before cutting inside to advance on goal was a joy, even if his precocious genius made Jacob feel old before his time.

He carried two dimpled tankards of foaming beer to the back of the bar. He and Oakes squashed against the wall next to a gaggle of Arsenal fans. They were disgruntled about their team's dropped point and vociferous about West Ham's craven willingness to settle for a draw.

'Cheers,' Oakes raised his glass.

'Here's to crime.'

'Speaking of which, I've looked into the death of Vernon Murray.' Oakes shot him a quizzical look. 'Did Miss Rachel Savernake put you up to this, by any chance?'

'How did you guess?'

The Scotland Yard man laughed. 'She's got you wrapped around her little finger.'

Jacob refused to rise to the bait. 'What did you find out?'

'Vernon Murray's death is being treated as an accident. Half a dozen witnesses have come forward. Nobody was seen pushing the man. He fell just as the train was coming in to the station. The driver couldn't stop before hitting him. The inquest should be open and shut.'

'It was Friday evening. The station must have been packed with people desperate to get home at the end of a week's work. Jostling to get to the front of the platform so they could squeeze into the next train. Nobody pays attention to anyone else in the rush hour. Other people are simply obstacles. Get your timing right, and killing someone is as easy as winking. One sharp jab against the spine, that's all it takes.'

'Maybe, but without evidence…'

'I asked you about Murray's father-in-law, a man called Baker. I'd like to find out if he was on the scene.'

'Then you'll be interested to know that Thomas Baker was in touch with the police last night.'

'Really?'

'He said he'd arranged to telephone Murray and got no answer. He'd heard on the news that there'd been a fatal accident at British Museum Station, and he was becoming concerned.'

'How decent of him. I expect he was heartbroken to discover his worst fears realised?'

'Naturally. He actually mentioned that this is his second grievous loss in a matter of weeks.'

'Poor fellow.'

Oakes's grin reminded Jacob of a card sharp about to play an ace. 'If you imagine he barged Murray onto the line, think again. Baker rang from Skegness.'

Jacob stared. 'It's October. What is he doing at the seaside?'

'He's rented a bungalow, a retreat where he can come to terms with the death of his wife.'

'And console himself with the company of a stream of young actresses.'

'Is that right?' Oakes downed the rest of his beer. 'I'll ask for discreet efforts to be made to check his alibi, but by the sound of things, he's taken care to ensure that it's watertight.'

'A racing certainty,' Jacob said grimly. 'Thanks for taking the trouble. Time for another round.'

As he returned bearing fresh pints, Oakes said, 'How is Miss Savernake these days?'

'Enigmatic as ever.'

'It amuses her to cultivate an air of mystery.'

Jacob wondered what lay behind the inspector's question. Rachel's beauty and intelligence were enough to bewitch any ambitious bachelor. A pity that she was ruthless through and through. Jacob didn't believe she had a romantic bone in her body.

'Nell Fagan mentioned that she spoke to you about her.'

Oakes inclined his head. 'The Fagan woman wants to take a leaf out of your book. Writing about the beauty with a flair for detection. I can see the headlines. Not that there's any chance of Miss Savernake playing ball with anyone as loose-tongued as Nell Fagan.'

'Nell told Rachel and me about Vernon Murray. Let me explain.'

He gave Oakes a potted summary of the events leading to the encounter with Murray outside the British Museum.

'Miss Savernake believed he was frightened?'

'And petulant because Nell hadn't paid him enough attention that morning. Her main concern was researching old newspapers. But yes, she thought he was afraid of something.'

'With good reason, it seems.'

'You think he had a premonition of his impending demise?'

'More than that,' Oakes said, taking another gulp of beer. 'A lot of information passes across my desk. Most of it earns no more than a cursory glance. Late on Thursday evening, there was a report of a hit-and-run accident in Notting Hill. Vernon Murray received a glancing blow from a car as he crossed the road to get to his home. He was knocked to the ground but apart from some bruising, he was none the worse physically. A police constable picked him up and dusted him down. Murray blurted out his belief that someone had deliberately tried to run him over. When questioned further, he clammed up and said he must have been mistaken. It was just the shock that had made him say such a thing.'

'Could he identify the vehicle?'

'He said not.'

'Surprise, surprise. That near miss explains the bruise on his cheek.'

'It also explains why I took your enquiry seriously when you rang me out of the blue. After one narrow escape, whoever wanted him dead made sure the second time around.'

'You're satisfied it wasn't a coincidence?'

'That kind of coincidence sticks in my gullet. All the same,

I'd never convince my colleagues in the absence of anything tangible to go on. Murray made a poor fist of things when he went to the Yard after his mother's funeral and accused Baker of murder. He was written off as a jealous mummy's boy who simply wanted a bigger inheritance.'

'But the Notting Hill incident, and now his death…'

'They prove nothing.' Oakes crumpled a beer mat in his palm. 'Your telephone call made me curious. This story of Nell Fagan's suggests that someone had a motive to do away with Murray. Someone who wanted to stop him kicking up a fuss about his mother's death.'

'In other words, Thomas Baker.'

'He's the obvious suspect. If not for the fact that yesterday evening he was one hundred and fifty miles away from British Museum Station.'

'Not to mention,' Jacob said bitterly, 'having an alibi for the death of his wife at Blackstone Fell.'

'I don't have enough evidence to justify devoting time to looking into the case.' Oakes stared gloomily into his beer. 'What does Miss Savernake make of Fagan's tale?'

'She's convinced that Nell didn't tell us the whole truth.'

'True to form,' Oakes said.

'Murray took fright after nearly being run over. When he denied all knowledge of Rachel, I believed him, but perhaps he was lying. My guess is that Baker had scared him off. But Nell was determined to write her story, and she didn't want to cancel a meeting she'd gone to such pains to arrange. Besides, she was keen to pick Rachel's brains. She compromised by telling Rachel only what she wanted her to know. And she served up plenty of red meat. A legend about vanishing men and a story of strange goings-on in a sanatorium would be enough for most people to gorge on. But Rachel Savernake is always hungry for something more.'

'Eloquently put.' Oakes was amused. 'What do you make of it all?'

The Arsenal fans were ratcheting up the noise. Guzzling beer, fuelling grievances, decrying the brutality of the other team's players.

Jacob said, 'It's like the football. There's been foul play. The difference is, I've no idea who is to blame.'

10

'Abide with me; fast falls the eventide.'

Nell Fagan sang lustily, if out of tune. She couldn't remember the last church service she'd attended; her instincts tended to the profane rather than the sacred. Clad in what passed for her Sunday best, she was clutching a dog-eared copy of *Hymns, Ancient and Modern* as if her salvation depended on it. She'd squashed in halfway up the aisle, next to Crawshaw, the landlord of The New Jerusalem. The hard mahogany pews of St Agnes Church were almost full. Blackstone Fell was scarcely a beacon of Christian virtue, but what else was there for sinners to do on a cold autumnal Sabbath?

'The darkness deepens; Lord with me abide.'

The walls of the church were plain, the architecture austere. The sole decorative flourish was a corbel table above the nave carved with grotesque heads which grinned down as if they were privy to the worshippers' darkest secrets. The sombre interior mirrored the rector's nature, Nell thought. How contrary and eccentric of him to choose this particular hymn; even she knew it was supposed to be sung at evensong. Outside, the sky was bright, but the windows were narrow and high, rendering this a place of shadows. Light was cast by the glow of flickering candles. The odour of hot wax filled Nell's sinuses.

Where is death's sting? Where, grave, thy victory?
I triumph still, if Thou abide with me.

Nell shivered. The stove at the back of the church wasn't enough to keep out the chill. The great and the good of Blackstone Fell – such as they were – occupied the front pews on either side of the aisle; the lower orders from the lower village knew their place. There was no difficulty in identifying the Sambrooks as they took their places beneath the pulpit.

The village doctor sat next to Denzil, who had greeted him like an old friend as he joined them moments before the service began. Although the professor had favoured Carrodus with a nod of welcome, Nell noticed that Daphne Sambrook ostentatiously ignored him. Her coarse hair and no-nonsense manner contrasted with the soft fair curls and delicate femininity of the rector's wife on the other side of the aisle.

Major Huckerby sat next to Judith Royle. Sitting in splendid isolation at the far end of the pew was the saturnine owner of Blackstone Tower. Nell's line of vision was interrupted by an inconveniently wide-brimmed hat, but the man had presumably recovered from yesterday's palpitations. Nell caught him sneaking a look at the rector's wife. Be careful, she thought darkly, or that fluttering heart will be the death of you. Yet she had to admit that, even in a drab grey coat and matching hat, Mrs Royle's golden frailty merited a second glance.

The young woman's head was bowed, but Nell saw her glance surreptitiously at her husband. It was as if she feared catching his eye. The Reverend Quintus Royle had a hooked nose and wild, shaggy eyebrows. Stern and cadaverous in his long black cassock, he marched towards the pulpit, footsteps echoing on the stone flags. He subjected his flock to a cold and penetrating stare, as if gazing into the villagers' souls. From the curl of his lip, he didn't like what he saw. His sermon was a doom-laden lament for the sins of the unrighteous, spiked with ominous quotations from the Book of Isaiah.

'Enter into the rock, and hide thee in the dust, for fear of the Lord.'

Nell watched the rector's wife shift uneasily, as if she thought her husband's fulminations were aimed at her. You didn't need to be Rachel Savernake to detect Judith's misery. For all his formidable manner and MA Cantab., Quintus Royle was a hellfire preacher. His corncrake voice rasped with passion, verging on fury.

'Woe unto the wicked! It shall be ill with him: for the reward of his hands shall be given him.'

Over afternoon tea at the rectory, Judith had dropped hints about her motives for marriage. Her father had died when she was a babe in arms, and after her mother's passing she'd been taken in by elderly relations who had a tumbledown cottage at Blackstone Foot. The family had no money to speak of, and she'd contemplated earning a crust as a lady companion. Or possibly as a governess. Like dear Peggy, Nell thought. Judith too had found a father substitute, but marrying your father wasn't a sensible idea. Peggy's character was much stronger; she would never allow a man like Quintus Royle

– or any man, come to that – to tell her what to do. Nell couldn't blame any woman for wanting to escape poverty, but she'd paid an extortionate price.

'And I will punish the world for their evil and the wicked for their iniquity.'

Quintus Royle's fearsome rhetoric reminded Nell of modern poetry. It sounded impressive and intimidating, even if you didn't understand what it meant. She gathered that the rector was warning his parishioners to save their souls before it was too late. Did his excoriations give some kind of masochistic satisfaction, even to those who refused to mend their ways?

'And I will cause the arrogance of the proud to cease, and will lay low the haughtiness of the terrible.'

The rector fixed his menacing scowl on the Sambrooks. If their consciences were itching, Nell saw no sign of it. The professor looked half-asleep and his son was lounging in the pew, as if utterly bored. One or two of the men in the congregation were taking a sidelong peek at Mrs Royle's trim form. In such a small community, a fetching woman was as conspicuous as Blackstone Tower. Nell wondered if any of the neighbours had gone further than merely coveting her from afar. If so, had Quintus Royle cottoned on?

At last the service thundered to a conclusion. Subdued worshippers began to shuffle out of the church. Nell's plan was to station herself at the lychgate and buttonhole the people she wanted to talk to. She raced to the door as the organist played the voluntary, but eagerness to get ahead of the crowd proved her undoing. As she rushed out into the open air, her damaged ankle gave way. Catching her toe on the uneven surface, she lost her balance. As she fell forward, her head banged against a corner of a lichen-encrusted gravestone.

The last thing she saw before losing consciousness was the bulk of Major Huckerby towering over her; the last thing she heard was Judith Royle's shriek of alarm.

'You're remarkably fortunate,' Dr Carrodus said. 'You took a fearful crack on your skull, but it only left a scratch. Concussion usually clears up soon enough. Not suffering brain fog, I hope?'

'No,' Nell lied.

'Glad to hear it. A blow like that can do untold damage, but as far as I can see, there's no lasting harm done. Plenty of bed rest in a darkened room, and by this time tomorrow, you'll be bright-eyed and bushy-tailed.'

Nell mustered a weak smile. Good-natured optimism was the doctor's stock-in-trade. They were in the large and well-appointed surgery at the rear of his house and Carrodus was in shirtsleeves, putting his stethoscope away in a drawer. She had a fuzzy recollection of Major Huckerby and Denzil Sambrook helping the doctor to bundle her here from the churchyard. She'd been a dead weight, but at least she wasn't dead. On coming round, she'd been sick, and when the waves of nausea receded, their legacy was a splitting headache. Never mind, Carrodus was right. It was frustrating that her plan to seize the initiative had misfired, but it could have been much worse.

'Thank you, Doctor.' Her voice was croaky. 'Just as well I'm like the cat with nine lives, eh?'

'You seem to be squandering them like billy-o,' he said in

genial reproof. 'Two falls in the past few days? The major remarked to the professor's son that Blackstone Fell doesn't seem to agree with you.'

'I hoped to talk to the Sambrooks,' she mumbled.

Carrodus raised his eyebrows. 'Not thinking of taking a cure in the sanatorium, Miss Grace? You may be unsteady on your pins, but I wouldn't put you down as a woman afflicted by bad nerves.'

Nell's head was swimming. So many questions cried out to be asked, but she'd better pipe down. Judith Royle had discovered her true identity, but it looked as if she'd held her tongue. Was it too much to hope that no one else in Blackstone Fell had tumbled to her secret?

'Can I offer you a cup of tea?' Carrodus pondered. 'Or could you manage a small tot of brandy?'

'Brandy, if you don't mind,' Nell said gratefully.

He grinned. 'Best medicine there is. You're a woman after my own heart, Miss Grace.'

Thank heaven he wasn't the miserable type who believed remedies only worked if they tasted vile. From a cupboard, he produced a bottle of Martell and two glasses, and poured a generous measure for each of them. They drank in companionable silence until he jumped to his feet.

'Just what the doctor ordered, eh? Should do you a power of good. Now if you'll excuse me, I must get on. Can you manage to walk back to the Lodge unaided, or would you let me take your arm, and see you home? We don't want you taking another tumble and crashing all the way down the slope to Blackstone Foot.'

'Thank you, Doctor,' she said, mustering what remained of her dignity, 'but I can cope.'

'Very well.' He helped her on with her coat, and handed her an ebony walking stick. 'Borrow this; it will help you to get about. Not that you should roam around until that ankle has healed.'

'It's very good of you.'

'All part of the service, Miss Grace. Remember what I said about bed rest.'

'How could I forget?' she said solemnly, taking her purse from her handbag. 'What do I owe you?'

He brushed the question aside. 'Put your money away. This is the Sabbath. I haven't treated you during working hours.'

'Most generous. If you're really sure…'

'My good deed for the day.' He gave a wry smile. 'After listening to the Reverend Quintus Royle lambast our morals, it's the least I can do if there's to be any hope for my benighted soul.'

'Is his tone always quite so… apocalyptic?'

'The rector has delighted in rebuking vice ever since I arrived in Blackstone Fell,' Carrodus said. 'I expect he'll be casting stones at sinners long after I've fled back to the den of iniquity whence I came. Namely, Islington.'

Nell could understand anyone wanting to shake the dust of Blackstone Fell from their feet. What puzzled her was why a young doctor had left London in the first place. On her way out of the surgery, she couldn't resist the urge to ask him.

'One night,' Carrodus replied, 'I went to a lecture given by Havelock Ellis and found myself sitting next to Denzil Sambrook. He'd come down to persuade his sister to return to Yorkshire. Denzil mentioned that the old village doctor was ready to take an overdue retirement and his practice was going for a song. Working in a small village sounded idyllic. And I suspect he wanted to do a bit of matchmaking.'

'Oh yes?'

'Strictly between you and me, he thinks his sister is turning into an old maid. Of course there's a shortage of eligible men in the neighbourhood, but Daphne is a strong-minded woman. It was only with the greatest reluctance that she agreed to give up her career as an artist and come back to Blackstone Fell. She certainly drew the line at romance with a humble sawbones.'

'She's an artist, you say?'

''Fraid her paintings are a bit too deep for me.'

'But Denzil Sambrook thought that you and she…'

Carrodus shrugged. 'It might have suited him to have a tame doctor for a brother-in-law. But I'm too frivolous for Daphne. I rather admire her, but we are very different.'

'What makes you admire her?'

'She's overcome tragedy. When she and Denzil were young, the professor's car crashed out on the moors. She was sitting on her mother's lap in the front passenger seat. Her mother was killed, and she and her father were injured by flying glass. He lost an eye and her face was badly scarred. Damn shame.'

'And her brother?'

'Denzil was in the back, fast asleep. He escaped unscathed. Not easy for a girl to cope with such a rotten experience so early in life. People say she's odd, but at least she's not surrendered to self-pity.'

'Are you glad you came to Blackstone Fell?'

Carrodus shrugged. 'In business terms, Denzil's advice was sound. There's no other doctor for miles, and I haven't done badly for myself.'

'Hence the Lagonda?'

He laughed. 'A chap must be allowed a little self-indulgence now and then. What else can I spend my hard-earned money on? It's different for Denzil. He's lived in Blackstone Fell since he was a child. He has the sanatorium to keep him occupied, as well as the Sambrook family trust. Personally, I hanker after the bright lights. Which is why I'm about to put the practice on the market and head back to London. Now, take care of yourself. And remember, plenty of bed rest!'

Blackstone Lodge was barely half a mile from the surgery, but Nell's homeward trudge was hard going. The brandy had dulled the ache in her head but each step along the lane was a painful reminder of the damage she'd done to herself in dodging the boulder. At least this time she only had herself to blame. Nobody had tried to kill her in the graveyard.

The brightness of the weather contrasted with the gloom of St Agnes Church, but she didn't see anyone out and about. The villagers took Sunday observance seriously.

The doctor's remarks about the Sambrooks intrigued her. She simply must make their acquaintance. As for Carrodus, he might just become a useful ally.

When at last she reached her front door, she delved into her bag for the key. As she bent her head, she saw something unexpected. Peeping from underneath the door was a crumpled piece of paper. Letting herself in to the Lodge, she bent down to retrieve the sheet from the floor.

The crinkly feel of the paper and the smell of rose petals

were as familiar as the typeface of the letters and words pasted onto it. Another anonymous message.

Meet me at the cave at sunset.

Judith Royle must be the author of the unsigned note, Nell told herself. That still left questions to be answered. Did the rector's wife realise that Nell had rumbled her trick with clippings from the *Daily Mail*? What was her purpose in delivering this message? Assuming, of course, that she was the person who had stuffed it under the door. Any of the worshippers from the church could have brought it here, given the length of time Nell had spent in the surgery. The only person she could definitely rule out was Dr Carrodus. She treated herself to another nip of brandy to help her think.

The trouble was, her brain was full of cobwebs. She assured herself the alcohol wasn't to blame. That bang on the head had muddled her.

Which cave? She only knew of one in the vicinity, at the base of Blackstone Fell. Nash, the tramp who had been questioned in connection with Alfred Lejeune's disappearance, had once lived there.

And Nash died there too, she reminded herself. Buried by a fall of rock.

Was Judith Royle seeking to lure her into a trap? An attempt to crush her to death with a boulder had failed, and that absurd anonymous note hadn't frightened her away. Had the rector's wife resolved to finish the job?

Nell groaned. The ache in her ankle meant that hobbling

out to Blackstone Fell would be an ordeal. The sensible choice was to follow Carrodus's advice and stay put, but safety first had never been her motto. Time was short. The sooner she sorted out this wretched business, the better.

She rebelled against the idea of Judith as a killer. The woman was frightened to death. No wonder, given that she was married to Quintus Royle. During the rector's rant from the pulpit, his eyes had gleamed with fury. If ever there was a suitable candidate for treatment in Blackstone Sanatorium, it was Royle. Judith must be desperate to escape her suffocating life in Blackstone Fell. Had she finally summoned up the nerve to confide in an outsider? Was she in need of help? If so, what information might she trade in return?

Nell asked herself what Rachel Savernake would do in her shoes. In the younger woman, she saw something of herself. Both of them were obsessively inquisitive and determined. Neither quailed in the face of danger. It was in their nature to take risks. With their lives, if need be.

Dr Carrodus's walking stick leaned against the table. Nell weighed it in her hand. It was made of ebony and tapered to a point capped by a steel ferrule. Hard and sharp. The brass handle would also come in useful if she encountered any funny business.

Her mind was made up. She'd be at the cave for sunset.

As Nell hobbled towards the Fell, she fought the still small voice of reason questioning her decision to venture out. What else could she do? Snuggle under her bedspread and wait for events to take their course? At least this way, if Judith told her everything she wanted to know, there was a chance of making sure justice was done.

In her bag, she had her Vanity Kodak, just in case anybody asked what she was up to, but the village was still deserted. She plodded over the clapper bridge and didn't pause for breath until she came to the fork in the path. Nearly there. Even if Judith didn't turn up at the cave, Nell had no intention of searching for her in the ravine. She'd heard too many stories of incautious visitors to Blackstone Leap ending up in a watery grave. No sense in making things easy for an enemy with murder in mind.

She strained her eyes for signs of life. Nothing. As the sun sank towards the horizon, she passed through a clump of sycamores. At last the mouth of the cave came into view. She clenched her fist in silent satisfaction; with any luck, she'd arrive before Judith Royle.

The cave was familiar to her. She'd noseyed around here previously, discovering that although the entrance was narrow, the hollow in the rock opened out once you squeezed inside, forming a small network of narrow passages of diminishing height which burrowed beneath Blackstone Fell. A succession of hermits had made it their home, long before Nash, the unfortunate tramp, had lived and died here.

Tightening her grip on the walking stick, she edged forward. There wasn't a soul in sight. A squirrel scampered up a tree trunk; she heard no other sound. Curiously, she sniffed the air. Yes, there was the smell of earth and grass, but was that a faint whiff of perfume?

At the entrance to the cave, she hissed, 'Mrs Royle?'

No answer.

On her previous visit, the light of day had afforded a good view of the cave's interior from outside. Now it was darker. A perceptible fragrance of lavender overlaid the mossy atmosphere. Nell recognised the scent as Judith Royle's. What if someone else knew the rector's wife had arranged to be here at sunset?

A vision sprang into Nell's mind of Judith's body sprawled out across the cave's jagged floor. She pictured a scarf knotted around the soft white neck. Or blood dripping from a savage head wound. Or...

Taking a small flashlight from her coat pocket, Nell shone it into the gloom. Thank goodness, she couldn't see a corpse. As she breathed out with relief, her beam caught a glimpse of a small rock.

The rock lay on the ground, a couple of feet inside the cave. Trapped beneath it was another crumpled scrap of paper pasted with cut-out letters.

Nell caught her breath. The sheet was upside down and she couldn't read what was on it. The rector's words resonated in her brain. *Enter into the rock, and hide thee in the dust, for fear of the Lord.*

Knees creaking, she put the walking stick down and bent forward to tug at the sheet. The flashlight revealed the message.

We can't go on like this.

She peered at the message in bewilderment.

'Can't go on like this?' she muttered to herself.

'Indeed we can't,' whispered a voice in her ear.

Nell twisted round to see a face emerging from the shadows, but was helpless to prevent a gloved hand clamping her neck with unexpected strength. She let out a frantic cry for mercy as a lump of rock was dashed against the back of her head: once, twice...

As she blacked out, her final memory was of her own hoarse singing in church.

Where is death's sting? Where, grave, thy victory?

11

Ottilie Curle was a diminutive, porcine woman with several chins. She wore an old-fashioned half mourning cap over her thinning hair. A short veil covered powdered cheeks, while the folds of fat around her throat were masked by a leather choker studded with pearls. A jet brooch was pinned to her black silk gown and gold bracelets glittered from her wrists. As Jacob was shown into the sitting room in Kentish Town, she was talking to Eunice Bell.

Before either the maid or lady of the house could utter a word of introduction, she turned to address him.

'You are Mr Hamish Parlane?'

Jacob was tempted to gush with admiration at her psychic powers, but restrained himself just in time. A séance was a serious undertaking. He mustn't betray the faintest hint of levity. Let alone cynicism.

'Miss Curle.' The Caledonian burr sounded convincing to his ears, as it should with the benefit of an afternoon's diligent practice. He wondered if the medium's refined, accentless tones were equally well rehearsed. 'This is a rare honour.'

They shook hands. Her pudgy fingers were stiff with rings to the knuckles, the skin so moist that Jacob wanted to wipe his palm dry. As Ottilie Curle's small, bulbous eyes measured him, his neck prickled. She reminded him of a pawnbroker examining a pledge of doubtful provenance.

In the corner of the room stood her servant Abdul, a muscular, dark-skinned man in a turban and red felt burnous lined with golden silk brocade. Nell Fagan had mentioned him to Jacob. The man was mute and supposedly a Moor, whatever that term meant in modern-day England. His arms were folded, his expression impassive, his sheer bulk forbidding. The medium didn't bother to introduce him. Apparently he played no part in the séance and there was no obvious reason for his presence. Presumably his role was to contribute an exotic touch to the proceedings. Or did Ottilie Curle believe she required a bodyguard?

Eunice Bell gave an anxious cough. She seemed awestruck, as if barely able to believe that the one and only Ottilie Curle had graced this humble villa with her presence.

'Poor Mr Parlane lost his…'

'Yes, yes,' the medium interrupted. 'I gather that you also seek the comfort of words from the Other Side.'

'Aye.' Jacob dropped his eyes. 'Without my beloved Flora, I am utterly bereft.'

'Quite so.' Ottilie Curle pursed fat little lips. 'You do understand that this is rather irregular? Unlike many of those who profess to be sensitives, my custom is to conduct each séance with a single person who desires communication from beyond the grave.'

Naturally, he thought, this was the secret of her success. No better way of evading exposure than making sure that, if her pronouncements were challenged, it was one person's word against another's. She didn't employ a confederate to help her to bring off startling effects while she was in a trance, and given that Abdul never spoke and might have a limited grasp of English, she wasn't at risk of betrayal or blackmail. Because she wasn't defensive about her gifts, she felt no need to engage in rowdy debates with sceptics or submit to being bound and gagged as a visible test of her powers when in a trance. She refused to work on any terms but her own. Take them or leave them.

And so she prospered. People were eager to interpret the simplicity of her methods and her insistence on giving individual service as a sign of good faith. If she'd been so vulgar as to advertise, her watchwords would have been *intimacy* and *exclusivity*. In fact, she benefited from word-of-mouth recommendations. Her charges were so exorbitant that prospective clients presumed that she must possess gifts to justify them. Whatever her skills in communicating with the spirit world, Jacob thought that one truth about Ottilie Curle was beyond dispute. She was a first-rate businesswoman.

'Aye,' he said. 'Aye, indeed. I am very much in your debt.'

So many mediums fell into the trap of over-elaboration, performing stunts with disembodied limbs and luminous household goods. Levitating hands, floating violins, and flying apples were much in vogue. Other charlatans – like Dinah Sugrue – regurgitated billowing offcuts of cheesecloth or muslin in the guise of ectoplasm. Ottilie Curle had no truck with showy spectacle or messy materialisation. Her speciality was straightforward. She spoke for the dead.

Jacob had interviewed people who had taken part in her sittings. He'd been taken aback by their unshakeable conviction that she possessed a genuine gift for conveying words of comfort from beyond the grave. Her background was uncertain and so was her age. Although she was grossly overweight, her skin seemed to be unblemished. She might be anything from in her late thirties to sixty.

She'd established herself at the head of her profession. In her early days she'd given tongue to the words of a wise Parisian seamstress, before Madame La Rouge was displaced by a young Indian girl called Maharani. Like women's fashions, her spirit guides changed with the seasons. Her latest otherworldly relationship was with an irascible man of law called Sir Roderick.

'Making contact with the Other Side is the most delicate of tasks,' Ottilie Curle said. 'You and I, Mr Parlane, have been denied the opportunity to discuss your tragic loss. Miss Bell has briefly indicated the sad circumstances, but I must emphasise from the outset that I cannot guarantee success in my attempts to make contact with this tragic young woman of yours.'

'My sweet Flora,' Jacob said in a dolorous tone. 'Yes, I appreciate the difficulty.'

He also appreciated the shrewd disclaimer. Mediums used methods like those of mind-readers at fairgrounds. They didn't need to press their subjects to lay all their secrets bare. Through subtle questioning, they elicited just enough information to make educated guesses about the dear departed. To the gullible and heartbroken, haphazard observations seemed quite magical in their accuracy.

Eunice cleared her throat. 'It is extraordinarily generous of you, Miss Curle, to make an exception at my request. As I said, Mr Parlane leaves for the Highlands tomorrow, so he had no time to engage you to conduct a separate séance.'

Jacob summoned an expression of youthful innocence.

When Nell Fagan first disclosed how much Eunice was spending to secure Ottilie's services as a medium, he'd whistled in disbelief. The sum amounted to a large chunk of the old woman's life savings; it was scant consolation that she had little time left to make use of them. Jacob was required to double the fee to be allowed to take part in the séance. He had no choice but to agree. Fortunately, Gomersall's determination to discredit this woman meant that the *Clarion* was willing to pay through the nose.

'I've heard so much about you.' This at least was true. 'Folk say you are a true spirit warrior, a modern Joan of Arc.'

'Folk?' Ottilie Curle enquired.

'Dear Miss Bell here, for one.' His accent was plausible, he thought; the rehearsals had paid off. He made a credible Scotsman of a certain class, never happier than when hunting deer or shooting grouse. Warming to his theme, he added, 'I really can't be doing with the naysayers.'

'Naysayers?'

Again the medium examined him. She made no attempt to hide her disdain and he cursed himself for not sticking to his plan to keep as quiet as possible.

'I mean the faithless puritans,' he said, trying to redeem himself. 'The Bible-quoters, the so-called rationalists.'

There was a chill in the room. Only the embers of the fire remained; an embroidered screen masked their dull glow. Heavy velvet curtains were drawn against the night and the other illumination came from a gooseneck lamp on the sideboard. Abdul's expressionless face was in shadow.

Ottilie Curle wrinkled her little snout behind the veil. Jacob wasn't sure whether she disliked his answer or had detected an unpleasant smell.

With undisguised anxiety, Eunice stuttered, 'I must… I must apologise. The lilies are… are past their best. I'm afraid I did wonder when…'

A large table stood between the two armchairs and sofa. At one end was a wind-up gramophone with a record ready to play, at the other an unlit candle in a brass holder. Between them on a crocheted mat stood a Wedgwood flower vase of green jasperware. A dozen white lilies were starting to wilt. The rottenness of decaying blooms tainted the air.

The medium's dismissive wave set her bracelets jangling. 'You merely did as I asked. The spirits inhabit a world far removed from our earthly realm. It is essential for them to sense they belong here. They must be made welcome.'

'Oh, yes, of course, I do understand,' Eunice said. '*Most* welcome, I'm sure.'

'Now I shall prepare myself. You will appreciate the paramount importance of my establishing perfect sympathy with my surroundings. If you would be so good as to remain silent.'

Without awaiting an answer, the medium breathed in, lowered her head, and closed her eyes. Nothing stirred in the room for five minutes. To Jacob it felt like an hour. Sombrely, he contemplated his shoes. Eunice Bell gazed at the other woman in wonder. Anyone would think Queen Mary had dropped in for a cup of char and a chat.

Expelling a low sigh, Ottilie Curle looked up at them. 'Very well. I am ready. The time has come. You may take your seats. I shall remain standing. It is arduous, but that is Sir Roderick's preference. Please restrain yourselves during the séance, whatever happens. To disturb me when I'm in a trance can do great harm. You might endanger my life.'

Jacob settled back against a firm cushion. His investigations had revealed that a séance – particularly a séance involving Ottilie Curle – could last for hours. Long, numbing periods of inactivity punctuated by brief flurries of melodrama. The spirits liked to keep people guessing. And fraudulent mediums aimed to catch clients off guard, to minimise the risk of their tricks being detected. He was thankful for small mercies; at least Ottilie Curle didn't indulge in table-tipping or jiggery-pokery with a Ouija board.

'Shall I extinguish the lamp?' Eunice asked.

Ottilie Curle inclined her head. Her every movement was deliberate, as if it came at a physical cost.

'Put the fire screen to one side and light the candle.'

Eunice did as she was told, taking infinite pains as she put a match to the braided cotton wick. Jacob's hackles rose. A dying lady was being treated like a servant and paying a fortune for the privilege. He found it a struggle to conceal his disgust at the way Ottilie Curle milked the bereaved.

'Let the music play.'

Eunice fiddled with the gramophone. The hiss was distracting, but Jacob recognised the opening bars of the music for an elegy by Tennyson. 'Crossing the Bar' had been his grandmother's favourite hymn. He'd sung it at her funeral. He scrambled to his feet.

Ottilie Curle stood stock still in front of them on the far side of the table. The candlelight flattered her plump features. Despite her lack of height, she had a commanding presence. When she began to sing, Jacob was surprised to hear a tuneful soprano. Eunice joined in and, digging into his memory to remember the words, so did Jacob.

Twilight and evening bell,
And after that the dark!
And may there be no sadness of farewell
When I embark.

'Sir Roderick,' Ottilie Curle called. 'Are you there?'

The question jerked Jacob out of a reverie. The spirit world hadn't seemed to be in the mood for conversation. His eyelids were heavy and if the fire had still been blazing, he might easily have dropped off to sleep. He fixed his gaze on the portly little medium.

A deep baritone voice filled the room.

'Yes, I am here. What of it?'

Sir Roderick sounded elderly, ill-tempered, and nothing like Ottilie Curle. Her lips had not moved. Quite an accomplishment, Jacob had to admit.

She said, 'We wish to talk to Nathan Hart.'

The old curmudgeon considered this request for an inordinate length of time.

'Very well.'

Eunice let out a gasp of relief. A long silence followed. The medium remained motionless.

'Auntie, may I speak to you?'

The voice that came through was young and masculine. The tone was firm but overlaid with a touch of anxiety.

Eunice put her hand to her mouth. It took a few moments for her to compose herself.

'Nathan, darling… is that, is that really you? I can hardly believe it.'

'Don't be silly. Of course it is.' A note of rueful amusement, precisely capturing the tone of a young fellow humouring a dear old fogey who worried about nothing. 'Not that I blame you for being bewildered. You've not heard me speak for such a long time.'

'Sixteen years,' the old woman breathed. 'Oh, Nathan… I've longed for this moment, and now I find I don't know what to say.'

'Please give my love and warmest wishes to Auntie Peggy. Not forgetting my dear Nellie. I do hope she is happy in her work.'

The medium had done her research, Jacob thought. She'd taken the precaution of checking up on the dead man's nearest and dearest. How would she cope with the dead lover of Hamish Parlane? Rely on meaningless generalities, he supposed. She was shrewd, but it would only take a single slip, one moment of overconfidence when she said something demonstrably untrue, and he would have his story.

Tears welled up in Eunice's eyes. 'I will tell her. Oh, Nathan, of course I will.'

'I wanted you to know that you have no cause to dread… anything. This is such a wonderful place.'

Tactful, Jacob had to admit. Ottilie Curle realised Eunice was dying. She was doing her best to sugar the pill.

'Oh, is it?' Eunice's cheeks were damp. 'I have been so afraid…'

'Nothing to be worried about, my dear old fusspot. Absolutely nothing, I swear to you.'

'It's just that…'

'Believe me, I know.' The voice softened. 'I want to be honest with you. Can you bear it, Auntie, if I speak bluntly?'

Honest. It was all Jacob could do not to click his tongue in reproof. The hypocrisy was bare-faced. Yet Eunice Bell was lapping it up.

'Please, Nathan. You must.'

The invisible presence allowed himself a low moan before he spoke again. 'In taking my life, I committed a mortal sin. None of us have the right to take decisions reserved to God and decide when our time on earth is at an end. But I was driven to it. The shame of being falsely accused suffocated me. I felt powerless to prove my innocence. I trusted Ormond Weaver and he played me false. Forgive me, Auntie, everything seemed hopeless. I just couldn't bear it any longer.'

'There's nothing to forgive,' the old woman whispered. 'The truth came out after you died.'

'Yes, Weaver's guilt was exposed and my good name restored. Instead of eternal damnation, I have experienced bliss.'

'Thank the Lord. The world knows you to be an honest man who was ruined by evil, destroyed by a tissue of terrible lies. I couldn't bear to think of you dead and gone, believing your reputation was in tatters. As for that wicked devil Weaver, he died a fugitive. He didn't live long enough to profit from his wrongdoing. Or for making you the scapegoat for his crimes.'

'Yes, he treated me foully. Thankfully, even he repented on his death bed.'

'Did he?'

Jacob saw the old woman smile in delight.

'Yes, as he lay dying in Botzen, he begged the physician

to summon a priest so that he could confess. He had a dreadful barking cough, but used his last moments to tell the unvarnished truth. The priest was Austrian, but his command of English was excellent. Weaver took full responsibility for his crimes. He was overcome by remorse for the cruel manner in which he had misused me.'

A happy-ever-after ending, Jacob thought. Carefully researched and skilfully crafted. An impressive work of fiction.

There was a lengthy pause. Jacob concentrated on memorising what had been said. He'd write it all up as soon as he got back to Exmouth Market.

'One day, Auntie,' the young man's voice said, 'you will discover for yourself. Sir Roderick will gladly confirm that on the Other Side, we understand everything.'

Lucky you, Jacob thought.

'How wonderful,' Eunice breathed.

Jacob hated the idea of giving an unscrupulous medium any credit whatsoever, but you didn't have to be a True Believer to admire Ottilie Curle's professionalism. She'd prepared thoroughly and so far her performance had left nothing to chance. Her methods reminded him of a line from a poem by Browning. *Less is more*. A sound philosophy in life, and also when it came to communicating with the Ones Above. A plain cook she might be, but despite her determination to eschew fancy garnishes and seasoning, Ottilie Curle served up an appetising dish. How could he deny to the *Clarion*'s readers that Eunice Bell was getting her money's worth? You only needed to look at the poor deluded woman's eyes, unnaturally bright even in the gloom, to see that she was in a state of ecstasy.

'I must go now, Auntie.' The voice was getting fainter. 'I am so glad that we have spoken. One day we shall meet again. Until then, be kind and be content.'

Eunice was crying again. 'Goodbye, dear boy.'

'Goodbye, Auntie.' The words were barely audible. 'Goodbye.'

Drained by the effort of communing with the unseen spirits of the dead, Ottilie Curle rested for fully twenty minutes. When she lifted her veil for a moment, the flickering light of the candle revealed beads of sweat on her brow.

Eunice wore an expression of pure rapture. Jacob wasn't sure he'd ever seen such joy on another face. In reporting this séance, he'd need to choose his words carefully. He sympathised with Gomersall's crusade against fraudulent mediums, but he couldn't bring himself to lie about what had happened this evening. Ottilie Curle had given a sick old woman happiness beyond price.

The medium rose.

At last, Jacob thought. The greatest show in Kentish Town resumes. The difference is that this time I'll be able to prove that she is making up her story as she goes along.

They repeated the ritual: music, hymn singing, the cry to Sir Roderick. On this occasion, the familiar seemed unwilling to respond.

'Sir Roderick,' Ottilie Curle called after several minutes of waiting. 'Have you deserted me?'

After a short pause, the baritone voice was heard. 'I am present.'

'There is a young woman by the name of Flora Kilbride. May we speak to her?'

A prolonged silence. Jacob itched with frustration. Keeping quiet was all very well for Abdul, but he felt an almost uncontrollable urge to ask how long he'd need to wait for some action. Ottilie Curle required payment in advance of a sitting and he'd gone to great lengths to ensure that she received the agreed sum in time. A trusted messenger had delivered a fat bundle of banknotes to her home in Kew that very morning. Surely he wasn't going to be fobbed off? He'd be furious if Sir Roderick said that Flora was unavailable or too busy washing her hair.

'Flora Kilbride?'

At last.

Jacob dug his nails into his palm, reminding himself of the need for patience. Ottilie Curle was very careful not to guarantee results, but his researches hadn't uncovered a single case in which she'd accepted a substantial fee without facilitating an encounter with a spirit visitor. She was too sophisticated a swindler not to deliver a degree of value for money.

'Yes.' The medium took a breath. 'I am accompanied by Mr Hamish Parlane.'

'Hamish Parlane?' Sir Roderick sounded querulous.

'Aye,' Jacob said. 'That's right.'

Another silence followed. Jacob forced himself to hold his tongue. This was the critical phase of the séance. He mustn't say anything to make Ottilie Curle suspect his motives.

'On the Other Side,' Sir Roderick said solemnly, 'there are no secrets.'

Nathan Hart told us that already, Jacob thought. In his meekest tone, he said, 'I just hoped for a wee word with Flora.'

A loud groan.

'Something is wrong.'

'With Flora?'

'Something is wrong,' Sir Roderick repeated.

'What is wrong?' Eunice cried.

Jacob shot her a worried glance. There was a chill on his spine. Things were not going to plan.

'There has been a breach of trust,' Sir Roderick growled.

Eunice moaned. Ottilie Curle didn't move a muscle. Surely the woman wasn't onto him? Jacob couldn't believe it. She didn't know anything about his background. She simply hadn't had time to investigate.

'I don't understand,' he said.

'The reek of duplicity is a poisonous stench,' Sir Roderick snarled. 'It corrupts the atmosphere.'

'Duplicity?' Eunice cried. 'What do you mean?'

'I mean,' Sir Roderick said, his voice rising, 'that we are in the presence of a liar and a scoundrel.'

Jacob's heart sank as Eunice let out a little squeal of dismay.

'Mr Parlane!' she wailed. 'What is he talking about?'

Before Jacob could think of anything to say, Sir Roderick replied.

'There is no Hamish Parlane.' He sounded frantic with rage. 'Flora Kilbride does not exist.'

Eunice was weeping now from misery, not happiness.

'I won't believe it. A friend of Nell's? Mr Parlane, tell him this isn't true!'

'His name is not Parlane.' Sir Roderick was hoarse with emotion.

A horrid choking noise filled the room. Ottilie Curle clutched her throat and stumbled towards them.

'Miss Curle!' Eunice cried.

The medium slumped onto the sofa. Her eyes were shut and she was breathing noisily. Anyone would think she was dying. Eunice Bell certainly did. Tears poured down her withered cheeks as she cradled the medium's solid head in her stick-like arms.

'She's sick! Where are my smelling salts?'

Abdul sprang to his mistress's side. He bent over her prostrate form, pulling away the veil before lifting his head and glaring at Jacob. Hatred filled his dark eyes. Just as well the man hadn't brought along his scimitar, Jacob thought.

This was all part of the performance, surely. Ottilie Curle had somehow found him out. Her collapse was nothing to do with supernatural agency, everything to do with outwitting an enemy. He'd been outfoxed by a mistress of deception.

He turned to Eunice. 'I'm sure…'

But there was no reasoning with her. Her distress shocked him. So did the disgust in her voice.

'For heaven's sake, Mr Parlane! I trusted you! What have you done to her? Don't just stand there, do something! Call an ambulance, for pity's sake. Miss Curle is dying – and in my sitting room!'

12

Jacob expected Monday morning's news conference at the *Clarion* to be an ordeal and so it proved. Gomersall was in a foul mood. His heavy investment in the séance had failed to yield a scoop. Worse, it had led to a telephone call from the news editor of *The Spiritual Sentinel*, a weekly catering for the most credulous True Believers. Its columnists venerated Ottilie Curle in the same way that contributors to *Picturegoer* idolised Hollywood stars.

'Odious little swine actually had the nerve to ask me for a quote,' Gomersall bellowed at the assembled reporters. He was roaming around like a caged beast, ready to pounce on anyone unwise enough to tweak his tail. 'Asked if I'd authorised an assault on Britain's best-loved medium and if so, whether I intended to resign. If not, when would I sack the guilty reporter?'

'Assault?' Carson, the legal correspondent, pursed his lips. 'An interesting point of jurisprudence. I'm not aware of any precedent in English law for a medium to recover damages for physical harm sustained while in a trance.'

'There's always a first time,' Plenderleith muttered.

'I went to the hospital,' Jacob said. 'Ottilie Curle was

released after a check-up. She told the doctor she didn't intend to press charges. The woman's got a nerve. I befriended one of the nurses. She told me they could find nothing the matter with her.'

'It's bad enough that she's pretending to be the injured party.' Gomersall glared at Jacob. 'I said I'd call back when my investigations were complete. Thankfully, this week's *Sentinel* has already gone to press. What I really want to know is this. How did she cotton on to you? What in the name of heaven did you let slip?'

A grim hush settled on the room. Barrett examined his fingernails, no doubt relieved not to be the target of Gomersall's wrath. Plenderleith wore his I-told-you-no-good-would-come-of-it expression. Others fiddled with their tobacco pouches and cigarette cases, hoping not to catch the editor's eye.

Jacob felt a sickliness in the pit of his stomach. In his early days at Clarion House, he'd been given the worst assignments, in vice dens and nudist camps; an apprenticeship was known in the trade as humiliation correspondent. He'd earned promotion, but although he was on good terms with his colleagues, his rapid rise must have provoked a degree of envy. Probably some thought he needed taking down a peg or two. Fleet Street was a mean street, no place for faint hearts or failure. He scented a sour tang of *schadenfreude* in the air.

'Nothing was said by anyone present to give the slightest hint I was a journalist. The messenger who took the money to Curle's house didn't know where it came from. As for Eunice Bell, she swallowed the story. Hook, line, and sinker.'

'Nell Fagan presented you as a friend of hers.'

'It was the only way to inveigle myself into the séance.'

Gomersall banged his fist on a convenient table. Jacob winced.

'The old biddy must have given the game away.'

'She had no idea that I'm a reporter. Nell impressed on Eunice the importance of sticking to the script. I was a friend of the family. Nothing more. Nell emphasised that her own name mustn't be mentioned. Her excuse was that if Curle thought that Eunice had been put up to organising the séance by a journalist, the whole business would prove a complete waste of time and money.'

'Ottilie Curle is as crafty as a cartload of monkeys.' Gomersall snorted. 'In another life, she'd have made a damn good newshound. When she was asked if a third party could take part at the last minute, I bet she smelled a rat. Wheedled away until Nell Fagan's name was mentioned, I shouldn't wonder. The old girl probably didn't even realise she'd let the cat out of the bag.'

Jacob rubbed his chin. 'Ottilie Curle has definitely investigated Nathan Hart's story in depth. Tons of detail came out during the séance, but nothing that couldn't be discovered through careful study of the newspaper reports into the Weaver Bank scandal and Weaver's subsequent death. She may not know that Nell Fagan attended Weaver's trial. But if she's looked into Nathan's life history, I'll lay you ducats to an old shoe that she found out about Eunice's connection with Nell – a crime reporter. So alarm bells rang.'

Gomersall nodded. 'Mediums feast on publicity, but Curle is different. With the *Sentinel* treating her like royalty, she doesn't need puff pieces in proper newspapers. In my opinion, she hates the press but keeps a close eye on everything we do. She's seen our stories about fake mediums. She probably knows that our chief crime reporter is a young fellow with more cheek than a baboon's backside. She must have loved taking the *Clarion*'s money and making you look like an idiot at one and the same time.'

Silence fell.

'I won't give up,' Jacob said.

'You certainly won't,' Gomersall said. 'The question now is how you can make amends. We're out of pocket and no nearer exposing Curle's séances as bogus. Make no mistake, lad. The onus is on you to set this mess to rights.'

Jacob looked around at his colleagues. Amusement mingled with sympathy on their faces. Most were simply thankful not to be in his shoes. He gritted his teeth. Oh well. Win some, lose some. He'd live to write another day.

'Absolutely, sir.'

'That's the spirit, lad. Only next time, make sure you nail the old witch. Otherwise, never mind about the dear departed. You'll be on the Other bloody Side yourself.'

Dark clouds were gathering overhead as Dr Carrodus rapped on the door to Blackstone Lodge. There was no answer. After knocking again without success, he peered in at the nearest window. The interior of the gatehouse was dark and he saw no sign of life.

He heard footsteps crunching down the mossy gravel of the drive. Looking round, he saw a man striding towards him, silver cane in hand.

'Lejeune! Good day to you.' He glanced up at the glowering sky. 'Not that the weather looks too good. How's that heart of yours today? Beating merrily, by the look of things.'

'Thank you, Carrodus. You were right, those palpitations were just a passing nuisance.'

'Capital! A bit of bed rest works wonders. Believe me, I swear by it.'

'Indeed you do.' There was almost a glimmer of a smile. 'I suppose I was overdoing things. Forgetting that I'm not as young as I was.'

'Fiddlesticks, you're as old as you feel. I'd say you're in pretty good shape, all things considered. Besides, it's not as if you have one foot in the grave. What are you, fifty or thereabouts?'

'Celebrated my golden jubilee a month ago,' the other man admitted. 'Not that there's much to celebrate about entering my dotage.'

'Fifty is no age these days,' Carrodus said. 'Have you clapped eyes on Miss Grace, by any chance?'

'Miss Grace?'

'The new tenant.' Carrodus indicated the Lodge. 'You may have noticed, she took a tumble in the churchyard yesterday. I thought I'd look in and see how she is.'

'Ah yes, I gathered there was a hoo-ha after the service. Saw you'd been called over. As it happens, I've never spoken to the woman. We exchanged nods on one occasion, but I've been rather preoccupied and...'

Carrodus looked at him enquiringly.

'Truth to tell, I feel rather awkward. The Lodge was in the hands of the Lejeunes for upwards of three centuries until I sold it. Seeing someone living there for the very first time brought it home to me. The ghosts of generations of my forebears must be looking down on me in disgust for selling off the Lejeune estate, slice by slice. But what else could I do? The upkeep of an estate is ruinously expensive. The family silver went decades ago. Now it's the land. Death by a thousand cuts.'

It was the longest speech Carrodus had ever heard him make.

'Times are hard, Lejeune. People on fixed incomes or reliant on capital are taxed to within an inch of their lives. It's little wonder that up and down England, so many great houses are falling into decay. Or being sold off. Nobody can blame you for doing whatever is required to make ends meet.'

'Good of you to say so. The difficulty is compounded by the fact that Blackstone Fell is scarcely Bloomsbury. There isn't a queue of purchasers ready, willing, and able to acquire property in an out-of-the-way spot like this. I'm thankful that young Sambrook made an offer.' A heavy sigh. 'It wasn't much money, but between ourselves, I bit his hand off. At least he wasn't deterred by all that rubbish about mysterious disappearances.'

The doctor nodded. 'You must find those old wives' tales especially painful, given what happened to your brother.'

The other man tapped his silver cane on the ground. 'Not that anyone seems to know what did happen to him.'

Carrodus coughed. 'I've never wanted to raise such a delicate subject with you, Lejeune. I respect the fact you prefer to keep yourself to yourself. Believe me, I don't want to cause offence, but I can't deny I'm curious about your brother's fate.'

'You don't offend me in the slightest, Doctor.' He hesitated. 'As a matter of fact, I meant to say it was damned decent of you to pop in to see me on Saturday at short notice. Specially considering that I've hardly spared you the time of the day since my wife's funeral.'

'Think nothing of it.'

'Put my rudeness down to our traditional misanthropy. I'm the last in a long line of cussed Lejeunes. For that reason, I can't bring myself to cry crocodile tears over Alfred. In the fifteen years before he went missing, I doubt if I saw him more than twice.'

'Did you ever form a theory of your own about Alfred's disappearance?'

A shrug. 'Your guess is as good as mine. Sad business, but after all these years we'll never know the truth. Selfish to say so, but it's just as well that he and I were never close.'

'Was he much older than you?'

'Yes, he'd already left school when I was born. He was an adult when I was still a grubby urchin. To make matters worse, he always had the attitude and interests of a crusty old bookworm. We had nothing in common and didn't keep in touch. His antiquarianism bored me stiff. My plant-hunting left him equally cold. I was sorry to hear of his death, but it didn't mean much to me. I'm no hypocrite. I won't pretend that I lost any sleep when I heard the news. Not like...'

His voice trailed away.

'Your late wife,' Carrodus said softly.

'I met Chiara shortly before news came through that Alfred was missing. It didn't make any difference. I'd no intention of rushing back to England. As one man to another, I don't mind saying I was besotted.'

'She was a beautiful woman.'

'I was luckier than I deserved.' His voice remained firm. 'As for Alfred's demise, I suppose he went roaming over the moor and lost his way. Easy to get sucked down in those bogs. I'd place a saving bet on his having been washed away at the Leap.'

The doctor respected the other man's refusal to pander to the cheaper emotions. Harold Lejeune was, he reflected, in some ways a man after his own heart. He felt the first spots of rain on his cheeks and shot another glance through the window of the Lodge. Still no sign of life inside.

'More than likely the same tragedy befell that chap who went missing around the time this place was first built. Mellor, wasn't that his name?'

'Alfred could have told you. Old legends were his department, not mine. I believe in the here and now, Doctor, not stories about strange disappearances from locked lodges.'

'I share your scepticism, Lejeune, but I don't mind admitting that mysteries fascinate me. And I'm not alone. One of my patients told me that everyone in the lower village has their own idea about the Puzzle of Blackstone Lodge. Human nature, you see. After a few mugs of ale have been polished off in The New Jerusalem, all sorts of bizarre explanations are apt to get an airing.'

'Glad I'm teetotal,' the other man said curtly. 'Much ado about nothing, if you ask me. Anyway, the Lodge belongs to the Sambrook family now. It's nothing to do with the Lejeunes any more.'

'I half-suspect Denzil of being nervous about the history of the place. He told me that he's hardly set foot inside since he bought it. He didn't expect to find a tenant until next spring at the earliest. And now I have knocked repeatedly and failed to rouse Miss Grace.'

He banged his fist against the door to prove his point.

'I hope you're not suggesting the woman has vanished without trace?'

The rain was falling in earnest as Carrodus shook his head. 'I doubt it. Strictly off the record, and bearing in mind that she's not registered with me as a patient, I can tell you that when I examined her yesterday, she stank of booze. A toper, sad to say. Oh well, I'd better be on my way before I get drenched. If you ask me, the woman is laid up inside, snoring her head off.'

'Dead to the world?'

'Dead to the world.'

'You lost the battle,' Rachel Savernake said that evening. 'Not the war.'

She and Jacob were drinking sherry in the sitting room of Gaunt House. He'd accepted an invitation to dinner, a chance to lick his wounds in the lap of luxury after a chastening twenty-four hours. Rachel had listened to his account of the disastrous séance without a flicker of emotion.

'You don't seem surprised by what happened.'

She shrugged. 'Nobody seems to know much about Ottilie Curle, but clearly she is as intelligent as she is unscrupulous. She gave Eunice Bell exactly what she wanted.'

'You make it sound as if she is performing a public service,' he grumbled.

'Isn't she? An old lady, close to death, given a few moments of unadulterated bliss? As for your little subterfuge, I'm sceptical about anything and everything connected to Nell Fagan. The woman is a loose cannon. There was every chance that the medium would see through you and seize the chance to rub your nose in the dirt.'

'You didn't say so when I told you my plan.'

'Would it have made any difference if I'd urged caution?'

He sighed. 'Not really.'

'Quite. This setback won't matter in the long run. You'll be better prepared next time. Now you've seen at first hand that you're up against a redoubtable adversary.'

'You sound as though you admire her.'

'I don't underestimate her. If I were you, I'd concentrate on investigating her background. There will be clues in her past, if only you can find them.'

'You sound very sure.'

He wondered what clues Rachel's own past might yield to the puzzle of her character. She'd arrived in London shortly after her twenty-fifth birthday, but her previous life on the island of Gaunt was shrouded in mystery. He was as curious as she was secretive, but he'd learned to let well alone where her private life was concerned. She would reveal what she wanted, when she wanted, and not a moment before.

'Decent sherry,' he said. 'Very smooth.'

'Glad it meets with your approval,' she said with a lazy smile. 'It's one of the finest amontillados in the world.'

'Blimey, I'm honoured. If you'd told me sooner, I wouldn't have gulped it down so fast.' He gave her a sheepish grin. 'Don't tell me Trueman's given up on experimenting with cocktails?'

'Not at all. I've sent him on an errand. This morning he caught the first train to Yorkshire.'

Jacob's eyebrows shot up. 'To keep an eye on Nell Fagan?'

Rachel shook her head. 'She'll have to look after herself. At least she made me want to find out more, especially after what happened to Vernon Murray. Trueman will act independently. Filling the gaps in her story.'

'About the men who vanished?'

'No, her little locked-room mystery was window dressing. A taster, to whet my appetite.'

'So you agree with me that both men sneaked out of Blackstone Lodge without being seen?'

'There's more to it than that, Jacob. Remember what I said to you.'

'About *Macbeth*?' He was no wiser.

'Yes, but there was something more pressing on Nell Fagan's mind than an old riddle about a locked gatehouse.'

'Something about the death of Ursula Baker, you mean?'

'Not necessarily. As for the Baker case, there's more to it than meets the eye.'

'Such as?'

'Let's assume that Baker sent his wife to the sanatorium as a prelude to her murder. A crime of this sort seldom occurs in a vacuum.'

'I don't follow.'

'Why did Ursula's husband choose Blackstone Sanatorium?'

'Why not?'

'An odd choice for the sickly wife of an aspiring London playwright. She had no family in the area, and it's a long journey if you want to visit.'

'She needed peace and quiet.' Jacob was in the mood to play devil's advocate. 'The remoteness of Blackstone Fell suited Baker down to the ground. He wanted her safely out of the way so he could paint the town red in the company of adoring young actresses.'

'The services of Professor Sambrook must cost a pretty penny. Why not send her somewhere cheaper? Baker doesn't sound the generous type.'

'Salving his conscience. Entrusting his wife's care to one of Britain's most eminent psychiatrists.'

'I've looked up Professor Sambrook. He's not produced original research since Victoria was on the throne. He's living off past glories.'

'Who can blame him? The sanatorium must keep his hands full. I'm sure he finds treating patients more rewarding than chewing over theories with fellow academics.'

'You may be right.' Rachel didn't sound convinced. 'Very well. Do we believe that Ursula Baker was deliberately killed?'

'There's so little to go on. If Baker was responsible, he's covered his tracks with depressing efficiency. If not for Vernon Murray's death…'

'Remember that he was nearly run over the day before. He was frightened. And the only person who thought his mother's death was suspicious.'

'Other than Nell.'

'And now Murray is dead and someone tried to crush Nell Fagan with a boulder. That shows a determination to tie up loose ends, and a distinctive modus operandi. A culprit whose methods represent variations on a single theme.'

Jacob waited.

'An attempt to commit the perfect crime,' Rachel said softly. 'Murder disguised as happenstance.'

'If Baker is telling the truth, he's hiding out of harm's way in Skegness. A resort that is only fifty miles closer to Blackstone Fell than it is to British Museum Station. Even if he knew Nell was on his trail, how did he shove the boulder over the cliff?

Or push Murray from the platform?' He pondered. 'Maybe they were accidents after all.'

'The long arm of coincidence?'

'Coincidences happen all the time.'

'True,' she said meekly.

He grunted. 'But?'

'An alternative explanation is that Baker is in cahoots with someone at Blackstone Fell.'

'Professor Sambrook?' He shook his head. 'Rather late in life to turn to homicide.'

'Nothing is impossible. He's earned distinction in one career. For all we know, he's been making a success of murder for decades.'

'You're joking,' he said. 'Aren't you?'

'Humour me, Jacob. If Ursula Baker was murdered while she was under the great man's care, is it likely that the crime came completely out of the blue?'

'What do you mean?'

'I wonder if other questionable deaths have been associated with Blackstone Sanatorium.'

He shook his head. 'The longest of long shots, surely?'

'I don't agree. But even if you're right, long shots give the greatest satisfaction, if they hit the target. It would be a huge story, enough to salvage Nell Fagan's career. As a freelance, she could name her price. I wondered why she was so willing to allow you to learn about Vernon Murray's allegation of murder. You're on good terms with her, but she's a professional rival. It may explain why she was selective in sharing what she knew. She wouldn't want you to break the story in the *Clarion* before she had a chance to find a home for it.'

'I wouldn't...' he began virtuously.

'Of course you would.' She allowed herself a flicker of a smile. 'There's a reason why where you work is known as the Street of Shame.'

'All this is pure speculation,' he said huffily.

'Impure speculation, surely? Anyway, I've every confidence in Trueman.'

'To do what?'

'To play two different parts. This afternoon, he was in Halifax, acting as my man of business. I'm taking the tenancy of a cottage in Blackstone Fell.'

Jacob's eyes widened. 'You're going up there?'

'Trueman telephoned an hour ago to report success.' She stretched luxuriantly in her chair. 'According to the agent, the village boasts a unique character and history.'

'You could say the same for Gomorrah.'

'Yes, the man fell over himself to secure the deal. The rent is modest. A pity Nell Fagan has already bagged the gatehouse, but one can't have everything.'

He shook his head in wonder. 'What else is Trueman up to?'

Rachel savoured the last of her sherry. 'Looking for someone to help him commit a murder.'

13

'Your very good health!'

All smiles, Trueman lifted his tankard of ale. The regulars at The New Jerusalem did likewise before turning their attention back to the dartboard. After demonstrating his prowess with the arrows, Trueman had stood everyone a round, hoping it might encourage the locals to thaw. Not much luck so far, but at least Dilys the barmaid was close to melting.

'Lovely car you have, Mr Mann,' she said. 'I told Mr Crawshaw to be ever so careful when he put it in the garage for you.'

She was a hefty young woman with a mass of red hair as bright as her smile. Her teeth showed a few gaps, and so did the buttoning of a blouse which fought a losing battle to contain her ample curves. Trueman rested his elbows on the well-scrubbed wooden counter and contemplated her figure with frank admiration.

'Wolseley Hornet Six, latest model. As it happens, I'm in the motor trade.'

A practical man, Trueman loved nothing better than tinkering with the engine of Rachel's Rolls-Royce Phantom. It was his idea to masquerade as a car dealer. A distant cousin of his worked in that line in Workington. He was acutely aware that he lacked young Flint's gift of the gab, but Rachel's confidence in him knew no bounds. She'd urged him to let his imagination rip. To soak himself in the make-believe world of a car salesman with murder on his mind. He'd agreed, because for Rachel he would do anything.

Dilys was impressed. 'Fancy that!'

'Interested in cars, are you?'

'I am, believe it or not. The doctor's just bought a Lagonda.' She beamed in triumph. 'A two-litre low-chassis speed model.'

'Well, well, you're quite the expert. Not just a pretty face, eh?' He made a mental note not to underestimate this young woman. 'Offered to take you for a ride, has he?'

'He's a very nice chap, I'll have you know.' She ran her eyes over Trueman's brawny frame. He was wearing a brown three-piece suit with rather loud checks. 'Not in the least stuck-up. Always the first to put his hand in his pocket when there's a flag day, or accept a bet in the saloon bar.'

'I'd offer to take you for a spin myself, but sounds to me like your head has been turned. The Hornet's nippy, but it doesn't compare to a Lag.'

'Oh, I don't know.' As she leaned closer, he inhaled her cheap scent. 'Maybe one afternoon, before we open the bar in the evening. Between you and me, Mr Crawshaw isn't a car driver, he's a slave driver. Me, I'm all for looking after the paying guests.'

'Customer service.' He took a swig of ale. 'First principle of business. I'm all in favour.'

'Booked in for a week, haven't you? Nice to have a couple of guests at this time of year.'

'Who else is staying here?'

'A single lady.' Dilys sounded disapproving. 'She arrived today, but she's not down tonight. I doubt she drinks. Not alcohol, anyhow.'

'Not my sort of lady, then.' He gave her a conspiratorial wink.

Dilys sniggered. 'This is a respectable house, I'll have you know.'

'Pity.' His expression was suitably roguish. 'The womenfolk of Blackstone Fell are real charmers, if you're anything to go by. Good sports, too, I bet. Just the tonic for a chap who is footloose and fancy-free and doesn't want to spend every hour of the day working his fingers to the bone.'

'You never know your luck, Mr Mann,' she said, flicking errant strands of hair from her eyes. 'Not that Miss Nee will be your cup of tea. For a start, she's getting on. Looks like a retired schoolmarm. On a walking tour, she said. She was out and about the moment she'd unpacked, but it can't be much fun in this weather. Who wants to go walking when you can go so much further in a nice motor car?'

'You're right there.' He smirked. 'You can get a lot further.'

The landlord plodded up the stairs from the cellar and cast a resigned glance at Dilys before trudging across the bar to throw more logs onto the fire.

'What about you, then?' Dilys demanded. 'Working in the area or here for a break?'

'Mixing business with pleasure, pet. My plan is to start selling cars in Yorkshire and I'm here to study the market. I'm partial to the countryside. The air's much cleaner than in Leeds or Bradford. Thought I'd take a gander around the neighbourhood.'

'You won't find much to see,' she said. 'Unless you count the moor and the Fell. Not forgetting Blackstone Tower, of course. I suppose you've spotted that?'

'I'll say. Can't miss it. Sticks out like a sore thumb. Who lives there?'

'Bloke called Harold Lejeune.' She made a face. 'Keeps himself to himself.'

'Stuck-up, is he? Like his house?'

Dilys tittered. 'Never seen him in here. A right misery, that one. The Lejeune family built the Tower, but he's not lifted a finger to stop it from going to rack and ruin. He doesn't come from this part of Yorkshire and if you ask me, he doesn't fit in to Blackstone Fell. His late wife was a foreigner, you know.'

'Came from Northumberland, did she?'

'Get away with you!' She was relishing the banter. 'No, a real foreigner, I mean. Italian. Lovely to look at, though I never talked to her. Go on, then, whereabouts are you from?'

'Distant parts.' He grinned. 'Cumberland.'

'Dad took us to the Lake District once,' she said. 'Ullswater. Rained cats and dogs all the time we were there.'

The main door of the pub swung open. Outside the rain was hammering against the cobblestones. A man wearing an ulster and a derby hat stepped over the threshold. When he shook his stumpy umbrella, the raindrops drenched the welcome mat.

'Wet in the Lakes, was it?' Trueman said cheerfully. 'You must have felt at home.'

'Take no notice of him, Major,' Dilys said as the man approached the bar. 'He thinks his name is Max Miller. Your usual, is it?'

'This one's on me,' Trueman said heartily as she delved

behind the counter for the major's personal pewter mug. 'I just got in a round, so you shouldn't be the odd one out. Specially not after braving the elements on a night like this.'

The major took off his hat and placed it on the counter. 'Decent of you, old fellow. Name's Huckerby.'

They exchanged a bone-crunching handshake. The major was powerfully built, although Trueman's shoulders were even broader.

'I'm Mann. Pleased to meet you, Major Huckerby.'

'Never mind the rank. We're all civilians nowadays.' Huckerby gave him a searching glance. 'Army man, by the look of you?'

'You're quite a detective.' Better tread with care, Trueman thought, this chap is another canny one. 'Yes, as it happens. Long time ago.'

'In the last show?'

'I was a Borderer, second battalion. Western Front.' Sometimes it was safer to tell the truth than to lie. It was so easy to get caught out. 'Led a charmed life until I got myself blown up in the trenches. I was invalided out with shell shock.'

'Bad luck.' Huckerby lifted his mug. 'What brings you here?'

As Dilys turned to deal with other customers, Trueman waxed lyrical about his hopes of expanding his activities on this side of the Pennines.

'Only snag is, I'm short of capital. As it happens, I'm in business with my father-in-law. He had a little garage and took me into partnership when I married his daughter. I was very much the junior man, and he kept a tight grip on the purse strings. I've built the firm up, and these days he's simply a sleeping partner, even though his profit share is three times mine. He refuses to give me free rein, so I'd like to set up on my own, but it's simply not possible. I've sunk everything I possess into his business. Victim of my own success, if you like. I'd buy him out if I could, but he won't hear of it.'

'Tricky, when it's a family concern.'

'Not that we're much of a family. Lately the old chap has gone into a steep decline. Confidentially, I think he's lost his marbles. The irony is that when we started out, he was the hard-headed one; I'd spent a year with my nerves in tatters. But the poor old boy never got over the death of my missus.' He coughed, as if embarrassed to show emotion. 'Betty passed away two years ago.'

'Sorry to hear that,' the major said gruffly. 'Must have been rough for you. Hard to deal with that kind of loss.'

'You never said a truer word.'

Huckerby took out his briar pipe and fumbled in his tobacco pouch with twitching hands.

'Matter of fact,' the older man muttered, 'I speak from experience. My own wife died last year.'

Neither of them said anything for a minute or two as the major puffed away at his pipe. Around them, the regulars were deep in conversation, while Dilys argued with Crawshaw and cast an occasional glance in Trueman's direction.

'My Betty's heart gave out,' Trueman said at last. 'Very sudden. One minute she was the life and soul of the party, the next…'

His voice trailed away. The major moved a little closer and murmured, 'My wife died suddenly, as well. Rather different circumstances, though.'

'Oh yes?'

The major sighed. 'No sense in beating about the bush. I'm afraid Gloria died by her own hand.'

'Ah.' Trueman frowned. 'I'm sorry.'

'Blasted rector is a puritanical old stick-in-the-mud. Didn't want to give her a proper Christian burial. Or a plot in the village graveyard.'

'Dear me, that's very hard.' Trueman hesitated. 'These cases – often it's far from clear whether the person really intends...'

Major Huckerby shook his head. 'That was the saving grace. She took a lethal dose of sleeping pills, but she didn't leave a note. The local sawbones told the inquest that she must have been confused. Damned decent of him. The coroner recorded an open verdict. But I knew Gloria. She meant it, all right.'

'Ah.'

'She had a stomach ulcer. Painful but not the end of the world. Unfortunately, she convinced herself she had cancer. The doctor is a good egg. He did his damnedest to persuade her she wasn't at death's door, but she was neurotic. Wouldn't listen to a word he said.'

Trueman shook his head sorrowfully as Huckerby drained his tankard and beckoned the barmaid. 'Same again, Dilys.'

'You two seem to be getting on like a house on fire,' she said.

'Turns out Mr Mann and I have plenty in common.'

As she pulled their pints, Dilys treated them to a coy smile. 'Two charming gentlemen, yes, I'm sure you'll have lots to talk about. Better leave you in peace!'

She moved away to deal with another customer. 'Nice girl,' Trueman commented.

The major gave him a sharp glance. 'I'm fond of Dilys. She's got her head screwed on.'

'I can tell that. Born and bred in these parts, I suppose?'

'One of a family of six. Her father drank himself to death, her mother's as deaf as a post after twenty years working on the looms in a cotton mill at Hebden Bridge. Over the years, Dilys has had her fun with the lads of the village, but she's got something about her. Sharp as a tack, I'd say, and not short of ambition. What she really wants is someone who's a cut above, someone who can give her a taste of the good life.'

'She mentioned the doctor, said he drove a Lagonda.'

'Young Carrodus? Popular fellow, easy manner. Bit of a gambler, but he has far too much sense to monkey around with his patients. Trouble is, there's a shortage of eligible bachelors round here, so when a stranger comes along…'

Trueman gave him a man-to-man smile. 'Understood. I take it you don't…'

'There was only ever one woman for me,' the major said heavily. 'When I lost Gloria, I lost everything.'

The pub door opened again and a tall man in a smart navy blue overcoat walked in. Trueman whispered, 'The doctor, by any chance?'

'No,' Huckerby replied. 'Denzil Sambrook. Scientific wallah. Father owns the sanatorium.'

'Sanatorium?'

'Local nickname is the Mausoleum. Ugly grey building out on the edge of the marshes. Walk towards the moor, and you can't miss it.'

The newcomer strolled over to join them at the bar and the major bought Sambrook a drink. Rather to Trueman's surprise, Dilys didn't have much to say to the young scientist.

Didn't Denzil Sambrook fall within the category of eligible bachelors? Perhaps his receding hairline and waxy pallor didn't appeal to her. Trueman, who was partial to a good vampire flick, reckoned there was a touch of Nosferatu about the fellow.

The major performed introductions. 'If you're in the market for a new car, Mann is your man, so to speak.'

Denzil Sambrook shook his head. 'I have a little runabout, but motoring doesn't appeal to me. Not like my sister Daphne. She loves tinkering with her Baby Austin. So much so that I doubt she'd dream of changing it for a newer model.'

Trueman laughed. 'Don't worry, I'm not one of those salesmen who can't take no for an answer. Find what a customer wants and then supply it, that's my motto. I expect it's the same in your line of country, Sambrook.'

Rather than answer, the scientist took a swig of beer. By the time they were ready for another round of drinks, Trueman had repeated for the newcomer's benefit his tale of the old man with diminishing faculties who stood between him and prosperity. This time he didn't mince his words. It was as if the alcohol had loosened his tongue and his new acquaintances were beginning to see him in his true colours. His father-in-law's obstructiveness and greed were making him desperate.

He lowered his voice. 'Just between the three of us, I don't mind admitting I'm at the end of my tether. Since poor Betty passed away, the old chap's nerves are shot to pieces. His mind simply isn't what it was.'

'Sounds like one for you, Sambrook,' the major said.

'What?' Trueman demanded. 'Don't tell me you treat this kind of problem?'

'When my father established the sanatorium,' Denzil

Sambrook said, 'his patients were mostly consumptives. They suffered from depression and he sought fresh ways to help them. He succeeded so well that his methods have been adopted in all four corners of the world. Ever since, he's continued to pioneer treatments for disorders of the mind.'

'Good Lord.'

'If only I'd realised the state Gloria was in,' the major said bitterly, 'I'd have begged you to take a closer look at her.'

'Don't reproach yourself,' the younger man said. 'Carrodus and I have told you time without number. Her death wasn't your fault.'

Trueman said, 'I'm in debt to both of you gentlemen. Perhaps, Mr Sambrook, we should talk further.'

The major coughed. 'He's Dr Sambrook, actually, old chap.'

'A doctor of philosophy rather than a medico.' Denzil Sambrook made a self-deprecating gesture. 'Are you free to come to the sanatorium at four o'clock tomorrow afternoon, Mr Mann? Very well. We can discuss what to do with your father-in-law.'

As the grandfather clock in the hall of the rectory struck seven the next morning, the Reverend Quintus Royle was dressed, breakfasted, and ready to take his dog for daily exercise. His belief that the early bird catches the worm was as fervent as his faith in the Scriptures. It was also a source of friction in his marriage, even though he and his wife had separate rooms.

Judith was an owl, not a lark. She loved to sleep in as late as possible, and getting any sense out of her before ten o'clock was the devil's own work. Quintus Royle blamed the old fools who had brought her up, sparing the rod and inevitably spoiling the child. It had been left to him to inculcate in her the habits becoming a rector's wife. A thankless task. After all these years, it was time to face the truth. He'd failed. Worse than that, she'd betrayed him.

Last night, his patience had finally snapped. The time for circumlocution was past. He'd decided to have it out with her. When he taxed her with her adultery, she'd screamed that he was a cruel and heartless beast. She wasn't always compliant; over the years, she'd bleated about certain of his proclivities, but this time she'd gone much further than ever before. When he called her a whore, she actually said that she hated him.

The slap on her cheek had been entirely unpremeditated. He was a man of God, a cerebral individual not given to violence. But he was only human. A mere mortal, and thus a sinner. Judith prated on endlessly about her feelings, but never concerned herself with his. When he hit her, she'd run upstairs in floods of tears. He heard the rattle of the lock turning in her bedroom door. Her racking sobs persisted, drowning out the sound of rain rapping the windowpanes. She was still crying when he retired, as was his invariable custom, at ten. The noise didn't stop him drifting off to sleep. His conscience was clear. That glancing blow to her face had not even drawn blood. She had provoked him beyond endurance. Her behaviour was shameful. Pure wickedness.

He patted the bull terrier's egg-shaped head. 'Time for your walk.'

Triangular eyes returned his gaze. The creature loves me more than my own wife, he thought. Judith had proved unable to give him a child. Something wrong with her innards; he didn't know the details and had no wish to enquire. Perhaps it was as well. At one time he'd yearned for a son, but what if the boy inherited her weaknesses? She would be sure to spoil a child, with calamitous results. He could not tolerate a milksop for an offspring. At least his dog was resilient and brave.

Once they were out of doors, he inhaled the fresh air. The grass and the leaves shone in the morning light. The downpour had washed the landscape, but this was no Eden. It would take more than a single cloudburst to cleanse Blackstone Fell.

He crossed the clapper bridge and let the dog off the leash. 'Go on, Moses. Have a run, boy.'

The bull terrier raced away down the track, leaving his master to muse on his misfortune in marrying a harlot. He'd fought against the growing suspicion that his wife's faithlessness had progressed from nursing infantile crushes on American film stars to the filthy reality of carnal relations with a man in the village. The indications had been there for some time, but he had refused to acknowledge them. Lately, however, it had become impossible for him to deny the truth to himself. She'd become more remote than ever. It was as if his very touch disgusted her. Yet they were man and wife. One flesh.

Last night, he'd come close to securing an admission of guilt. In the end she'd kept her luscious lips buttoned, but it wasn't her silence that inflamed his temper. It was the glint of contempt in her beautiful eyes.

And they were beautiful. Even now, after everything that had gone wrong between them, he found her loveliness beguiling. But her allure was tainted. How could he ever trust her again? She was the Messalina of the Pennines.

Who had cuckolded him? He'd agonised about the culprit's identity, not daring to contemplate the unspeakable possibility that Judith had consorted with a servant or someone from Blackstone Foot. The rector's wife would be quite a trophy for a low-browed lecher, some brute of a peasant. For all her faults, he could not believe that Judith would stoop so low. Who, then? In the upper village there were just a handful of plausible candidates. Not the professor; that was unthinkable. His son was a very different matter. Yes, the culprit must be one of four men. Denzil Sambrook. Young Carrodus. Harold Lejeune. And Major Huckerby.

His hands shaking with anger, he tramped along the path towards the Fell, whistling for Moses. The bull terrier was nowhere to be seen.

'Moses! Here, boy!'

There was no sign of him. Quintus Royle gnashed his teeth. The black dog was trained to obey. The rector prized fidelity. He was close to the base of the Fell and as he passed through the clump of trees, the mouth of the cave came into view. He called again.

'Moses!'

He was answered with a faint growl. The dog couldn't be far away. Had he entered the cave?

'Moses!' He approached the cave. 'Moses!'

Still the dog failed to come rushing back to him. He felt his temper rising. It was unaccountable.

Quintus Royle would not see sixty again, but he prided himself on retaining a spry physique. If he needed to enter the cave, so be it. Breathing hard, he got down on his haunches and peered into the darkness.

'There you are!'

Moses was still growling, as if on guard. Whatever he was guarding was bulky and broken.

Quintus Royle moved forward and squeezed himself into the opening of the cave. He stared, unsure whether to believe his eyes.

Moses had found a blood-soaked corpse.

14

'Morning,' Trueman said as he walked into the back room of The New Jerusalem where food was served to paying guests.

A tall woman with iron-grey hair sat reading the *Bradford Telegraph & Argus*. An unopened copy of the *Witness* lay on the tablecloth, next to her coffee cup and an empty toast rack. Her back was straight, her build spare. She gave an unintelligible grunt and didn't look up.

'Rotten weather when I arrived,' Trueman persisted. 'Hoping for better luck today. I don't know this part of the country and I fancy taking a walk to get my bearings. I'm here on business, mainly, but all work and no play makes Jack a dull boy, eh?'

The woman took no notice. He tried again.

'The name's Mann, by the way. Hugh Mann. Human, you see? Don't laugh, I've heard all the jokes a hundred times before.'

The woman lowered the newspaper and peered at him through small, rimless glasses. A severe but intelligent gaze, Trueman thought. She didn't pretend to be amused by his feeble quip. If, as Dilys suspected, she was a retired schoolmistress, she'd brook no tomfoolery in the classroom. Her round face was weather-beaten, her leathery cheeks and bony hands spotted with age. It was tempting to diagnose a dried-up spinster, but he had learned from his sister's disfigurement. A quick glance never gave you a proper measure of a person. The woman's features were nicely proportioned and her bone structure striking. Thirty years ago or more, she must have attracted plenty of suitors. And she'd not forgotten how to brush off men who tried to soft-soap her.

'If you'll excuse me.' She dropped the newspaper on the table and got to her feet. 'This belongs to Mr Crawshaw, but he won't mind you taking a look. I'm afraid the news is parochial, but they don't take the *Times* here and the *Witness* is unreadable tosh. Good day to you.'

With that, she was gone. Moments later, Dilys arrived to take his order for breakfast. Mrs Crawshaw was a martyr to arthritis, and Dilys helped in the kitchen as well as serving behind the bar. Trueman contented himself with idle chit-chat while he polished off the last of his Yorkshire ham.

'Enjoy your chat with the major last night?' she asked.

'Good bloke, that,' Trueman said, wiping his mouth with a cotton napkin. 'Not in the market for a new car, mind. Nor was Dr Sambrook, more's the pity.'

'He's one of these intellectuals,' Dilys said. 'Too clever for me.'

'Not your type, eh?'

She shrugged. 'The major, now, he's a real gent. Such a terrible shame about his wife.'

'You liked Mrs Huckerby?'

There was a momentary hesitation. 'I hardly knew her.

They never used to come in here. It's only since the tragedy that I've got to know the major. Since she died, he's got into the way of drowning his sorrows.'

'An occasional drink is a great solace,' Trueman said.

'After he's had a few, he gets downcast. I do my best to cheer him up, but grief's a terrible thing, Mr Mann.'

'It is that. And don't stand on ceremony, you can tell I'm not one of the nobs.' He grinned. 'Common as muck, that's me. So go on, pet. Call me Hugh. Hugh Mann, get it?'

He'd taken the precaution of masquerading as his cousin from Workington, whose full name was Hubert Mann and who was invariably called Hugh. Rachel had urged him to borrow a verifiable identity, in case someone bothered to check up on him.

She laughed. 'All right, Hugh Mann.'

'That's more like it.' His amusement faded. 'Shame about the major. His wife had nervous trouble, I gather?'

'So they say. She was a quiet one. Stand-offish, some folk said.'

'I imagine they were a devoted couple.'

'You never know what goes on behind closed doors,' Dilys said darkly.

'Was there any… talk, then?'

'Oh no,' she said hurriedly, 'I'm sure I don't mean to imply anything. Her death was such a shock, that's all. She looked a bit frail and washed-out, but some women do, don't you find?'

'Present company most definitely excepted,' Trueman said gallantly. 'You're a genuine Yorkshire rose, if you don't mind my saying so. Even if by rights you ought to come from the Red Rose county, with that wonderful head of hair.'

'You're a right charmer, Hugh Mann,' she said, running a hand through her unruly mop. 'And no mistake.'

He steered the conversation back to the topic of the late Mrs Huckerby. 'Terrible way for anyone to end it all. Self-poisoning, I gather?'

'It was awful,' she said. 'Nothing was proved, but everyone reckoned she topped herself. She collected the tablets the doctor prescribed until there were enough to make sure she'd never wake up again. There was a lot of talk in the village. We've had nothing like that since old Mr Barrass the cobbler hanged himself from a coat hook.'

'Folk always gossip, don't they? Shocking. Must make it even harder to cope with the grief. Rough on a man, when he loses his wife.' Trueman gave a philosophical shake of the head. 'But life goes on.'

Dilys nodded in vigorous assent. 'Exactly what I've told the major. He's not such an old buffer yet, and he keeps himself fit. Army training, I suppose. He's in here most nights. Not that I'm complaining. Good for business.'

Trueman gave her a wicked grin. 'Who can blame him? Bet he enjoys the scenery.'

She smiled. 'Flattery doesn't always get you everywhere.'

'Sorry to hear that, pet, but hope springs eternal.'

'Less than twenty-four hours since you signed the visitors' book, and already you're taking liberties!'

'I bet the major is one of your secret admirers.' He winked at her. 'Maybe not so secret, eh?'

She winked back. 'Jealous, are you?'

'Helpless in the clutches of the green-eyed monster.'

She laughed. 'Well, you're not as smart as you think you are, Hugh Mann. The poor major can't get over what happened.

Believe it or not, he's even talked about making contact with his wife in the spirit world.'

'Get away!'

'As true as I'm standing here. You know, séances and whatnot. I heard that he and the rector fell out over it. Mr Royle reckons all this spiritualist malarkey is unchristian. He's a rum one, the rector, and no mistake. I feel sorry for that poor wife of his. She wouldn't say boo to a goose. But I suppose he's right, it's a load of malarkey. Not that I'd say so to the major. Only the other week he was bending Dr Sambrook's ear about the afterlife. Not what we expect in The New Jerusalem. People are usually more interested in whether Bradford City will beat Bradford Park Avenue.'

'I don't suppose,' Trueman said as she paused for breath, 'a scientist would sympathise with the idea of getting in touch with the dead.'

She spread her arms. 'I can't make him out, that Dr Sambrook. Got his head in the clouds, if you ask me.'

'I bet you're much smarter, when it comes to things that really matter.'

'Get away with your bother. Off to work now? Or are you on the skive?'

'Treating myself to one or two well-earned days off work, pet. I'll have a look-see at the village, maybe climb up the Fell. Good to get a breath of air after yesterday's storm. And this afternoon, I've got an appointment at the sanatorium.'

Her eyes opened wide. 'You're not...?'

'It's about my father-in-law,' he said. 'Since my missus died, he's gone downhill fast. By the sound of it, Blackstone Sanatorium is ideal for anyone who has trouble with the nerves.'

She shrugged. 'I wouldn't know.'

He feigned anxiety. 'You don't think they are quacks, do you? I'd hate my father-in-law to go anywhere that wasn't…'

'Oh no,' she said quickly. 'Ever since the place was built, folk have called it the Mausoleum, but only because it's an eyesore. The professor has always been very close about his work.'

'What about his daughter? Are you friends? Two lasses who grew up in a small village?'

She gave him a hard stare. 'Daphne Sambrook's older than me, I'll have you know. We've never had anything to do with each other. The local kids used to make fun of her after the accident.'

'Accident?'

'It was when she and her brother were kids. The professor bought a new Daimler, but as he was driving along the lane that crosses the moor, he lost control on a bend.'

Trueman tutted. 'Daimlers, eh? I bet he braked too hard and the wheel rim collapsed. It wouldn't be the first time.'

'Mrs Sambrook was killed. The professor lost an eye and Daphne was badly scarred. For a year after the accident, she didn't utter a word. The professor set up a family trust to care for her. But she's a tough one. She made a very good recovery, though you can still see a livid mark on her brow.'

'And she is deputy matron at the sanatorium?'

'That's what they call her. From what I can make out, her main job is to look after the books. She isn't a scientific type. She came back not long before Dr Carrodus bought his practice here. There was gossip that her brother wanted the two of them to make a match of it. Not that it was ever likely.

The doctor is jolly and she's always had a sharp tongue. She's never bothered to get to know folk in the village. Even so, it doesn't cost anything to be civil, does it?'

'Snob, eh?'

'It's not so much that. We have a saying round here.' She cleared her throat. '*Nobbut a mile between Foot and Fell, and far apart as Heaven and Hell.*'

Trueman raised his eyebrows. 'Meaning what, exactly?'

'Meaning we've got nowt in common with the posh folk in the upper village. The likes of the Lejeunes and the Sambrooks. And the rector and his wife, for that matter. They keep themselves to themselves.'

'What about the staff at the sanatorium?'

'The professor has always forbidden them from talking about what goes on there. Anyone who opens their gob gets the boot.'

'Sounds mysterious.'

'You can understand why they want to keep things hush-hush. People who go there to be cured pay a lot of money. Or their families do. Nobody likes to hang out their dirty washing in public? I mean it's not nice, is it, if folk know you've gone doolally?'

'Ah. They want discretion.'

'That's the word. And that's what they get.'

'The treatment usually sets them right, then, does it?'

'I expect so,' she said. 'Otherwise people wouldn't keep coughing up, would they?'

His admiring gaze lingered on her. 'Sounds like the Sambrooks have cornered the market. An outfit like that must be a real gold mine. They must be rolling in it.'

'The professor's a boffin, got his head in the clouds. He

doesn't care about money, always goes around looking like a scruffy old tramp.'

'Not like his son, eh? That suit he wore looked like a Savile Row job.'

'It's not just his clothes,' Dilys said. 'In his own way, he sees himself as a lord of the manor.'

'Well, he does live in a manor, doesn't he?'

'That isn't the half of it, believe me. He and his family trust have started buying up land and houses. They even bought Blackstone Lodge from Harold Lejeune.'

'Blackstone Lodge?'

'Yes, the gatehouse of the Tower. Been in that family since the place was built, but the Lejeunes ran out of money years ago. You can't live on a view. There's a whisper going round that Harold wants to get rid of the Tower.'

'Didn't I hear about some sort of legend?'

'Sharp ears you've got,' she said. 'Yes, there's an old tale about the gatehouse. Men have vanished from there without trace.'

'Good grief!'

'Harold Lejeune's own brother went missing just before war broke out. I was only a kiddie at the time, but there was a big to-do about it. Alfred Lejeune, his name was. Went into the Lodge and never came out again. Or so they say. They searched the moor and the Fell, but he was never found.'

'So that's how Harold came to own the Tower?'

'Not that it's done him much good. By all accounts, he never wanted to come back to England. He lived on the Continent for years before his brother was declared dead.'

'Is that right?'

'Yes, he went out there to hunt rare plants. That's where he met his wife. I heard he didn't really want to live in the Tower at all. The grounds are a wilderness. He's never even planted a bed of his precious flowers.'

'What do you think happened to Alfred Lejeune?'

'I haven't the foggiest,' she said cheerfully. 'But I do know what will happen to me if I don't get these plates washed.'

Trueman got up. 'I'd better leave you to it.'

'Nice to have a chat,' she said. 'If you want to know about Blackstone Lodge, you'd better have another chinwag with Major Huckerby.'

'Why's that?'

'If I remember rightly, he was the last person to see Alfred Lejeune alive.'

Trueman walked outside to get his bearings. The sky was morose, with a cold wind sweeping across the desolate landscape. The moors stretched out beyond the writhing trees, all stunted bushes, gorse thickets, and tangles of bramble and bracken. Ahead of him loomed the sanatorium. Its windows were high and narrow, while the sombre slate roofing and dark-grey stonework were enough to make the most carefree soul despair. *Mausoleum* captured the building's melancholy, if not the impression of aching loneliness. It stood apart from the lower village, like a leper colony.

Standing at the point where the lanes crossed, he could see Blackstone Tower rearing up in the distance, a man-made rival to the Fell. Built three hundred years earlier, it had something in common with the sanatorium, Trueman thought. They both looked like monuments to misery.

He shook his head. Not like him to indulge in flights of

fancy. Best to leave that to Jacob Flint. He made his way back to The New Jerusalem and took the Hornet out of the garage.

Although he meant to avoid Nell Fagan, he ought to take a quick look at the upper village and work out the best route to Rachel's cottage. Halfway up the hill, he passed his fellow resident. She was striding back towards the inn and staring straight in front of her. He waved, but she took no notice. Miserable as sin, that one.

Moments later, a police car raced past, on its way towards Foot. A Lagonda followed close behind. Trueman slowed down. Something was amiss in Blackstone Fell.

Approaching the bend at the top of the hill, he saw the gatehouse to his right. Major Huckerby and another man were having a smoke under the archway. Right outside Nell Fagan's front door, Trueman thought.

The major spotted him and raised his hand. Trueman braked hard.

'Morning!' he shouted.

'Heard the news?'

Trueman jumped out of the car. 'What news?'

'The rector found a body in the cave beneath Blackstone Fell.'

'A body?'

One thought filled Trueman's mind: *Rachel was right.*

'I hear it's the woman who took a tenancy of the Lodge.' The major used his pipe to indicate the gatehouse. Trueman shot a glance at his companion. 'Sorry, forgetting my manners. Let me introduce you to Harold Lejeune. His family have owned the Tower since it was built. Lejeune, this is Mann, he's staying at The New Jerusalem. In the motor trade.'

They shook hands and Trueman gestured in the direction of the Tower. 'Remarkable home you have.'

'White elephant. The upkeep has bled me dry ever since I came here. The sooner I see the back of the place, the better.'

'You're dead set on leaving the village, then?' the major asked.

'Absolutely. The damp has crept into my bones.' He rapped his cane on the ground. 'Bad for my health. I need to get back to the sun. This business about a dead woman is the last straw. Thank God I've already sold the Lodge. People will start gossiping about absurd legends again.'

'You must admit, Lejeune, it is extraordinary,' the major said. 'Your brother's disappearance. That old case, centuries ago. And now this. It does make you wonder.'

'Damnable nonsense. We're even getting trippers!'

He glared at Trueman.

'Steady on, Mann is a damned decent fellow.' The major turned to Trueman. 'Another guest from The New Jerusalem was here a few minutes ago. A woman. Wanted to know what was up. Rather got Lejeune's goat, didn't she, old chap?'

The answer was a disagreeable grunt. 'I don't care for nosey parkers.'

The major tried to lighten the mood. 'I say, Lejeune, perhaps you should start offering tours of the Tower. Earn a few bob, eh?'

The other man scowled as Trueman said, 'What about the woman who died? What happened to her?'

'Sounds as though she was poking around inside the cave and precipitated a fall of rock. The hollows inside the Fell are a death trap. An old tramp used to live there before the war, believe it or not. Poor devil met a similar fate.'

'Do you know who the dead woman is?'

'Called herself Cornelia Grace,' the major said. 'Met her a time or two. Don't wish to speak ill of the dead, but she struck me as rather… well, brash. Another nosey parker, you might say. What did you make of her, Lejeune?'

A shrug. 'Never spoke to the woman.'

'She tripped up in the churchyard after the service on Sunday. Sambrook and I helped her to the doctor's surgery. Carrodus told her to rest, but she struck me as the cussed type. Not one to obey doctor's orders. Perhaps she injured herself while she was inside the cave, and before she could get out, part of the roof gave way.'

'She had to be dug out?' Trueman asked.

'From what Carrodus said, it was scarcely an avalanche. Just a few chunks of rock fell down. It was her misfortune to be struck on the head. Wrong place at the wrong time, I'm afraid.'

Another accident, Trueman thought. Just like Vernon Murray. The boulder toppled from the Fell didn't crush Nell Fagan, but she'd given the killer a second chance.

'When did this happen?'

'I had a word with the doctor before I bumped into Lejeune here. After the rector raised the alarm, Carrodus examined the body and talked to the local constable. They aren't sure about time of death. There will be a post-mortem, of course. Nasty business.'

'Very.'

'What's more, Carrodus mentioned an extraordinary thing.'

'Oh yes?'

Trueman leaned closer. The major's breath smelled of stale beer.

'This came from the local constable, who looked inside the Lodge.' The major pointed to the gatehouse door. 'Went through her things to see if he could identify a next of kin. Long story short, it seems the woman was living here under an assumed name.'

Trueman feigned amazement. 'Good grief!'

'Turns out that her Christian names are Cornelia Grace, but her surname is Fagan. On the QT, it seems she's a newspaper reporter from London.'

'Crikey, what was she playing at?'

'Carrodus asked the very same question, and he won't be the only one,' the major said. 'What in the name of heaven brings a Fleet Street hack to Blackstone Fell?'

15

'You read my mind,' Rachel Savernake said into the telephone. 'There's no time to lose. Tomorrow, we catch the early train to Yorkshire.'

Trueman was calling from Halifax. He'd met the land agent handling the tenancy of the vacant cottage at Blackstone Fell, and broken the news that Rachel insisted on proceeding immediately. The deal was done on the spot. She was free to move in.

'Nell Fagan had a fall on Sunday. Tripped over in the churchyard after attending the service. Curious. I wouldn't have said she was the religious type.'

'She wanted to spy on the locals.'

'One of them outwitted her. I'm told the village doctor warned her to rest. She should have taken his advice.'

'She hated toeing the line,' Rachel said. 'That stubborn streak cost her life. How much do we know about what happened?'

'Nothing. According to Huckerby, she hadn't been seen since Sunday. The doctor said he'd called at the Lodge yesterday to see how she was faring, but there was no answer.'

'So she may have been missing for more than twenty-four hours?'

'Yes, but she isn't the first person to have died in a rock fall in the cave at Blackstone Fell. Everybody tells me her death was an accident.'

'Of course. It's the simple explanation. Comforting, too. Especially so far as the murderer is concerned. I can't swallow the idea that she was simply unlucky.'

'Me neither.'

'Any joy with the register of visitors to The New Jerusalem?'

'Not yet, but tonight I may do a bit of sleepwalking. While everyone is tucked up in bed and dreaming sweet dreams, I'll nip downstairs and study the book. I'll make a note of the names and put it back before people wake up.'

'Watch out for creaking floorboards.'

'Don't worry. I know which ones to avoid.'

'Tell me about the other people you've met so far.'

He summarised the conversations he'd had since arriving at Blackstone Fell. 'So I haven't met the rector and his wife yet,' he concluded. 'Or Professor Sambrook and his daughter, but I should see them later, when I ask them to take care of my inconvenient father-in-law.'

'Perhaps on a permanent basis?'

'In Blackstone Fell,' he said, 'anything is possible.'

'Nell Fagan is dead?' Jacob Flint tightened his grip on the receiver. 'You mean she was murdered?'

He was at his desk in Clarion House. As Rachel told the story, he felt his stomach churn. He and Nell hadn't been close friends, but he'd enjoyed her company. Exuberant, irrepressible, a woman full of life. Now someone had snuffed it out, and her remains were lying on a cold slab two hundred miles away.

'The news will kill Eunice,' he said. 'She and Peggy were the closest to family that Nell had.'

'You can't talk to them. They will hear soon enough.'

'No need to worry,' he said bitterly. 'After the fiasco of the séance, I'm the last person to break bad news in Kentish Town.'

'Discovered anything more about Ottilie Curle?'

'That woman is as elusive as her spirit guides. Nobody admits to knowing who she is or where she comes from.'

'People who hide their past usually have a very good reason,' Rachel said quietly.

'I won't give up.'

'Good. Tomorrow morning, we take the early train to the north. If you'd wish to join us for dinner this evening before we go, you'd be welcome.'

Jacob knew Rachel well enough to recognise a summons when he heard one. And to understand that she didn't take no for an answer.

'You're spoiling me. Luckily enough, I'm not doing anything tonight. Seven o'clock?'

'Perfect.'

'I suppose I'm singing for my supper again?'

She laughed. 'Am I so transparent? I must work harder at preserving my mystery. Yes, while we are away, I need you to do some more digging.'

'Into what?'

'Martha's spent hours at Somerset House,' Rachel said. 'Looking through death certificates.'

He thought for a moment. 'Investigating the deceased of Blackstone Fell?'

'Excellent, Jacob,' she said. 'We'll make a detective out of you yet.'

Rachel buttered a crumpet. She was sitting at the kitchen table, having tea with Hetty.

'Cliff is doing a first-class job. Anyone would think he was born to the stage.'

The housekeeper shook her head. 'I can hardly credit it. My own husband, the man who never utters a word more than he needs. Strutting around like Sir Henry Irving.'

Rachel reached out and squeezed the older woman's hand. 'We dreamed of this, don't forget, all those years on the island. Dreamed that one day we'd be as rich as Croesus, free to amuse ourselves however we pleased.'

'You're the one who inherited the Judge's fortune.'

'We always agreed,' Rachel said. 'We're in this together.'

The housekeeper pulled her hand away to rub her eyes. 'I'm sleeping badly.'

'Cliff told me.'

'I wake up in the small hours and my cheeks are wet with tears.'

'What's wrong?'

A sob choked Hetty's voice. 'I'm afraid.'

Rachel gave her a sharp look. She couldn't remember a time when this woman hadn't been there to lean on. Or an occasion when she'd given in to despair.

'Of what?'

'I'm afraid we'll be ruined. I've not had a decent night's

sleep since we left Mortmain Hall. That made me realise the risks we run. One day everything will come crashing down on our heads.'

'All the more reason to make the most of every waking moment.' Rachel pushed the tub of butter across the table. 'Go on, have another crumpet.'

Hetty Trueman sighed. 'What's become of us, Rachel? Martha is playing the sleuth. Cliff is pretending to be a motor car salesman. Tomorrow we'll be in a godforsaken backwater. With a murderer on the loose.'

'Perhaps more than one,' Rachel said lightly.

'Once upon a time, life was wretched.' Hetty took a breath. 'To all intents and purposes, Judge Savernake kept you as a prisoner. I was at my wits' end, Cliff was shell-shocked, Martha had acid thrown in her face. We've paid back the people who made our lives hell. We got what we wanted. We escaped from Gaunt, we don't need to…'

'Don't we? Aren't we always escaping from something?'

A derisive snort. 'That's too deep for me.'

Rachel put her elbows on the table. 'The other day, you called me an addict. It's true, but murder isn't my only addiction. I can't live without excitement. For so long, I lived in my imagination. Now I crave the thrill of the unexpected. Puzzles, mysteries – the more outlandish, the better. Each time we cross the street outside, we take our lives in our hands. Why dread the risks? I'd rather embrace them.'

'But…'

'I need to face down danger, Hetty, don't you see? It gives me a purpose, makes me feel alive. Selfish, yes, but we can't change who we are. Martha understands. Even Cliff has come round.'

'If I know Cliff…'

'You know him best of all. But you also know I haven't corrupted either of them. They enjoy tasting freedom, you can see for yourself.'

Hetty grunted. 'Seeing isn't believing. I've heard you say that more than once.'

Rachel pretended to flinch. 'Touché.'

'I don't find danger liberating. Not in the slightest. Deep down, I'm a coward.'

'You're the bravest woman I know.'

Hetty sighed. 'You're always impossible to argue with.'

'And your glass is always half empty.' Rachel's eyes met Hetty's. 'Please. Trust me.'

'Oh, I trust you, all right.' The housekeeper's lips formed in a faint and reluctant smile. 'With my life. You know that.'

'Well, then.'

'I'm not like you.'

'I don't ask you to be.'

'Nell Fagan has died. Before her, Murray. Even so, this Blackstone Fell business, you treat it as a game.'

'Because life is a game.'

'On this earth, we all lose in the end.'

'Maybe.' Rachel shrugged. 'But I play to win.'

Trueman arrived at Blackstone Sanatorium in good time for his appointment. A stout fence, six feet in height, separated the grounds from the moorland. There were no signs, nothing to give a clue to the building's purpose. This was a place of secrets.

He rang the bell at the main gate. An unseen dog began to

bark. A canine alarm system, he thought. Effective enough. The racket persisted until he was admitted by a tall woman in a uniform which matched the grey stonework. She had a foreign accent, German probably. He tried to engage her in conversation, but her responses to his cheerful overtures were brusquely monosyllabic. Defeated, he squashed his heavy body onto a rickety wooden chair in the draughty entrance hall and feigned interest in a tattered copy of the *Illustrated London News*.

The sanatorium's interior was no more uplifting than its external appearance. The air had a faint tang of carbolic. The walls were whitewashed and stark, the corridors radiating from the lobby long and straight. A nurse bustled past, not sparing the visitor a second glance. The squeak of her shoes on the linoleum set Trueman's teeth on edge.

Denzil Sambrook hurried down the steps to the lobby. In a sombre black three-piece suit, he reminded Trueman more than ever of the old vampire films. This time Dracula was on his home ground. In his castle.

'Afternoon, Mann.'

'Good to see you again.'

'Let me take you upstairs. You must meet my father. The professor insists on seeing everyone who wants us to take a new patient.'

Trueman followed him up the stairs. The upper floor of the sanatorium seemed mainly devoted to office space. Sambrook stopped at an imposing door which bore the professor's name. He knocked, a distinctive double rap, and waited for a moment before entering.

Wilfred Sambrook sat behind a vast mahogany desk, leafing through documents in a magenta folder. Trueman was taken aback by the old man's fragility. He looked as though a puff of air would blow him over. When Denzil made the introductions, he said hello but did not get up or offer to shake hands. He closed the folder and settled back in his large leather chair, contemplating a wisp of cobweb on the ceiling.

'Impressive place you have here,' Trueman said. 'Very quiet.'

The professor inclined his head. 'A peaceful environment is essential if I am to do my work.'

'Blackstone Fell is certainly off the beaten track.'

'Our patients benefit immeasurably if they are removed from everyday preoccupations. It is essential to reduce the pressure on a disordered brain.'

'You accept patients from all over the country, I believe?'

'Mental disturbance knows no geographic boundaries.' The professor fixed his good eye on Trueman. 'We treat the sick with the delicacy of skilled surgeons. The difference is that the diseases we fight exist only in the mind. There are no telltale spots or rashes or bleeding. Our patients' disorders are real and they are serious. But they are invisible.'

'All the more terrible for that, eh?' Trueman said.

Denzil said, 'Tell the professor about your father-in-law.'

'He's just not himself, sir. Not since my late wife died, sir. He was devoted to Betty.'

'Describe the symptoms.'

Trueman threw a nervous glance towards Denzil. 'Excuse me, sir, but I have to ask. Everything I say within these walls is treated in confidence?'

'Of course!' The old man's voice rose. 'My son and I are men of integrity.'

'Very good, thank you.' Trueman exhaled. 'You see, it's like this. My father-in-law suffers from strange fancies. Delusions, you might call 'em.'

'Be specific. What kind of delusions?'

'Arnold and I always got on so well while Betty was alive. He took me into the firm, made me a partner, even though I had no capital. It was only right and proper that he took the lion's share of the profits. Since Betty passed on, he's not done a hand's turn in the business. I wouldn't mind, but…'

'Yes, yes,' the old man interrupted. 'And the delusions?'

'Sorry, sir. You see, this is really difficult for me. I'd never dream of coming to a place like this if I wasn't at the end of my tether.'

'A place like this?'

'A nut… sorry, I can't find the right words.' Trueman put on a brave smile. 'Selling cars is one thing. It's not like talking to a famous… well, psychiatrist.'

'Get on with it.' The great man was losing patience.

'Absolutely. You see, sir, it's like this.' Trueman hesitated. 'I mean, it sounds ridiculous, but the old chap has got a bee in his bonnet. I scarcely dare say it, but I must. He actually believes… that I want to kill him.'

For a few moments, nobody spoke. The professor nodded several times, as if he'd received confirmation of a long-held theory. Denzil Sambrook's face gave nothing away.

'These are specific delusions?' The professor rapped on his desk, an unexpectedly forceful gesture. 'Chapter and verse, give me chapter and verse.'

Trueman swallowed. 'Arnold used to come round to our house for dinner. Every Thursday evening, regular as clockwork. Now he refuses to cross the threshold. At first I thought he was simply upset. When he let something slip, I began to understand. He's afraid of being poisoned.'

'Nonsense, surely?' Denzil said.

'Of course, but he questioned my cook, and she was so deeply offended that she handed in her notice. That isn't the half of it. He refuses to drive any of our cars. Our mechanic tackled him privately. According to him, the old fellow is afraid someone has tampered with the brakes.'

The professor steepled his fingers together. 'Interesting. There was a case in Wales, I recall, which bore certain similarities to the situation you describe…' His voice trailed away as he dredged the recesses of his memory.

Denzil said, 'Did anything specific provoke these fears?'

'His strange fancies began after Betty died.'

'What happened to her?'

'Heart failure.'

'Does weakness in the heart run in her family, by any chance?'

Trueman pondered. 'Do you know, I think it does.'

'Can you give particular examples?'

Trueman racked his brains. This was a question for which he hadn't prepared. He wiped a line of sweat from his forehead. The effort of playing a part was taking a toll. He told himself it didn't matter. The Sambrooks would be familiar with people in his position showing signs of stress.

'Her aunt dropped down dead all of a sudden. And then there was a cousin…'

'Very well. So your father-in-law has no reason to hold you responsible for his daughter's death?'

'Good grief, no!' Trueman added virtuously. 'We were a devoted couple, Betty and me. Never a cross word.'

'I'm sure,' Denzil said crisply. 'In that case, what makes him behave like this? Has anything you've said or done prompted these irrational fantasies?'

Trueman bit his lip. 'I suppose… given that we're speaking under the seal of the confessional, so to speak, I ought to put my cards on the table.'

The professor said, 'That is a *sine qua non*.'

'You see, sir, since I lost Betty, I've been beside myself. Working every hour God sends, while her old man pockets most of the money. It's very hard.'

'Go on.'

'I have my needs. As men of the world, I'm sure you two gentlemen understand.'

The professor turned his good eye to the cobweb again. Denzil frowned. Neither of them looked in the least like men of the world.

Trueman coughed. 'Recently I met a young lady, and… well, to be blunt, she told me last week that she's in the family way.'

'Ah,' Denzil said.

'I intend to do the decent thing, but it's not easy. Arnold has met Lily and he doesn't approve. Called her a whore. The other day, he came right out with it. A lot of bile, it was quite shocking. Even to me.'

'As a man of the world?'

'Exactly. He actually had the nerve to accuse me of getting rid of Betty. Outrageous! He said that I'd got away with murder and now I was planning to do away with him. Said I only cared about the money.'

Professor Sambrook said, 'Your father-in-law, does he display any obvious signs of neurosis?'

'I'm not sure what the obvious signs are, sir, but I'm the only one who knows him well enough to realise he's got a screw loose. If you'll pardon the expression. This rotten slander about Betty. Let alone the idea that I want him dead.'

'His behaviour has not given rise to concern on the part of others?'

'Not as far as I'm aware, sir. You see, he isn't a sociable fellow. Not like yours truly. His wife died years back, and Betty was an only child. The apple of his eye.'

'Treating such a case is fraught with difficulty.'

'I understand, sir.'

The professor closed his eyes. Trueman coughed, but got no response. Time for a little pathos, he decided.

'I'll be honest with you, sir. I try to put a brave face on things, but I'm at the limit of my endurance. When I came to Blackstone Fell, I'd even considered… well, I was wondering whether the world would be better off without me, if you follow my drift.'

The professor said nothing.

'I don't mean to speak out of turn, but it might just be a godsend that I happened to bump into your son last night.'

The professor's breathing became noisier. Was his mind wandering? Surely he hadn't fallen asleep?

Denzil Sambrook said, 'My father tires easily these days. We'd better leave.'

'My father slept badly last night,' Denzil Sambrook said as he closed the door to the professor's room. 'He's suffered from insomnia for many years. Let me take you to see my sister. She is our deputy matron. A courtesy title, frankly. Her job is to look after administrative matters. She will explain whether we can accommodate an additional patient.'

'How many patients do you have at any one time?' Trueman asked.

Denzil paused before replying. 'We are highly selective. Our courses of treatment are demanding. Increasingly, we concentrate, so to speak, on quality rather than quantity.'

'I understand.'

Trueman wiped a line of sweat off his brow. By nature he was a man of action, accustomed to relying on his strength and determination. Rachel had placed her faith in him, but he couldn't help wondering if he'd bitten off more than he could chew.

'Sorry, this whole affair is such a strain…'

'We are accustomed to the most difficult cases.'

'They don't come much more difficult than my father-in-law, I can tell you.'

Denzil Sambrook led him down the short corridor, halting in front of a door marked with his sister's name. He repeated his double knock, and a woman's voice told them to come in.

Daphne's room was much smaller than her father's. Vivid abstract paintings hung on the wall rather than framed scrolls. The extravagant shapes and patterns seemed to Trueman like representations of a disordered mind. He suspected that Rachel, whose love of modern art he'd never understood, might be taken with them.

The woman behind the desk lacked the high intellectual brow of the male Sambrooks; hers was disfigured by the scar. Her haircut and plain, shapeless dress seemed to emphasise that she didn't care about her looks.

Denzil performed the introductions. 'I mentioned Hugh to

you this morning. The patient is his father-in-law. Appears to be suffering from paranoid delusions, triggered by the death of his daughter. He is under the mistaken impression that Hugh wants to do away with him.'

'How did you hear about the sanatorium, Mr Mann?'

Rachel had anticipated this question. She and Trueman had discussed how, as a car dealer with murder on his mind, he ought to respond. If nothing untoward was happening here, his answer didn't matter. On the other hand, if the Sambrooks were somehow concerned with disposing of inconvenient individuals such as Ursula Baker, a great deal hinged on what he said.

'Someone mentioned this place to me. Said it would be worth my while to take a trip to Blackstone Fell.'

'Really? And who was that, may I ask?'

Daphne's manner was polite and enquiring. Her brother's expression made Trueman feel like a specimen under the microscope. In his head, Trueman heard Rachel's words of warning.

'Don't prevaricate. Be discreet, but not defensive. People believe what they want to believe. It's extraordinary what they will swallow if you speak with sufficient confidence.'

He beamed. 'Chap I met in a pub.'

Daphne frowned. 'A pub?'

'It was down in London. In my job, I get around the country, you know.'

'Naturally. Whereabouts in London?'

'Covent Garden.'

'And the chap's name?'

Trueman rubbed his nose. 'Let me think.'

Daphne Sambrook eyed him thoughtfully. 'Let me explain

why I press you on this, Mr Mann. My father's work has attracted some controversy over the years. There are those – even within our own profession – who disapprove of his methods.'

'I say, Daphne…' her brother began.

She ignored him. 'It's important for us to be aware of what people are saying about us.'

'Baker, that was it,' Trueman said. 'Youngish chap. Arty type.'

'A playwright,' Denzil said.

'Ah yes, poor fellow,' his sister murmured. 'I'm sorry to say that his wife passed away. It was very tragic.'

'Yes,' Trueman said. 'He did mention that. Rotten shame.'

Denzil Sambrook said hurriedly, 'Her death was entirely unconnected with the treatment she was receiving, of course.'

'Of course,' Trueman said. 'Matter of fact, Baker sang your praises.'

'That was good of him,' Daphne said quietly.

'You can't beat personal recommendation,' Trueman said. 'Not that Baker told me much about the sanatorium and… how things work, so to speak. Mind you, a nod's as good as a wink to a blind horse, eh?'

Daphne peered at him curiously. She exchanged glances with her brother, although Trueman couldn't interpret their meaning.

'I realise,' he said, 'your services won't come cheap.'

'I'm afraid that's right,' Daphne said. 'The sanatorium is rather exclusive. At any one time, we care for only a small number of patients. The regime here is intensive and sophisticated, and reflects the latest advances in scientific thinking.'

'Glad to hear it. In this life, you get what you pay for. My motto is, you can't make a Rolls-Royce out of parts from a Model T.'

'How very true.'

'Go on, then, how much do you charge?'

Daphne named a weekly rate that made even Trueman blink. 'Naturally, we understand that not everyone can afford to fund a loved one's treatment in the sanatorium. Our charges reflect the unique service that my father and brother provide.'

I bet, he thought, taking out his wallet.

'Put your money away, Mr Mann,' Daphne said briskly. 'I'm sorry to tell you that just at the moment, we are not able to take on any more patients.'

16

Jacob reclined on the settee in the sitting room of Gaunt House. Nell Fagan's death had ruined his day, but a glass of Château Pavie 1921 provided a touch of solace. He was no wine buff, but it was the most stunning Bordeaux he'd ever tasted.

'You were right about Nell, and the risk she ran,' he said.

Rachel shrugged. 'Even cats run out of lives in the end.'

'I can't believe I'll never drink with her again.' He sighed. 'Or cringe at the stench of her cheroots. You don't suppose she might simply have had an accident?'

'Do you?'

'No,' he admitted. 'If only...'

'Speculation will get us nowhere. We must look ahead. This time tomorrow, I'll be in my new cottage. A cat among the pigeons at Blackstone Fell.'

'One of those pigeons is a murderer.'

She smiled. 'At least one.'

'You sound excited.'

'Of course. You know me.'

He laughed, thinking *I wish I did.*

Martha refilled his glass. She was wearing a sleeveless

beaded chiffon gown, the epitome of chic. Her chestnut hair was done in a finger wave and pulled into a bun at the nape of her neck. The style was borrowed from June Collyer, one of her favourite actresses. In the low light, Jacob thought she looked more entrancing than any Hollywood star. With artful make-up, the damage to her face was invisible.

'Thanks, Martha. You're looking very glamorous.'

Her smile was flirtatious. 'Cinderella's last hurrah. I've spent hours spent poring over dusty documents. Tomorrow, it's back to the housemaid's uniform.'

'How did you fare at Somerset House? Any needles in the haystack?'

Rachel said, 'I asked Martha to apply four criteria in searching the records. First, to prioritise deaths within the past two years. Second, the death must have occurred at Blackstone Fell, even if not at the sanatorium itself. Third, the deceased shouldn't be a local resident. Finally, the cause of death must be capable of amounting to murder. I'm tempted to rule out cancer, for instance. But we can't take anything for granted. We're dealing with an ingenious killer.'

'You're convinced that Ursula Baker was murdered?'

'Her son is dead. So is the woman he asked to investigate his mother's death. They had survived apparent attempts to kill them within the past few days. Circumstantial evidence, yes, but men have been hanged on less.'

'Men have been hanged by mistake,' Jacob pointed out.

Rachel gave him a withering glance. 'Listen to what Martha discovered.'

'I found three strong candidates,' Martha said. 'All within the last eighteen months. Two men and one woman. They hailed from different parts of the country. Wales, Brighton, and

Oxford. Two cases were certified as heart failure. One fellow of seventy-five died of old age. According to the records, each time the place of death was Blackstone Sanatorium.'

Jacob turned to Rachel. 'What are you asking me to do?'

'Martha will give you the names of the dead. Your job is to find out who had a good reason to kill them.'

Trueman shaved in his room above the bar before going downstairs. He felt crushed by a sense of failure. Daphne had put the name of his mythical father-in-law on a waiting list, but said it might be weeks before they could take on another patient. When he emphasised his desperation in the face of his father-in-law's wild accusations, she simply replied that they could make no promises.

Thank goodness he'd taken Rachel's advice and masqueraded as his cousin. Surely they wouldn't go so far as visiting Workington to check his bona fides?

Nothing had been said to suggest that the professor disposed of his patients, with or without his son's assistance, in return for their outrageous fees. Trueman told himself he wasn't cut out for this kind of work. Distracted, he nicked his chin with the cut-throat razor for the first time in years.

Nell Fagan was dead and he was no further forward. He needed some beer inside him.

He'd presumed that the death of a stranger would be the talk of The New Jerusalem, but when he walked into the bar, this wasn't the case. The regulars were preoccupied with their darts, dominoes, and shove ha'penny, while the landlord stonewalled his conversational overtures before joining a couple of cronies to argue about football.

His hopes rose when Dilys emerged from the back room. 'Wondered if it was your night off,' he said, as she poured him a second pint.

She cast a resentful glance towards Crawshaw. 'Chance would be a fine thing.'

'I heard talk about that woman who died up at Blackstone Fell.' He shook his head mournfully. 'Shocking business.'

'Isn't it just?' Dilys's eyes shone with excitement. 'She'd rented the Lodge, you know. Nobody ever lived there before. Nobody dared. It stood empty all those years when the Lejeunes owned it. Being scientific folk, the Sambrooks have no use for old wives' tales – and look what's happened!' Dilys leaned towards him. 'She came in here, you know, the deceased.'

'Is that right?' He allowed his gaze to linger on the barmaid's figure. She still hadn't mastered the knack of buttoning her blouse properly.

'Oh yes, served her myself. Smoked like a chimney, she did. Horrid cheroot things. And she liked a drink. You can always tell.'

'I bet you can.'

'Called herself Grace, she did, but not wishing to speak ill of the dead, there was nowt graceful about her. Cornelia Grace, that's how she introduced herself. But it was a lie. I heard on the grapevine, she was an impostor.'

'Get away!'

Dilys was thrilled to share exclusive gossip. 'From what I hear, her real name was Fagan. And guess what?'

Looking suitably agog, Trueman breathed, 'Go on!'

'She was a newspaper reporter. Came from London.'

'Good grief. What was a newshound doing in this neck of the woods?'

'Folk say she was going to write about the Lodge and its strange past. Why else would a journalist want to rent the place?'

'What happened to her, exactly?'

'Sounds like she went noseying around in the cave. Maybe she disturbed the rock. It's not safe, but she was a stranger. She wouldn't have known.'

'Bad luck, that. To be there just at the moment the cave roof crumbles.'

'I'll say.' Dilys shook her head. 'I bet it'll be a long time before Dr Sambrook finds another tenant for the gatehouse. You can guess what folk are saying.'

'What's that?'

Her expression was conspiratorial. 'There is a curse on Blackstone Lodge!'

Jacob washed down Hetty's shepherd's pie with more than his fair share of the Château Pavie. During the evening, the conversation ranged far and wide, taking in Alfred Hitchcock's new film about murder in a theatrical troupe, Oswald Mosley's latest attempts to seduce the Labour Party, and the score for *Bitter Sweet*. Wine and good company helped to distract him from imagining Nell Fagan's cold and lonely end.

Rachel was in sparkling form, witty, perceptive, and scathing by turns. Jacob never ceased to be amazed by the sheer breadth of her knowledge. He couldn't think of a single reporter on Fleet Street who was so well informed. Let alone one who was so entranced by the puzzles of *The Waste Land*. Tonight her excitement was palpable. The prospect of unravelling the tangle of Blackstone Fell exhilarated her, made her come alive.

'What do you plan to do there?' he asked as the clock chimed ten.

She stretched in her chair. 'Too soon to say.'

'You must have some idea.'

'An investigation is like a drive in the night-time. You have a destination in mind and a map, but still you're in the dark. There may be bumps in the road. The headlamps show the way ahead, but you can only see so far. You need to trust your sense of direction to make sure you'll get there in the end.'

He hiccupped. 'That's quite profound.'

She shrugged. 'You look drowsy. Not surprising after you've drunk so much. Before you go home, we have something for you. A little present.'

Martha handed him a book in gift wrapping. 'Light reading to keep you out of mischief while we are away.'

He blinked. 'I don't know what to say.'

Rachel laughed. 'Just say good night, Jacob.'

Martha accompanied him to the door. She gave him an exercise book.

'Rachel asked me to write this out for you,' she said. 'A summary of what I discovered at Somerset House. Plenty there to get your teeth into.'

'I'll start work on it right away.' He stood at the top of the stone steps that ran up to the front door. The weather was mild, the sky clear, the stars bright. 'I'm glad Rachel asked me over. Much better than being on my own. After what happened to Nell…'

'What's done is done,' she said. 'We can't undo the past.'

The light from the street lamp caught the damaged side of

her face. 'You're getting as bad as Rachel,' he said ruefully. 'Always in the right.'

'We'd better start thinking of fresh ways to surprise you.' She leaned forward and dropped a light kiss on his cheek. 'Goodnight, Jacob. Sweet dreams.'

He was rooted to the spot. He'd never felt the touch of her lips before. How should he respond? As he asked himself the question, she took a step back and closed the door.

Back in his flat at Exmouth Market, Jacob felt pleasantly woozy. It wasn't merely the wine. It was Martha's kiss. She had a teasing sense of humour and she wasn't in the least romantic. And yet.

He enjoyed the company of women, but he'd never known anyone like Rachel Savernake. Or Martha Trueman, come to that. Rachel's good looks were matched only by her ruthless determination to go her own way. She didn't need anyone other than the Truemans. He amused her, but he wondered if she simply saw him as a useful idiot. Of course she was desirable, but her wealth and beauty put her out of reach. As for Martha, what did she want from life? Was she happy to remain forever in Rachel's shadow? There was still so much about the strange ménage in Gaunt House that he struggled to understand.

Yawning, he opened the exercise book. Martha's round handwriting was neat and careful. She and Rachel had grown up together on that remote northern island. They'd been forced to educate themselves. No governess for them, not like Nell Fagan.

A picture flashed into his mind of Nell, crumpled on the

floor of a dark cave, head smashed by sharp, heavy rocks. A freak accident? No. Murder, it must be. Clenching his fist, he told himself that he owed it to her to find the killer.

On the first lined page of the exercise book, Martha had written three names.

Clodagh Hamill

Violet Beagrie

Joshua Cuthbert Flood

Yawning, he read Martha's brief notes. All three deaths had occurred within the past fifteen months, starting with Clodagh Hamill. She'd died at the age of forty-nine, whereas Violet Beagrie was just twenty years old. They were recorded as dying of heart failure and coronary thrombosis respectively. The cause of Flood's death was noted as old age.

Clodagh Hamill's home address was in Woodstock Road, Oxford. Beagrie came from a village outside Brighton, while Flood lived on the Welsh coast. Clodagh Hamill's occupation was stated as 'housewife', whereas Flood was a retired merchant. Beagrie was simply described as a spinster.

Three human beings, with nothing to connect them except that their lives had come to an end at Blackstone Sanatorium.

And, perhaps, that they had been murdered.

For a big, muscular man, Clifford Trueman was light on his feet. At two o'clock he left his room, closing the door noiselessly behind him. He wore a dressing gown as well as pyjamas and had a satchel over his shoulder and a torch in his hand. Bending double to avoid cracking his head on the old beams, he crept along the narrow passageway.

There were several vacant guest rooms. The Crawshaws'

room was at the far side of the small landing, just above the staircase. No servants lived in; Dilys returned each night to the cottage where she lived with the rest of her family. Trueman paused outside the landlord's door and was reassured by a faint rumble of snoring. Glancing over his shoulder, he saw a tiny strip of light under the door of the room beyond his at the far end of the passageway.

The other guest must be awake. What was the woman up to?

This wasn't the moment to find out. He sneaked down the wooden steps, avoiding the floorboards which creaked loudest on his way to the front of the inn. The register sat in its customary place on the counter. He'd brought paper and a pencil so that he could make notes while downstairs. This seemed preferable to taking the register up to his room and then bringing it back again, which ran the risk of an additional trip up and down the stairs. But with someone awake upstairs, he changed his plan.

He opened the register. The other guest had signed in as Margaret Needham of Camden Town. Her handwriting was firm and considerably more legible than his own casual scrawl. Whether the details she'd given were as fictitious as those of Hugh Mann in Workington remained to be seen.

Rachel wanted to know the names and addresses of everyone who had stayed at The New Jerusalem over the past two years. Trueman flicked back through the book. Just as well that this wasn't the Savoy. For long stretches of time, there were no guests at all. He and the Needham woman had signed in on a new page. The information he sought covered most of the two preceding pages.

Taking a razor from his satchel, he slit the two pages at the edge and removed them from the book. A neat job. Nobody would notice unless they examined the register. He slipped the sheets into his satchel and retraced his steps.

That thin line of light from the other guest room was still visible. Perhaps Margaret Needham was as much of an insomniac as Professor Sambrook. Trueman closed the door behind him and breathed out.

Mission accomplished. He took off his dressing gown and put his ear to the wall, but no sound came from the room next door. Sitting on the edge of his bed, he scanned the signatures of those who had previously enjoyed the hospitality of The New Jerusalem. Only one name meant anything to him: Thomas Baker.

'Let's see what Rachel makes of all this,' he said to himself.

Taking a foolscap envelope from his case, he slid the two sheets inside. He sealed the envelope and wrote on the front in his untidy hand.

Miss Rachel Savernake,
Hawthorn Cottage,
Fell Lane,
Blackstone Fell

Tomorrow she'd be here. Cliff Trueman wasn't soft-hearted, but he almost felt sorry for whoever had killed Nell Fagan. They had no idea what they were up against.

17

Trueman was in good time for breakfast. This morning's challenge was to persuade Margaret Needham to engage in conversation.

What was she doing here? Was the walking tour a blind? As he hurried down the stairs, careless this time of whether they creaked or not, an unwelcome thought struck him. Was she another prospective customer for the services of Professor Sambrook and Blackstone Sanatorium?

She was already seated at the table when he walked into the room. Her face was the colour of clay. His hearty greeting was dismissed with the briefest nod.

'Bad business up at the Fell yesterday,' he said.

No answer.

'Poor woman. What a way to go, eh? Buried by a fall of rock.' He tutted. 'Tragic. Absolutely tragic.'

Margaret Needham devoted herself to smearing marmalade over a thick slice of toast. She ignored him as she began to eat.

'Strange that she went inside the cave,' he mused. 'It's a death trap, they tell me. Avalanches and whatnot. Dangerous village, Blackstone Fell. You and I had better keep our eyes peeled, eh?'

He was rewarded with a reaction: a withering stare. She swallowed a mouthful of coffee. Definitely haggard, he thought.

'Funny, I hear she was a newspaper reporter. Staying in the village under a false name. Peculiar, don't you think?'

After a few moments, he tried again. 'Can't imagine what brings someone like that up here, can you?'

Margaret Needham kept on eating.

'Young Dilys told me she was writing a story about some old mystery. You look like a lady who keeps her ear to the ground, if I may say so. Heard any whispers?'

She finished her toast before contemplating him with thoughtful grey eyes.

'If you'll excuse me,' she said in a clipped tone. 'This death is, as you say, a tragedy, but I detest idle gossip and scandal-mongering.'

She was gone before he could muster a suitable reply.

'Hey, where's the fire?' George Poyser demanded, as Jacob brushed past him in the entrance lobby of Clarion House.

Jacob pulled up sharply. 'Sorry, I'm due to catch the Oxford train shortly. I'll miss the conference. Can you give my apologies?'

'Don't tell me Ottilie Curle is conjuring up phantoms among the dreaming spires?'

'I'm following up a different story. A lead I owe to Nell Fagan.'

'Nell Fagan, eh? Couldn't believe it when I heard she was dead. The woman seemed indestructible.' Poyser sniffed, as if hoping to catch the smell of a story. 'You don't think there's something fishy about what happened to her?'

Jacob had no desire to set the Fleet Street rumour mill in motion. 'If I did, I'd be heading for Yorkshire, wouldn't I? This is a story she was chasing herself.'

'So what takes you to Oxford?'

Jacob tapped the side of his nose. 'Ask no questions and you'll get no lies.'

Before Poyser could interrogate him further, he raced off through the maze of corridors and obscure staircases to a remote cubbyhole at the back of the third floor. The little room was occupied by Percival Vaughan and the overflowing piles of books, magazines, and miscellaneous clutter that he insisted on describing as his research material.

Percy was the *Clarion*'s obituarist, a jolly little man with a pink face and gold pince-nez whose delight in his job was enviable if disconcerting. He prided himself on a knowledge of the deceased which extended far beyond those illustrious enough to command column space in the *Clarion* when they died. Gomersall had poached him from the *Times* and although his position was only part-time, he filled his days by freelancing for specialist periodicals, recording the lives of the famous and the forgotten with the same unflagging zeal.

'Come in, young man, make yourself at home. Immaculate timing. I've put the finishing touches to a piece on Aubrey Faulkner for *The Cricketer*. Bowled a mean googly, but malaria finished his career. Gassed himself, poor devil.'

Jacob's colleagues gave Percy a wide berth, since once he'd cornered you, escape was all but impossible. Percy wasn't really a bore, in Jacob's opinion. For all the surface bonhomie, the man was achingly lonely. Before the war, he'd been a subeditor. He'd served on the Western Front and come home without a scratch, only for his wife to succumb to the Spanish flu. His first obituary took the form of a love letter to her. Since then, he'd lived for his work. He prided himself on doing honour to the dead.

'Clodagh Hamill, Violet Beagrie, Joshua Cuthbert Flood.' He read the names off the sheet of paper in Jacob's hand. 'All the dates of death within the past eighteen months.'

'Ring any bells?'

Percy's dismay was almost comical. 'Nothing springs to mind, I'm very sorry to say.' As he studied the sheet, his brow cleared. 'Might Violet Beagrie be one of the Sussex Beagries?'

'No idea. Who are they?'

'Horatio Beagrie was a leading light in the East India Company, you know.'

'Before my time, I'm afraid.'

'Ha! Very good!' The little man beamed. 'It's not such a common name. Let me do a bit of digging.'

As Jacob turned to go, he said, 'I suppose Horatio made a pile of money?'

'Absolutely. Thanks to Horatio, the Beagries became one of the richest families in the county.'

The late Clodagh Hamill's home was a villa set in grounds laid mainly to lawn and a stiff walk from Oxford station. The windows were shuttered and the house gave every appearance of being empty, but Jacob never gave up easily. He rang the bell and within a few seconds a plump young housemaid opened the door.

'Good day to you,' Jacob said breezily. 'I wondered if I might be able to see Mrs Hamill?'

The girl's smile was pleasant. 'I'm afraid she won't be back for another fortnight.'

Jacob gaped. He'd been about to express his dismay at the sad news that the former mistress of the house was dead.

'Oh really?'

'Yes, didn't you know? The honeymoon is due to last six weeks.'

'Ah, I see.' The housemaid gazed at him expectantly as he absorbed this revelation. At least she hadn't shut the door in his face. 'Goodness, that's longer than I expected.'

There was a wistful expression in her eyes. 'Must be lovely. I don't blame them for making the most of their trip. Florence, Rome, the Amalfi coast…'

'How wonderful.' He coughed. 'I suppose that Mr Hamill…'

His voice trailed away, mainly because he couldn't think of how to end his sentence. Luckily, the housemaid was far from averse to conversation.

'How marvellous that he managed to find true love after going through such a terrible time. He put up with so much for so long.'

Jacob nodded sagely, guessing that she was a little in love with her employer. 'Can't have been easy.'

'It certainly wasn't!' She thought for a moment. 'Not that I'd ever wish to speak ill of the dead, of course.'

'Of course you wouldn't,' Jacob agreed. 'I bet it wasn't easy for you, either.'

'I don't mind admitting,' she said, 'I thought about giving in my notice. Between you and me, that is. I mean, she wasn't a well woman, but even so.'

'Even so,' Jacob confirmed. 'Actually, I never knew the details. What exactly was the matter with her?'

For the first time, a doubtful look came into her eyes. 'I don't suppose I should talk out of turn. What did you want, by the way?'

'My father's an old friend of the family. He said that, any time I was passing, I ought to look them up.' He grinned. 'Not that Papa knew about his chum's delightful servants, or he'd never have mentioned it.'

The housemaid blushed. 'Get away with you. I'm sorry you've been disappointed.'

'About not seeing the Hamills? Not at all! Please don't think I'm being forward, but I wonder, would you fancy a quick cup of tea? I'd love to catch up on all the news. Something I can pass on to Papa when I get back home tonight.'

She scarcely hesitated before saying yes.

As he waited on the windy platform for the London train, Jacob reviewed the information he'd teased out of Marjorie the maid. She was courting, but over the weekend Frank, who looked after the garden at the villa, had earned her displeasure by flirting with a kitchen maid who worked in Summertown. To be taken out for tea by another young man was the perfect way to restore self-esteem. It was also sufficient, Jacob suspected, for her to give the gardener a second chance. He wouldn't be surprised if within the next year Frank and Marjorie followed Patrick Hamill and his new wife to the altar.

Hamill was managing director of a local brewery. An Irishman, he'd come over to England after marrying a girl from the same small village in Wicklow. Clodagh Hamill was a pretty colleen, but the couple's disappointment at their failure to start a family was compounded by her persistent hypochondria. By the sound of it, she'd become old long before her time.

'He couldn't do anything right as far as madam was concerned,' Marjorie said as she tucked into a slice of cake. 'I felt so sorry for the poor man. He did his best to cheer her up, but she had a headache whenever it suited her to play the invalid.'

Whenever she retired to her bed, Clodagh Hamill devoured the outpourings of Ruby M. Ayres and Ethel M. Dell. Her husband's methods of amusing himself were rather different. While he was away on his increasingly frequent business trips, his wife believed he'd developed a fondness for an occasional flutter at the tables as well as for female company.

'If you ask me,' Marjorie said darkly, 'she drove him to it.'

Clodagh was jealous of a succession of her husband's secretaries. When he engaged a young blonde-haired woman called Alice, it was the final straw. Marjorie had overheard – 'you simply couldn't help it, they were shouting at each other' – a furious row. It culminated in Clodagh Hamill returning to her room and insisting that she was at death's door. The local doctor barely concealed his view that she was a neurotic malingerer, but her dutiful husband insisted on her having the best possible treatment.

'Sent her to an expert, he did,' Marjorie explained. 'A professor with a sanatorium somewhere in Yorkshire.'

'That must have cost a few bob,' Jacob said.

'I'm sure it did, but that's Mr Hamill for you. Generous to a fault.'

His wife's treatment had come to a sudden end with her death from heart failure. The news had startled Marjorie. Perhaps Clodagh Hamill wasn't such a hypochondriac after all.

The second Mrs Hamill was Alice, the former secretary. The servants had been invited to the wedding. That was the sort of man Patrick Hamill was, Marjorie explained. Kind and considerate. And it had been so interesting to go to a wedding in a Roman Catholic church.

What it boiled down to, Jacob reflected as the train pulled in, was this. Patrick Hamill was unhappily married and in love with a younger woman. He and his wife were Catholics, so he could not solve his problem by seeking a divorce.

Instead, he'd sent Clodagh Hamill to Blackstone Sanatorium.

'Home sweet home,' Rachel said, after giving the taxi driver a lavish tip and closing the door of Hawthorn Cottage behind her.

Martha looked around the hall. 'The Sambrooks have done it up better than I expected. The Lodge is a dingy hovel, judging by Nell Fagan's photograph.'

'They didn't seriously expect anyone to take a tenancy of a gatehouse with such a dark history, that's the difference.'

As they inspected the ground floor, Hetty ran her finger

along the top of a large mirror and found a trace of dust. She gave a grunt of disapproval.

'I thought the agents sent in a cleaner? Looks as if they have skimped.'

'They don't meet your standards at Windsor Castle, let alone in west Yorkshire,' Rachel said. 'For a rented cottage in a windswept village, this is rather cosy. And the artwork is an unexpected bonus.'

Three large framed paintings dominated the living room. They were garish abstracts, wild whirls of red, blue, green, and yellow. The contrast with the conventional décor and furnishings elsewhere in the cottage was jaw-dropping.

'Well, well,' Rachel murmured, peering at the tiny signatures. 'These are all Daphne Sambrook's handiwork. I didn't expect to find a would-be Kandinsky in Blackstone Fell.'

Martha screwed her face up, trying to make sense of the paintings. 'Are they any good?'

Hetty made a scoffing noise, but Rachel said, 'She has an artist's eye.'

'Do you think she realised Nell wasn't a photographer?' Martha asked. 'Perhaps Daphne told Judith Royle that Nell was an impostor and put her up to producing that home-made anonymous letter.'

Rachel shook her head. 'Nell hadn't met Daphne at that point.'

'But she was renting the Lodge from the Sambrooks, so they'd probably heard something about her from the agent.'

'Why would Daphne confide in Judith?'

'How else would Judith know that Nell was a journalist?'

'A good question. Someone told her – but who? And why?'

Martha gave up. 'Speaking of journalists, thank goodness you made sure there is a telephone. We can keep in touch with Jacob.'

Rachel smiled. 'He has his uses.'

Hetty snorted. 'A law unto himself, that young man. You never know what scrape he'll get himself into next.'

'Why not get some rest, Hetty?' Rachel said. 'Don't forget, in an hour's time you will be at death's door.'

Hetty looked to the heavens, as if tormented by a bothersome offspring.

'Cheer up,' Rachel said. 'I predict a miraculous recovery. Now I must get out and about. First port of call, Blackstone Tower.'

Jacob settled in his seat on the train, and unwrapped his gift from Rachel. It proved to be a slender volume by Robert Ganthony dating back more than a quarter of a century. The title was a mouthful: *Practical Ventriloquism: Being a Thoroughly Reliable Guide to the Art of Voice Throwing and Vocal Mimicry by an Entirely Novel System of Graded Exercises.*

Glancing at the list of contents, he noticed that Rachel had marked one section with an asterisk: *Dark Room Séance*. He flicked to the relevant passage. One sentence was underlined:

There are a variety of little comedies that can be acted in the dark.

You could say that again. He'd skimmed through the whole book by the time the train arrived at the terminus. As he jumped down to the platform, he told himself that after his humiliation at the pudgy hands of Ottilie Curle, Rachel expected him to fight back. Frustrated by his lack of progress, she'd decided to give him a clue that even an obtuse crime reporter couldn't fail to interpret correctly.

A medium who relied on spirit communication rather than producing ectoplasm must be adept at throwing her voice. Sir Roderick sounded nothing like Ottilie Curle, but that merely demonstrated her skill as a ventriloquist. Ganthony's advice was cogent, but Jacob hadn't drawn the obvious conclusion, that the woman who had made a fool of him was a professional rather than a talented amateur. Nobody acquired such proficiency without extensive training. The veil suggested a woman mourning for the dead, but also made it impossible to see any slight movements of her lips.

Jacob knew Rachel well enough to guess what her gift was meant to convey. He ought to concentrate on Ottilie's flair for ventriloquism rather than her work as a medium. Who had taught her, and where had she learned her craft?

Leaden clouds threatened a downpour as Rachel Savernake strode purposefully past the rectory and St Agnes Church. There was no danger of getting lost. Her destination loomed ahead of her, ominous and unmistakeable. What had possessed Robert Lejeune to build a home as dark and ugly as the Tower?

She halted beneath the archway, outside the entrance to the gatehouse. There was nobody in sight, and she gave the door an experimental push. It didn't budge. Either the police or the owners had made sure the Lodge was locked. A pity, but she'd find an excuse to look inside. She wanted to test her theory about the disappearances of Edmund Mellor and Alfred Lejeune.

Black poplars flanked the drive. On the gatehouse side, a brook wound past the trees before disappearing underground. As she approached the Tower, its dark stone and sheer height seemed increasingly forbidding. Rachel stared at the upper windows. Nobody was watching her approach.

The views from the Tower must take your breath away. You could look across to the Fell, and down towards the lower village, the moor, and the sanatorium. What might one witness from such a vantage point?

The oak front door was heavy and imposing. The ancient iron knocker took the form of a unicorn. Robert Lejeune's choice, she had no doubt. She gave a little nod of satisfaction before rapping half a dozen times. There was no answer. She walked round to the back of the Tower, peering through each of the ground-floor windows in turn. No sign of the man she sought, inside or out.

Spots of rain moistened her cheeks as she surveyed the grounds to the rear of the Tower. The estate was a wilderness of brambles, gorse thickets, elms, and sycamores. Couldn't the fellow afford a gardener? Or had his wife's death so sickened him that he no longer cared about his surroundings? The Lejeunes had lived at Blackstone Fell for more than three hundred years, but old money didn't last forever.

Science was the future, or so people said. Ancestry counted for nothing; tradition didn't pay the bills. If you believed what you read in the papers, tomorrow belonged to the Sambrooks. They had already snapped up the gatehouse. How long before they got their hands on Blackstone Tower?

Not for its history, not because they needed somewhere to live, but simply because they could?

Back at Clarion House, Jacob headed straight for Percival Vaughan's lair. The obituarist greeted him with undisguised glee.

'You're in luck. It turns out that Violet was indeed the great-niece of Sir John Beagrie. Is the name familiar to you?'

'Sorry, no.'

Percy stuffed an ancient briar pipe. '*Sic transit gloria mundi*. As it happens, I wrote his obituary. Not that there was much to say. He led a quiet life. A confirmed bachelor, if you know what I mean.'

Jacob nodded sagely.

'He was descended in a direct line from Horatio Beagrie, who made a fortune out of the East India Company's opium smuggling. They would ship it from Bengal to China. In the old days...'

'About Sir John,' Jacob said firmly.

'Ah yes. His only connection with the Orient was an obsessive love of Japanese woodblock prints. He devoted his life to building up the finest collection in private hands anywhere in Europe. Sotheby's auctioned it last spring.'

'Was it worth much?'

Percy named a figure that took Jacob's breath away.

'You live and learn. I'd no idea Japanese prints were in such demand. When did Sir John die?'

'Last winter. He was seventy-three. His great-niece predeceased him by a matter of weeks.'

Jacob remembered the summary in Martha's exercise book.

'Before she reached her twenty-first birthday. I don't suppose you have any idea who inherited Sir John's estate?'

'I took the liberty of dropping in for elevenses with my friends at Somerset House.' The records office was Percy's second home. 'Sir John's will was complicated, with many charitable bequests. He was a generous man who supported many worthwhile causes. Even so, the residue was substantial. Violet was his only close living relative. Her death meant that the Beagrie fortune went outside the family.'

'Who was the lucky heir?'

'His name is Eric Livingstone. I've come across him. Dashing fellow, rather a dandy. He edits *The New Magazine of Art* and I contribute the occasional death notice to his pages. He commissioned me to write Sir John's obituary. He mentioned their shared love of Japanese prints, but I had no idea they were on terms of such… intimacy.'

'Tell me about Livingstone.'

Percy drew on his pipe. 'The magazine is his pride and joy. The original *Magazine of Art* was splendid. Ruskin was a contributor, but revenue never matched reputation, and it ceased publication a good twenty-five years ago. Livingstone decided to revive it. Admirable ambition.'

Jacob sensed a note of reservation. 'But?'

'He's no businessman and frankly the magazine is a pale echo of the original. But Livingstone is a born gambler. He's spent heavily to keep it going. I expected he'd be forced to abandon the unequal struggle. Of course, I never dreamed he'd come into a small fortune.'

'He kept quiet about his inheritance?'

'Oddly enough, yes.'

'Why is it odd?'

'Livingstone is the last person you'd describe as a dark horse. He oozes charm. Sir John must have taken quite a fancy to him to make him his heir in the event of the girl's demise. I suppose he felt abashed by his good fortune. Profiting as a result of tragedy.'

'Violet Beagrie was an orphan?'

'Indeed. If she'd lived a little longer, she'd have inherited her great-uncle's residuary estate, and Eric Livingstone would still be short of money. Makes you think, doesn't it?'

'Yes,' Jacob said, 'it definitely makes you think.'

18

'Thomas Aquinas, on the other hand…' the rector of Blackstone Fell said.

'Please, Quintus.' Judith Royle gave a tinkly, nervous laugh. 'I'm sure Miss Savernake has better things to do than listen to you harp on about Thomism.'

As the rain slanted down, the Royles and Rachel were sheltering under the timber roof of the lychgate of St Agnes. Rachel had encountered the rector after peeking inside the church. At first he ignored the intruder, but her eager questions about the finer points of theology prompted an impassioned discourse on the Book of Isaiah. If Quintus Royle disdained the opposite sex on principle, he wasn't immune to breathless flattery on a subject dear to his heart.

As Rachel unobtrusively shepherded him out of the church, Judith had caught sight of them. She could barely hide her amazement at finding a young stranger hanging on to her husband's every word. Rachel might have been lapping up a broadcast by George Bernard Shaw or Father Knox.

The rector glared at his wife. Rachel took no notice. 'How wonderful to be blessed with such learning. To have that special insight into God's mysterious ways must have been a great comfort to you yesterday.'

He frowned. 'Yesterday?'

'Forgive me if I said something indelicate,' Rachel said meekly. 'The taxi driver mentioned that dreadful affair at the cave. I hear you discovered the body of one of your parishioners.'

'Hardly a parishioner.' The rector became abrupt. 'She hadn't been in the village for five minutes.'

Without another word, he strode through the rain towards the church. His wife said in a low voice, 'The woman in question was living in Blackstone Lodge.'

She gestured across the lane towards the gatehouse, prompting Rachel to gasp.

'The Lodge? Good heavens! Then what happened...'

Judith interrupted. 'It was a tragic accident. She was poking about inside the cave at the very moment the roof fell in.'

Rachel put her hand to her mouth. 'Crushed to oblivion? It doesn't bear thinking about!'

'I'm afraid it's not the first time someone has died there,' Judith said. 'Even in Quintus's time, a tramp was killed in the cave. The rock is unstable. The landscape can be treacherous, Miss Savernake. Please do take care.'

'Believe me,' Rachel said earnestly, 'I will.'

'What brings you here, may I ask? Very few visitors come to Blackstone Fell in autumn.'

'I am a student of folklore,' Rachel announced.

'Folklore?'

'I can see from your dubious expression, Mrs Royle, that you regard the legends of England as the preserve of crusty old bores. Believe me, few subjects are so perfectly suited to illumination as a result of feminine insight.'

Judith frowned. 'Is that so?'

'Most certainly! Long before our sex was extended the courtesy of the right to vote, a woman was elected president of the Folklore Society. Her monographs—'

'I don't see…'

'I must apologise, Mrs Royle.' Rachel smiled. 'I get carried away on my hobby horse. I'm quite the evangelical, if that isn't a blasphemous term in the presence of a rector's wife. I've become entranced by the legend of Blackstone Lodge. An astonishing story. High time it received scholarly examination. Two men disappeared from the very same spot, more than three hundred years apart, never to be seen again!'

'My husband will tell you, the story is balderdash. On each occasion, there was a perfectly innocent explanation for what happened.'

'But this latest incident, the death of the first person to have lived there!' Rachel's voice trembled with excitement. 'A calamity for the wretched woman, of course, but it raises fascinating questions…'

'She was a journalist called Fagan,' Judith snapped. 'A newspaper reporter from London.'

'Good gracious!'

'The woman came here under false pretences, masquerading as a photographer named Grace while she wormed her way into our trust. A brazen deceit.' Judith paused. 'When I confronted her, she claimed she wanted to write a story about the Lodge's curious history.'

She looked Rachel straight in the eye.

'Incredible!' Rachel returned her gaze. 'How on earth did you discover her secret?'

The rector's wife gave a little start. Her cheeks had a pink tinge, as if she felt she'd said too much. She made a fuss about consulting her watch.

'It's... a long story, Miss Savernake. Unfortunately, I'm afraid I have another appointment. Perhaps we can talk further on another occasion.'

'Wonderful!'

'I make it a rule to invite newcomers in the parish to tea.' Judith lowered her voice. 'Between you and me, Quintus isn't sociable by nature. He'd rather sit in his study with his books and his Bible. But as he often reminds me, we have our position in Blackstone Fell to think about. Would you like to come to the rectory tomorrow?'

'How very kind, I'd love to.' Rachel indicated their surroundings with an airy gesture. 'Dare I hope that you'll invite any of our neighbours in this lovely village? I'm dying to meet them.'

'I've drawn a blank as regards Clodagh Hamill,' Percy Vaughan said. 'Not much luck with Joshua Cuthbert Flood, either. He was a retired businessman from the Midlands, but more than that, I can't say.'

'Don't worry,' Jacob said, 'you've excelled yourself. As for Mrs Hamill, I found the information I wanted.'

'Is this anything to do with our editor's crusade against the spiritualists?' Percy shook his head. 'Between you and me, I'm not convinced that all séances are shams. Fact is, I'm in a similar line myself.'

'You are?'

'Absolutely. The business of getting to know the dead, making sense of what we've lost. Look at the late Sir Arthur Conan Doyle, God rest his soul. A true believer, and a man with a fine mind. That reminds me…'

Jacob said quickly, 'Do you know anything about Ottilie Curle's background?'

Percy was anguished. 'Sorry, not a sausage.'

'How about ventriloquism?'

'Ah.' Percy brightened. 'Now you're talking! Fascinating characters, ventriloquists. Did you know they go all the way back to the Oracle at Delphi and the Witch of Endor? Not to mention Elizabeth Barton. The Mad Maid of Kent, they called her.'

'You're a walking encyclopaedia,' Jacob said hastily. 'I was wondering about variety performers who were skilled ventriloquists.'

'Ah, the music hall! I used to love taking my wife out to places like the Poplar Hippodrome. Arthur Prince and "Sailor Jim" made us laugh till we wept. Marvellous the way the dummy sang while his master smoked a cigar. Not to mention Fred Russell and "Coster Joe". I remember…'

'Is it possible that Ottilie Curle was on the stage before she began to conduct séances?'

'Sorry. It's an unusual name. I doubt I'd have forgotten.'

Jacob doubted it too. 'Not to worry.'

'Wait!' Percy clapped a hand to the side of his head. 'You don't think she had anything to do with Curly Charles?'

'Who?'

Percy clicked his tongue. 'How quickly they forget! Curly Charles was all the rage at one time of day.'

'What did he do?'

'He hailed from the north country. Made his name at the Leeds City Varieties before coming to London. I'm going back long before the war, mind. You're too young to have seen him perform. He had a sweet little daughter in pigtails. She was part of the act.'

'As a human dummy?'

'Not at all! She was a talent in her own right.'

Jacob's interest quickened. 'What happened to them?'

Percy shook his head. 'It was a great shame. Both of them suffered from ill health. Curly died, but what became of his daughter, I've no idea.'

'You didn't write the father's obituary, by any chance?'

'Good Lord, no. This was the best part of thirty years ago.'

'What was the daughter's name?'

'Matilda, I suppose. At least the act was known as Curly and Tilly.'

'Tilly?'

They looked at each other as the same thought struck them.

'Words can't express my gratitude, Doctor. I don't know what we'd have done if you'd not answered my cry for help.'

When Rachel wanted to sound effusive, she didn't opt for half measures. Dr Carrodus responded with a modest shake of the head.

'I never could resist a damsel in distress, Miss Savernake. Please think nothing of it.'

They were in the hall of Hawthorn Cottage. Rachel had summoned him as a matter of urgency, explaining that her housekeeper had collapsed in a heap, and looked as white as chalk. Carrodus had picked up his black bag and raced next door, only to find disaster averted. Hetty was lying on the couch, accepting a glass of water from Martha, and saying that she really didn't know what had come over her.

'I can't claim any credit, Miss Savernake,' he said good-humouredly. 'Take my word for it. Your housekeeper is as strong as an ox. It was just a fainting fit. Simple as that, let me assure you.'

'Oh goodness! I'm afraid I've wasted your precious time. What must you think of me?'

'Heavens, it's no trouble. Better safe than sorry. Her blood pressure is a touch on the low side, but a good night's rest will do the trick. Tomorrow morning, she'll be bright-eyed and bushy-tailed.'

Rachel begged him to stay for a cup of tea, insisting it was the least she could do after he'd come rushing to her aid like a knight in shining armour. Once Carrodus was ensconced in the sitting room, she explained at considerable length her devotion to English folklore. As the rain hammered down outside, she was conscious of his scrutiny. Yes, he was a doctor, but he was also a bachelor who saw no need to disguise his interest in a good-looking newcomer to the village.

She steered the conversation towards Blackstone Lodge and the sensational death of its tenant.

'Did you come across her by any chance?' Rachel asked.

'More than once. The poor lady was accident-prone. Hurt her ankle on the Fell and then made matters worse by going headlong in the churchyard on Sunday. I treated her in my surgery and told her to get plenty of rest.'

'If only she'd heeded good advice!' Rachel gave a lavish sigh. 'What do you think happened to her?'

'Blessed if I know,' Carrodus said. 'She was a heavy drinker, I'm sorry to say. Reeked of alcohol. My best guess is that she knocked back a few glasses of gin to ease the pain, and then wandered over to the Fell in a fit of bravado. If her leg gave way suddenly and she clutched at the cave wall to save herself, perhaps she precipitated the rock fall.'

'It sounds plausible.' Rachel shook her head. 'Mrs Royle tells me she was a journalist.'

'So I hear. Extraordinary behaviour, to take a false name and pretend to be a photographer. Why not tell the truth?'

'Yes, why not?' Rachel breathed.

Carrodus fiddled with the knot in his tie, unexpectedly bashful. 'Well, I'd better say no more. Good to meet you, Miss Savernake. I'm sure we'll meet again.'

'Thank you, Doctor.' Rachel gazed at him in admiration. 'I look forward to it.'

As darkness fell, there was a knock on the door of Hawthorn Cottage. Martha answered and Daphne Sambrook introduced herself. Martha brought her into the living room to meet Rachel, and left the door ajar on her way out. In the absence of a Dictograph, you couldn't beat good old-fashioned eavesdropping.

'No tea for me, thank you, Miss Savernake. I simply wanted to see for myself that you find everything satisfactory. We don't have much experience as landlords, and my brother prefers to leave the tenancy arrangements to our agent. Given that we're near neighbours, the very least I could do was to call on you.'

Rachel made polite noises about the cottage before

pointing to the abstracts on the wall. 'Your own handiwork; how wonderful! You have a rare eye for colour.'

Daphne Sambrook flushed with pleasure. 'That's kind of you. Once upon a time I hoped to pursue a career as an artist.'

'It's not too late!'

'I was lucky enough to win a scholarship to the Slade, much to Father's displeasure. He shares Freud's attitude to women, but art is in my blood. My late mother loved sketching with pen and ink. Her example inspired me. Unfortunately, I couldn't sell my work, and I like my comforts too much to want to starve in a garret.'

'It's a man's world,' Rachel said sadly.

'It doesn't need to be, Miss Savernake. As you may have gathered, my father built the sanatorium out on the moor. He promised a generous allowance if I trained in bookkeeping while trying to establish myself as a painter. I loved London, and I go there whenever I can, but last year I moved back to Yorkshire with my tail between my legs. My father and brother are men of science, not business. They needed help with managing the sanatorium and the family trust which owns this cottage.'

'What a shame.' Rachel gazed at the paintings. 'Your work has a distinctive flavour, but do I detect a seasoning of Mondrian and Kandinsky?'

'You flatter me, Miss Savernake. I could never hope to compare with the masters. In my younger days, I went through an idealistic phase. I studied theosophy and experimented with automatic drawing. Expressing my subconscious through my work.' Daphne gave a wry smile. 'My father and Denzil aren't impressed. They ridicule my efforts, and won't have them on the walls of the Manor. So I seized the opportunity to inflict them on the tenant of Hawthorn Cottage.'

'So delightful. I hope you still find time to paint?'

Daphne shook her head. 'My tastes have changed. Right now, my artistic fumblings seem like the indiscretions of youth.'

'What a shame. I suppose the sanatorium keeps you very busy? Such marvellous work your father and brother do. Helping those who are deeply troubled.'

'I'm no psychiatrist,' Daphne said briskly. 'My job is to balance the books.'

'A place that size must cost a fortune to maintain. At least it seems large enough to accommodate a good many patients.'

Daphne hesitated for a moment before saying, 'My father is highly selective as regards the people he treats. He prefers to specialise in certain conditions.'

'Disorders of the mind are so frightening, aren't they? I imagine that sometimes—'

'I'm sure you'll appreciate that I can't discuss my father's work.' Daphne was pleasant but firm. 'We owe a duty of discretion to our patients and their families.'

'Oh, please forgive me. I don't mean to pry.' Rachel indicated their surroundings. 'This cottage is so charming. I gather your family has bought Blackstone Lodge too?'

Daphne gave a crooked smile. 'We've lived here for thirty years and even now the villagers treat us like outsiders. My father is too wrapped up in his studies to care, but Denzil has hit upon a different approach. He's started seeing himself as a sort of lord of the manor.'

'And now you're landlords of the manor,' Rachel said playfully.

Daphne didn't return her smile. 'Father set up the family trust after we lost our mother in a car crash. He and I were both hurt in the same accident. This scar on my brow is a permanent reminder. The trust was meant to make sure my brother and I wouldn't go hungry if we were orphaned. Lately Denzil has come up with the idea of owning land through the trust. He has very progressive ideas about politics and society.'

'What sort of ideas?'

Daphne pretended to stifle a yawn. 'To be honest, I can't make much sense of them. Sometimes I wonder if he's simply trying to reinvent the feudal system for the modern age.'

'I suppose he dreams of acquiring Blackstone Tower?'

'That monstrosity? Yes, I'm sorry to say you're right.' A mischievous gleam came into her eyes. 'It seems regrettably Freudian to me. I tease him about Tower envy.'

Rachel giggled. 'And is Mr Lejeune willing to sell?'

'If a price can be agreed. I don't blame him. If it was left to me, I'd have the place demolished. Mind you, it's in such poor condition that nature should do the job anyway over the next few years.' Daphne looked thoughtfully at Rachel. 'But I'm talking far too much. That's quite enough about us. What brings you to Hawthorn Cottage?'

Rachel expounded on her love of folklore with practised ease, but her attempts to probe into the Lodge's strange history earned no reward.

'Father and Denzil say I have a secret romantic streak which clouds my judgment,' Daphne said sardonically, 'but not even I put any credence in the so-called curse. There must be a rational explanation for why those men disappeared. I expect they left the Lodge when no one was looking, only to meet a miserable end. On the moorland marshes or at Blackstone Leap.'

'If he sells the Tower, will Harold Lejeune leave Blackstone Fell?'

'I expect so. Most people would be glad to see the back of the place.' Daphne checked herself. 'Sorry, forgetting my manners. I mustn't prejudice you against your new home on your first day here.'

'The death of the poor lady from the Lodge must have come as a dreadful shock to you.'

'We never actually met. Frankly, I was amazed that anyone wanted to live there. I presumed she must be rather odd. Naturally, I'm sorry about what happened, but it was nothing to do with her tenancy of the Lodge.'

'Buried under a small avalanche after putting her head inside a cave.' Rachel was mournful. 'How horrible.'

'I gather she was rather clumsy, poor woman. Dr Carrodus tells me she fell over twice in a matter of days and hurt her leg.' Daphne got up. 'Now I'd better leave you to settle in.'

'Thank you so much for coming.'

'Good to meet you, and welcome to Blackstone Fell.' Daphne gave a rueful smile. 'Please take better care of yourself than our last tenant.'

19

Trueman slipped out of The New Jerusalem at twilight. The rain eased to a drizzle as he strode up the path that led to the clapper bridge. He branched off along the track that ran through the trees in the direction of Fell Lane. While reconnoitring the area, he'd discovered that the rear gardens of the surgery, Major Huckerby's house, and the rectory were bounded by stone walls, each with a gate affording access to the path. In contrast, the rear garden of Rachel's cottage was bounded by a thick hawthorn hedge.

He'd identified a gap in the hedge. Wide enough for a child to squeeze through with ease, it presented a greater challenge for a man of his bulk. At the cost of a few scratches, he made it. The garden comprised a bumpy lawn and a scattering of azaleas. The curtains of the cottage were drawn, except for those at the rear bedroom window. A light was shining, the pre-arranged signal that Rachel had a visitor.

He settled down to wait.

Ten minutes later, the light went out and the kitchen curtains were pulled together. He hurried forward, and knocked three times on the window. Martha opened the back door, and soon his clothes were drying as he gulped down a mug of tea and listened to Rachel's description of Hetty's supposed fainting fit.

'She played her part to perfection. Sarah Bernhardt couldn't have done better.'

For once in her life, Hetty blushed. 'I didn't do anything.'

'We found out what we wanted,' Rachel insisted.

'Namely?' Trueman asked.

'Remember the death certificates Martha picked out. They had something in common. Not just that Hamill, Beagrie, and Flood all died in the sanatorium last year or this. Each death was certified by Dr Carrodus.'

'You think he…?'

'He's popular with his patients, half the battle for a village doctor who wants to get on. But he's not much good at his job. His diagnostic skills are indifferent and his remedy for everything is bed rest.'

'He's not stupid.'

'I agree, but my impression is that he's more interested in enjoying himself than in medicine. He has a taste for the good life.'

'Driving a Lagonda, for instance?'

'Exactly. Our little experiment with Hetty shows how easy it is to pull the wool over his eyes. His examination of her was cursory in the extreme.'

'I expect he saw through me,' the housekeeper said. 'He was just humouring us because he took a shine to you.'

'Possibly.' Rachel didn't waste time on false modesty. 'Alternatively, he may be suggestible. Whatever is going on at the sanatorium, it's convenient for the Sambrooks to have a tame doctor at their beck and call. Someone whose word is unlikely to be questioned.'

'Do you think Daphne is in cahoots with her father and brother?'

'There are tensions between them. She doesn't seem content with her lot.'

'That's women for you.' Trueman said, poker-faced. 'What did you make of her?'

'If I were a psychiatrist, I'd say she craves excitement.'

'No shortage of that at Blackstone Fell. Is she a potential ally?'

'Too early to tell. Now, what have you been up to?'

When he'd finished his account, she asked, 'Do you think the Sambrooks are suspicious of you?'

'Yes,' he said grimly. 'I can't put my finger on it, but I felt as if I'd run into a blank wall. It's as if they were waiting for me to come out with something to reassure them. Evidence that my story was genuine.'

'Have they checked up on the real Hubert Mann?'

'I rang my cousin today. Nobody has been poking around in Workington, asking tricky questions. If the Sambrooks don't believe my story, it's for some other reason.'

'Don't sound so glum. We must be patient and see if they rise to the bait. Any luck with the records at The New Jerusalem?'

'Here you are.'

From his coat pocket, he produced the envelope. She slit it open and glanced at the names and addresses on the two sheets from the guest book.

'Excellent. Jacob is due to call later. We can compare notes.'

'This woman who is staying at the inn,' he said. 'My fellow guest. In the small hours, there was a light in her room.'

'An insomniac?' Rachel said. 'What's her name?'

'Dilys thought she was called Miss Nee, but her full name is Margaret Needham.'

'*Margaret* Needham? Where is she from?'

'She gave an address in Camden Town. If you ask me, she's up to something.'

'What makes you say that?'

'For someone on a walking tour, she's taking a very close interest in what goes on in the village.'

'A woman has died in unusual circumstances. A little curiosity is pardonable, don't you think?'

'This morning I saw her from my window. She came out of the inn and turned up the lane towards Blackstone Fell. I sprinted up the path and managed to get to the lychgate just in time to catch a glimpse of her disappearing up the drive to Blackstone Tower.'

'Interesting.'

'As I caught my breath, Huckerby came along. We got talking, mainly about his late wife. It's as if he's haunted by her.'

'Mrs Huckerby's death was definitely suicide?'

'Or murder?' Martha suggested.

Trueman shook his head. 'I can't believe he killed her. Where's the motive? In her last days, Gloria Huckerby became a hypochondriac. Maybe she took an overdose by mistake. More likely she thought that by taking an overdose, she was sparing herself a horrible, lingering death.'

'I wonder if he's interested in spiritualism,' Rachel said.

He allowed himself a smile. 'Yes, the man's lonely. He was genuinely devoted to his wife, that's clear. I'm sure he's tempted by the prospect of making contact with her beyond the grave.'

'Excellent. What about Margaret Needham?'

'While Huckerby and I were talking, she came back down the drive. Gave me a funny look, as if she realised I was keeping an eye on her.'

'She's a shrewd woman.'

'You seem very sure,' Martha said.

'We already know something about her.'

Martha raised her eyebrows. 'We do?'

'Yes,' Rachel said. 'Remind me of a popular nickname for women called Margaret.'

Light dawned in her companions' eyes.

'Peggy!' Martha exclaimed.

'Yes. Nell Fagan's old governess followed her to Blackstone Fell.'

'A little angel, she was,' Cora Wynn said sentimentally. 'Such a bonny girl.'

Her eyes misted over as she took a restorative sip of stout. She and Jacob were refreshing themselves in a pub near Sadler's Wells. He'd been given her name by the *Clarion*'s drama critic, who was too young to remember Curly and Tilly and whose tastes ran more to Somerset Maugham than forgotten acts of the music hall.

Cora was a tiny, immaculate woman in her seventies. She and her late husband had enjoyed a long career on the stage, never scaling the heights, but seldom out of work. Although she'd retired as an actress, the theatre ran in her blood. She freely admitted that she loved nothing better than reminiscing about the good old days.

'She performed with her father?'

'That's right, dearie. He was a jolly good ventriloquist, was Curly.'

'Can you remember his real name?'

She considered. 'I think it may have been Curle. Yes, Charlie Curle, that was it.'

Jacob barely restrained himself from hugging her. 'His daughter's nickname was Tilly. What was that short for?'

'She was always just Tilly. Matilda, I suppose.'

'Or Ottilie?'

Cora Wynn shrugged her thin shoulders. 'Sorry, dearie, I haven't the foggiest. I'm not much use to you, I'm afraid.'

'Believe me, this is a tremendous help. Curly taught his girl to be a ventriloquist?'

'Very good she was, too. It was a stone cold certainty that she'd be a star one day.'

'What happened?'

'She took ill, dearie. And then her father had a stroke, and that was that.'

'When was this?'

'Now you're asking. It's more than twenty-five years since I last saw them. I can only go on backstage gossip.'

'Fair enough, it's a hundred times more reliable than a leader article in the *Witness*.'

Cora hooted with laughter. 'What I heard was that Curly worried himself sick about the girl. His wife had died years before, you see. It was just the two of them. And then he passed on as well.'

'How old was she at that point?'

'Fourteen or fifteen, at a guess.'

'And eventually she got better?'

'I suppose so, dearie, but the illness finished her on the stage.'

'Because she'd lost her father?'

'That was bad enough, but her looks suffered terribly, or so I heard.'

'In what way?'

'Trouble with her glands, dearie. Thyroid, if I remember rightly. Her eyes always tended to bulge, poor thing. And she put on an awful lot of weight. Someone said she ended up like a little rubber ball. What with Curly's death as well, two terrible blows, she didn't really have a chance.'

'No,' Jacob said softly.

Cora drained her glass and allowed herself a ruminative belch. 'Poor soul. I wonder what became of her?'

'You guessed, didn't you?' Jacob cradled the telephone receiver in his hand.

Rachel sounded amused. 'I prefer to call it deduction rather than guesswork.'

'So that's why you gave me the book.'

'Everything we know about Ottilie Curle suggests she is genuinely skilled. Even confidence tricksters don't reach the top of their profession by chance or good luck. So what was her special gift? A talent for throwing her voice is easier to acquire than the ability to communicate beyond the grave.'

'The faulty thyroid accounts for her weight and prominent eyes.'

'You told me her hair was thin, another sign. The choker she wears probably disguises a damaged neck.'

'I wonder if her father's death inspired her interest in spiritualism.'

'I expect so. Well done, Jacob. Your next task is to find her and make a bargain. Any joy with Martha's list of names?'

He gave a concise report. 'So the question is whether you can identify any connection between Blackstone Sanatorium and these two men. Patrick Hamill and the magazine editor.'

'Let me check the information from Martha and Trueman.' She was silent for a few moments. 'Congratulations, Jacob. The New Jerusalem attracts guests from far and wide. Patrick Hamill of Woodstock Road, Oxford, spent a night there a week before the date of his wife's death.'

'Bullseye!' Jacob exclaimed.

'You've hit the target twice. Ten days before young Violet Beagrie died, a visitor from Wimbledon booked in for a couple of nights. He signed in as Mr E. Livingstone.'

Jacob was jubilant. 'An aspiring murderer, I presume?'

'He has a case to answer, yes.'

'The pieces of the puzzle all fit together!'

'A rather unoriginal observation, Jacob,' she said languidly. 'I'd say we have a cocktail recipe with vital ingredients missing.'

He felt deflated. 'I don't follow.'

'Hamill and Livingstone wanted rid of inconvenient people. But how exactly did they engineer the deaths of their unloved ones?'

'By despatching them to Blackstone Sanatorium.'

'As simple as that? The Sambrooks don't advertise discreet assassination in the personal column of the *Times*.'

'Surely the answer is up there in the Pennines?'

'Tell me this. Trueman is eager to commission a murder, so why have the professor and his son failed to rise to the bait?'

'They are simply being coy. Playing hard to get. Probably to justify charging a massive fee.'

'There's more to it than that. Connections still waiting to be found.'

'What can I do?'

'Keep searching.'

'For what?'

'For a signpost pointing prospective murderers to Blackstone Fell.'

20

Rachel rose early the next morning. Soon she was loping down the muddy path towards Blackstone Foot, glad of the warmth of her cashmere coat. The rain had eased off but the air was cold and damp, and leaden clouds threatened another downpour.

Opposite The New Jerusalem, a narrow alleyway ran between terraced houses and the scrubland separating the lower village from the moor. Pulling her hat down over her eyes, she stationed herself there, and waited.

Her patience was rewarded when the door of the inn opened and a woman stepped out. Tall, angular, grey-haired, she matched Trueman's description. Rachel skipped across the slippery cobbles.

'Miss Needham!'

A fierce stare. 'What is it?'

'My name is Rachel Savernake. I'd like to talk to you about Nell Fagan.'

The woman looked pale and tense, Rachel thought, but she was extraordinarily self-possessed. If she was shocked at being accosted, the only clue was a barely visible tightening of her thin lips.

'I don't understand.'

When in doubt, play for time. 'I think you do, Miss Needham.'

'Nell Fagan, you say?'

'You knew her better than anyone. She told our mutual friend Jacob Flint that when she was a child, you became her governess. After her parents died, you continued to look out for her, and you've remained close ever since.'

There was a pause. 'You're very well informed, Miss Savernake.'

'There is a great deal that I don't know. You were in her confidence, and I hope to persuade you to help me.'

The woman took a step back. Rachel could almost hear her mind working. The click, click, click of calculation. Is it worth prevaricating? And if not, how far to trust a stranger with the truth?

Rachel prompted her. 'Her death must be a grievous blow.'

The other woman breathed in, as if reaching a decision. 'Nell gloried in living dangerously, Miss Savernake. I was devoted to her, but at the same time, I despaired of her, and told her so a thousand times. If her liver had failed, I'd have been heartbroken but unsurprised. For to die like that, though, it doesn't bear thinking about.'

The words rushed out like water after the breach of a dam. Rachel suspected that this woman seldom revealed her thoughts, far less her innermost feelings. Peggy Needham was a Victorian who didn't believe in betraying weakness.

'Why did you come to Yorkshire?'

'To beg Nell to return to London.'

'Why?'

'She was risking her life. Do you know that someone had already tried to kill her on Blackstone Fell?'

'With the boulder? She said it may have fallen by accident.'

'Nell had a gift for persuading herself that what she wanted to believe was the truth,' Peggy Needham said grimly. 'It was obvious that she was in danger.'

'She was a crime correspondent. Taking risks came with the job.'

'She wasn't simply reporting a crime or writing about a trial,' Peggy said. 'She was flying solo, trying to solve a murder. You know about Ursula Baker?'

'Who supposedly died of heart failure?'

'Correct. Nell believed the woman was killed at Blackstone Sanatorium. She wanted to bring the culprit to justice. A murderer would have no peace unless he silenced her.'

'You're sure it was a man?'

'Who else could it be? I wanted to make Nell see sense. I pleaded with her on Friday, to no avail. I hoped that after calling on you, she'd change her mind. No luck. I arrived here too late.' She bowed her head. 'I'll blame myself to the end of my days.'

'What makes you think she was murdered?'

'I can't swallow the idea of another supposed accident. Nell's death is too convenient.'

'I agree.' Rachel looked her in the eye. 'What do you intend to do?'

Peggy Needham returned her gaze. 'I failed to save Nell's life.'

'It wasn't your fault. She was a grown woman. Responsible for her own decisions.'

'Whatever the truth, I owe it to her to find out who killed her.'

'If she was murdered,' Rachel said, 'you're risking your own life if you play a lone hand.'

A long pause.

'I'm not a young woman, Miss Savernake. Unlike you, I don't have fifty years ahead of me. I can afford to take a chance in order to see that Nell isn't written off as a careless drunkard. She deserves justice. I owe it to her to make sure she gets it.'

Her tone was defiant, the set of her jaw uncompromising.

'I understand,' Rachel said.

Peggy Needham stared at her.

'What is more,' Rachel said, 'I can help.'

Jacob Flint had kept out of his editor's way since the debacle of the séance, but when Walter Gomersall marched into his office, there was no escape. Jacob hastily removed his feet from the desk. He'd just come off the telephone after speaking to John Lester, a former colleague who had recently retired to the Welsh coast.

'Any progress with the Curle woman?' Gomersall demanded.

'I'm working on it.' The editor's grimace indicated that this was inadequate reassurance. 'Hopeful of a breakthrough any time now.'

'What sort of breakthrough?'

'Too early to say,' Jacob said quickly. 'Strange business. Nell Fagan's death is a further complication.'

Gomersall glowered. 'Don't blather, lad. What has Nell

Fagan got to do with it? Other than that her aunt booked the séance where you made such a fool of yourself?'

'Exactly,' Jacob said enigmatically. 'Wheels within wheels. If you'll just give me a few days.'

'You haven't got a few days,' Gomersall snapped. '*The Spiritual Sentinel* goes to press tonight!'

'One thing at a time,' Jacob said. 'I'm confident that story will be spiked.'

The editor stared at him. 'We're their sworn enemies. Why would they give up a chance to stick a knife in our gizzard? Don't tell me you're getting messages of encouragement from the spirit world?'

'I'd love to say more,' Jacob lied, 'but of course I must protect my sources.'

Gomersall groaned loudly. 'Have it your way. But if the *Sentinel* publishes that story...'

He stomped out, banging the office door shut behind him.

Half an hour later, Peggy Needham and Rachel were in the sitting room at Hawthorn Cottage. Hetty lit a log fire and Martha served coffee before both made themselves scarce. Their next task was to make the acquaintance of the servants in the neighbouring houses and pick up nuggets of gossip from below stairs.

On the walk up from the lower village, Peggy remained deep in thought. Now the two of them sat in armchairs, eyeing each other like rival grand masters before a chess tournament.

Peggy made the first move. 'You wanted to know why I came here, Miss Savernake. May I ask you the same question?'

'Before she first came to Blackstone Fell,' Rachel said,

'Nell Fagan approached me. She expressed an interest in collaborating. You were her confidante. I presume she told you?'

'Nell didn't tell me everything,' Peggy Needham said quickly. 'But yes, she mentioned that you're something of an amateur detective.'

Rachel shook her head. 'A term I detest. But I admit to a weakness for mysterious murders.'

'I gather you've had one or two dazzling successes. She described you as a conjuror who performs tricks for her own amusement, not for an audience. But she said that... you and she hadn't hit it off.'

'Because she told me a pack of lies.'

A sigh. 'Nell was like her late father, a natural storyteller. I love playing with words as much as she did. But she was always inclined to embellish the truth.'

'She went too far by implying that she knew something to my discredit. Pure fabrication.'

'She lost her job and couldn't find another,' Peggy snapped. 'Did you need to complain to her editor?'

Rachel shrugged. 'Her technique for tempting people into indiscretions was to provoke them. With me, she chose the wrong person.'

Peggy sipped her coffee before replying.

'I won't beat about the bush, Miss Savernake. Your treatment of Nell made my blood boil. For a woman of her age to be blackballed by Fleet Street editors was a catastrophe. You wrecked her career. Yet she never bore a grudge. I admired that about her, even though I'm very different. She said it was her own fault for being pig-headed. Blackstone Fell began to obsess her. That story was her passport to regaining credibility as a crime reporter, but even she realised she'd bitten off more than she could chew. So she persuaded this young man Flint to arrange a second meeting with you.'

'Against my better judgment, I agreed. On condition that she was entirely frank with me.'

'I'm sure she was,' Peggy said vehemently.

'Unfortunately not. She told me about the disappearances from Blackstone Lodge, and described Vernon Murray's suspicions concerning the death of his mother. But I was convinced that she was withholding important information from me.' Rachel leaned back in her chair. 'So I sent her off with a flea in her ear.'

Peggy glared at her. 'What information did she keep back?'

'If I knew the precise answer to that,' Rachel said carefully, 'her deception wouldn't have been so frustrating.'

The other woman sniffed. 'If you doubted her, why come to Blackstone Fell?'

'As you say, she told a good story. Evidently she was in jeopardy. That evening, I tried to question Vernon Murray, but he gave me the slip. Minutes later, he fell from the platform at British Museum Station.'

Peggy's eyes widened. 'Murray is dead?'

'He went under a train.'

'Did he jump deliberately? Was he pushed?'

'Nobody witnessed anything untoward.'

'If this man Baker…'

'Baker has an ironclad alibi. The police are satisfied it was an accident.'

'Do you agree?'

'No.'

'You think he was murdered?'

'When I saw him, he was frightened. Someone had already tried to run him over. His mistake was to give them another chance. They took full advantage.'

For a moment, Peggy closed her eyes. 'Just as Nell gave them a second chance.'

'Perhaps.'

Peggy shot a sharp glance at her. 'And now you want to find out what happened to Murray and Nell?'

'Yes.'

'Nell said your father used to be a judge at the Old Bailey. Hence your interest in crime?'

'I promise you,' Rachel said harshly, 'Judge Savernake was very different from me. All I inherited from him was enough money to please myself how I spend my time. Parties and the social whirl repel me, and I don't long for the shackles of marriage. I love solving riddles. As for justice, it fascinates me.'

'So you did inherit a lawyer's mind?'

'Justice and the law are different beasts. Laws are two a penny, justice is rare. Much rarer than people like to believe.'

'You're a cynic.'

'I confess to an unhealthy interest in murderers, especially those who masquerade as respectable. Provided they are intelligent enough to cover their tracks. Taking another person's life breaks the ultimate taboo. By killing someone, they risk their own necks. I always ask myself: *why*?'

Peggy drank some coffee. 'Please go on.'

'Nell Fagan's story fascinated me, despite her reluctance to reveal the whole truth.' Rachel considered the older woman. 'How much did she tell you?'

Peggy put her cup down. 'Nell didn't share everything with me, Miss Savernake.'

'You were the person she trusted most.' Rachel paused. 'Tell me about her.'

'When we met, I was nineteen and she was five. Randolph Fagan, her father, was a prolific novelist and playwright.'

'I have read one or two of his thrillers. Larger-than-life stories.'

'He was a larger-than-life man who dreamed of becoming a second Dickens, but settled for making a great deal of money. He'd married young, and his wife had numerous miscarriages before Nell came along. It wasn't an easy birth. Aileen Fagan was frail and more preoccupied with her health than her child's upbringing. Eventually I was engaged to look after the little girl. From the day I arrived in the household, Randolph Fagan insisted on treating me as one of the family, rather than a hired hand.'

She fell silent, lost in memories.

'And that suited you?' Rachel said.

'Perfectly. I had no living relations except for my aunt and her daughter Eunice. Nell was a delightful child, always up to mischief. We had a blissful time together, but Randolph died far too young. He left a good deal of money and he was remarkably generous. So much so that even I was well provided for.' She hesitated. 'I regarded it as a moral duty to do my utmost for Nell, but it was no hardship. Her mother went into a slow decline, but at least Nell and I had each other. Over time, despite the age difference between us, we became more like sisters than governess and charge. Like her father, she was unreliable and drank too much, but she wasn't short of charm or courage. I wasn't blind to her failings, but

I was always on her side. We understood each other. I should have persuaded her to stay in London. If only…'

'If only?' Rachel interrupted. 'The most futile phrase in the language. You didn't fail her, any more than I did. What we owe her is to find out what happened.'

Peggy Needham gave a wintry smile. 'Are you suggesting we should become partners in crime?'

Rachel lifted her coffee cup, as if in a toast. 'Why not?'

'I'm a spinster, advanced in years. You could say I've led a sheltered life. Hardly the stuff that detectives are made of.'

'I disagree,' Rachel said. 'I suspect we have more in common than you realise.'

'You flatter me, Miss Savernake.'

'Not at all. I'm interested that you're so definite in your belief that Nell was murdered.'

'It's my nature to be definite,' Peggy said dryly. 'I have no time for woolly thinking, for caveats and disclaimers. Nell used to tease me for it.'

'You're a woman after my own heart,' Rachel said. 'All the same, I'd like to know what makes you so certain.'

'While I don't have absolute proof that she was murdered,' Peggy said after a pause, 'there is strong circumstantial evidence.'

'I'm all ears.'

Peggy cleared her throat. 'On Sunday afternoon, Nell was followed as she walked in the direction of Blackstone Fell.'

'Who followed her?'

'Unfortunately, I don't know. All I can tell you is that it was a man, not a woman.'

'Go on.'

'When I came up here to Blackstone Fell, I was shocked

to find that I'd arrived too late. Nell was already dead. I was distressed and confused. I stammered a few questions, but my thoughts were scrambled. Everyone was more than happy to treat her death as an accident. The sheer complacency horrified me. That night, I couldn't sleep. I made up my mind that I'd try to find out what had really happened to her.'

'How did you intend to go about that?'

'I made the assumption that the murderer is associated with the sanatorium. The least likely culprit, so to speak, is Harold Lejeune.'

'What makes you say that?'

'Lejeune has nothing to do with the sanatorium, and precious little to do with anyone else in the village. Nell never even spoke to him. Ever since his wife died, he's pined away in that grotesque Tower. An architectural obscenity, but its height makes it unique. Nobody has a view of the surroundings remotely comparable. As far as I can gather, he has nothing to do with his time but stare out from his windows. It occurred to me that he may have seen something.'

Rachel waited.

'Yesterday morning, I visited the Tower. He was reluctant to answer the door, let alone talk to me.'

'You persisted?'

Peggy allowed herself a faint smile. 'I'm a determined woman, Miss Savernake. I made up a piece of nonsense, banking on the fact that he wouldn't know that Nell was already dead when I got here. I said I was a birdwatcher. With my field glasses, I'd seen someone following Nell Fagan through the trees, towards the cave. I'd also trained my glasses on the Tower, to watch an oystercatcher circling the roof. I said I'd caught a glimpse of Lejeune at one of the upper windows. I pretended to be confused about whether to tell anyone what I'd observed. So I wanted to know if he could corroborate my story.'

'What did he say?'

'At first he blustered, but I wasn't giving up. If only to keep me quiet, he admitted seeing Nell as she left the gatehouse and limped down Fell Lane. At the same time, he noticed a man on his own in the churchyard.'

Rachel leaned forward. 'Go on.'

'This man didn't go out through the lychgate. Instead, he left by the back gate, behind the Lejeune family mausoleum. That gate gives on to a track which winds round the back of the houses and joins up with the path you and I came up a few minutes ago. The track goes through a clump of trees, and Lejeune lost sight of the man.'

'And?'

'That was all. The man was walking briskly. He would have had time to reach the cave before Nell got there. Although he took the longer route, she was moving slowly because of her damaged ankle.'

'Did Lejeune describe this man?'

Peggy clenched a small, age-spotted fist. 'His description was infuriatingly vague. No help at all. He could only confirm that he definitely saw a man, rather than a woman.'

'How tall was this man? Thin, fat, young, old?'

'Fairly tall. More than that, Lejeune couldn't or wouldn't say. The fellow he saw wore a trilby and an overcoat. His age was unclear. As far as I can make out, it might have been Denzil Sambrook, Dr Carrodus, or Major Huckerby. I can't absolutely rule out Professor Sambrook or even the rector.'

'The rector found the body.'

'That doesn't prove innocence. You're more familiar with these things than me, Miss Savernake, but I gather it isn't unknown for murderers to return to the scene of their crime.'

Rachel pursed her lips. 'What else did Harold Lejeune tell you?'

'Nothing. What's more, he urged me not to mention to anyone else what I'd seen.'

'Why?'

'I felt he told me as much as he did because he wanted to earn my trust. If I implied someone was responsible for Nell Fagan's death, he said, it would be a very serious matter. He mentioned slander, but I said I couldn't leave matters there. In the end, he promised to make some enquiries himself and let me know what he found out. We could then decide together what to do.'

'How very helpful.' Rachel rubbed her nose. 'So we have another prospective partner in crime?'

'I doubt it.'

'Don't you believe him?'

'The story I made up caught him off guard. Once he'd blurted out what he'd seen, his priority was to persuade me to keep my mouth shut.'

'You said he couldn't *or wouldn't* tell you more. Do you think he was hiding something?'

A thin, humourless smile. 'Thanks to Nell, I'm accustomed to dealing with people who prefer invention to the truth. Perhaps I read too much into things.'

'Perhaps you're more perceptive than most. What is your opinion?'

'I feel sure he recognised the man in the churchyard. The man who may be a murderer.'

'He's protecting someone?'

'Certainly not a friend. I say that because as far as I can tell, none of the neighbours are his friends. But I'm sure he was feigning ignorance.'

'Or simply being tactful?'

'He doesn't have a reputation for tact.'

'Perhaps he wants to satisfy himself that the man was up to no good before revealing his name to a stranger.'

Peggy finished her coffee. 'Your guess is as good as mine.'

'So what is your guess?'

'Harold Lejeune is desperately short of money. You only have to look at the state of Blackstone Tower to realise he must be on his beam ends. Why else would he sell a gatehouse that has been in his family for three hundred years?'

'What is your conclusion?'

Peggy put down her cup. 'I suspect he intends to try his hand at blackmail.'

Jacob dialled the number Lester had given him. Within a minute, he was talking to that rare creature, a jovial editor. Alec Hughes presided over the *Barmouth Advertiser* and was a golfing pal of Lester's. He had a booming voice and Jacob pictured a rotund, red-faced individual, fond of long, liquid lunches at the nineteenth hole.

'Joshua Flood, you say?' Hughes demanded.

Jacob heard gulls squealing in the background. He loved the seaside and had fancied travelling to mid-Wales to sample the salty air on Barmouth promenade. But time was against him.

'I gather he made a pile of money manufacturing hollowware in Birmingham before moving to Wales.'

'Yes, I knew of him by reputation. This is a popular spot with Brummies. He'd come here on holidays as a boy. After the war, he sold his business, and built a big house overlooking the estuary. Gorgeous location.'

'Sounds idyllic. He died about a year ago, I understand. I wanted to trace his family.' Jacob paused before lowering his voice. 'Sorry, can't say more. All rather confidential at this stage.'

'Don't worry, I won't pry into a fellow hack's enquiries. Glad to help. Any pal of Lester's is a pal of mine. As for Joshua Flood, he was a crusty old bachelor. Never married, no children.'

'Really?' Jacob was surprised. He'd imagined Flood as an aged miser, forever threatening to change his will to disinherit the latest relative who had displeased him. 'What happened to his estate?'

'Apparently a lifeboat rescued him from the sea when he was young. He never forgot it. So he gave the bulk of his money to the local branch of the Lifeboat Institution.'

'The Lifeboat Institution?' Jacob couldn't keep the amazement out of his voice. When a rich man dies in suspicious circumstances, money is the obvious motive.

'Extremely good cause,' Hughes said reproachfully. 'Well, they got the lion's share of the cash, anyhow. Three quarters of the residue. Pal of mine is on the committee, that's how I happen to know. Extremely generous. Though I gather the old man's mind was failing long before the end came. Nervous trouble.'

'Who looked after him?'

'He wasn't short of servants. And his late sister's son organised a nurse for him.'

'So he had a nephew?'

'Yes, name of Walker. The fellow did his best for his uncle, tried to get him proper treatment. When the nurse couldn't cope, he arranged for Flood to go to a sanatorium up in the wilds of Yorkshire where he could be treated by an expert.'

'How thoughtful.'

'Exactly. At least they patched things up before the end came. I gather that Alan Walker had been a disappointment to the old chap. He seemed quite content to work as a chef in a London club, instead of joining the family business. Simply had no desire to go into hollowware.'

'Dear me,' Jacob said. 'A chef, you say? I don't suppose you know where he worked?'

''Fraid I can't remember, young man.' Hughes chortled. 'Memory's not what it was. They'll be putting me out to grass, like Lester, before I'm much older.'

'I'm sure you're good for plenty more front-page scoops,' Jacob said. 'Do you happen to know if Joshua Flood looked after his nephew in the will?'

'Oh yes, that's where the other quarter of the estate went. My pal in the Lifeboats joked that it was a pity the nephew redeemed himself, but he can hardly complain, can he?'

'How much was Walker's share worth, then?'

Hughes pondered. 'Maybe two hundred thousand.'

'Pounds?' Jacob gripped the receiver more tightly. 'Good grief.'

'It's not so surprising,' Hughes said. 'There's a lot of money to be made in hollowware. As for Walker, he can afford to buy his own restaurant now. Lucky fellow, eh?'

'Very lucky,' Jacob said.

'Has Harold Lejeune arranged to meet you again to discuss the outcome of his enquiries?' Rachel asked.

Peggy Needham shook her head. 'Perhaps he hopes I'll lose interest and leave the field clear for him. Of course, he hasn't a clue about my connection with Nell.'

'You're sure of that?'

Peggy frowned. 'Absolutely. Lejeune holds the key to her murder. So I must go back to the Tower.'

'I called there yesterday afternoon. There was no answer.'

'Do you think he was inside? Lying low? If he thought I'd turned up again, he might be avoiding me.'

'I saw nobody at the window. He may have been hiding. Or perhaps he was out.'

Peggy's expression was grim. 'Calling on the neighbour he suspected of murdering Nell?'

'If you're right, he's playing with fire,' Rachel said. 'A murderer facing blackmail knows he can't be hanged twice.'

21

'Judith Royle is a nervous wreck,' Martha said.

She'd arrived back at the cottage moments after Peggy left. She and Rachel were drinking tea at the kitchen table.

'You talked to her maid?' Rachel asked.

'Her name is Myrtle, and she is nineteen. She's about to hand in her notice. Nobody can bear to stick it there for long. The Reverend Royle is beastly to his servants, but they get off lightly compared to his wife. He treats her like a slave, at least when he's not closeted in his study. Myrtle hears him ranting and raving behind closed doors when he's supposed to be preparing his sermon.'

'He has an Old Testament view of the world,' Rachel said languidly. 'Perhaps he's adapted Stanislavski's techniques to rural preaching and tries to get into the right frame of mind.'

'Sounds to me as if he's got a screw loose. He's driven his wife to the verge of a breakdown.'

'A prime candidate for the sanatorium?'

'Funny you should say that. According to Myrtle, the professor's son has called round more than once. Last week, she overheard Dr Sambrook talking to the rector.'

'Touting for business?'

'Far from it. He insisted there was nothing wrong with Judith's state of mind. She was simply overworked and under the weather.'

'Had the rector asked him to examine her?'

'Myrtle reckons so. The rector is horrid about Judith, says she lacks moral fibre. He was furious when Sambrook wouldn't back him up. Judith tried to calm him down, but that only fanned the flames. He called her a harlot to her face.'

'Charming.'

'If you ask me, Quintus Royle is the one who should be in the sanatorium.'

'Judith likes to play the delicate little deer. Lovely, and persecuted. I suspect her of having read *Bambi*.'

'You think it's a pose?'

'Not entirely. The rector is a brute. He only has himself to blame, but that doesn't mean she hasn't strayed.'

Martha nodded. 'Myrtle says she's not one to talk out of turn.'

'Naturally. But...?'

'But the rector and his wife sleep in separate rooms, and she reckons young Sambrook has taken a shine to the lady.'

'Does she reciprocate his interest?'

'Myrtle thinks so, but doesn't have anything concrete to go on. Not that the gossip-mongers lose sleep about evidence before they spill their poison. People in Foot love spreading mischief about the posh folk in Fell. Rumour has it that when Dr Carrodus arrived in the village, Judith set her cap at him. If so, she didn't get far. He's friendly enough, but Myrtle says there's nothing more to it than that.'

'Unless they are adept at covering their tracks.'

'He must be scared of wagging tongues. A doctor has to mind his reputation. It isn't wise to misbehave with a patient.'

'Especially one so highly strung. How does she get on with her other male neighbours?'

'The professor, the major, Harold Lejeune? Myrtle isn't interested in them, and she can't imagine Judith Royle being any different. As she says, they are positively ancient.'

'Ah, the prejudices of youth. Don't forget, Judith married a much older man.'

'And look how that turned out,' Martha said tartly.

'True. You've done very well.' A key rattled in a lock. 'Is that Hetty at the door? Let's see what she's discovered.'

Over lunch, Hetty regaled them with an account of her conversation with Dora, the elderly woman who had served as the major's housekeeper since before the war. Dora combined an unswerving devotion to her employer with a jaundiced opinion of most of his neighbours, not to mention the people who worked for them.

'So you see,' Hetty concluded mournfully, 'I didn't find out anything important.'

'You're far too hard on yourself.' Rachel leaned back in her chair. 'Now we know the late Chiara Lejeune spoke poor English and didn't mix with the locals any more than her husband did. When Chiara fell ill and died, there was a short-lived wave of sympathy for Lejeune, but he became more reclusive than ever. The Tower is looked after for him by two elderly sisters from the village.'

'Who are as much use as a headache,' Hetty interrupted.

'These slatterns don't mix with anyone other than their widowed brother, who helps Lejeune with odd jobs. Dora has never set foot inside Blackstone Lodge and doesn't know anyone who has, at least until the Sambrook family bought it. She believes the place is cursed and blames the hoodoo on unspecified shocking behaviour by the Lejeunes of long ago.'

'Ridiculous superstition,' Hetty sniffed. 'Not that I said so to her face.'

'Ever the diplomat,' Rachel said. 'Let's turn to Dr Carrodus. He's hinted to his own servants that he's got itchy feet and is tempted to return to the bright lights of London. They suspect he has a young lady waiting for him in the capital. His housemaid recently chanced upon a box of luxurious satin undergarments and some wrapping paper in a cupboard in his bedroom.'

'Perhaps he intended them for Mrs Royle,' Martha suggested.

'That would take some explaining to Quintus, but possibly she never gives her husband the chance to find out what she wears next to her skin. There's a widespread belief that she tried to seduce Carrodus, but he refused to succumb to her overtures. The villagers have a flexible moral stance. They'd tolerate the doctor conducting an irregular liaison with the rector's wife, if it meant he stayed in Blackstone Fell to dispense pills and sympathy with his usual bonhomie.'

'I took to him,' Hetty said unexpectedly. 'There was nothing wrong with me, but the way he talked when he examined me was a real comfort.'

'His powers of diagnosis are as reliable as Ottilie Curle's contacts with the spirit world. Patients are like the bereaved. They believe what they choose to believe. As regards Dora's beloved Major Huckerby, he's lived here since marrying a local woman over twenty years ago. People are sympathetic towards him because of Gloria Huckerby's tragic end, but it's an open secret that lately he's spent too much of his time drowning his sorrows.'

'Dora told you there was bad blood between Huckerby and the rector,' Martha said. 'What caused the rift?'

'Old Royle was furious that Judith made a big song and dance about consoling the major after his bereavement. Constantly baking him cakes and suchlike. Not that the rector has anything to be jealous about. Dora says the major has too much sense to be interested in a flibbertigibbet like Judith Royle.'

'He's a lot older than her,' Martha said.

'He's much younger than the Reverend Quintus Royle,' Rachel said. 'Alcohol is taking its toll, but he's still a fine figure of a man. For all his unhappiness, he puts on a brave face.'

'Dora is adamant,' Hetty said. 'There's nothing between the two of them.'

'Judith is bored with the drudgery of being a rector's wife. Daphne Sambrook may have a romantic streak, but in Judith's case there's no doubt of it. I'm sure she'd enjoy conducting an elaborate deception. If she and Huckerby were engaged in an illicit liaison, they'd go to great lengths to make sure none of the servants knew about it.'

'People always underestimate how much servants know,' Hetty said darkly. 'Dora's worried sick about the major's drinking. She's afraid he's destined for an early grave. She asked the doctor to have a quiet word, but it did no good. Last month the major tripped as he was staggering home up the hill from The New Jerusalem and split his head open. Only a few evenings ago, she found him slumped in his chair. He stank of whisky and was talking to himself about his wife. Saying how empty life was without her. Dora was so embarrassed, she crept out of the room.'

'Why did Mrs Huckerby take an overdose?' Martha asked.

'She imagined she was dying of cancer. Dr Carrodus did his utmost to convince her the symptoms weren't serious. Said it was simply a stomach ulcer, but she wouldn't listen.'

'So Gloria Huckerby was the one patient who lacked complete faith in the doctor?' Rachel said. 'A cruel irony.'

'Harold Lejeune's wife died of stomach cancer a few weeks earlier. They weren't friends, but the news knocked Mrs Huckerby sideways. The trouble is, the major blames himself for her death. There's no reason why he should feel guilty, but that's grief for you. You get strange fancies.'

'It's high time,' Rachel said, 'for him to try making contact with the Other Side.'

'Thank you for seeing me, Miss Curle,' Jacob said.

He kept any hint of triumph out of his voice, although after his humiliation at the séance, he itched to offer Ottilie Curle mocking congratulations on her swift return to full health. Gaining admission to the Pythoness's lair had proved simpler than he'd expected. He mustn't slip up now.

'Did I have a choice?'

Her voice was low, her demeanour subdued. Jacob detected a north country edge to her accent that had been absent the last time they'd met. She was wearing a voluminous blue gown and her feet were bare. This time she hadn't put the choker around her neck, and the dull red scars of surgery were plain to see.

A French housemaid had admitted Jacob within a minute

of his arrival. He'd said he wanted to discuss his proposed article for the *Clarion* about the stage career of Curly and Tilly. As simple as that.

'Not really,' he admitted.

His hostess hadn't invited him to take a seat. They were in the vast living room of her split-level penthouse atop an art deco block of flats in Primrose Hill. The only exotic touch was a vast divan, the colour of a ripe plum. At the far end of the room, a spiral staircase of wrought iron twisted up to the floor above. The servant Abdul stood on the lowest step, staring at Jacob. He was wearing white linen trousers and nothing else. His bare chest and arms rippled with muscular menace.

'If you know about me, and also about Curly and Tilly,' she said, 'even a mathematical dunce could add two and two together.'

'You admit that you are Tilly Curle?'

'I admit nothing,' she said with a flash of contempt.

'But...'

'Why have you come? Hoping to extract an extra pound of flesh to avenge the ghost of Hamish Parlane?' She raised the left sleeve of her gown to reveal a flabby arm. 'Here you are. Take a slice.'

'I want to talk to you. I want to be fair.'

'Fair?' she scoffed, pulling the sleeve back over her arm. 'I know what fairness means in Fleet Street. You'll give me a chance to tell my story, put forward my point of view? On an exclusive basis, naturally? Before Walter Gomersall crucifies me in his editorial columns, seizing the high moral ground in the way that only bloodsucking newspapermen can?'

'I understand your reservations about journalists,' Jacob said, feeling rather pleased with his command of understatement. 'Presumably you make an exception for *The Spiritual Sentinel*? Please hear me out. My editor didn't instruct me to come here. He doesn't know anything about this meeting. Or about Curly and Tilly.'

The bulbous eyes stared at him. 'Is that true?'

'If you don't believe a word I say,' Jacob retorted, 'why ask?'

'How can I possibly trust you after you spun such a web of lies? Pretending to be a young Scot who had lost his lover?' She glared. 'Why should I listen to you?'

'Because you've nothing to lose,' he retorted. 'You've checked my background. Use your instinct. Wouldn't you rather give me a chance to talk to you than throw me out and wait for the volcano to erupt?'

'Aren't you taking a risk?' She gestured towards the dark-skinned man on the staircase. 'Be warned. Abdul is very protective of me.'

'I'm sure.' Jacob took a step forward. 'Cora Wynn told me about you and your father. It's a sad story; I sympathise.'

Ottilie Curle had long practice in disguising her feelings. 'Cora, yes,' she said in a neutral tone. 'A nice lady, if overly fond of her glass of stout.'

He smiled. 'Cora hasn't changed.'

For a few moments, the medium closed her eyes. There was a curious dignity about her, Jacob thought. Even without the melodramatic trappings of a séance, even at a moment when the lie she'd been living was finally exposed to the light, she showed no sign of crumbling or pleading for mercy or forgiveness. This was a moment she'd expected for years. Perhaps in some peculiar way she was relieved that the truth was finally out.

She gestured to the divan. 'You may as well take the weight off your feet.'

'Cora admired you and your father,' he said, settling himself down. His hostess did not join him. Abdul remained on the step, glowering at him. 'She said you'd go far. As you have, in a different direction.'

'Not so very different,' she murmured.

'I suppose not. Skill at ventriloquism is a precious gift for an aspiring medium and you are highly skilled. Your lips hardly move, and the veil covers them in any case. You're also adept at holding an audience in the palm of your hand. You learned young, from an expert teacher. To lose him and suffer serious illness yourself must have been a devastating blow.'

She inclined her head. 'I won't deny it.'

'Did you start off in this line because of your father? Did you try to make contact with him on the Other Side?'

'You're a sceptic, Mr Flint, so I won't bore you with the turmoil I went through. At one point I expected to die. My father made a lot of money, but by the time I made some sort of recovery, it was all gone. So were my looks and my health. It would have been easy for me to surrender to the cruelties of Fate. To this day, my energy levels fluctuate wildly. Conducting a séance is utterly exhausting. I might have sought comfort in the bottle. Instead I explored the spirit world.'

'Did you ever believe in it?'

'You won't understand, Mr Flint.'

'You'd better explain in words of one syllable.'

There was a long pause. When at last she began to speak, her voice trembled.

'Your editor decries me as a charlatan who profits from the heartache of others. So be it. Nothing I can say will prise open minds that are firmly closed. I maintain that I have brought joy to a great many people whose lives were scarred by loss and loneliness.'

'But you relied on invention.'

'Isn't the same true of Austen and Dickens?' she demanded. 'Fiction supplies a gift of happiness when cruel reality drives us to despair. Even self-destruction.'

'Your clients are credulous. Naive.'

'Imaginatively receptive.'

Jacob shrugged. 'Go on.'

'I have always been certain that I remain in close proximity to my father. I'll hold firm to that belief until the day I join him on the Other Side. Or whatever you care to call it. Over the years, I've had my share of curious experiences that defy rational explanation. So, Mr Flint, I am content to adopt Hamlet's view. There are more things in heaven and earth than are dreamt of in your philosophy.'

Jacob kept quiet for a few moments.

'How did you find out who I was? Through Nell Fagan?'

'Please understand, Mr Flint, that the more famous I became, the greater my fear of exposure. Careful research is more important to a medium than a journalist. Once I discovered Miss Bell's connection with a crime reporter, I was on my guard. Nell Fagan was unable to witness the séance, but when I learned about the young man who was desperate to attend, I smelled a rat. It wasn't difficult for Michael and me to discover the truth.'

He frowned. 'Michael?'

Ottilie Curle's smile was bleak. 'Call yourself an investigative reporter? You don't have a clue, do you?'

'My psychic powers are at a low ebb.'

'Very well, Mr Flint. Against my better judgment, I'll take you into my confidence.'

She nodded towards Abdul. 'Let me introduce you to Michael Keegan, my beloved husband. His father was a seaman from Africa. One night in port he met a Liverpool lass, then he sailed away and was never heard from again.'

22

The grandfather clock in the rectory drawing room chimed three as Rachel and Judith Royle were joined by Major Huckerby and Dr Carrodus. The doctor's practice evidently didn't keep him fully occupied. There was no sign of Quintus Royle. Judith murmured something about him working in his study and said he might join them later. Rachel guessed from Dora's gossip that his antipathy towards the two other men would keep him at his desk until they had gone.

Judith's face was blotchy, her eyes reddened. She looked as though she'd been sobbing her heart out. The two men exchanged quick glances. As Myrtle the housemaid served tea, the major took command.

'Delighted to make your acquaintance, Miss Savernake.' He considered her quizzically. 'May I ask what induces a young lady from London to rent a cottage in such an obscure part of the world?'

He gestured to the windows, which looked out over the sloping grounds of the rectory. The rector's bull terrier was prowling around the orchard. The mean dwellings of Blackstone Foot were huddled in the valley below and the moors stretched away as far as the eye could see. The dark, weighty clouds seemed to have reached bursting point.

'Miss Savernake is a devotee of folklore,' Carrodus said lightly. 'Once she heard about the curse of Blackstone Lodge, wild horses couldn't have stopped her from racing up here. Her housekeeper was so overcome with excitement that she fainted. Her poor mistress was afraid she'd dropped dead on the spot.'

Rachel smiled. 'You're making fun of me, Doctor.'

Carrodus grinned. 'I don't have much time for old wives' tales, but you might persuade me to reconsider my scepticism. Tragedy befell the very first person to occupy the Lodge. It's extraordinary; maybe there's something in the old riddle after all. Major, you were on the scene when Lejeune's brother went missing, weren't you? Did he really vanish into thin air? Come on, spill the beans!'

'Nothing to tell.' Huckerby seemed put out by the doctor's levity. 'The man entered the Lodge, but what happened to him afterwards, I simply can't say.'

'What exactly did you see?'

Judith Royle lifted a teacup. Her hand was trembling.

'I was out walking as he came down the drive and unlocked the door to the gatehouse. I was taken aback, since I'd never seen anyone enter the Lodge. I tipped my hat to him, but as usual he took no notice. Miserable as sin, that fellow. I'm sorry to say that bad manners run in the blood of the Lejeunes.'

As Rachel watched, the cup slipped from Judith's grasp and fell against the side of an occasional table on its way to the ground. The bone china shattered and hot tea splashed over Judith's skirt and onto the carpet.

She squealed in horror and dissolved into tears. Carrodus leaped to his feet and rang the bell. Myrtle came running back in, only to yelp with dismay at the sight of her weeping mistress and the mess she'd made.

'Better get that cleaned up,' the major said.

Rachel put her arm round Judith Royle's thin shoulders, and the rector's wife gave a low cry.

The maid returned with a cloth. Close behind her was the rector, his gaunt features twisted with anger as he took in the scene.

'For goodness sake, woman,' he thundered. 'What have you done now?'

Judith stepped away from Rachel. For a terrible moment it looked as though she might fall to her knees and beg forgiveness.

'Can't you even manage to hold a tea cup?' the rector demanded. 'What's wrong with you?'

He turned to the visitors. Carrodus studied the pattern in the carpet as intently as if reading about a new Lagonda in *The Autocar*. The major was summoning his last reserves of military discipline to stare into space. Rachel returned the rector's ferocious gaze until he blinked and looked away.

'I must apologise to you all,' Quintus Royle said. 'I see that it is no longer possible even to invite parishioners to tea without turning the occasion into an Aldwych farce.'

Huckerby coughed. 'I think we'd better go.'

The doctor sprang to his feet. 'Least said, soonest mended, eh? Thank you for the invitation, Mrs Royle. Let me know if I can be of any service to you.'

This remark drew a small wail of misery. Carrodus winced, but moved towards the door and the major followed. Glad of an excuse to escape, Myrtle scurried out to retrieve hats, coats, and umbrellas.

Rachel murmured a farewell before joining her neighbours on the front path outside the rectory. It had started to drizzle. From the back of the house came the roar of the bull terrier's bad-tempered demands to be let back into the house.

'Shocking behaviour,' Huckerby said to the doctor. 'His manners are getting worse by the day.'

Carrodus shook his head. 'Bad business, but what can one do? I'd better be off. Good to see you again, Miss Savernake. Hope that next time we meet in… pleasanter circumstances.'

As he hurried through the gate, the major turned to Rachel. 'You must have gained an unfortunate impression of our village, Miss Savernake. One minute, a visitor dies in a cave. Next, there's a brouhaha in the rectory.'

'I believe everything happens for a reason, Major,' she said in low, earnest tones. 'Whatever tragedies befall us, there is some great design. I… no, I must apologise, you don't want to listen to my chatter.'

'Please continue. I'm interested.'

She gave him a sad, sweet smile. 'My enthusiasm for folklore has led me down countless byways. Lately, I've become convinced that our mundane lives are enhanced by greater understanding of psychical phenomena.'

Huckerby frowned. 'Spiritualism, do you mean?'

She put a hand to her mouth. 'Oh dear! You disapprove. I should have known better. A soldier is concerned with the here and now, not the hereafter.'

'You do me an injustice, Miss Savernake. Believe me, I'm as broad-minded as the next man.'

'Really?'

His expression darkened. 'I lost my wife, you see. She was under the weather and persuaded herself that the outlook was grim. Officially her death was an accident, but the local gossips will tell you she knew exactly what she was doing when she swallowed those pills. Hand on heart, I can't disagree.'

'How awful for you!'

'I long to speak to her, just for one last time. To try to understand why my love wasn't enough for her. Why she thought life was too hard to bear.'

Impulsively, Rachel clutched his hand. 'You poor man!'

'Perhaps you can understand why I've come to believe that the logic of the spiritualists is difficult to resist.' The major gently detached his hand from hers. 'Of course it goes against the grain to believe in ectoplasm and table-turning, but even scientists like Denzil Sambrook have to admit that if we discount the spirit world, so many things become difficult or impossible to explain.'

Within moments, the drizzle had become a downpour. Rachel opened her umbrella. 'I ought to hurry back to the cottage before I'm washed away, but we must talk again. There is someone I'd like you to meet.'

Jacob gaped at the man at the foot of the spiral staircase. 'You aren't a servant?'

'Isn't every husband some kind of servant?' the man asked. His accent was catarrhal Scouse, his tone sardonic.

'You can speak!'

'Nineteen to the dozen, given the chance.' There still wasn't a flicker of expression. 'I met Tilly at the old Empire, when she was still trying to get back on the stage. I never met a woman with such courage and determination. I was a magician's assistant. Tilly said I'd make a better ventriloquist's dummy.'

'Two outsiders,' Ottilie said. 'As far as others were concerned, neither of us looked quite normal. We were in love, but we didn't fit in with the world at large. It was as if somehow we weren't quite respectable. Work was hard to come by. I had time on my hands and I became obsessed by the idea of communicating with the dead.'

Jacob nodded. 'So you hit on the idea of turning a pastime into a lucrative career?'

'You make it sound cold-blooded,' Ottilie said. 'For us, it was a question of survival. Thankfully, the gullibility of the British public knows no bounds, as you gentlemen of the press are well aware. People are credulous because they are ignorant and fearful of the strange and unfamiliar. The irony is that they are entranced by the outlandish, even when it scares them stiff.'

Her husband made a derisive noise.

'As for Michael,' she continued, allowing herself a faint smile, 'they also serve who only stand and wait. In the presence of a Moor who never utters a word, people presume he is either deaf or can't understand a word of English. So they loosen their tongues the moment I step out of the room. The information he gathers is priceless.'

Jacob indicated their surroundings. 'You've done well for yourselves.'

'We earned it,' she said. 'And now, Mr Flint, do you intend to wreck everything and send us back to a rented room in Bootle?'

He shook his head. 'I have a proposition to put to you.'

★★★

'That was quick,' Martha said as Rachel shrugged off her sodden clothes. 'Did the mad vicar throw you out?'

'We jumped before we were pushed,' Rachel said.

Thunder growled outside as she recounted the events at the rectory. Rain hammered against the windowpanes. The storm was like a wild animal, trying to force its way in to the cottage and devour them.

'Quintus Royle really is insane,' Martha said. 'He must be.'

'He's been slipping downhill for a long time. Holding himself together through sheer force of personality. His status in the community offers protection. Who would dare to challenge the rector? Now he is losing control. The decline is gathering pace. As if someone has pushed him towards the precipice.'

'Judith has provoked him?'

Rachel's expression tightened. 'Whatever she has done, it can't excuse him from beating his wife.'

Martha stared. 'Did she accuse him of...?'

'No, it was nothing she said. When I put my arm round her shoulder, she gave a cry of pain. I touched her on a very sore spot. My guess is that her upper arm is badly bruised.'

'A man of God resorting to violence?' Martha shook her head. 'Nell Fagan said he was a sarcastic bully. But inflicting physical harm? Hurting his own wife, in his own home?'

'Stranger things have happened,' Rachel said tersely. 'He's not completely taken leave of his senses. He is careful to leave no visible marks.'

Martha touched her damaged cheek, an instinctive reaction. She knew what some men were capable of.

'Suppose you are right,' she said. 'What can anyone do about it?'

'The rector has a taste for the Book of Isaiah,' Rachel said. 'He'd do well to remember chapter 63, verse 4.'

Martha looked blank.

'The day of vengeance is in mine heart.'

Lightning flashed over Hawthorn Cottage as a loud knock came at the door. Peggy Needham was on the threshold, soaked to the skin. Martha showed her in, and she stood dripping in the hall. The gale had smashed her umbrella into pieces, but she refused Rachel's offer of a replacement.

'Thank you, but it won't last five seconds in this storm. I can't accept your hospitality either. The river is threatening to burst its banks, and I must get back to The New Jerusalem in case the lane floods. But I wanted to see you urgently. I'm desperately worried about Harold Lejeune.'

'What's wrong?' Rachel asked.

'I tracked down his servants, the sisters. They live in a hovel in Blackstone Foot. An unpleasant pair. They were reluctant to speak to me, but I made it clear I wasn't taking no for an answer.'

'Quite right.'

'They haven't seen Lejeune in the past couple of days. When his wife was alive, they spent a lot of time away from Blackstone Fell, but in recent times he's become a hermit. The women have no idea where he may be.'

'His bed was slept in?'

'The bedroom door is locked. The servants haven't been inside for two or three days.'

'Curious.'

'But not unusual. He often sends them away before they have finished cleaning the place, which suits them down to the ground. I went to the Tower again just now, but there's no sign of life.'

'Just as there wasn't when I called.'

There was a deafening crash outside the front door. The women looked at each other, like soldiers in a trench, hearing a grenade explode.

'A slate from the roof,' Rachel said calmly. 'Thank you for letting me know, but there's nothing more we can do today.'

Peggy's expression was grim. 'Except hope that Harold Lejeune hasn't found his way into Blackstone Lodge. The last thing we need is another inexplicable disappearance.'

23

Rachel woke at dawn. Furtive rays of light sneaked through chinks in the curtains, as if ashamed of the frenzied violence of the night before. For hour after hour last night, the rain had roared and the wind had howled, but she'd grown up on a small island and she'd heard worse. Nothing compared to the demented rage of a tempest whipping the Irish Sea. By the small hours, the storm was exhausted.

'We got off lightly,' Martha said after they had inspected the cottage. 'If the roof had been torn away, we might have drowned in our beds. A couple of buckets will take care of the leak in the box room ceiling.'

Rachel went outside. Jagged fragments of slate were scattered over the ground. In the lane, the potholes had become puddles, while an uprooted beech tree blocked Dr Carrodus's driveway. In the distance, Blackstone Tower remained unmoved and as forbidding as ever.

Where was the Tower's owner? He held the key to the mystery of Nell Fagan's death, Rachel was sure. The first task was to find him.

Breakfast was interrupted by the arrival of Daphne Sambrook. She'd set off early for work, but on seeing the slates strewn over the ground, she wanted to check the state of the cottage.

'The Manor took a pounding last night,' she explained as Rachel filled an extra cup from the coffee jug. 'A drainpipe snapped and crashed to the ground. Lucky nobody was underneath it at the time. A dovecote blew over and the pergola is broken.'

'It's good of you to take the trouble to come round,' Rachel said.

'I'd hate anything serious to go wrong here.' Daphne sounded rueful. 'To lose one tenant is bad enough.'

'Yes,' Rachel said. 'To lose two might look like carelessness.'

Daphne gave her a quizzical look as she gulped down her drink. 'I must get over to the sanatorium. I'll ask the agent to make sure the roof is repaired soon.'

'Thank you. Speaking of losing people, I haven't managed to speak to Harold Lejeune so far. I don't suppose you've seen him lately?'

'I don't keep tabs on the man, I'm afraid. He is such a recluse that he makes even my family seem gregarious. The last time I saw him was in church on Sunday, but we didn't speak. Truth to tell, I can't recall that he and I have ever had a proper conversation.'

'I'd like to ask him about the history of Blackstone Lodge,' Rachel said.

'Good luck.' Daphne looked at her curiously. 'Do remember that in view of what happened to his brother, it's a rather delicate subject.'

'I'll be the soul of tact.' Rachel added wistfully, 'I'd love to see inside the Lodge.'

Daphne shrugged. 'You're welcome to take a look as far as

I'm concerned. I gather the agent has already sent the dead woman's belongings back to London.'

'It's kind of you to indulge me.'

'Not at all. Please don't build up your hopes. You won't find anything of interest. My brother looked around the place, of course, before an offer was made to Harold Lejeune. It's a poky little hole. I was astonished when the agent found a tenant.'

'Do you keep the key at the Manor?'

'Yes, the new keys were made yesterday. We keep a couple and the agent has one.'

'New keys?'

Daphne frowned. 'Someone broke into the Lodge the other day. We had to get the locks changed again.'

'Again?'

'Yes, the old lock had rusted up from disuse, so the agent had a new one fitted after we completed the purchase. After the rector discovered the poor woman's body, the local constable found the door to the Lodge had been forced open. The place was in a mess.'

'How extraordinary! When did this happen?'

'Presumably between the time she left the Lodge and when her body was found. Nobody saw anything suspicious, but that's hardly surprising. It would have been easy enough to force the lock under cover of darkness.'

'Why would anyone want to break in?'

'No idea. A burglar would find richer pickings elsewhere in the village. The Manor, for instance. Thankfully for us, this village isn't a den of thieves. There's occasional pilfering by servants, of course.'

'Of course. Was anything stolen?'

'Not as far as we can tell. The late Miss Fagan wasn't a tidy person, but there was no obvious sign that any of her possessions had been taken. Perhaps it was just the work of a young ruffian who wanted to brag to his friends or someone who was unpleasantly inquisitive.'

'Like me?' Rachel became bashful. 'You must think I'm such a dreadful nosey parker.'

'At least you have the good manners to wait for an invitation, as well as a genuine reason to investigate. I don't give much for your chances of solving the mystery of the disappearances, but if you make some extraordinary discovery, we'll have the benefit.' Daphne's smile was wan. 'Who knows? The Lodge may become a Mecca for sightseers.'

Trueman had taken a chance the previous night and telephoned Rachel from The New Jerusalem. The inn was deserted, and it would be madness to climb up to Hawthorn Cottage and back through the thunder and lightning. Rachel described her conversations with Peggy Needham, and explained that Harold Lejeune was missing. He knew better than to ask what was going through her mind. She'd tell him in her own good time.

As he put down the receiver, Dilys popped her head round the door of the cubbyhole where the public telephone was kept. She wanted to see he was all right. Peggy had arrived back at the inn looking like a drowned rat, she said, and gone straight to bed.

In the morning, his fellow guest didn't come down. As Dilys served liver and bacon, she explained that she'd persuaded the older woman to have breakfast in bed.

'Not that she's got any appetite, mind, poor thing. She's getting on, and she should never have been out in the storm. I dread to think of anything happening to her while she's staying here. One visitor to the village has died this week. Any more tragedies and we'll be getting a bad name.'

'We wouldn't want that,' Trueman agreed heartily. Privately he thought the reputation of Blackstone Fell was already beyond redemption.

Before long he was striding across the moors. The landscape was washed and clean after the storm. Sunlight glimmered, pale and uncertain, through gaps in the fleecy clouds, but even now a stiff breeze nipped his cheeks. The ground underfoot was sodden. As he squelched along the rough path between tufts of coarse grass and dense patches of heather, he was glad of his stout boots as well as the scarf Hetty had knitted for him last Christmas.

The solitude appealed to him. There wasn't a living soul in sight. In the distance he saw the sanatorium, silent and unwelcoming. How many people did Professor Sambrook and his son care for? When he'd called there, he hadn't seen a single patient. Denzil Sambrook hadn't offered to show him round. Perhaps it was taken for granted that he didn't care about the standard of facilities and treatment, as long as his inconvenient father-in-law was removed. Why not take his money, then? He couldn't pinpoint a moment, a stray word or gesture, when he might have given himself away.

The air smelled of wet earth. A curlew cried in the distance and he saw a flock of linnets flying over the marsh. The path traced a winding route between reedy tussocks. The way was marked by short wooden posts. This wasn't a good place to put a foot wrong. Beyond the reeds lay a black stretch of low, boggy ground. This was a place where mist lingered. A man who lost his bearings also risked losing his life.

He stopped to pick up a stone and weighed it in his huge palm. Like a cricketer, he bowled it into the quagmire. The stone kissed the shivering surface, and his sharp ears caught a faint sucking sound as it vanished from sight.

Trueman wasn't given to strange fancies. Yet as he stood on the lonely path and stared at the dark marsh, he couldn't restrain a shudder. Into his mind came a picture of Harold Lejeune, screaming in terror as he was swallowed alive by the swamp.

Rachel devoted an hour to exploring Blackstone Lodge. Once she'd finished, she took care to arrange everything so as to remove any evidence of her intrusion. Daphne Sambrook had done her a good turn by allowing her to borrow the key to the gatehouse, and satisfy herself that her theory about Edmund Mellor and Alfred Lejeune was correct.

Harold Lejeune's disappearance was a very different matter. She was no closer to finding him. As for the break-in which had baffled Daphne, Rachel had a shrewd idea of who was responsible, and why, but for the moment there was no proof.

She locked the Lodge and walked down the drive to the Tower. As she lifted the unicorn door knocker, she recalled that the mythical creature stood for purity, innocence, and freedom. Virtues in short supply at Blackstone Fell.

Once again there was no answer. This time she didn't keep trying. Wherever the man was, she doubted it was in his own home. For the next forty minutes, she poked around the grounds on the off-chance that the wilderness concealed a place of shelter where he might, for some extraordinary reason, be hiding. An old ice house, perhaps, or some nook in a neglected grotto where he might have taken refuge from the storm.

There was nothing.

She set off back towards the Fell. The churchyard was deserted, the rectory quiet. The rector wasn't out shooting at blameless birds. Even his dog had stopped barking. Rachel recalled touching Judith Royle's sore shoulder, and the woman's stifled gasp of pain. Why marry a beast like Quintus Royle? Desperation, she presumed, plus the mirage of security. Coupled with an orphan's longing for paternal kindness.

Outside the surgery she saw Huckerby and Carrodus. Despite the autumn chill, both men were in their shirtsleeves and panting hard. They'd shifted the uprooted beech tree onto the verge.

'Need to make sure the doctor can get through in his Lagonda if he's called out,' the major explained.

Carrodus's expression became grave. 'After yesterday afternoon's fracas, I'm afraid the next emergency may come close to home. I don't mind admitting I'm worried about Mrs Royle.'

'Rotten show, that tea party,' the major said gruffly. 'Embarrassing for all concerned.'

'But you weren't entirely surprised?' Rachel asked.

'The rector's never been a charmer,' Carrodus said, 'but I'd say his behaviour has got much worse lately. It would take the Sambrooks to diagnose his state of mind. At a guess, there's a touch of schizophrenia allied to a persecution complex that's gathering momentum.'

'What can be done?'

'There's the rub. A professional man needs to walk on eggshells. Can't interfere between man and wife.' An unexpected gleam lit his eyes. 'Every time one tries to help, with the very best of intentions, one risks making matters worse. I'd hate to… precipitate a crisis.'

Rachel changed the subject abruptly. 'I don't suppose either of you has seen Harold Lejeune?'

Carrodus said, 'Not had your fill of our local curmudgeons, Miss Savernake?'

She smiled. 'I'm curious. Nobody seems to have seen him for a couple of days.'

The major indicated the puddles in the lane. 'I wouldn't be surprised if he moves away before winter sets in. There's nothing to keep him here. If you ask me, he'll go back to Italy. Bolzano, where he met his wife. I don't think they ever really wanted to leave.'

'Would he vanish on a whim?'

A shrug of the shoulders. 'Strange cove, Lejeune. Wouldn't put anything past him.'

As Rachel reached the clapper bridge, Quintus Royle emerged from the path to the lower village, the bull terrier at his heels. She gave a curt nod, but he ignored her and strode away in the direction of the rectory. Lost in thought, or simply rude? She didn't care. The man was an odious bully, but at this precise moment he was not her main concern.

The sun had come out, but it wasn't warm and the river was still swollen from the previous day's deluge. She crossed the bridge and took the fork in the path that led to the cave at the base of the Fell. Her keen eyes spotted a windhover in search of prey. As she watched, the kestrel swooped into the trees, moving in for the kill. Instinctively, she checked inside her coat pocket, and felt the reassurance of cold steel. She had brought her revolver.

Her brisk pace slowed as she passed through the clump of sycamores and the mouth of the cave came into view. Listening intently, she heard only birdsong and the rustling of small creatures in the undergrowth. As she reached the cave, she scanned her surroundings, but saw nothing untoward. She took out the gun, shrugged off the coat, and squeezed her lithe frame through the gap.

There was nothing to find. Certainly no trace of the owner of the Tower. A few days ago, a woman had died on this very spot, but the only clue to her fate was a heart-shaped smear of blood on the ground. Rachel exhaled. Nell would still be alive if she'd revealed everything she knew. But that was history, it couldn't be changed. All that mattered now was to uncover the secrets of Blackstone Fell.

She wriggled out of the cave, keeping tight hold of the gun in case someone outside hoped to give her an unpleasant surprise. As soon as she was able to stand upright, she scanned her surroundings with an intensity the kestrel might have admired. Still there wasn't a soul to be seen.

Following the path to Blackstone Leap, she edged down the slope towards the ravine. The trees were packed close together, and she heard the rush of water. As she moved out of the brightness and into the shade, she saw the river tumbling at pace through the narrow cleft in the land.

At first glance, the Leap was nothing special. The peat-stained river was more like a babbling brook. There were no wild rapids, no towering waterfalls, no apparent cause for fear. The stream was barely three feet wide. The temptation to jump across was hard to resist.

But seeing wasn't believing. The Leap was deadly. Fifty yards upstream, the river was much wider; its narrowness here was an illusion. Thanks to a quirk of geology, the terrain had turned the river on its side. Instead of carving a straightforward course through the silt, it flowed down into a tight vertical shaft in the rock, twisting and turning, gouging passages and tunnels far below the surface. The banks were bare overhangs and the riverbed simply didn't exist. In its place was a mass of fast and powerful currents, hissing inside a chasm.

The stones on the edge were too slippery to give a proper foothold. If you fell into the crevasse, you'd be dragged down. Nobody knew the depth of the water swirling in the void. If you didn't get trapped in an underwater hollow, there was every chance you'd be smashed into pieces as the turbulence dashed your limbs against the hidden rocks.

Over the centuries, many people had died here. There were no marked graves, because the bodies were rarely found. One thing was certain in Rachel's mind. Anyone who believed that Edmund Mellor and Alfred Lejeune were among the casualties of Blackstone Leap was mistaken. But was it possible that the river had claimed a recent victim? If so, did she have any hope of finding the body?

Frustration boiled up inside her. She'd unravelled some of the tangled threads of the mystery of Blackstone Fell, but there was still much to do. She felt so close to the final truth, yet so far.

She trudged along by the riverside. Presently she came to the far side of the ravine. The channel broadened out and half a dozen large stepping stones offered a route to the other bank. The water seemed to be taunting her, daring her to jump. Slick wet moss made the stones treacherous. If she skidded or lost her balance, the rain-fattened river would sweep her downstream to be devoured by the hungry gorge.

'I'll make a deal with the devil,' she murmured to herself. 'It's not the first time, after all. If I cross the Leap and survive, I solve the case. If I slip, old Nick can do his worst.'

Hetty accused her of being rash and headstrong. Why prize logic and then behave irrationally? To be fearless was often foolhardy. All this was true. But for Rachel, life was nothing without taking chances. She didn't think twice.

She took a breath and skipped over the stepping stones. One, two, three, four, five, six. Lucky, but safe. In the blink of an eye, she'd reached the opposite bank and won her bet.

Yes, that was it! She'd gambled and won. A Eureka moment. A heady sensation, as if she'd downed Trueman's most potent cocktail in a single gulp. She had half a mind to fire the revolver in jubilation. She'd done more than keep her footing as she crossed the river. At one and the same time she'd stumbled onto the secret of Blackstone Sanatorium.

Rachel danced along the path through the ravine. She was brimming with a renewed sense of purpose. Finally she saw the wood for the trees. Her brain whirred as she made the connections that had previously eluded her. Ursula Baker, Clodagh Hamill, Violet Beagrie, Joshua Cuthbert Flood. Three women and one man of varying ages, each from a different part of the country. They had all died at Blackstone Fell, but what stroke of ill fortune had brought them here? The people who wanted them out of the way all had something in common. She'd been slow on the uptake, but now she understood.

Still there was nobody else in the ravine. She followed the river's winding course as it broadened out. The ravine became shallow and the path departed from the bank, rising above the mass of small boulders on either side of the river before heading in the direction of the clapper bridge. The canopy of leaves and branches thinned. The light filtering through made the water gleam like the village doctor's smile.

The sun glinted on a streak of black. Something was trapped between the rocks at the water's edge.

Rachel stopped in her tracks.

She breathed out. Was this what she'd been searching for? She scrambled down the muddy slope to get a better view.

Yes, it was a broken mess of flesh and bone.

She'd found what was left of a man after Blackstone Leap had spat him out.

24

'One tragedy after another,' Major Huckerby said. 'Anyone would think there's a jinx on Blackstone Fell.'

He and Rachel stood on the clapper bridge. The sun gave the peaty brown water of the river a bright, meretricious sheen. Dr Carrodus was talking to the ambulance driver, who was about to remove the remains Rachel had discovered. As the pair watched, the ambulance set off, and Carrodus ambled over to join them.

'Poor Lejeune,' he said heavily. 'I wouldn't wish that fate on anyone.'

'I suppose,' Rachel said diffidently, 'there isn't any doubt that it is Harold Lejeune?'

Carrodus stared at her. 'His face was very badly knocked about, as you saw. Barely recognisable. Even so, I have no doubt. I examined him only the other day. The hair, the build, a gap in his teeth, everything tallies so far as I could tell.'

'Do you know when he slipped into the water?' Rachel asked.

The doctor shook his head. His eyes were tired, and the good humour had drained out of him. He seemed stunned by what he'd seen. Certifying death in the quiet surroundings of the sanatorium was one thing, Rachel supposed. Encountering a corpse pulverised by nature in the raw was quite different.

'Impossible to tell,' he said curtly.

'It's a miracle you found him,' the major said. 'If someone is lost in Blackstone Leap, they are seldom seen again. I suppose the storm is responsible.'

'How do you mean?' Rachel asked.

'It swelled the river into a raging torrent. If the body was trapped underwater, the sheer force of the current must have dislodged it.'

'I wonder how he came to be in the water.'

The major shook his head. 'It beggars belief. Lejeune wasn't a stranger, like the journalist who died in the cave. He knew the dangers of Blackstone Leap.'

'The other day he complained of heart palpitations,' Carrodus said. 'Mind you, he seemed in pretty good shape to me. I can only hazard a guess. Perhaps he had some sort of seizure while he was walking above or beside the river. If he lost his balance, it would be easy to plunge into the water.'

'The last of the Lejeunes.' Huckerby sighed. 'Who is the next of kin, I wonder? When you were treating his wife, did you pick up anything about his family?'

'No, he never talked about himself. Or the brother who disappeared.' The doctor turned to Rachel. 'You must wonder what sort of village this is, Miss Savernake. I'm beginning to ask myself the same question. Now, I must be off. Your summons came before I finished visiting my patients.'

He walked off down the lane towards his surgery, swinging his black bag to and fro in a regular rhythm, as if to help him make sense of the inexplicable twists of fate.

As Rachel watched, Judith Royle came round the bend

in the lane. She wasn't wearing a coat and was evidently flustered as she said something to Carrodus.

'I suppose she saw the ambulance driving past the rectory,' Huckerby said. 'Wondering what the fuss is all about.'

As Carrodus spoke to Judith, Rachel and the major were too far away to eavesdrop.

But even if they'd stood a hundred yards further back, they couldn't have failed to hear the woman's scream of horror. And as they watched, Judith dropped to the ground in a dead faint.

'Everyone in the village is on edge,' the major said. 'Understandable.'

He'd invited Rachel to join him for lunch, a rich oxtail soup prepared by the faithful Dora. His housekeeper was a wizened old lady who was, Rachel suspected, the person in Blackstone Fell least ruffled by the latest fatality.

The rector's wife had come round shortly after passing out, only to begin sobbing uncontrollably. The major had helped Carrodus to take her to the surgery. He'd left her in floods of tears as Carrodus prepared a sedative.

'The news left Mrs Royle distraught,' Rachel said, putting down her spoon. 'Were the two of them on good terms?'

The major shrugged. 'Not as far as I know. As I've said, Lejeune was an odd fellow. Didn't seem comfortable with village life, never made any attempt to fit in. He and his wife were happy to wait in the South Tyrol for years until his brother was presumed dead. I suppose he felt under an obligation to keep the Tower in the family.'

Rachel wiped her mouth on a napkin. 'Perhaps.'

'Not that it matters now. He's gone to a better place.' The major shook his head. Rachel guessed that his thoughts were drifting to the death of his wife.

She took a breath. 'I was wondering...'

'Yes, Miss Savernake?'

'This may seem a peculiar suggestion,' she said.

'Try me.'

'I mentioned yesterday that there is someone I'd like you to meet.'

'Yes?'

'I wonder if you'd care to attend a séance?'

'You've bewitched the major,' Martha said. 'He's eating out of your hand.'

'There's no doubt he's fascinated by the idea,' Rachel said. 'It bothers him that a military man isn't supposed to have any truck with mumbo-jumbo like spiritualism. I reminded him that he isn't in the army now. Why not open one's mind to new experiences? He's desperate to communicate with Gloria. It just needed one final push. Ottilie Curle's renown is such that even the major has heard of her.'

'How can you be confident that he'll persuade his neighbours to take part? A rector, a doctor, a professor, a...?'

'He's got a better chance than a stranger like me. The major has lived here a long time. Nobody seems to dislike him, even though he drinks too much. Besides, everyone's shaken by recent events. With any luck, the chance to see a famous medium and not pay a king's ransom for the privilege will—'

She was interrupted by a fierce knock. Martha opened the door and they saw Peggy Needham on the step, breathing hard. Rachel took her into the sitting room while Martha put the kettle on. As Peggy sat down, her shoulders were hunched with tension.

'I hear you found Harold Lejeune's body,' she said. 'Word has reached The New Jerusalem. The girl Dilys told me she got it from the postman. I had to come here, to see if it is true.'

'Yes, the corpse washed up close to Blackstone Leap. He'd spent a considerable time in the water.'

'How long, do you know?'

'The doctor is vague. So much damage was done.' She recounted her conversation with Carrodus and the major. 'The theory that he suffered a seizure of some kind is plausible, but I think we can discount it, don't you?'

Peggy nodded. 'Too convenient.'

'Precisely. A man with a secret dies just before he reveals what he knows. Death by accident is impossible to swallow.'

'You agree that he was murdered?'

'I'm sure of it.'

Martha came in and served tea and scones before making herself scarce again.

'Picture this,' Rachel said. 'Someone took him unawares, struck him on the head, and then bundled him into the river. The blow needn't have been fatal. The killer could safely leave the rest to Blackstone Leap. The body took such a battering from the water that no one will be able to prove that one particular wound was inflicted deliberately, before the rocks and the current did their worst. A clever crime, difficult to detect. But for the storm, the body would probably never have been found. He'd have joined Edmund Mellor and Alfred Lejeune in the pantheon of mysterious disappearances from Blackstone Fell.'

Peggy stared at her. 'Do you think his death is connected with theirs?'

'Oh no. The old stories are simply helpful camouflage for a contemporary murder.' Rachel buttered a scone. 'What do you make of it?'

'It's a desperate blow,' Peggy said in a low voice. 'I'm convinced that Lejeune knew who murdered Nell. His death surely proves it. He needed money and tried to blackmail the man he saw following her, and paid for it with his life.'

'If he did see a man.'

'What do you mean?' Peggy asked sharply.

'Suppose he lied to you. What if he actually saw a woman? Rather than indulging in blackmail, he may have been trying to protect her.'

Peggy stared. 'Protect her? Who do you have in mind?'

'There are only two realistic candidates. Daphne Sambrook and Judith Royle. The rector's wife is the clear favourite.' Rachel described Judith Royle's scream on hearing that the body had been found. 'She is an emotional woman, very highly strung. Even so, her reaction was melodramatic.'

'She'd known Lejeune for years. It's a terrible way to die. The news must have come as a shock.'

'There was more to it than that. Everyone has told me that the man was desperately unpopular. Yet her horror seemed genuine.'

Peggy's astonishment was evident in her voice. 'Are you suggesting that Harold Lejeune was conducting an affair with Judith Royle?'

'If so, it explains one or two things that puzzled me. Not only her hysterical response on learning of his death.'

'He must have been twenty years older than her.'

'Considerably younger than her husband, however, and I have no doubt that she is attracted to father figures. I gather that the late Chiara Lejeune was a beautiful woman who was devoted to her husband. I suspect there was a touch of charisma in his personality that many women found appealing.'

'Charisma?' Peggy sounded outraged.

'Magnetism, force of personality, call it what you will. He seldom deployed his charms in Blackstone Fell, but I can imagine weaker characters being drawn to someone of that type. A strong man. Persuasive when he wanted to be.'

'It sounds extraordinary. Are you guessing? Or do you have evidence?'

'I imagine that if a rector's wife sleeps with one of her husband's parishioners, they will go to great lengths to cover their tracks. So – proof, no. Pointers, yes.'

'Such as?'

'He talked about leaving Blackstone Fell. She was desperate to escape her suffocating existence with Quintus Royle. I suspect they planned to start a new life together, closer to the Apennines than the Pennines.'

'Is that all you have to go on?'

Rachel said drily, 'You described me as a conjuror, Miss Needham, so you must expect me to keep one or two aces up my sleeve.'

'If you're right, the prime suspect is the jealous husband.' Peggy took a bite of her scone. 'The rector. Whatever happened to "thou shalt not kill"?'

'He's more than capable of committing murder. It's not impossible that this was an unpremeditated crime. If he encountered the man who had cuckolded him, it's more than likely there was an altercation. He is an older man, but far from feeble. If enraged or provoked, he might have landed a blow that knocked his victim over and into the river.'

'Is that what you believe happened?'

'As a hypothesis, it has some merit. But I doubt it's correct.'

'What, then?'

Rachel shrugged. 'I suppose you will argue that this is a case of a blackmailer getting his just deserts?'

Peggy wiped the crumbs from her mouth. 'My head is spinning, Miss Savernake. I'm not sure what to think any more.'

'Of course, it's possible that Lejeune was blackmailing the rector. Negotiating Judith Royle's release from the marriage on favourable terms. If he was short of money, a little nest egg courtesy of Quintus Royle would come in very handy.'

'Your imagination is even richer than Nell's,' Peggy said ruefully. 'I'm struggling to keep up.'

Rachel smiled. 'Don't do yourself down. Women make that mistake too often. You've shown a great deal of ingenuity.'

Peggy leaned forward. Her cheeks were regaining their colour. 'So do you think that he was killed because—'

A sudden noise made them freeze. Martha had opened the window to let in some air, and the noise seemed to come from somewhere in the upper village.

Moments later, there was a second bang. It sounded like a small explosion.

Peggy stared at Rachel, who sprang to her feet and flung open the front door.

In the distance, a woman screamed.

★★★

'The rectory!' Martha said. 'The reports came from there.'

'Quintus Royle has a rifle,' Rachel said. She turned to Peggy, who was standing in the hall. 'I must go and see what's happened.'

'I'm coming too,' the older woman said.

'Stay here. It will be safer.'

'I told you before. I've had my life. What happens to me now doesn't matter. I want to be in at the death.'

Rachel looked into her grey eyes. 'Watch out. Those words may be truer than you think.'

'I don't care,' Peggy said defiantly. 'Remember what we said? Partners in crime?'

'Very well, we'll go together. Martha, wait here. Hetty may be back soon. We don't want her wandering into the line of fire.'

'You don't think the rector's going on the rampage?' the maid asked. 'If he's lost his mind?'

'For once,' Rachel said, 'I'm not sure what to think.'

She didn't bother to slip on a coat before going outside. Peggy followed close behind.

Someone was running towards them on Fell Lane. It was Myrtle, the Royles' maid. She was sobbing and flailing her arms around like a demented dervish.

'What is it?' Rachel demanded as they reached her.

Myrtle slumped to the ground. She was crying uncontrollably and seemed unable to gasp out anything coherent.

'Look after her,' Rachel told Peggy. 'I need to go in.'

This time there was no argument. Peggy put her arm round the woman, and murmured words of comfort as Rachel approached the rectory.

The front door was open wide. Rachel strode down the path but stopped at the threshold. She listened intently, but there was nothing to hear. A deathly silence. In the air, there was a whiff of cooked mutton mingled with the smell of cordite.

She moved into the hall. The door of the morning room was wide open. Rachel looked inside.

Sprawled across the blood-drenched carpet, just inside the door, lay the body of the Reverend Quintus Royle. His head had been blown off.

Judith Royle's remains were sprawled over the same chair that Rachel had occupied during the disastrous tea party. The rector's rifle was close to her feet. It didn't take astute detection to realise what had happened. She'd killed her husband as he tried to escape. Then she'd thrust the gun barrels at her face and managed to reach the trigger.

25

Jacob lifted the register from the counter in the lobby of The New Jerusalem. Taking a fountain pen from his pocket, he signed his name with a flourish, and blew on the ink to help it to dry.

Dilys squinted at the book in bewilderment.

'That's funny,' she said. 'It looks as though someone has cut out a couple of pages. Do you see, Mr Flint? They made a neat job of it, but you can just about see the tear.'

'How mysterious,' he said disingenuously. 'An autograph hunter, perhaps. Had any famous guests recently?'

'Not as far as I know. We're booked up solid right now, mind. I've never known anything like it. Specially not at the back end of autumn.'

He treated her to an admiring glance. 'Perfectly understandable, given the local attractions.'

She laughed. 'I bet you think flattery will get you everywhere. I'm not sure you can compete with Mr Mann. He's in the motor trade, up in Cumberland. Promised to take me out for a spin in his Wolseley tomorrow.'

'Ah. I know when I'm beaten,' Jacob said.

She pouted. 'You may live in London, but you sound like a Yorkshireman to me.'

'Born and bred. Always glad to get back to God's own county.' He beamed. 'And where better than The New Jerusalem?'

'Well, you're not on your own. There's an older lady staying here, likes to keep herself to herself. And we're expecting two more, any time now. A Miss Curle and her servant. They are from London. You might have come across them.'

'Very big place, London,' Jacob said. 'The name Curle rings a bell, though. I've escaped from the Smoke for a few days. An acquaintance of mine rented a cottage up by the Fell and she told me how nice it is round here.'

'Oh yes?' A note of disappointment entered her voice. 'That would be Miss Savernake, I suppose?'

Jacob gave a cautious nod. 'You know her?'

'The milkman told me she's taken Hawthorn Cottage.' Dilys considered him. 'Extremely handsome lady, by all accounts. Old Bob was smitten, and he's sixty if he's a day. Close friend of yours, is she?'

'More of an acquaintance, to be honest.' Jacob sighed heavily. 'She's keen on folklore. Superstitions, séances.'

'Bob heard on the grapevine that she's investigating our local curse.' Dilys leaned closer and lowered her voice. 'Two men vanished from Blackstone Lodge and were never seen again. It all happened ages ago, but she wants to solve the mystery.'

'Word gets around quickly in these parts,' Jacob said. 'Hard to keep any secrets, I should think.'

Dilys chortled. 'Worried your past will find you out? Well,

let me share a secret with you. This morning your friend Miss Savernake stumbled across a dead body.'

Jacob's eyes widened. 'Good heavens, did she really? Who did it belong to?'

'Mr Harold Lejeune from the Tower.'

'What happened to him?'

'Drowned up by Blackstone Leap.' Dilys indulged herself with a theatrical pause. 'The question is – did he jump, or was he pushed?'

'Good grief.'

'That's not the half of it.' Dilys's cheek was almost touching his. Her musky scent was cheap and pungent. 'There was a terrible tragedy up at the rectory only this afternoon. The grocer's lad was telling me before you rolled up. Mrs Royle, the rector's wife, shot her husband with his own rifle and then she killed herself. The police are there now.'

Jacob's mind was whirling. 'Anyone would think I've turned up in Chicago by mistake.'

'Terrible, isn't it?' Dilys allowed herself a moment's solemn reflection. 'Makes a change, anyway. Normally, we get a bit of excitement here once in a Preston guild. The grocer's lad says Mr Lejeune was in love with Mrs Royle, and threw himself into the Leap because they could never be together. She had a fit and thought she couldn't live without him. So she shot the rector and herself.'

Jacob shook his head. 'Passions run high round here.'

'I'll say!' She grinned. 'The landlord has a different idea. He thinks the rector murdered Mr Lejeune.'

'Murdered?'

'Knocked him out and chucked him in the water, that's right. Mr Crawshaw never cared for the Reverend Royle, mind. Leastways, not since he preached a sermon about the evils of alcohol.'

Jacob exhaled. 'Never a dull moment in Blackstone Fell, eh?'

The door of the inn swung open. Abdul – must remember to keep calling him that, Jacob told himself – stood there in his robes and turban. He had a suitcase in either hand. Behind his bulky figure, Jacob glimpsed the dumpy figure of Ottilie Curle.

Abdul stood back to allow the medium to sweep into the inn. She was draped in furs and her bracelets were jangling. When she glanced at Jacob, there was no flicker of recognition in her eyes. She could certainly act, he thought.

Dilys stared at the newcomers.

'You can say that again,' she said in an awestruck voice.

Jacob scribbled half a dozen suitably breathless paragraphs about the deaths of the Royles and Harold Lejeune in his room before rushing downstairs again to telephone his office with his scoop.

His mood was jubilant, the misery of the séance in Kentish Town long forgotten. Ottilie Curle had made sure *The Spiritual Sentinel* didn't print a word about that unfortunate episode. In writing his story, he'd given his imagination free rein, but Gomersall would lose no sleep over that. Lashings of melodrama and touches of mystery were what their readers craved. As for the fuzziness about matters of detail, it was enough to hint that the pernicious laws of libel prevented the *Clarion*'s man on the spot from revealing everything he knew.

Hurrying back upstairs, he caught sight of a formidable figure looming above him on the landing. Clifford Trueman turned on his heel and returned to his room. Jacob followed and tapped on the door. Trueman opened up, his craggy features dark with menace, and waved him inside.

'Rachel wants us to act like perfect strangers, remember,' he hissed.

'You heard about all this bloodshed at the rectory?' Jacob whispered.

Trueman nodded. 'Can't talk now. I'll be in the bar later. Talk to people, pick up what you can. We need to keep a safe distance from each other.'

'Understood.'

'There is one thing.' From the top of a chest of drawers, Trueman picked up a brown paper parcel tied up with string. 'Rachel wants this. You'll see her before I do. Make sure she gets it.'

Jacob weighed the parcel in his hand. 'What is it?'

Trueman gave him a crooked grin. 'A newspaper.'

'Cut and dried,' Sergeant Margetson repeated, lifting his tankard of beer. 'Cheers, young man.'

The bar of The New Jerusalem was full to bursting and the locals were in such raucous form that his words were barely audible. The sergeant and the village constable had adjourned here after concluding their enquiries into the fatalities at the rectory. They were men in their fifties, coasting towards retirement, and not prepared to allow a bloodbath to get in the way of their evening's refreshment. Jacob had plied them with alcohol and quizzed them about the investigation. He discovered nothing that Dilys hadn't already told him.

'Glad to hear your inspector's satisfied,' Jacob said. 'Quick work, wrapping the case up in a few hours.'

'We're not slouches round here,' PC Fowler said, with an admonitory jab of the forefinger. 'Tell your London friends.'

'I come from Yorkshire myself,' Jacob said. 'Leeds.'

The constable sniffed. 'Better a Loiner than a Lancastrian, I suppose.'

'The eternal triangle,' the sergeant said ruminatively. 'Royle discovered that his wife was misbehaving with this other chap. In a fury, he bumped off the lover. When she realised what he'd done, she had nothing left to live for. First chance she got, she took her husband's rifle and shot him before topping herself. Like I say…'

'Cut and dried,' Jacob murmured. 'Open and shut.'

'That's the size of it.' The sergeant took another swig of ale. 'You work for the *Clarion*, eh? Got up here sharpish, I'll give you that.'

'Instinct,' Jacob said shamelessly. 'As my old mum used to say: first up, best dressed.'

'Was Lejeune's death a simple accident?' Major Huckerby asked rhetorically. 'Or did the rector get wind of something going on between his wife and the other fellow? Everyone has jumped to the conclusion that Judith Royle was mixed up with Lejeune in a sordid intrigue. Was it true? I don't suppose we'll ever know.'

He, Carrodus, and Trueman were standing at the far end of the bar counter, out of earshot of Jacob and the policemen.

Trueman had resolved to keep quiet and make sure his companions' glasses were replenished regularly.

'She was an unhappy woman,' the doctor said. 'I don't mind admitting, when I moved to Blackstone Fell, she paid me too much attention for my own peace of mind. I had to make it clear, very gently, that I wasn't interested.'

The major filled his pipe. 'Between ourselves, I had a rather similar experience with her after I lost Gloria. Loneliness, that's what I put it down to. When Daphne Sambrook came back here, I thought the two women would make friends. But they had so little in common.'

'Daphne is a bluestocking,' Carrodus said. 'And Judith Royle was more interested in men than other women.'

'What did she say to you in the surgery this morning, after she came round?'

'She was embarrassed that she'd keeled over in the middle of the lane. Said she had no idea what came over her. The shock of hearing about Lejeune's death, so soon after that Fagan woman died in the cave, was simply too much for her. I told her she was anaemic and needed to take it easy and get a good night's rest.'

'Was that all?'

'She begged me not to tell her husband what had happened,' Carrodus said. 'Naturally I gave her my word.'

'Did she seem heartbroken about Lejeune's death?'

'At the time, it didn't occur to me that she had any… personal reason for grief. I understood why she was afraid of Royle. He'd have made her life hell simply for making a fool of herself in public.'

Huckerby nodded, his expression grave. 'What do you think led to her… taking such drastic measures?'

'If the rumour-mongers are right, and she was in love with Lejeune, his death may have sparked a confrontation. Perhaps the rector provoked her.'

'She didn't strike you as mentally unbalanced?'

Carrodus gave an emphatic shake of the head. 'I'd never have allowed her to go back home if I thought so. I'd have wanted an expert opinion from Professor Sambrook or his son.'

'Speak of the devil,' the major said. 'Here is young Sambrook.'

Denzil Sambrook pushed through the crowd to join them. Trueman signalled to Dilys for another round.

'What are you drinking, Dr Sambrook?'

'Double whisky.' Sambrook sounded weary and bad-tempered. 'It's been a long day. The old man has been utterly…'

He made a noise signifying frustration and disgust.

'Can't be easy,' Carrodus said sympathetically, 'working with a genius. Especially if he's your own father.'

'Genius! Ha!' Sambrook glared. 'Those were the days! If they ever existed.'

'Come, now.' The doctor eased into his bedside manner, calming and persuasive. 'You really don't mean that. Your father's reputation…'

Sambrook interrupted him with a loud groan. 'Believe me, I know all about his ruddy reputation. I've had it rammed down my throat all my life. The fact is, he's an old man. Stuck in the past. In his dotage, frankly. It's getting to a point where I really wonder if it's right for him to carry on. Or pretend to carry on, that would be nearer the mark.'

Huckerby and Carrodus exchanged shocked glances.

Trueman composed his features into an expression of puzzled sympathy.

'If you're worried about him,' the doctor said, 'I could take a look-see.'

Sambrook shook his head. 'In his current mood, he wouldn't wear it. That's the trouble. He still thinks he's in his prime, though he does nothing all day but rewrite lectures he gave thirty years ago. Thanks for the offer, Carrodus, it's decent of you. But I've said too much already. Better leave it there.'

'I take it that even in the rarefied surroundings of the sanatorium,' Carrodus said drily, 'word has reached you about all the excitement in the upper village?'

Sambrook seemed relieved to change the subject. 'Extraordinary business.'

'I was saying that if I'd had any clue that Judith Royle was a risk to herself or anyone else, I'd have asked for your professional opinion.'

'The rector took it upon himself to do just that. Frankly, the woman was riddled with neuroses.' Sambrook shrugged. 'A weak personality, thrown together with a dominant male with evident traces of psychosis. I hear she was misbehaving with Lejeune. A man cut from the same cloth as the rector.'

'The poor creature couldn't help herself,' the major said glumly.

'Quite. Ah, thank you, Dilys.' Sambrook raised his tumbler and said wryly, 'Your health, gentlemen. Here's to natural selection.'

The major frowned. 'I say, old fellow, that's in rather poor taste.'

Sambrook knocked back the whisky as if it were lemonade. 'Unlike the Glenfiddich. Now, Major, let's call a spade a spade. None of us liked Lejeune. Or the rector. As for the woman, she was her own worst enemy. In all candour, you can't tell me that the world is poorer without them.'

Carrodus contemplated his short, neatly manicured fingernails. The major reddened.

'You're a man of science, Sambrook; you see the world in terms of strict logic. But hang it all, whatever their faults, those three people were human beings. What happened was a tragedy.'

'The manner of their deaths was brutal, I agree. I'm strongly opposed to unnecessary bloodshed.'

'But?' Carrodus asked quietly.

Sambrook emptied his glass. Trueman caught Dilys's eye and she poured another double for him.

'If the war taught us anything, it's that human life is as cheap as chips. That's something a man like Quintus Royle could never understand, never accept. But it's true. Christianity cultivates human weakness. For society to prosper, we can't afford to delude ourselves, or indulge in sentimentality and religious cant.' The other men watched as he swallowed some more whisky. 'I'm not saying anything new or revolutionary. Plato realised what society needs to survive and progress. Fewer degenerates and more intelligent minds. Good creation.'

The major's bushy eyebrows lifted. 'Damn it, man, scientists aren't a race apart from the rest of us. I didn't care for the fire and brimstone the rector poured from his pulpit. But when it comes to picking who lives and who dies, I'd rather put my trust in God than men with test tubes.'

'So you oppose birth control? Facts don't change, Major, simply because people don't dare to face them. You don't need to be a scientist to understand. I stand with H.G. Wells, George Bernard Shaw, Harold Laski, Maynard Keynes…'

'Self-righteous socialists!' the major snapped.

'Progressives,' Sambrook retorted. 'Science is morality. Socialism is its natural ally. As for eugenics, we know it works for dogs and cows and the loveliest roses. Why not take advantage of it for ourselves?'

Carrodus coughed. 'This is getting a bit deep for me, Sambrook. Do your principles permit you to attend tomorrow evening's séance?'

'Séance?'

'The major has scored a coup. Tell him, Huckerby.'

The major made a visible effort to master his emotions. 'Your tenant in Hawthorn Cottage, young Miss Savernake, is a friend of Ottilie Curle, the country's foremost medium. She kindly offered me the chance to host a séance at my home. Normally the woman charges a fortune, but it seems she owes Miss Savernake a favour.'

Sambrook groaned. 'You're not hoping to make contact with your late wife's spirit?'

The major flushed. 'I'm prepared to approach these delicate matters with an open mind.'

'Without prejudice,' Carrodus said with a faint smile. 'A scientific attitude, quite commendable.'

Sambrook took another drink. 'Are you taking part in this nonsense, Doctor? I wouldn't have put you down as the credulous type.'

'It's a unique opportunity. Ottilie Curle is the leader in her field. The woman is probably the worst kind of charlatan, but when the major offered me the chance to see her in action, I bit his hand off.'

'I bumped into your sister as I was leaving the house,' Huckerby said. 'She was equally glad to accept my invitation.'

'People think Daphne has her feet on the ground,' Sambrook snorted. 'Believe me, she often gets carried away with ridiculous fancies. I wouldn't be surprised to learn she is a secret spiritualist.'

'If you're so sceptical, why not come along tomorrow evening?' the major said. 'See for yourself. Isn't that what scientists are meant to do? Evaluate the data?'

'I might just take you up on that, Huckerby.'

'Please be my guest. Miss Savernake emphasised that the medium is more than happy for dyed-in-the-wool sceptics to attend. She doesn't fear scrutiny of her methods. Your sister said she might persuade the professor to join us.'

Sambrook yawned. 'The old boy is losing his grip on reality, so it wouldn't surprise me. He certainly has nothing better to do with his time. Very well. I'll bring him along.'

'Sounds like quite a party,' Trueman said in a wistful tone.

'You're welcome to join us, Mann,' the major said. 'I'm sure Miss Savernake won't object.'

'Thanks awfully.' Trueman rubbed his chin. 'She sounds like an unusual young lady.'

Sambrook said, 'My sister has met her. She believes there is more to her than meets the eye.'

'Damned attractive, too,' Carrodus said pensively. 'I wonder why a young woman like that is burying herself away in Blackstone Fell?'

Huckerby took a swig of beer. 'For all her interest in folklore and the spirit world, she's made of stern stuff.'

'What makes you say that?' Sambrook asked.

'Lejeune's corpse was in a wretched state when she found it. The damage done by water and stone was appalling. Even Constable Fowler turned green at the sight of the remains. Yet Miss Rachel Savernake didn't turn a hair.'

26

'The local bobbies are congratulating themselves,' Jacob announced the next morning. 'They reckon they have cracked the case.'

'Aren't our policemen wonderful?' Rachel said.

They were sitting at the kitchen table at Hawthorn Cottage. Jacob had turned up in time to tuck into one of Hetty's lavish cooked breakfasts while Rachel made do with a slice of toast. For once, he thought her appearance lacked its customary touch of chic. She was wearing a chunky Fair Isle jersey and twill trousers.

He pointed to the parcel he'd handed her. She'd put it on the shelf without bothering to unwrap it.

'Aren't you going to look inside?'

'Not for the moment.'

'Trueman said it's a newspaper.'

'I expect he's right.'

When she was in this kind of mood, he'd learned not to push his luck. All would be revealed when it suited her.

'Lucky I arrived in the village ahead of the pack,' he said. 'The *Clarion* has a front-page splash and a headline to make any editor's mouth water.'

'*Murder at the Vicarage*?'

'How did you guess? A rector, a beautiful woman, adultery, two murders, and a suicide. The tranquillity of an idyllic English village shattered to smithereens. What more could our readers possibly ask for?'

'Idyllic?'

Jacob pulled a face. 'Touch of journalistic licence. In my defence, it was bright sunshine when I arrived yesterday afternoon. After all the mayhem, it was as if order has been restored in Blackstone Fell.'

'Except that it hasn't,' Rachel said.

'I'm disappointed, frankly.' He gave a theatrical sigh. 'You've been here seventy-two hours and what's happened? Far from tying everything up, you've got more loose ends than a bowl of spaghetti. Meanwhile, the local morgue is running short of slabs.'

'I can only apologise for my indolence.'

'Do you believe Judith Royle and Harold Lejeune were lovers?'

'Yes.'

'Did Quintus Royle kill Lejeune?'

'I very much doubt it.'

She told him about Peggy Needham's account of her conversation with Lejeune and the blackmail theory.

'If that's true, then perhaps he was killed by the person he tried to blackmail.'

'That seems to be the obvious conclusion.'

He glanced at her suspiciously. 'And when Judith learned that Lejeune was dead, she couldn't face life without him?'

'A poor decision,' Rachel said quietly. 'But yes, it seems

likely. She couldn't bear the prospect of remaining chained to the rector and Blackstone Fell.'

'Quintus Royle scared everyone witless, according to the barmaid. Dilys says people blame him for what happened.'

'Husbands have to be good for something, even if merely to serve as scapegoats,' Rachel said. 'Isn't that right, Hetty?'

The housekeeper snorted and cleared the plates away with a clatter.

'Last night Trueman spent a long time in the company of Huckerby, Carrodus, and Denzil Sambrook,' Jacob said. 'He doesn't seem to be missing his cocktails. Young Sambrook was putting away the whiskies as if there was no tomorrow.'

Rachel said, 'Did you meet Peggy Needham?'

'We bumped into each other as I was getting out of my taxi. We exchanged a few words, but she was obviously stunned by what happened in the rectory.'

'It wasn't a sight for the squeamish. Anyone would be shaken.'

Except you, he was tempted to say. 'Peggy didn't go down to the bar last night. Neither did Ottilie Curle or…'

'Abdul,' Rachel prompted.

'Abdul. They seem to be sticking to their side of the bargain.'

'So I should hope.'

'I wonder if Trueman will persuade Sambrook to take his father-in-law as a patient.'

Rachel shook her head. 'It no longer matters. We have the key to the deaths at the sanatorium.'

Jacob's jaw dropped. 'You've found it?'

'Joshua Flood's nephew was the last link in the chain.' She smiled. 'A single telephone call to London was all it took to confirm my theory.'

'Are you going to let me in on the secret?'

'I'm sure you can work it out for yourself. Not that you made much of a fist of solving the locked-room puzzle.'

He laughed. 'And you did?'

'It wasn't such a challenge.' She smiled. 'Peggy Needham is due to join us shortly. We can tackle the riddle of Blackstone Lodge together. Thanks to Daphne Sambrook, I also have a key to unlock that particular door.'

Peggy arrived at the cottage twenty minutes later. She looked as if she hadn't slept a wink.

'I telephoned my cousin from the inn before I came out. Eunice's maid answered. She was in a state of some distress. Eunice was sick during the night and the doctor was called out. He's changed her medicine, but the prognosis is far from hopeful. Nell's death has hit her very hard. I worry that she's lost the will to live.'

'Do you intend to go back to London?' Rachel asked.

'When you told me about this evening's séance, I promised to be there.' There was a resolute set to Peggy's jaw. 'I must see this through; I owe it to Nell. Tomorrow, I'll catch the train home and go to my cousin.'

'Thank you,' Rachel said. 'My own promise was to unravel the mystery of Blackstone Lodge.'

Peggy shook her head. 'Forgive me, Miss Savernake, but I can't quite believe that you've answered a question that has defeated everyone else for over three hundred years.'

'Please call me Rachel. I don't care to stand on ceremony. Especially not with a partner in crime.'

'And I am Peggy.' A thin smile. 'Never Margaret.'

'You'll be glad to hear that I owe a great deal to Nell Fagan. Her account of the historic disappearances from Blackstone Lodge was so scrupulously detailed that the glimmering of an idea came to me at once. Jacob, like many others, supposed that both Edmund Mellor and Alfred Lejeune had got out of the gatehouse and perished elsewhere. Perfectly plausible, but to my mind unlikely. Especially given that there was an alternative explanation.'

'You gave me a clue,' Jacob said. 'The problem was, it didn't help. You placed a lot of emphasis on the year that Mellor vanished. You said the date of 1606 was significant, and we talked about *Macbeth*, a story about killing a king. I've kept turning it over in my head, but I'm still none the wiser. Can you make any sense of it, Miss Needham?'

Peggy shook her head. '*Macbeth* is a marvellous play, so rich in atmosphere. I studied it in my younger days and I must have watched half a dozen performances. But what is the link with Mellor and Alfred Lejeune?'

Martha came into the room and handed Rachel a small flashlight.

'Thank you.' Rachel turned to Peggy and Jacob. 'It's time to go to the Lodge. You can see for yourselves.'

They trooped past the rectory in silence. A young police constable stood guard outside the porch. A press photographer skipped up and down the lane, taking pictures from every conceivable angle of what his paper would no doubt delight in calling The House of Death. A handful of villagers had gathered by the lychgate. They'd taken off their hats, and their heads were bowed.

Rachel came to a halt once they crossed the road. Blackstone Lodge stood in front of them, on the other side of the lane, with the Tower rising up behind.

'The gatehouse is like a strange kind of folly,' Jacob said. 'The Tower is bizarre, but at least it has a purpose. People have lived there for centuries. There's no rhyme or reason to the Lodge.'

'I don't agree,' Rachel said. 'Remember when it was built. Think about life in England at the time.'

'When Shakespeare was writing *Macbeth*?' Jacob shook his head. 'You've lost me again.'

Rachel smiled. 'Peggy, would you like to give our friend a short history lesson?'

The older woman cleared her throat. 'A new King of England and Scotland had ascended the throne. *Macbeth* paid homage to him, a monarch obsessed with the supernatural. He wrote a book about demonology, and was terrified of witches. Above all, James was tormented by insecurity. His predecessor Elizabeth had put his own mother to death. To the end of her life, the Virgin Queen refused to name an heir. In Scotland, James had witches tortured and burned at the stake. Shakespeare was desperate to keep on the right side of royalty, and flattery was part of his stock-in-trade. So he portrayed the three old hags in his play as weird and malevolent, while the man who kills a king descends into madness and dies.'

'Very good,' Rachel said. 'You're getting warm.'

'I'm afraid it's as far as I can go.' Peggy gave a pebble a disconsolate kick. 'Robert Lejeune came from a family loyal to the Crown. His father was a member of parliament. Did he build the Tower and Lodge as a tribute to the king?'

'He had a more practical purpose in mind,' Rachel said. 'Let's go inside.'

Even on a bright day, the interior of the Lodge was dark and oppressive. Peggy's eyes glazed over as she took in their surroundings. Jacob guessed that they both had the same mental image. Nell Fagan in this musty, claustrophobic room, preparing to limp out into the cold autumn air for the very last time. How and by whom, he wondered, had she been tricked into going to her death in a dank and lonely cave?

There were only two chairs. Rachel waved to her companions to sit down. Her eyes were shining as she prowled around the room, like a magician preparing to produce a flock of doves from a silk bandanna.

'To fathom the secret of Blackstone Lodge, we must understand the turmoil of those days. The new king's fears weren't confined to witchcraft. He dreaded spies, rebels, and conspirators. With very good reason.' She lowered her voice as she began to recite. '*Remember, remember, the fifth of November. Gunpowder, treason, and plot.*'

'What does Bonfire Night have to do with Blackstone Lodge?' Jacob asked.

'More than you may think. Catholics felt betrayed by James after he came to power in England. Following a brief honeymoon of hope, their dreams that he'd stamp out religious persecution crumbled to dust. Those who regarded him as a tyrant decided to assassinate him. The mood was febrile, the threat to the king serious. The more conspiracies that were discovered, the harsher the punishments meted out. So Guy Fawkes and his comrades hatched a plot to blow up

Parliament. An act of terror on an unimaginable scale. The aim was to destroy not only the king but the might of the English establishment.'

Peggy said, 'Guy Fawkes came from York, didn't he?'

'As did the Mellors and the Lejeunes,' Rachel said. 'Edmund Mellor, like Guy Fawkes, spent time in the Iberian Peninsula. Whether he and Fawkes met there, we'll never know. They were both dissidents. Mellor's father was an ecclesiastical lawyer who made himself unpopular. I expect the family were recusants, people who refused to take part in Anglican services. The Lejeunes were firmly on the other side of the fence.'

'Robert and Edmund were friends,' Jacob objected.

Rachel shrugged. 'One thing we know about the Lejeunes is that they don't bother much about friendship. Those were tumultuous, violent times. A fervent supporter of the king would be bitterly hostile towards a papist bent on regicide.'

'In that case, why did Robert offer Edmund hospitality? And why did Edmund accept?'

'I can hazard a guess,' Peggy said. 'Robert was a spy. He knew Cecil – the man who discovered the Gunpowder Plot – so perhaps he belonged to Cecil's network of agents.'

'Edmund wasn't part of the Gunpowder Plot,' Jacob said.

'So far as we know,' Peggy said. 'He'd been out of the country and when he came back, he was out of touch. Robert probably thought he posed a threat to the defence of the realm. By nature Edmund was hot-headed and rash. But he walked straight into a trap.'

Rachel gave her a little clap. 'Bravo! If the king's men regarded Edmund as an ally of Guy Fawkes, hoping to launch another assassination attempt, they'd want him dead. Edmund would be wary and fearful, so Robert Lejeune's personal connection with him was invaluable. He won Edmund's confidence, and swore he'd be safe in Blackstone Fell.'

'How did he manage that?' Jacob asked.

'By pretending to be a secret sympathiser with the Catholic cause. To the outside world, he took care to appear loyal to the monarchy. The Tower has a door knocker in the shape of a unicorn, a symbol favoured by King James. But Robert persuaded Edmund that in fact, he was playing a double game. In those double-crossing days, that was just about plausible. But it wasn't true.'

'You think Robert murdered Edmund?'

'Before I came here, I thought it likely. Now I'm certain.'

'Was he capable of such savagery? Duping a childhood friend and then disposing of him?'

'It was a cruel world. Do you know what happened to Fawkes and his fellow conspirators?'

'Of course,' he retorted. 'They were executed.'

'That doesn't capture the sheer savagery of their punishment. They were tied to wooden hurdles and dragged through the streets. On the scaffold a noose was put round their necks. Then they were stripped, emasculated, disembowelled, and cut into quarters. Two men who were shot before they could suffer the same fate weren't spared public disgrace. Their bodies were dug up from the ground. They were exhumed simply in order to cut off their heads and display them on spikes.'

Jacob's throat suddenly felt dry. 'Barbarous. And all in the name of God and the King?'

Rachel shrugged. 'They were different times. Who are we to

judge from the comfort of the present day? Isn't it the height of smug self-indulgence to say we would be more civilised?'

'What makes you so sure that Lejeune committed murder?'

Rachel pointed to the decorated wooden surround of the fireplace. Jacob squinted, but he couldn't make any sense of the jumble of letters.

aabaaabbaabaaababaaaabbbb

'I don't understand.'

Rachel looked at Peggy. 'You love history. Any ideas?'

The older woman pondered. 'It's not… a Baconian cipher?'

'Congratulations. You've scored another bull's eye.'

'A Baconian cipher?' Jacob asked.

Peggy took pity on him. 'Even if Bacon didn't write Shakespeare's plays, he did invent a method of conveying secret information at around the time of the Gunpowder Plot. Robert Lejeune was in his circle. He would have been familiar with the technique. Strictly speaking, it wasn't a form of cipher, but a form of steganography.'

'Never heard of it.'

'It does have one particular virtue.'

'Oh yes?' Jacob said, with the resignation of a classroom dunce.

'Steganography,' Rachel said, 'doesn't simply disguise what is being said. It conceals the very fact that there is something secret to be discovered. For example, a sardonic message masquerading as an elaborate piece of interior design.'

'And Robert Lejeune left a secret message here?'

'Yes.' Rachel smiled. 'Above an alcove where a fire might burn. A cryptic reference to the Gunpowder Plot. His message was simple: EMRIP.'

'EMRIP?'

Peggy put a hand to her mouth. 'Of course! Edmund Mellor RIP.'

'Ask yourself why Edmund Mellor entered the Lodge in a furtive manner,' Rachel said, 'and one answer springs to mind. He wanted to hide. Not from Lejeune, whom he trusted. Urged on by his host, he hoped to avoid discovery from his enemies, the anti-papists enraged by acts of terror aimed at overthrowing the establishment.'

'He was like a priest lurking in a priest hole,' Peggy said.

'Precisely. Robert Lejeune was a false friend. He offered to help Mellor and instead lured him to his death. He designed and built the Lodge for that specific purpose. It was a place of execution.'

Jacob stared. 'This isn't a vast Jacobean mansion with wide wings and endless passageways. Not an obvious place for a priest hole.'

'That was the beauty of his plan,' Rachel said. 'And no doubt the reason he was able to persuade Mellor that he'd be safe, once he locked the door of the Lodge. The priest hole is so inconspicuous, no one was likely to find it. And nobody did, at least not until Alfred Lejeune came along. He was an antiquary, and I expect his reasoning was the same as mine. The cipher is an impudent clue.'

She pointed. 'The priest hole, like so many others around the country, is beneath the fireplace.'

'Have you examined it?' Peggy asked.

'Yes. One of Nell's photographs of the Lodge showed the cipher. Blurred, but just about decipherable. As soon as I made sense of it, I knew where to look. When I borrowed the key from Daphne Sambrook, I cleared the rubbish out of the fireplace and poked around.'

She beckoned them to join her. The base of the fireplace comprised uneven chunks of stone. Propped against the wall was a lengthy strip of ironwork pitted with rust, a combination of hammer and crowbar.

'I found the crowbar inside the fireplace,' she said. 'It looks as if it might date back to when the Lodge was built. Edmund Mellor probably used it. Alfred Lejeune certainly did.'

Peggy peered at the back of the fireplace, and pointed to a tiny gap in the stone. 'Is that the entrance to the priest hole?'

'Let me demonstrate.' Rachel lifted up the crowbar and inserted the claw into the gap. Gritting her teeth, she levered up an irregular section of stone. Once it began to move, it swung open with an ease that took Jacob by surprise. The stone was thinner than he'd expected, and there was a rusty bracket beneath, as well as an iron stave. The stone came to rest against a jutting point on the upper part of the fireplace.

'Don't get too close,' Rachel said, as he moved forward to squint into the space she'd revealed beneath the fireplace. 'The stone is delicately balanced. One nudge, and you'll knock it down again.'

'The gap is large enough for a man to wriggle down into,' Jacob said. 'Provided he breathes in. By the look of it, the hole is at least six feet deep.'

Rachel switched on the flashlight to illuminate the space beneath the fireplace.

'Nobody could stay there for any length of time,' Peggy said. 'It's too tight.'

'No,' Rachel said, 'but there is more to this priest hole than meets the eye. There is a second secret space, hidden beneath the first. Edmund Mellor would be familiar with the principle, but if not, Robert Lejeune will have explained the trick. There are double priest holes of this kind up and down the country. If searchers managed to discover the first priest hole, they'd see it was empty. They seldom realised that someone was hiding out of sight in a lower chamber.'

'Cunning,' Jacob said.

'The unique feature of Blackstone Lodge's priest hole,' Rachel said, 'is that the second chamber wasn't constructed as a place of safety, but as a death trap.'

Jacob stared into the dark hole in the ground, his imagination whirling.

'The bottom of the priest hole appears to be solid rock,' Rachel said, 'but the rock is simply a wafer-thin covering. Below it is an iron flap. I believe that Robert Lejeune advised Edmund Mellor to haul himself down into the hole and tug on the iron stave, to close the stone covering. He may have lit a candle, otherwise it would be pitch black. Not that it mattered. Mellor's next task was to open the iron flap. Shall I give you a demonstration?'

Jacob and Peggy nodded in unison. Flashlight in one hand and the crowbar in the other, Rachel lay down on the ground by the edge of the hole, and it dawned on Jacob why she'd chosen to wear a jersey and trousers.

'Peggy, would you rest your hand on the stone, so that it doesn't fall down when I'm underneath it?'

The older woman did as she was told.

'Jacob, grip both my ankles, tight as you can. Whatever you do, don't let go if you want to see me again.'

'Is this a good idea?' he asked.

'Too dangerous,' Peggy whispered. 'If you fall…'

'I have every confidence in Jacob,' Rachel said calmly. 'It's not difficult. Besides, his life is at stake too. If he drops me into the abyss, Trueman will send him down to keep my corpse company.'

Jacob swallowed. 'If you're certain.'

'I am.'

'Very well.'

He got down behind her, gripping one of her ankles in each hand. Rachel eased herself forward into the space and thrust the crowbar downwards.

Jacob craned his neck to glimpse what was happening below the fireplace. Rachel's upper body was poised over the gap. He was conscious of her slender ankles between his fingers, her trim figure right in front of him.

Suddenly the floor of the priest hole gave way like a trapdoor swinging open, to reveal a vertical shaft beneath. Jacob winced at the foul smell. He was staring down into a long, fetid drainpipe.

Peggy let out a little moan of horror. 'Those poor men!'

'Seen enough?' Rachel said. 'Thank you, Jacob, you can reel me in.'

He pulled her back. They scrambled to their feet and dusted themselves down.

'What's down there, do you think?' he asked.

'My guess is that Robert Lejeune dug a hole in the underground rock. As you've seen, the Lodge is built on a slight incline. A brook runs close to the drive, by the poplars, before disappearing below ground for a little way. Robert probably cut out a channel for it. The first time I came here, I dropped a pebble into the hole, and there was a faint splash. Perhaps there are slight gaps on either side of the bottom of the chamber, and the water runs through a gully. If there's a storm, the water level rises, but never high enough to come close to the top of the chamber. Let alone to flood the priest hole.'

'You think Edmund Mellor's remains are still there?'

'And Alfred Lejeune's. Whatever is left of them. Escape would be impossible. Below the priest hole, it's a sheer drop.'

'Presumably Alfred's researches led him to deduce Mellor's fate, just as you did,' Peggy murmured. 'He decided to check to see if his hypothesis was correct.'

'Yes. He locked the door of the Lodge behind him, so that nobody could disturb him, but he made two mistakes that proved fatal. He didn't take anyone into his confidence and he didn't take enough care. I expect he was so excited when he realised the purpose of the crowbar and discovered the priest hole that he couldn't resist the urge to investigate further. The cover came down over him, and he dropped through the trap.'

Jacob's face was as ashen as Peggy's.

'Never to be seen again,' he said.

27

Rachel led the way back to Hawthorn Cottage. Jacob glanced at Peggy. Her eyes were glazed with misery. After passing the church, they saw Major Huckerby approaching from the other direction. At his heels was the rector's dog.

He tipped his hat. 'Morning, Miss Savernake. I've got a new companion, you see. Someone needed to look after Moses. He's always been a moody brute, but perhaps a change of home will improve his temper.'

'I'm sure it will. May I introduce you to my friends, Miss Needham and Mr Flint? They are staying at The New Jerusalem and will join us this evening.'

Huckerby shook their hands. 'Do you know when the medium is due to arrive?'

'She and her servant are here already. They too are at The New Jerusalem.'

'My word. No room at the inn, eh? Someone else is staying there, a motor dealer called Mann. Hulking fellow; you wouldn't want to meet him in a dark alley, but he's agreeable enough. Lost his own wife a while back, so I took the liberty of inviting him to come along tonight.'

'Splendid. I look forward to seeing him, however ugly he

may be. Did you manage to persuade Daphne Sambrook's brother and father?'

'Yes, I've inveigled them into putting in an appearance. Young Denzil promised to bring the professor. Be prepared for snorts of derision.'

'Miss Curle is accustomed to dealing with those who lack faith.'

Huckerby sighed. 'Do you really think there is a chance she will be able to make contact with Gloria?'

'I must be honest,' Rachel said. 'I expect that what happens this evening will test you to the limit. Tomorrow, everything will look different in the cold light of day.'

'You certainly know how to handle a car, Hugh!' Dilys cried as the Wolseley swung round a sharp bend in the lane that snaked across the moor.

Trueman pulled up on the crest of a rise in the ground. The smell of bracken was everywhere. They were a few hundred yards away from the path skirting the deadly quagmire. The sanatorium was ahead of them. To their left, Blackstone Fell rose in the distance. He stared at its man-made rival. From here, the Tower looked forlorn, as if mourning the death of its owner.

'Cars are like women,' he said. 'You need to treat them with respect. Otherwise, they misbehave.'

'I bet your favourites have plenty of fire under their bonnets!'

'How did you guess?'

'This drive has been lovely,' she said. 'I'm so glad of a breath of air after everything that's happened in the village.'

'Hard to believe, isn't it? I was saying as much to the major last night.'

'The pair of you had a long chinwag, didn't you?'

'He strikes me as a decent chap.'

'Oh, he is. Such a shame about his wife.'

'What was she like?'

'A gentle soul, quietly spoken. Didn't think she was better than the rest of us just because she lived in Fell, not Foot. She thought the sun shone out of the major, they were a lovely couple. But there always seemed to be something wrong with her. A cough or a headache or a pain in the back.'

'She was a hypochondriac?'

'If that's what you call it. When Mrs Lejeune took ill, it affected her badly, even though they weren't close friends. She started getting symptoms, I don't know the details. She reckoned she was dying. Stopped listening to what her husband said.'

'Sad business.'

'Very. The major was terribly cut up when she died. I still like to think it was an accident. Mr Crawshaw tells me I'm a fool. He says that for all his faults, the rector knew a thing or two. Whatever the doctor said, she killed herself. And the major has never been the same since.'

'Poor devil.'

'He does his best to keep cheerful. I love to see him so often, but when it comes to the booze, he's his own worst enemy.'

'So are a lot of people,' Trueman said. 'I bet the doctor would say the same.'

She nodded. 'Dr Carrodus is very sympathetic. I've heard him more than once telling the major not to blame himself for what happened to Mrs Huckerby. Not that the major takes any notice. He just gets in another round of drinks.'

'Dr Sambrook was knocking them back last night. He wasn't in the best of moods.'

'He's getting to be as grumpy as poor Mr Lejeune.'

'Maybe his patients are giving him a rough time.'

She sniffed, but said nothing.

'What is it?' When she hesitated, he pointed to the wide-open countryside. 'You don't have to watch what you say with me, you know. Nobody is eavesdropping. And I'm no blabbermouth.'

'No,' she said slowly. 'I'm sure you're not. It's just that… I'm starting to think there's something funny going on at the sanatorium. It's not like it used to be.'

'How do you mean?'

'They've got rid of a lot of the staff. Go back a couple of years, and nurses would come in to The New Jerusalem for a drink after their shift. One or two of them lived in Blackstone Foot. But they've gone and the people who do work there are stand-offish. We never see them.'

'Denzil Sambrook still drinks at the inn.'

She shrugged. 'Apart from the doctor and the major, he hasn't got any other friends, as far as I know. And they aren't really close. Just people to booze with.'

'He seems to have fallen out with his father.'

'I wouldn't know about that. The professor has always kept himself to himself.'

'And he doesn't have much of a good word to say about his sister.'

'He finds her embarrassing. Just because she's rather plain and has that dreadful scar.'

'Really?'

'Oh yes. I've overheard him, talking about physical perfection. Anyone would think he's Conrad Nagel!'

'Has he always been like that?'

Dilys considered. 'It's got worse lately, but he's always had some funny ideas.'

'So I gather.'

'The other day, he asked me about Blackstone Tower. Whether I'd like to live there.'

'Really? What did you say?'

'I thought it was some kind of joke. I said Mr Lejeune would never want me there, and I certainly didn't fancy being under the same roof. Dr Sambrook just laughed.'

'Was he drunk?'

'He'd certainly had a few. He said buying the Lodge was just the start. Harold Lejeune would sell the Tower before long. He asked if I thought he'd make a good lord of the manor.'

'And did you?'

'I know better than to upset the regulars, Hugh. Doesn't matter if they are patting my backside or talking nonsense about Blackstone Tower. When he asked if I fancied working there, I just gave him a sweet smile and said I'd better get on with cleaning the glasses.'

'So he wanted to employ you?'

She shrugged. 'So he said. But I didn't understand what he had in mind, and he's never mentioned it since.'

In mid-afternoon, Trueman arrived at Hawthorn Cottage. Peggy Needham had returned to The New Jerusalem. The horrors of the past few days had left her with a bad head and she wanted to take a nap so as to be ready to take part in the séance.

'You came in the Wolseley?' Rachel asked.

He nodded. 'As instructed.'

'Good. Quite apart from collecting our friend from the station, this evening's entertainment won't finish until late. I don't want Peggy Needham tripping up on her way back to The New Jerusalem and breaking her neck. You'd better give her a lift. Now, what have you been getting up to?'

Trueman reported his conversations in the bar as well as his trip across the moors with Dilys.

'She's got a soft spot for you,' Martha said.

'She can have him,' Hetty said, without looking up from her knitting.

Rachel glanced at the clock. 'Time to go.'

Trueman jumped from his chair. 'See you later.'

'What about Denzil Sambrook?' Jacob turned to Rachel as the door closed behind the chauffeur. 'Why would he talk to her about Blackstone Tower?'

She stretched languidly in her armchair. 'We already knew that he is eager to add the Tower to the family trust's portfolio of properties.'

'If it was left to me, I'd raze it to the ground, along with that vile death trap, the Lodge. I can't imagine why he wants to buy such an eyesore, but Lejeune's death will make it easier for him to lay his hands on it.'

'Marginally, perhaps. But perhaps not. Probate lawyers are capable of snarling things up for years. In any case, even before he died, Lejeune was preparing to desert Blackstone Fell for warmer climes. Probably in the company of Judith

Royle. He was simply haggling over the price. I suspect they'd soon have reached a compromise, greedy as he was.'

'Greedy?'

'Yes,' Rachel said. 'His greed for money lies at the heart of this whole murky business.'

'So you think he was blackmailing...?' Jacob began, only to be interrupted by a knock at the door.

Martha showed Ottilie Curle and Abdul into the sitting room. The medium cast a sceptical eye over Daphne Sambrook's garish paintings. She and Rachel shook hands. Abdul bowed.

'Mr Flint has told me something about you, Miss Savernake,' the medium said. 'But I must say your motives seem as mysterious as anything in the spirit world.'

Rachel smiled. 'Thank you for humouring me.'

'Jacob Flint left us with little choice,' Ottilie Curle said wryly. 'What you propose is quite extraordinary.'

'Put it down to my taste for the theatrical,' Rachel said. 'Now, perhaps the two of you would like to join me next door, so that I can explain what I'm hoping to achieve? Jacob, perhaps you can entertain Martha while we await our next visitor.'

'Peggy Needham?' Jacob asked.

Rachel smiled. 'Not Peggy. One of our old acquaintances.'

'Checkmate,' Martha said, moving her bishop.

'Well done.' Jacob frowned at the board. 'I never realised you were such a good player.'

'Rachel taught me when we were on Gaunt. She needed an opponent and we spent hours together, learning the moves and the methods of the masters. I can give her a game, but mostly she wins. Once in a blue moon, though, she makes a mistake.'

'Just to show she's human?'

'She's human, all right.'

He leaned back in his chair. 'Tell me about Gaunt.'

'Our life on the island belongs to the past. We don't like to talk about it.'

'It's only natural for me to be curious.'

'Don't be,' Martha said. 'There are enough mysteries in the world to keep you and Rachel out of mischief. Or at least fully occupied. Have you worked out what's going on at Blackstone Sanatorium?'

'I hadn't realised that Denzil Sambrook is an advocate of eugenics.'

Martha made a disgusted noise. 'I hate that sort of thing. Those folk, they'd have no room in their utopias for the likes of me.'

He looked at her damaged face. So often these days he forgot about it. 'I'm sure that…'

A knock came at the door and Martha leaped to her feet. 'Here he is.'

'Who?'

He had his answer moments later. Inspector Philip Oakes from Scotland Yard put his head round the door.

'I don't understand,' Jacob said a couple of minutes later.

Oakes had no sooner taken off his hat and coat and said hello than Rachel had whisked him into the front room, giving Jacob no time for the questions he was desperate to ask.

Martha said, 'I wish I had a pound for every time I've heard you say that.'

'It makes no sense. This isn't Oakes's bailiwick. Scotland Yard hasn't been called in by the local chief constable.'

'Right on both counts.'

'Then what is he doing here?'

'He made some enquiries on Rachel's behalf in London. She asked him to drop everything and get up to Blackstone Fell.'

'He's a busy man. He won't...'

'She can be very persuasive. Nobody knows that better than you and me.'

'He can't butt in here without even consulting the local force.'

'I expect he's told them he's taking a short break to meet some friends in the south Pennines.'

'What about protocol?'

'Rachel doesn't give two hoots about protocol.'

He sighed. 'Suppose she presented him with enough evidence to arrest someone for something. Oakes plays by the rules. Wouldn't he still need to involve the local police?'

'Rachel has no confidence in them. She thinks Oakes is shrewd. What's more, he's taken a shine to her.'

He blinked. 'You think so?'

'It's as plain as the nose on your face, Jacob.' She smiled. 'No offence intended. The inspector is smitten, I promise you. But don't worry, Rachel can handle him. No need to be jealous.'

'I'm not jealous!' His cheeks felt hot. 'It's just that... it doesn't make sense. Oakes knows that if he arrested someone in connection with whatever is going on at the sanatorium, he'd be on a sticky wicket. Unless he means to bring in PC Fowler and Sergeant Margetson?'

'You're forgetting something,' she said.

'What?'

'Someone was murdered in London.'

He stared.

'At British Museum Station,' she said. 'Don't tell me you've forgotten poor Vernon Murray?'

28

'Welcome,' Major Huckerby said as he and Rachel came back into his drawing room. 'You all have drinks, I see? Excellent. My thanks again to Miss Savernake for inviting Britain's most gifted medium to Blackstone Fell and making this remarkable occasion possible.'

Trueman and Oakes led a murmur of appreciation. Rachel blushed prettily. She'd changed into an evening gown, a swirl of black velvet beneath a sequinned bodice with flowers of blue and pink and green. Her skin was pale and flawless. This evening she looked about nineteen, Jacob thought. A picture of innocence.

The major locked the door, saying, 'Don't want the servants barging in.'

The curtains were drawn, but the gas lamps glowed brightly and a log fire was blazing in an inglenook. Some of the furniture had been cleared away to make room for ten high-backed chairs. They were grouped together in a semicircle around a small table, on which stood a vase of fragrant gladioli and a candle in a silver stick. A grandfather clock with a rosewood case ticked away at the back of the room. Sporting prints and cartoons from *Punch* adorned the walls. A stuffed trout stared out from a glass case on the top of a chest of drawers. Stretched out on the parquet floor was a Persian rug of red and gold.

Their host fussed around like a mother hen, guiding everyone to their seats. There seemed to be a definite plan to the arrangements, but Jacob couldn't fathom what it was. Rachel had evidently given Huckerby detailed instructions. All the signs were that she had him eating out of her hand. If Jacob was sure of anything, it was that she hadn't taken the major fully into her confidence.

At the far end of the semicircle sat Professor Sambrook, exuding vague disapproval. He'd hardly said a word as introductions were performed, and his glazed expression resembled that of the stuffed trout. Was he thinking Great Thoughts, Jacob wondered, or simply gaga?

Rachel had described Jacob and Oakes as friends from London. Peggy and Trueman, the last to arrive, were introduced as guests at The New Jerusalem who longed to watch a famous medium at work. The small talk had been stilted, as if people were embarrassed to indulge in the frivolity of a séance after the horrors at the rectory.

The professor sat at the far end of the semicircle, resting his chin in an age-spotted palm. Beside him was Peggy; then came Denzil Sambrook. There was a vacant chair on either side of Jacob. Daphne Sambrook, Oakes, Dr Carrodus, and Trueman completed the audience.

Jacob's spine tingled. He had no idea what Rachel was up to. It amused her to keep him in the dark, to challenge him to keep up with her leaps of imagination.

He noticed the village doctor casting a sardonic glance first in his direction and then at Oakes. Carrodus probably assumed they were two of Rachel's admirers. In a sense, he was right.

Professor Sambrook's eyelids were drooping. Any minute now, he would fall asleep. What if he snored during the séance? Rachel had probably told Peggy to jab him in the ribs. The old governess was ramrod-straight in her chair, determined not to miss a moment. Her pallor and the bags under her eyes suggested she hadn't slept for a week. Exhausted, Jacob thought, and no wonder. Nell Fagan's death was a devastating blow, while the horrors of the gatehouse and the rectory were enough to knock the strongest woman sideways.

Denzil Sambrook lounged in his seat. He had the demeanour of a wise man condescending to the juvenile fancies of his intellectual inferiors, while wishing he was elsewhere.

His sister was taking closer interest. Her eyes darted from one face to another. In a low-cut red Chanel gown and matching lipstick, she'd made a considerable impression on Jacob. She'd already asked him how he came to know her new tenant, Miss Savernake. He repeated the lines Rachel had drummed into him, saying they'd bumped into each other at a party in London. Now he watched as she murmured something in Oakes's ear, and guessed she was putting the same question. The inspector smiled amiably as he palmed her off with another lie.

Carrodus and Trueman were exchanging pleasantries, perhaps picking up where they'd left off in the inn the night before. They fell silent as the major cleared his throat and took a step forward.

'In a moment,' he said, 'I shall turn down the lights and Miss Curle will make her entrance. She will be accompanied by Abdul, her servant. At that point, she will ask each of us to hold hands with the person or people at our side and continue to do so throughout the séance. She tells me that the physical connection we make with each other is crucial to the success of the evening. However strong the temptation to speak or cry out, please restrain yourselves. I must implore you to maintain complete silence until Miss Curle concludes the séance.'

The major paused and lowered his voice. 'Otherwise, you risk causing her terrible harm.'

He lit the candle and doused the gas lamps before taking his place between Jacob and Denzil Sambrook. At the same time Rachel sat down on Jacob's right. She caught his eye and gave him a faint smile.

Ottilie Curle and Abdul entered the room. Their attire was familiar to Jacob from that humiliating night in Kentish Town. Once again, the medium's bracelets were jangling.

'Good evening,' the medium said. 'Please, would you all hold hands?'

Huckerby took Jacob's left hand. On his other side, he was conscious of Rachel's small hand slipping into his. Her grip was even tighter than the major's.

'Thank you, ladies and gentlemen.'

Ottilie Curle paused. In the flickering light, Jacob detected a bead of sweat on her brow. What must be passing through her mind? For once she was performing a script written by someone else.

'Please understand that never before have I agreed to undertake a séance in the presence of so many people. Including, no doubt, certain individuals whose scepticism and, I dare say, prejudices about communication with the spirit world are deeply entrenched. What you make of this evening's séance is a matter for you. I ask simply this. Please remain silent and *do not move* while I am in a trance. Should you do so, the danger to my wellbeing will be profound.'

There was a short pause before she added in a hushed voice, 'My life, ladies and gentlemen, is in your hands.'

Jacob felt Rachel squeezing his fingers. Was she afraid he'd laugh out loud? She ought to have more faith in his self-control. He forced himself not to glance in her direction.

A slight movement made him conscious of Denzil Sambrook, shifting irritably in his chair. The professor's eyes were closed. His daughter seemed to be concentrating intently, but in the gloom Jacob detected a faint smile playing on the village doctor's lips. Major Huckerby leaned forward, taking in every word. Peggy Needham's face was a mask. Was she remembering her cousin's attempt to make contact with that dead young man, Nathan Hart?

This time there was no gramophone. Instead, Ottilie Curle began to hum the tune of 'Crossing the Bar'. She was naturally musical, Jacob thought. Her conduct of the séance made more sense now he knew she'd grown up on the stage. She had a flair for giving an audience what they wanted.

Except that this time, it was what Rachel Savernake wanted to give them.

The medium fell silent and closed her eyes. Jacob guessed that this time she'd proceed more quickly than she had in Kentish Town. The Sambrooks in particular would not show infinite patience.

So it proved. Within a couple of minutes, she summoned Sir Roderick.

'I am here,' the deep baritone voice replied.

Oakes let out a little gasp. Playing the naive visitor to perfection, Jacob reflected.

'We wish to talk to Gloria Huckerby,' the medium said.

There was a long pause.

'Someone else is calling,' the old man's voice said. 'Someone else who wants to be heard.'

Jacob cast a quick glance at Huckerby. The major stiffened in his chair. Was he disappointed? Wasn't this what he'd been led to expect?

Ottilie Curle said, 'Who wishes to be heard?'

'A woman.'

In the glow from the candle and the fire, Jacob saw Daphne Sambrook frowning. Surely the medium hadn't summoned the spirit of Judith Royle?

'What is her name?'

Another pause.

'Cornelia Fagan.'

Nell! What was going on? Jacob increased his pressure on Rachel's hand. She paid no attention. Her gaze was fixed on the small woman in front of them.

Jacob looked round and saw Huckerby shake his head. Denzil Sambrook let out a very audible sigh. The professor seemed to be asleep. Carrodus and Daphne Sambrook exchanged puzzled glances with each other. Trueman and Oakes didn't move a muscle.

'Cornelia Fagan,' the medium intoned. 'Do you wish to speak to us?'

Jacob's throat felt dry. Of course it was all a charade, yet there was something oddly compelling about this strange little woman as she threw her voice and acted a part.

'Yes, I most certainly do.'

It was uncanny. The woman might never have met Nell, but she'd captured her voice with remarkable precision. The husky tone, the faint slurring of the words.

'Why do you wish to speak?'

'I wanted to return to Blackstone Fell. I have unfinished business here.'

Jacob shivered. He couldn't help it.

'What do you mean?'

'Murder has been done.'

'Do you mean that someone murdered you?'

'Yes.'

A long pause. The light was flickering, but Jacob could see distress etched on Peggy Needham's face. She'd been devoted to Nell. Why was Rachel putting her through this ordeal?

'But I am not the only victim,' the disembodied voice said. 'There were others before me.'

'Other people have been murdered in Blackstone Fell?'

'Yes.'

The fire blazed as merrily as before, but Jacob felt a chill descending on the room. An exotic piece of theatre was now confronting harsh realities. Even the professor had opened his eyes. Denzil Sambrook no longer looked disdainful. The major was aghast.

'Who has been murdered?' Ottilie Curle demanded.

There was another silence. Jacob felt Rachel's hand clasped in his, as if they were lovers. His heart beat faster.

'The first victim,' Nell Fagan's voice said, 'was Gloria Huckerby.'

29

In the darkened drawing room, the only sound came from the ticking clock. Nobody moved or uttered a word. Jacob had forgotten about Gloria Huckerby's death. Suicide, wasn't it? Or perhaps an accident. Nobody had talked about murder.

The major seemed to be paralysed. Jacob tightened his grip on the man's hand. To judge by his features, Huckerby was horror-stricken. But was he genuinely surprised? Or did his expression reflect guilty knowledge; was he simply shocked because he'd killed his wife and now the truth was out?

Rachel had prepared the major to expect startling revelations, but this surely wasn't it. In a few moments, he'd aged ten years. Jacob was conscious of Rachel keeping firm hold of his right hand. On her pale face, he saw no hint of emotion. It was as if she too were in a trance.

'Gloria Huckerby,' Ottilie Curle repeated. 'But she wasn't the last to be murdered, was she?'

'No,' Nell Fagan's voice said.

'Who else was killed?'

'Clodagh Hamill.'

A pause. Jacob held his breath.

'And?'

'Joshua Flood.'

'And?'

'Violet Beagrie.'

Another pause. There was something deeply menacing about the small, veiled figure. Jacob couldn't take his eyes off her.

'Was there anyone else?'

'Ursula Baker.'

'Is that all?'

'Vernon Murray.'

The major made a low, inarticulate noise. He couldn't believe his ears, Jacob thought, but did Huckerby's astonishment spring from what he'd heard or because his sins had found him out?

Ottilie Curle stood motionless in front of them. Jacob felt a spurt of admiration for the power of the woman's personality. Her ability to command an audience enabled her to pour out this extraordinary sequence of claims in the course of a supposed trance, and still have people hanging on her every word, rather than leaping to their feet in bewilderment and rage. She wasn't so much a medium as a mesmerist.

It couldn't last, but for the moment her audience was stunned and still. The professor kept blinking, as if unsure whether he was awake or dreaming. Peggy Needham was transfixed by the sound of Nell's voice, so cleverly captured by ventriloquism. Denzil Sambrook and Carrodus seemed to share the major's disbelief. Daphne remained as impassive as Oakes, Trueman, and Rachel Savernake.

'Why were they killed?' Ottilie Curle asked.

'They got in someone's way.'

Nell's booming tone filled the room. She would have loved this, Jacob thought. Building the suspense, holding a rapt audience in the palm of her hand.

'Whose way?'

'Patrick Hamill wanted rid of his wife in order to marry his secretary.'

'Joshua Flood?'

'Alan Walker wanted a share of the old man's wealth.'

Ottilie Curle paused. A touch of showmanship, no doubt, but there was an intense look of concentration on her face. Making sure she's remembered the names in the right order, Jacob supposed. She had plenty of experience at memorising a script, but she hadn't had much time to rehearse today.

'What about Violet Beagrie?'

'Money again. Eric Livingstone stood to inherit a fortune if the girl died in time.'

'And Ursula Baker?'

'Her husband Thomas only married her in order to become her heir. The mistake he made was to antagonise her son. Vernon Murray discovered what had happened. So he had to die as well.'

Denzil Sambrook cleared his throat. 'Look here. This farrago has gone far enough. Too far, frankly.'

'Be quiet,' Peggy Needham hissed.

Others stirred in their seats. Major Huckerby, Daphne Sambrook, the village doctor. The professor was frowning.

'Show some respect,' Peggy said.

'Respect?' Denzil laughed, a noise that tore through the solemn atmosphere like a firecracker at a funeral. 'This whole pantomime is utter tosh. I recognise some of those names. They were patients at the sanatorium. And their relatives.'

The major was on the edge of his seat. 'Leave it, Sambrook,' the older man muttered. 'You'll get a chance to speak when the séance is at an end.'

'It needs to end right now!' Denzil's voice rose. 'This is an outrage. I don't have the faintest idea what kind of hocus-pocus is going on, but I cannot tolerate a slur being cast on my professional reputation.'

Abdul took two long strides, so that he stood right in front of Denzil, just as the scientist was getting off his chair. The servant's fists were balled. Jacob swallowed hard. It was play-acting, but Denzil wasn't to know that. The man looked as if he was about to seize Denzil by his scrawny throat and give him the beating of his life.

'Quiet!' Peggy whispered.

Denzil subsided back into his chair, like a deflated sausage balloon. He folded his arms and glared at the medium. Her eyes were still shut tight.

Abdul lifted a meaty finger to his lips before taking a step back.

'Are you still there?' Ottilie Curle cried. 'Will you speak again?'

'I am here,' Nell's voice replied.

'Walker and the others each wanted someone dead,' Ottilie said. 'What brought them here? How did they learn of Blackstone Fell?'

'They all have something in common.'

'Can you tell me what it is?'

A lengthy pause.

'The Hermes.'

★★★

The Hermes.

A bell rang in Jacob's mind. As he racked his brains, he was vaguely aware of people shifting in their chairs. Hadn't Nell herself mentioned the name, when describing how Vernon Murray accosted Baker, by Leicester Square?

'The Hermes,' Ottilie Curle repeated. 'Where is it?'

'In London.'

'And what is it?'

'A club which takes its name from the god of gambling.' Nell chuckled. 'A poor man's Crockford's. As well as the casino, they have a restaurant where the members can dine. Walker was their chef.'

'And Hamill?'

'He was a member. So were Livingstone and Baker.'

'Anyone else?'

The room was hushed. To Jacob, the tick of the grandfather clock sounded deafening.

'Yes.'

'Who was it?'

A pause.

'Dr Carrodus.'

Daphne Sambrook let out a cry of dismay. Everyone was looking at the doctor. He threw back his head and burst into incredulous laughter.

Rachel released Jacob's hand and sprang to her feet. 'Major, would you turn on the lights?'

Huckerby, in a daze, did as he was told. Ottilie Curle

opened her eyes. The professor was shaking his head, as if he'd just been assured that the moon was made of green cheese. Carrodus couldn't stop laughing.

'Are you all right, Doctor?' Daphne Sambrook demanded.

'Oh,' he said, wiping his eyes. 'It's too absurd. I simply can't credit...'

Denzil Sambrook snapped, 'Is there any truth in this twaddle, Carrodus?'

'Utter balderdash, old fellow.' The doctor pushed a hand through his hair. He was breathing hard, but making a visible effort to remain as amiable as ever. 'Please accept my congratulations, Miss Savernake. You put on quite a show for us. I've not seen anything like it since I last went to the music hall.'

'I don't understand,' Major Huckerby said.

'You're not the only one,' Denzil Sambrook said. 'This is an absolute disgrace. We've been lured here under false pretences.'

'For once,' his sister said, 'I have to agree. Miss Savernake, I can't imagine what you thought to achieve by persuading a so-called spiritualist to spout a load of slanderous piffle.'

'Never mind that,' the major snapped. 'What I want to know is this. My late wife's name came up first, remember? She wasn't a patient in Blackstone Sanatorium. On the contrary. How can anyone possibly suggest she was murdered? It doesn't make sense.'

Rachel looked him in the eye. 'I regret to say that it does. Her death was the catalyst for everything else that has happened in Blackstone Fell.'

'How do you mean? Who can possibly have murdered her? You're not suggesting I fed her those sleeping pills?'

'Certainly not,' Rachel said. 'When I say she was murdered,

I am bound to accept that the crime could never be proved in a court of law. For what that's worth.'

'What, then?'

'She became a guinea pig in an experiment.'

Colour rose in the major's cheeks. 'Don't talk in riddles, woman!'

Rachel lowered her voice.

'Your wife was well looked after in her final weeks. Dr Carrodus was extremely attentive. He supplied her with drugs to make her comfortable.'

'She wasn't seriously ill!' the major said.

'Exactly. The fear that she would suffer the same protracted and painful death as Chiara Lejeune haunted her. In her mind, mild symptoms became exaggerated. Her anxieties were nurtured like tender plants. She was encouraged to fear the worst.'

'I begged her to see sense!' the major exclaimed.

'Of course you did.' Rachel turned to face Carrodus. 'But she trusted her doctor more. He was sympathetic and did everything he could to give her the impression that he was hiding the truth from her. To persuade her that her dread was justified, simply by saying the opposite in a highly unconvincing tone.'

'I say!' Carrodus said.

'This is utterly ridiculous,' Denzil Sambrook said.

'Really?' Rachel demanded. 'The doctor is renowned for his bedside manner. His medical skills are modest, but he has the knack of winning his patients' trust, of persuading them that he's on their side. Even when he isn't. When all he wants is the pleasure of watching them suffer. Enjoying the power of life and death.'

'That's enough!' Carrodus rose to his feet. 'I'm not staying here to be slandered. Goodnight, everyone.'

'Sit down,' Rachel said.

Carrodus was nonplussed. 'Who on earth do you think you are? You can't order me about.'

'You heard Miss Savernake,' Trueman said. 'Do as you're told.'

He sprang up, and at the same moment, Abdul interposed himself between the row of chairs and the door.

'What are you doing?' Carrodus demanded.

'You are not going anywhere,' Rachel said. 'You will hear me out.'

'This is an absolute disgrace. You'll be hearing from my solicitor. And if you don't get out of my way, I'll call the police.'

'No need.' Oakes fished a warrant card out of his pocket. 'I am a detective inspector at Scotland Yard.'

'What? Is this some kind of depraved joke? A game?'

'I wish it was,' Oakes said. 'Your name is on the death certificates of the patients who were mentioned just now, those who died at Blackstone Sanatorium.'

'Of course. I'm the attending physician at the sanatorium. They died of natural causes.'

'I don't believe that to be true. Exhumation orders will be applied for, naturally, so we can see if you killed them with morphine or by some other means.'

Carrodus stared at him. 'Killed them? Why should I kill them?'

'Because you were paid large sums of money to do so,' Oakes said. 'The Hermes is where, on your regular trips to London, you encountered fellow gamblers. Men who wanted to rid themselves of people they saw as nothing more than a neurotic nuisance.'

'Tommyrot!'

'You were able to offer the perfect solution. Pack them off to Blackstone Sanatorium and all your troubles will be solved. For a pretty price. After all, Lagondas don't come cheap.'

Denzil Sambrook shouted, 'Carrodus! Is there anything in this? For God's sake, tell me it's a wicked lie.'

At his side, the professor was shaking. The old man seemed incoherent and distressed. His daughter got to her feet. Her voice was steady, her manner intense yet controlled.

'I don't believe a word of it. As everyone is aware, Dr Carrodus and I have never seen eye to eye, but the suggestion that he is guilty of murder is arrant nonsense. Anyone would think he is some kind of monster. He's no more capable of killing a patient than I am.'

She addressed Rachel. 'As for you, young lady, I bitterly regret that you ever set foot in Blackstone Fell. Who you are and what your motives may be, I can't begin to imagine. I must ask you to pack your bags and go back to wherever you belong first thing tomorrow. Sorting out the mess you've created will be a nightmare, and we don't want any further interference or sensation seeking. A séance! This has been a wretched charade. Even if it was meant to entertain in some perverse way, it's heartless and cruel.'

Rachel considered her coolly, but said nothing.

'Thank you, Daphne,' Carrodus said quietly. 'I'm much obliged.'

Turning to Oakes, Daphne said, 'I can't believe you're a detective. Your card must be bogus. Why on earth would you come here? This is Yorkshire, not London.'

'I happen to be investigating a murder committed in London,' Oakes said calmly.

He turned to the doctor. 'Lawrence Carrodus, I am arresting you on suspicion of the murder of Vernon Murray at British Museum Station on Friday last. You do not have to say anything, but—'

30

Carrodus didn't wait for Oakes to finish. He swung his fist and connected with the detective's jaw, knocking him off balance. He put his hand inside his jacket, but Trueman was too quick for him. The big man seized his arm and with no apparent effort twisted it sideways. The doctor screamed in agony and fell to his knees. A small Colt revolver fell from his grasp onto the rug.

As Trueman held him down, Abdul picked up the gun. Oakes struggled back to his feet, and Abdul tossed it to him. The detective caught the Colt one-handed, with as much nonchalance as if fielding at first slip in a village cricket match.

'You're wasting your time,' Trueman hissed in the doctor's ear. 'The major locked the door, remember? Even if you got out, it'd do you no good. Last thing I did before I came in was to let down the tyres of your Lagonda.'

The doctor swore at him. His face was crimson with pain and fury.

'I don't believe it,' Denzil Sambrook looked aghast. 'I simply don't believe he is capable of such crimes.'

'Is that a professional diagnosis?' Rachel asked sardonically. 'You know that he likes to play games of chance. Murder gave him the ultimate thrill.'

Major Huckerby moved forward. 'Is it true, Carrodus? Did you frighten Gloria to death?'

'She was weak,' the doctor panted. 'She died by her own hand. Everyone knows that. She was a suicide. A coward.'

Huckerby lifted his arm, as if about to strike Carrodus, but Oakes took hold of his wrist.

'Leave it, Major,' he said. 'We will deal with him. The local officers will be here soon. I arranged for them to wait with the man they have stationed on guard at the rectory.'

'He drove my wife to... no, I can't bear to think of it!'

The major stumbled back to his chair and put his head in his hands. Peggy Needham leaned across and clapped him on the shoulder.

'Bear up, Major. At least justice will be done.'

Carrodus's breath began to come in jerky gasps.

'There's something wrong with him,' Daphne Sambrook said.

Trueman eased his grip. 'He'll live.'

'His breathing doesn't sound right,' she insisted, picking up her handbag. 'Let me take a look. It's hard for him to take in air. He may need treatment, medication. You don't want to have a dead man on your hands. Not after all this.'

She crouched down over the doctor's bent figure. Rachel sprang forward and knocked something from her hand. It spun away out of Daphne's reach. Jacob caught his breath as he realised it was a hypodermic syringe.

Daphne looked up into Rachel's eyes. 'You fool! I was only trying to help.'

'I doubt it,' Rachel said. 'Did you decide the time was ripe for desperate remedies?'

'What are you talking about?' Daphne's cheeks were red with temper.

'There's a popular theory that injecting an air bubble into a vein causes death by undetectable means, but you'd never do it with such a small syringe. Surely a member of such a distinguished family of scientists should conduct her research with greater care?'

'Disgraceful! You suggest that I'd kill the doctor! Even if he has done all those terrible things, I wouldn't stoop so low…'

'Save it for the jury,' Rachel snapped.

'What do you mean? The doctor and I may not be friends, but I'd never dream of causing him physical harm.'

'I beg to differ,' Rachel said. 'You can see him falling apart, and you don't want him to incriminate you.'

Denzil Sambrook stepped forward. 'For goodness sake, woman, have you taken leave of your senses? This is my sister you're talking about, not some Johnny-come-lately village sawbones.'

'The sister you spent a lifetime patronising,' Rachel said. 'For all her vices, I'd say she's worth ten of you. At least she has guts and character. A pity she made such rotten use of them. Her biggest mistake was to fall in love with a man who developed a passion for killing.'

'Fall in love!' Daphne exclaimed. 'With Dr Carrodus? Now I know you are raving. I thought your interest in folklore was absurd, but this is insane.'

The doctor groaned as Trueman tightened his grip on his shoulders. Abdul and Oakes were watching to see if Carrodus made any further attempt to get away.

'Is it really so ridiculous?' Rachel asked. 'You first met the doctor in London. He's a good-looking man and you were instantly attracted.'

'Pure invention!'

'You were the woman he'd been looking for all his life. Intelligent, with a strong personality fashioned by the experience of being patronised by your own family. An ugly duckling, put in the shade by your brother's academic attainments. A sad disappointment to the father whose careless driving killed the mother you adored.'

The professor murmured something. He was quite incoherent, Jacob thought. This was why so little was seen of him. His mind must have been failing for years, the intervals of lucidity becoming shorter and less frequent.

'You're making a vile accusation, Miss Savernake.' Daphne put her hands on her hips. 'As if the doctor would pay me the slightest notice.'

'I don't wish to give Dr Carrodus any credit,' Rachel said. 'He is a callous murderer who has forfeited any claim to mercy, but at least he had the sense not to be deceived by superficial impressions. He saw a truly formidable woman. The two of you became inseparable.'

'Inseparable? From a man I detested?'

'Your supposed mutual antipathy was a crude blind. It never rang true. Why dislike such a popular fellow for no apparent reason? No, he was someone you could bend to your will. The perfect foil.'

'Are you seriously accusing me of complicity in this wild story you've put before us?'

'You were the driving force,' Rachel said. 'I imagine that was so from the moment the pair of you met. When you came across each other at the Hermes.'

'The Hermes?' Denzil Sambrook raised his voice. 'This gambling den you spoke about? Now I know you're mistaken, Miss Savernake. Daphne is too strait-laced.'

'How little you know of your sister,' Rachel said. 'Scotland Yard have confirmed her membership. I expect she found it exciting to mix with a different class of people. Perhaps she's always led a secret life. Some people do.'

She threw a fleeting glance at Trueman, but he remained poker-faced. Jacob thought it was almost as if the two of them were sharing a private joke.

Rachel turned to Daphne. 'You encouraged the doctor to leave London and join you at Blackstone Fell. I suppose you engineered his first meeting with your brother. At a lecture given by Havelock Ellis, wasn't it? Prating on about eugenics, presumably?'

Denzil said, 'You can't be serious. Carrodus was genuinely interested.'

'It's not difficult to hoodwink an obsessive,' Rachel said brusquely. 'His first patient was Chiara Lejeune. Soon it became obvious that she was dying. I imagine he was thrilled by the power he was able to exercise. Regulating her doses of medicine, adjusting the precise level of misery or relief that his patient experienced.'

'Repulsive fantasy!' Daphne Sambrook spat out the words, but the fight was seeping out of her, Jacob thought, like the air from the Lagonda's deflated tyres. Rachel had too many answers.

'Repulsive, yes. Fantasy, no. Everyone praised the doctor's bedside manner. He had the gift of winning people's trust. Manipulating their perceptions. He shepherded Gloria Huckerby into an early grave. The taste of power was sweet, but not enough. He had extravagant tastes, and gamblers need money. Your connection with the sanatorium offered the perfect opportunity. You both knew Alan Walker, and once he told you about his potential inheritance, he became your first client. The sanatorium is on its uppers...'

'That's not true!' Denzil Sambrook said.

'Time to stop pretending.' Rachel nodded towards the professor, who was whimpering quietly as Peggy held his hand for comfort. 'Your father is not the man he was. I needn't labour the point. You are more concerned with pursuing your own fantasies. Your sister decided which patients were admitted, and she made sure the bulk of the fees were paid directly to her and her lover.'

Denzil glared. Without looking directly at his sister, he muttered, 'Daphne, tell her that isn't true.'

'None of it is true,' Daphne said. 'I'm being put through hell. Humiliated in public, with a tissue of lies.'

Rachel ignored her. 'The doctor recruited victims from people he cultivated at the Hermes. He eased their passing in return for eye-watering sums of cash. It all made for efficient business. There was one setback, when Vernon Murray got wind that something wasn't right. He didn't understand what you were up to, but he made so much fuss that he had to be silenced. Luckily the doctor has a very fast car. He raced down to London and after one failed attempt, managed to eliminate Murray. Unfortunately for him, the damage was done. Murray had spoken to Nell Fagan, and she involved me.'

Carrodus, still on the floor, groaned again.

'Otherwise, all went well. A fraction of the money went through the books, to be funnelled into the family trust and keep Denzil occupied with his daydreams about eugenics.'

'Daydreams!' Denzil shouted. 'How dare you? I'll have you know…'

'What, exactly? You have a vision of Blackstone Fell as your own private fiefdom, don't you? Where the elect, presided over by your good self, are served by minions such as Dilys from the inn and fellow believers you've brought in from the Continent. Meanwhile the sanatorium will become a place for study and experiment at the expense of the worthless folk shoved there by relatives who never want to set eyes on them again.'

'You simply don't have any conception of what I have in mind. It's a new world…'

'I told your sister to save her excuses for the courtroom. Put your theories in a book and see how many it sells. There may be a few takers. Others who believe they count for more than the people who don't share their prejudices.' Rachel turned back to Daphne. 'Not that you care for your brother's political nonsense, do you? You don't want to create a better world. Just one tailored to your pleasure.'

'There was never likely to be room for me in Denzil's

rural utopia,' she said. 'I'm not a shining example of good creation.'

'Rubbish,' Denzil said impatiently. 'Blood is thicker than water.'

Daphne made a derisive noise.

'You and the doctor didn't mean to stay here much longer,' Rachel said. 'London has more to offer than Blackstone Fell. Casinos, for a start. You'd made a small fortune and you were ready to spend it.'

'You think you know everything, don't you?'

'I wonder how your brother and father fitted into your plans. Presumably they didn't. Were they going to be your next victims?'

'Daphne!' her brother cried. 'It can't be true!'

For answer, Daphne Sambrook leaped at Rachel and tried to rake her fingernails down the pale porcelain cheeks. Rachel was ready for her. With a swerve of her body and a shove with her right hand, she sent Daphne tumbling to the floor.

Daphne lay silent for a moment before scrambling back to her feet. She dusted herself down and fumbled for her handbag. Rachel stepped in between her and Oakes.

'It would have paid them back, wouldn't it, for all the times they condescended to you, and treated you as a nobody? Not to mention that car crash which killed your mother and scarred you for life? How satisfying to have the last laugh.'

With a swift movement, Daphne reached into her handbag. Jacob gasped, expecting her to pull out a gun, but instead she found something tiny that she stuffed into her mouth. He watched as she gulped it down.

'Stop that!' Oakes shouted, trying to push past Rachel and seize hold of Daphne.

'Let her be,' Rachel said.

'Too late,' Daphne said. 'You were right about the last laugh.'

31

'I came to say goodbye,' Rachel said the next morning.

She'd waited outside The New Jerusalem until Peggy Needham emerged, clad in a thick coat and woollen scarf and carrying her alpenstock. Her appearance was haggard, her movements stiff, her grey skin hardly distinguishable from the colour of her hair or the clumps of mist drifting in from the moor.

'I must congratulate you on bringing those foul creatures to justice,' Peggy said. 'Nell told me she'd never met anyone like you. Now I believe it.'

'Justice takes many forms.'

'You deliberately obstructed the policeman. He might have saved Daphne Sambrook's life, prevented her from taking poison.'

'Carrodus is alive. More or less. That is enough for the police to secure the information they need to bring charges against his clients. Thomas Baker and the rest of them.'

'So all's well that ends well?'

Rachel looked at her. 'You are returning to London now?'

'There's no rush.' Peggy stared across the street. 'When I

finally got back last night, there was a telegram waiting for me. Eunice died yesterday afternoon.'

'I'm sorry. It's hard for you. Losing two people you were so close to, within such a short space of time.'

'Eunice's death was inevitable. Nell was the one with plenty to live for.'

'She died doing something that mattered to her.'

Peggy shot her a sharp glance. 'Yes.'

'And you?' Rachel asked. 'You don't look well.'

A faint smile touched the pale, dry lips. 'Your honesty is refreshing. As usual, you are right. I have a tumour on my brain.'

Rachel nodded. 'I thought it might be something like that.'

'You did?'

'You were unavailable to see Nell the day she returned from Blackstone Fell because of a medical check-up. She was desperate to see you, but she waited until the next day, which struck me as out of character. She wasn't a patient woman.'

'No.'

'That check-up must have been significant. You claimed you were fine, but you haven't looked well since I met you.'

'You are very perceptive, Miss Savernake.'

Rachel said nothing.

'I thought I'd go for a stroll. Clear my head.'

'You won't wait for the fog to lift?' Rachel asked.

'The murk is like the fuzziness in my brain.'

'May I walk with you?'

'Of course.'

They headed down the alley opposite the inn and within a couple of minutes they were out of the lower village and in the open countryside, with the mist swirling in from Blackstone Moor. Even as they approached the crossroads, the sanatorium was barely visible.

'What does the future hold for the Sambrooks?' Peggy asked.

'The professor is a sick man. He should be his son's first priority.'

'And the sanatorium?'

'Doomed. Like Denzil Sambrook's dream of becoming lord and master of Blackstone Fell.'

Peggy shook her head. 'He wanted to transform an English village into his own personal laboratory, somewhere he could test his theories to destruction.'

'That's the trouble with lofty intellectuals. So often they turn out to be extremely stupid.'

'You are an intelligent woman. And if I may say so, beautiful. Why devote yourself to a sordid business like murder?'

Rachel shrugged. 'To say I devote myself to seeing justice done sounds too pretentious.'

Peggy gave her a keen look. 'What does justice look like?'

'A good question.'

They walked on in silence, the cold air nipping their cheeks. Rachel slowed her natural pace. Peggy was moving slowly, as if carrying a heavy load on her back. Only doggedness propelled her forward.

'The medium may be a fraud, but the way she caught Nell's tone of voice was uncanny,' Peggy said. 'I wondered if anything would be said last night about the part Harold Lejeune played in this business.'

'It wasn't necessary.'

'You think he blackmailed Carrodus?'

'No,' Rachel said. 'He didn't see anyone following Nell on her way to the cave.'

'The whole story was a fabrication?'

'Yes.'

Peggy hesitated. 'What makes you say that?'

'I believe he murdered Nell.'

Neither of them spoke until they reached the crossroads. Out on the moor, the mist was thickening.

'Which way would you like to go?' Rachel asked.

Peggy pointed to the path that Trueman had taken two days before. As they moved forward, she said, 'What possible reason would Harold Lejeune have for killing Nell?'

'She was suspicious of him.'

'Why? You can't possibly believe he was complicit in Carrodus's activities? The doctor attended to his late wife and her death was a catalyst for all the later killings. I thought Lejeune was left distraught? At least until he found some consolation with Judith Royle?'

'I'm certain that he knew nothing about what the doctor and his mistress were getting up to at the sanatorium. As everyone said, he kept himself to himself.'

'What, then? As far as we know, Nell never even spoke to him.'

'That may well be true.'

Peggy halted. 'You're teasing me.'

Rachel gave a faint smile. 'I'm sorry. It's a bad habit of mine, as Jacob Flint knows. I realise the seriousness of what I'm saying.'

'Go on.'

'I think Nell recognised him.'

'She never mentioned having met the man before.'

'Not directly.'

Peggy lapsed into silence. They walked on for two or three minutes before Rachel said, 'You can probably guess what I'm going to say.'

'Try me.'

'Nell took a photograph of him on Fell Lane. I'm sure she couldn't believe her eyes when she realised who she'd seen. But the photograph supplied the proof that she wasn't dreaming.'

'Who was it?'

'The man who called himself Harold Lejeune was really the disgraced financier, Ormond Weaver.'

Peggy stopped in her tracks. 'Ormond Weaver? The crook who set up Weaver's Bank and ruined poor Nathan's life?'

'Yes.'

'Impossible. He died before the war, in Austria-Hungary. As for Harold Lejeune, he was no banker. His hobby was hunting rare plants. We know he was the last of a long line of Lejeunes at Blackstone Fell, going back to the man who built that beastly death trap in the gatehouse.'

'Can we be sure about all that?' Rachel shook her head. 'There are established facts, yes, but we've been asked to take too much on trust. What we know is that Weaver fled to the Continent and was last heard of in a town called Botzen.'

'Yes.'

'The major mentioned that Lejeune talked about going back to the town his wife Chiara came from.'

'In Italy.'

'Yes, a town by the name of Bolzano.'

There was a pause.

'You see,' Rachel continued, 'Botzen became Bolzano after the war. It changed hands following the collapse of Austria-Hungary and became part of Italy.'

'What exactly are you suggesting?'

'Harold Lejeune went plant-hunting in the Dolomites, not long before hostilities broke out. Botzen, as it then was, is a cosmopolitan town, a gateway to the Dolomites. About that time, Weaver fled there. We know that Chiara ran a small guest house. That's where she and Weaver met. No doubt Harold Lejeune stayed there.'

Peggy looked her in the eye. 'You're saying that Harold Lejeune died of diphtheria, not Weaver?'

'Yes. It doesn't require much imagination to paint in the blanks. Weaver was a renowned charmer. Chiara fell for him, but he was on the run. Then Lejeune turned up and took a room. Perhaps he talked about his background to a fellow countryman. Conveniently, he fell ill and died. It wouldn't be difficult for an experienced fraudster to steal Lejeune's papers, and pass off the corpse as his own. They were about the same age and build, and the authorities probably regarded one Englishman as very much like another.'

Peggy snorted. 'Hard to swallow.'

'I disagree. For all we know, Lejeune mentioned to Weaver that his brother Alfred had just inherited a dilapidated tower in a remote Yorkshire village and that the pair of them were all that remained of their family. At first it wouldn't have seemed important. All Weaver wanted was to escape the British justice system. By faking his death, he accomplished his aim.'

'Why take such a risk?'

'It wasn't much of a risk. I don't know when the news of Alfred's disappearance from the gatehouse reached him, but it's immaterial. Perhaps he supposed his brother had also done a bunk for some reason, and might turn up later. Seven years must elapse before a missing person can be presumed dead. And within a short space of time, war broke out. The couple had to stay put in the South Tyrol.'

'If what you say is true,' Peggy said, 'why did they return to Britain?'

'Who knows? The fascists were tightening their grip on Italy. It was becoming a less comfortable place to live. Perhaps the inn ran into difficulties, perhaps Weaver was homesick. He may have thought that, if he could claim ownership of Blackstone Tower and then sell it, he'd make enough money to fund a lavish retirement elsewhere. Of course, once he saw the place for himself, he realised that it wasn't exactly Chatsworth or Blenheim.'

'To come back to this country would be a huge gamble,' Peggy objected.

'Ormond Weaver was as much a risk-taker as Dr Carrodus. Time had passed. There had been a world war. Weaver's Bank, the scandal and the trial, they were all forgotten.'

'Not by those who were ruined by Ormond Weaver.'

'Blackstone Fell is out of the way. Weaver's wasn't a large bank with branches in every town. I doubt if anyone living within twenty miles of here ever banked with them. The new occupants of Blackstone Tower were reclusive and spent much of their time travelling overseas. It's significant that the supposedly passionate plant hunter never bothered with the garden. A bad mistake, but he got away with it for long enough. He must have thought he was safe. But then his wife died, a shattering blow.'

Peggy stared into the mist. 'I can't find it in my heart to grieve for the woman. She knew he was a scoundrel, a man who profited from the misery of so many of his victims.'

'Like Carrodus and Daphne Sambrook?' Rachel sighed. 'After Chiara's death, I imagine Judith Royle set her cap at him. Crooked as he was, he didn't lack charm, when he wished to exercise it. That's how he deceived Nathan Hart and everyone else. I doubt he ever lost the knack. Judith was a good-looking young woman, desperate to escape the rector's tyranny. They began a dangerous liaison.'

'Did Quintus Royle find out? Is that why he killed Weaver?'

'One step at a time.' Rachel gestured towards the marsh. 'Let's not sink into a quagmire of supposition. Nell had seen Weaver on trial at the Old Bailey. She liked to boast that she never forgot a face. Perhaps she recognised him at once. Failing that, she would at least realise that his face was very familiar. It would nag at her. They didn't speak to each other, but I'm sure she had the presence of mind to take his photograph. Unfortunately, Weaver had a first-class memory too. She told me he'd stared at her from the dock.'

Peggy shook her head. 'It was a long time ago. Seventeen years! I can't believe he could possibly remember her.'

'Why not? He worked closely with Nathan Hart. He would know something about Nathan's family. I expect he was well aware of the connection with Nell, and that she had a job in Fleet Street. Sitting in the gallery of the court, Nell wouldn't have concealed her loathing. If anything sticks in the mind, I imagine it's the experience of being on trial, when so much is at stake. He'd know who she was, and why she detested him. I don't suppose he was ever troubled by conscience. More likely, the fact that someone knew him for what he really was made him furious.'

'What you're suggesting is extraordinary.'

'So much in life is.'

'Do you think he pushed the boulder from the top of Blackstone Fell?'

'Yes. I think he sensed that she'd recognised him that morning. That afternoon, he spotted her heading for the Fell, and decided to seize the moment. He climbed to the summit by the other track, and tried to kill her.'

Peggy shook her head. 'If you're right, the story he told me was a pack of lies.'

Rachel looked at her, but said nothing. For a little while, they walked on along the path.

'I suppose Lejeune or Weaver or whatever we call the man told Judith Royle that Nell was onto him. Hence Judith's crude attempt to drive Nell away from the village.'

'Agreed. He may have been on his way to see her at the time Nell spotted him. My guess is that they used to meet at the cave.'

'Really?'

'Where better? The rector's wife could hardly allow herself to be seen trooping down the drive to Blackstone Tower at regular intervals. Far less coming back with a smile on her face and a spring in her step. At least the cave offered a little privacy.'

'What about the anonymous note Judith showed to Nell?'

'A piece of crude improvisation. As we know, Nell saw straight through it. I am sure it was Judith's idea rather than her lover's. She made her own paper, and I imagine she communicated with him through notes made up of letters and words cut from the *Daily Mail*. A simple subterfuge, but all part of the excitement.'

'Weaver must have known he'd never be safe. Not while Nell remained alive.'

'Correct. She returned to London before he could work out a plan, but she made it clear to Judith that she was coming back. When she did, he found a way to lure her out to the cave. My theory is that he used one of the unsigned notes Judith had sent him. She was a highly strung woman, I'm sure he had a stock of useful material. Nell knew the risks, but she fell into the trap. The prospect of Judith spilling the beans was impossible to resist. Weaver saw her leave the gatehouse from his vantage point in the Tower, and although he took the longer route to the cave, she was limping, and he was able to beat her to it. And then he beat her to death and faked a rock fall.'

Peggy exhaled. 'Pure evil.'

'He no longer owned the gatehouse, so he broke in and looked for her camera and any incriminating photographs. For all I know, he destroyed them. I expect he congratulated himself on committing the perfect murder. Not that it did him any good.'

'No.' Peggy sighed. 'Is it possible that his death was a sheer accident?'

'Too convenient an explanation. He was a risk-taker, but I doubt he was given to jumping over Blackstone Leap.'

'Murder, then?'

'It will never be proved, but yes.'

'So Quintus Royle did discover that his wife had betrayed

him and wanted to leave. For such a proud man, the humiliation would be unbearable. I suppose he accosted Weaver and knocked him into the water?'

'No. The lovers guarded their secret well. At least until Judith gave the game away by becoming hysterical when she heard that Weaver was dead.'

Peggy stopped and put her hands on her hips. 'Well, then? What do you think happened?'

'Do you really want to know?'

'Of course.'

Rachel sighed. 'If you insist.'

'Why wouldn't I?'

'Because you murdered Ormond Weaver.'

32

Peggy was silent for a full minute, gazing into the gloom. The fog was all around them. It lay over the moor like a shroud, blanketing out sound. The air was cold and moist. Rachel felt the damp seeping into her bones. Eyes lowered, she waited for the other woman to speak.

At last Peggy lifted her head, as if seeking divine inspiration. She tightened the knot in her scarf.

'So I'm a murderer, am I? Aren't you afraid to be out here with me? We're all alone. I may be an old woman, but if you're right, I'm also desperate. Anything could happen.'

She raised her alpenstock as if to reinforce the point. Her voice struck Rachel as extraordinarily steady. Or perhaps it wasn't so extraordinary. Peggy Needham was formidable.

'You won't murder me.'

'You're a very confident young woman. If you're right, and I'm a desperate killer, I might bash you on the head and then drag your limp body into the bog. You'd never be found.'

Rachel shook her head. 'Please don't attempt it. I have no wish to hurt you. As I said, I can't prove that Ormond Weaver was murdered. Let alone that you were responsible.'

'I'm curious. What makes you accuse me?'

'It starts with Nell Fagan. Originally she imagined me as a tame amateur sleuth, a useful collaborator. In her opinion, Jacob Flint hadn't fully exploited his acquaintance with me, and she thought she could do better. What she didn't realise was that Jacob has learned the hard way not to take liberties with me. She made the mistake of doing precisely that, so I threw her out. After she came to Blackstone Fell, she was torn about what to do.'

'Torn?'

'Nell was convinced that Vernon Murray's mother had been murdered at the sanatorium, but felt she couldn't handle things on her own. Involving the police was out of the question – they would take the case out of her hands, and she'd lose any chance of glory and professional redemption. She wanted my help in exposing the culprit. As she guessed, the legend surrounding the disappearances of Blackstone Lodge interested me, though I didn't find the riddle hard to solve. Two strong stories were within her grasp, concerning the sanatorium and Ormond Weaver. But she knew her life was in danger.'

'Because of the incident with the boulder?'

'Yes, although she probably thought that Ursula's killer – whoever that was, perhaps Denzil Sambrook – pushed it. Possibly she didn't realise that Weaver had recognised her, even though Judith Royle had somehow discovered her true identity.'

Peggy nodded. 'She didn't always think clearly. Seeking your assistance was a panic move.'

'Last Thursday, before she met Jacob, she had her photographs developed. On Friday morning, she went to the British Museum, and checked issues of the *Globe* and

Clarion from 1914. I believe she was looking for photographs of Ormond Weaver after his arrest, to confirm her memory of his appearance. Allowing for the passage of time, she satisfied herself that she hadn't been mistaken. The man she'd photographed in Blackstone Fell was Weaver. Perhaps she discovered that the town Weaver supposedly died in now belongs to Italy. The pieces fitted together. Harold Lejeune was an impostor. And that was the news she brought to you, wasn't it?'

'If I denied it, would you believe me?'

'No.'

'Very well. You are quite right.'

'Thank you.' Rachel paused. 'The news was a devastating blow to you. You'd always believed that Weaver didn't live to profit from his crimes, or from making a scapegoat of Nathan Hart. And then you discovered that he'd pulled off an exchange of identities and was living in peaceful seclusion up in Yorkshire.'

'He'd got away with murder,' Peggy said. 'Quite literally. He murdered poor Nathan as surely as if he put a gun to his temple and pulled the trigger.'

Rachel nodded. 'Justice had failed you. You didn't have long to live, so you decided to take matters into your own hands. Nell must have had at least an inkling that you were determined to make Weaver pay for what he had done to Nathan.'

'Perhaps.'

'You made her swear not to tell me about Weaver. She'd already arranged for Jacob to attend the séance, and you thought it would be helpful to reinforce the notion that Weaver, like Nathan, was safely in his grave. Neither of you felt it prudent to cancel the meeting with me, given the lengths she'd gone to in arranging it. Safer to tell me half a story rather than none.'

'It seemed logical,' Peggy admitted.

'Nell wasn't as good a liar as she liked to think. It was clear to me that she was hiding something, contrary to our express agreement. I was also curious about her choice of words.'

'In what way?'

'She was strangely elliptical when she talked about Harold Lejeune. For instance, she referred to "the owner of Blackstone Tower", rather than using his name. It was as if that name stuck in her gullet. Despite her best efforts, she provoked my curiosity, as well as my anger.'

'Ah, I see.'

'I doubted that Judith Royle would recognise Nell as a crime reporter. If someone tipped her off, who could it be? Someone much more worldly-wise. In other words, not her husband or the professor. The major was a possibility, Denzil Sambrook and Carrodus were more likely. As well as Harold Lejeune. Even at that early stage, the idea of Lejeune and the rector's wife conducting an intrigue crossed my mind.'

'You have a vivid imagination.'

'One of my many faults. A quick temper is another. If I'd persuaded her to tell me the whole truth instead of sending her packing, she might be alive today.'

'You shouldn't blame yourself.'

'I don't,' Rachel said flatly. 'Any more than you should. I suppose you were in a state of turmoil. Your cousin was dying, and so were you, Nell was erratic and a man you hated had suddenly come back to life.'

Peggy snorted. 'My understanding is that detectives aren't

supposed to care about things like that. Their concern is to solve a mystery.'

'People are the greatest mystery,' Rachel said. 'Ignore human nature and you solve nothing. Nell was clearly in danger. Vernon Murray's death confirmed my suspicion. I decided to find out for myself what was going on in Blackstone Fell. I sent Trueman on ahead, and he told me about the other guest at The New Jerusalem.'

'And?'

'You gave yourself away.'

'How?'

'Before I come to that, did you tell Nell you wanted to come to Yorkshire?'

'Yes. She did her best to dissuade me, but the more I thought about it, the more it seemed the right thing to do.'

'She rushed back here, but her thinking remained confused. Should she challenge Weaver? Was she at risk from the Sambrooks? She was brave, but hopelessly impulsive.'

'Nell never had a strategic mind,' Peggy said quietly.

'She was murdered in the cave before you arrived. Another death for you to avenge. I suppose you were satisfied of Weaver's guilt?'

'Although Nell wasn't sure who had tried to kill her with the boulder, I was morally certain it was him. She hadn't got close enough to discovering what was going on at the sanatorium to become a threat to Ursula Baker's murderer. Like you, I presumed Weaver was in cahoots with Judith, and that was why she knew who Nell was. Whether the woman was his mistress, or just a shoulder to cry on, I neither knew nor cared. I came here because of Weaver, nothing else.'

'When you arrived at The New Jerusalem, you told Dilys that your name was Nee. Trueman assumed that she'd misheard. I thought you'd indulged yourself in a touch of black humour.'

Peggy nodded. 'How perceptive of you.'

'Miss Nee,' Rachel said. 'A simple anagram of Nemesis.'

'Childish of me, wasn't it? And to think that by amusing myself, I committed a cardinal error.'

'There was more than that. Your report of your alleged conversation with Harold Lejeune didn't ring true.'

'No? I'm sorry you think so. I was rather pleased with myself. I thought what I said was plausible.'

'Why would he take you into his confidence? You claimed that he quickly came to regret saying too much, but he wasn't the sort who would unburden himself to a stranger in the first place. You were actually the last person who claimed to have seen him alive. The question I asked myself was – is she lying? And if so, why?'

Peggy heaved a sigh. 'What answer did you come up with?'

'You wanted to destroy Weaver. I think you deduced that he received secret messages from Judith when they arranged their trysts, so you came prepared. You brought a copy of the *Daily Mail* to Blackstone Fell. The New Jerusalem doesn't offer its guests the privilege of reading that particular newspaper, but you wanted to mimic the style of anonymous note that Judith Royle showed to Nell. You concocted a message designed to lure Weaver to Blackstone Leap.'

'That explains…'

'Why your mutilated copy of the *Mail* went missing from your room? Now it's my turn to make a confession. I asked Trueman to borrow the room key from the rack in the lobby while you were out. He had a snoop round and found the evidence we needed to corroborate my guesswork.'

Peggy closed her eyes for a moment.

'Before that, Trueman witnessed you walking down the drive to the Tower, but you had no intention of calling on Weaver, did you?'

A shrug of the shoulders. 'There's no point in pretending, is there?'

'None whatsoever. My guess is that at that point, he was already dead and you were simply giving the impression that you were unaware of the fact. I suspect you'd been there before and pushed the note under Weaver's door. Not that it matters. He was bound to be suspicious, but he'd killed Nell and must have been nervous. Sure enough, he rose to the bait and went to the ravine.'

'He wasn't entirely stupid,' Peggy said. 'He came armed with a revolver. But I'd hidden behind the rocks. I tripped him up with my alpenstock and then smashed his temple with it.'

She proffered the stick to Rachel for inspection. 'Look closely and you'll see the faint traces of dried blood. I washed most of it off, obviously, but I didn't want to clean away all the evidence. I wanted to be able to see it and remind myself of what I'd done to him. For Nathan's sake.'

Rachel examined the stick before passing it back. Peggy dug it into the soft ground and leaned on it.

'You relieved him of his revolver, I presume, and hurled it into the river. You also shoved his body into the water. He'd never have been found, but for the bad luck of the storm swelling the river and bringing his remains to the surface.'

'There's no point in wasting your time with pathetic denials,' Peggy said. 'You've discovered all my guilty secrets.'

'I'm afraid I have,' Rachel said.

'There's nothing more to be said, then.'

'Except for one thing. The true motive. The fundamental reason why Ormond Weaver had to die.'

'What do you mean?'

'You had a special reason to hate the man. He was to blame for Nathan Hart's downfall and disgrace, and his suicide while the balance of his mind was disturbed. And Nathan Hart meant a great deal to you.'

'So did Nell. So did all the children Eunice and her mother cared for.'

'There was more to it than that.'

Peggy was motionless. 'Go on.'

'Nathan Hart was your son, wasn't he? The child you had by Nell Fagan's father, the child you loved but were never able to acknowledge in public.'

The two women looked at each other. The air was still. The fog was all around, pressing in on them, a malign, smothering presence. Visibility was shrinking. They could see no more than six or seven yards.

Peggy breathed out. 'How did you find out?'

'Randolph Fagan was as popular with the ladies as he was with so many readers. No doubt he could be extremely charming when he was so inclined. You came to live in his home, an intelligent young woman, but perhaps not worldly-wise. There was a meeting of minds, which became something rather more.'

A faint smile. 'A delicate way of putting it. I was passionately in love. Randolph was the first and only man for me, but he made it clear that he could never abandon Aileen. Ailing Aileen, he used to call her, but he did care for her. She was a self-centred hypochondriac, but the irony was that he died long before she did. It was the day after I told him I was expecting his child. I have often asked myself if his heart attack was caused by… but no, that way madness lies.'

'It wasn't feasible for you to raise your son as your own?'

'My father was a vicar in a rural parish, my mother equally devout. They had strict moral standards.'

'Always a hindrance.'

'The shame of discovering that their daughter had borne a child out of wedlock would have killed them. Eunice and her mother were the only people I let into my shameful secret. They were utterly trustworthy. They agreed to bring up the baby, and I would become an honorary aunt. It was the best I could do for all concerned. As for my parents, they went to their graves ignorant of the fact that I'd slipped from the pedestal they'd put me on, and that they had a grandson.'

'To answer the question you put, the child's name pointed me to the truth.'

'Nobody else has ever made the connection.'

'Because they weren't looking for it. You shared Randolph Fagan's love of word play. His last novel was *The Mystery of Hannah Tart* and in his honour the name you gave the boy was an anagram of Hannah Tart. Nathan Hart.'

'Very astute.' She bit her lip. 'He dedicated that book: *To the love of my life*. Nobody else knew I was the one he meant. If he did have me in mind.'

'I'm sure he did.'

'That's generous of you.'

'There was also a psychological clue. You and Eunice were exceptionally devoted to Nathan. Nell Fagan regarded him as a younger brother. As indeed he was. A half-brother, at any rate. The four of you were so close, I felt there might be something more to it than the natural affection you all showed the other children Eunice looked after. When Nell told you that the man you regarded as responsible for your son's death was still alive, you decided that it wasn't enough to hand him over to the proper authorities. He had to die.'

'The proper authorities?' Peggy made a scornful noise. 'Who stood by and let Weaver escape the consequences of his crimes? I had no faith in their ability to punish him with the severity he deserved.'

'So you decided to kill him.'

'Yes,' she said. 'I suppose you think that was very wicked.'

Rachel considered the old woman. She was propping herself up with the alpenstock. She looked very sick. It was a wonder that she'd walked this far.

'In your shoes, I'd have done the same.'

A weak smile played on Peggy's lips. 'You'd have made a better job of it.'

There was a long pause.

'What do you want? Should I submit myself to... the proper authorities?'

'I've achieved what I came here to do. Today I shall go back to London. I suggest you do the same.'

'What about your friend, Mr Flint?'

'You needn't worry about him. He has enough stories to fill the *Clarion* for a month. As far as he is concerned, the rector killed Harold Lejeune in a fit of jealous rage.'

'I see.'

Rachel waited for a few moments, then extended her hand. 'Come on. We'll go back to the inn together. After that, you won't hear from me again.'

Peggy sighed. 'I've never met anyone like you, Rachel Savernake.'

'Perhaps it's just as well.'

'You like playing God, don't you?'

'I'd never be so presumptuous. It's simply that life is a mystery I long to solve.'

'Very well. At least, you step in when God is otherwise engaged. You understand my plight, and I'm grateful. But I can't accept your proposal. My late father drummed into me that actions have consequences. I've taken a man's life.'

'If we are to believe Denzil Sambrook, life is cheap.'

'Sambrook is a deluded nincompoop, we both know that. No, there is nothing left for me in London. Like you, I've done everything I came here to do.'

'Where will you go, then?'

Peggy Needham gazed into the fog. 'I think I'll go for a walk. I'm tired of following the beaten track. I shall cut across the moor.'

Rachel looked at her. 'You know that...'

'Yes, I know.'

Rachel proffered her hand. Peggy took it in a claw-like grip and held on for a few moments before letting go.

'Goodbye. I wonder what you will do in future.'

'Get into more mischief, I expect. Goodbye.'

Peggy smiled wanly and strode between the marker posts, off the path and into the moorland. Her movements were slow and uncertain. Within moments her stout shoes began to sink into the sodden, unstable ground. Undaunted, she kept moving forward.

Rachel kept watching. Presently the fog wrapped Peggy in its clammy embrace and she was lost from sight.

33

'Carrodus has hanged himself in the prison cell,' Oakes said. 'Used his own bootlaces. It was in the local lock-up. Shocking case of negligence.'

'It's for the best,' Rachel said.

They were in the living room at the back of Hawthorn Cottage, together with Jacob Flint and the Truemans. A roaring fire was keeping them warm.

'You think so?' Jacob asked. 'Doesn't it make prosecuting Thomas Baker and the rest of his clients almost impossible?'

'Carrodus and Daphne Sambrook played a dangerous game, committing murder on behalf of others. Daphne was too shrewd to expose herself to the risk of blackmail or underpayment by the people who wanted her to do their dirty work.' Rachel turned to Oakes. 'Search her files. She will have kept something in black and white from each of them that ties them to the crimes.'

'An insurance policy?' the detective asked.

'Exactly. Without it, Carrodus was at risk. If any of the bodies were ever exhumed and excessive traces of morphine or whatever else he used were found, the argument would be that he acted entirely on his own initiative, committing murder out of sheer lust for killing.'

'That was part of it. The desire for power.'

'Oh yes. But he liked money as much as Daphne did.'

'I've wired Gomersall,' Jacob said. 'He's so pleased with the scoops that he's called a halt to his crusade against spiritualism. On condition that Ottilie Curle gives us an exclusive about abandoning her work as a medium and slipping into graceful retirement. She and her husband are going to America. Starting a new life.'

'And your headline?' Rachel asked.

'*The Spirits Spoke of Murder*.' He coughed. 'I've kept your name out of it, naturally. Of course I did have to indulge in some journalistic…'

'Lies?' Trueman growled.

'Licence,' Jacob said, assuming an expression of injured dignity. 'Truth is stranger than fiction. I had to make some things up to be sure the story was believable.'

'Of course,' Rachel said.

'What about Denzil Sambrook and his father?' Martha asked.

'They face ruin,' Rachel said. 'Daphne was in charge of the family trust's finances, and she'll have made sure that the funds were channelled out of her brother's reach. So much for his fantasy about buying up Blackstone Fell and turning the village into a laboratory for his social experiments.'

'Huckerby tells me that Sambrook admires Stalin's determination to bring prosperity to the people of Russia,' Trueman said. 'Maybe he and his father will end up there.'

'They should remember their Aesop and take greater care about what they wish for.'

'I bumped into the major on my way here,' Jacob said. 'He's in a state of shock about what happened at his house last night. How Carrodus betrayed Gloria.'

'Time will be a healer.'

'In the *Clarion*, he cuts a heroic figure.'

'Rightly so. Our task would have been harder without him.'

'He won't give any other reporters the time of day.' Jacob grinned. 'His flirtation with the spirit world is dead and buried. I've encouraged Dilys to keep an eye on him.'

'She'll do better than that,' Trueman said. 'With any luck, he'll take her away from this benighted place.'

Rachel gazed out of the window. Through the gaps in the trees, she saw the moors in the distance. The fog was beginning to clear.

'I missed Peggy Needham this morning,' Jacob said. 'I wanted to say goodbye.'

'I saw her myself. She was going for a walk in the countryside.'

'In this weather? She needs to be careful. The marshland is treacherous in the fog. If she gets lost...'

'You needn't worry about her,' Rachel said. 'She is a strong-minded woman. Someone who knows exactly which path to take.'

Cluefinder

Cluefinders enjoyed a vogue during 'the Golden Age of murder' between the world wars, but the cluefinder in *Mortmain Hall* was the first to appear, so far as I know, for more than half a century. I was delighted by the response to my resurrection of this device, and so many readers asked me to create another that I found it impossible to resist the challenge of including a cluefinder to *Blackstone Fell*. Here is a selection of pointers to the solution of the various mysteries.

Nell and Weaver recognised each other

Page 11: *a long, hard stare at the pair of them. Nell felt as if she were being hypnotised*

Page 61: *I watched him lying through his teeth*

Page 69: *I never forget a face*

Page 99: *Miss Fagan requisitioned back numbers of the Globe and the Clarion from as long ago as 1914*

Weaver's imposture

Page 138: *he lay dying in Botzen*

Page 291: *he'll go back to Italy. Bolzano, where he met his wife*

Carrodus's lack of an alibi for the attacks on Vernon Murray

Page 9: *I'm late for my weekly clinic at the sanatorium and after that I've got a long drive*

The gambling connection between Carrodus and his clients

Page 83: *Baker's method of coping with distress was to squander his wife's riches on actresses and roulette*

Page 84: *outside a casino club off Leicester Square. Baker emerged arm in arm with a pretty young woman*

Page 84: *making sure that in his misery he didn't spend too much time and money at the Hermes*

Page 159: *Always the first to put his hand in his pocket when there's a flag day, or accept a bet in the saloon bar*

Page 165: *Bit of a gambler, but he has far too much sense to monkey around with his patients*

Page 217: *he'd developed a fondness for an occasional flutter at the tables*

Page 224: *Livingstone is a born gambler*

Page 262: *He seemed quite content to work as a chef in a London club*

Rachel realises the link

Page 294: *She'd gambled and won. A Eureka moment*

The murderer's alias

Page 160: *Not that Miss Nee will be your cup of tea*

Page 241: *Dilys thought she was called Miss Nee, but her full name is Margaret Needham*

The secret of Nathan Hart's name

Page 59: *Jacob studied the long line of books bearing Randolph Fagan's name. The first title was The Clue of the Cobweb, the last The Mystery of Hannah Tart*

Page 252: *Nell was like her late father, a natural storyteller. I love playing with words as much as she did*

Peggy's liaison with Randolph Fagan

Page 255: *He left a good deal of money and he was remarkably generous. So much so that even I was well provided for*

Peggy's personality and motivation

Page 252: *she never bore a grudge. I admired that about her, even though I'm very different*

The doctor's modus operandi: preying on weakness

Page 281: *Now he is losing control. The decline is gathering pace. As if someone has pushed him towards the precipice*

Page 291: *An unexpected gleam lit his eyes. 'Every time one tries to help, with the very best of intentions, one risks making matters worse. I'd hate to... precipitate a crisis.'*

Page 313: *'She didn't strike you as mentally unbalanced?'*
Carrodus gave an emphatic shake of the head. 'I'd never have allowed her to go back home if I thought so.'

The locked-room mystery

Page 15: *the only decorative touch was a carved design on the ancient wooden fireplace surround: aabaaabbaa-baaababaaaabbbb*
Page 68: *Mellor senior was a church lawyer who fell out of favour with the authorities and died when his son was fifteen. Edmund had seemed destined for the law, but after developing a yen for travel, he spent years in the Iberian Peninsula*
Page 69: *he was a hothead and a malcontent*
Page 70: *His father persuaded him to enter government service in London, and gave him an entrée into high society. He mixed with the likes of Bacon and Cecil*

Acknowledgements

I researched this novel in between lockdowns and found writing it an enjoyable exercise in escapism during the pandemic winter of 2020–21. Blackstone Fell is imaginary but real-life locations which contributed geographic inspiration were Salomons Tower in Kent, Hardcastle Crags and Bolton Strid in Yorkshire, and Kinver Edge in Staffordshire.

This is a work of fiction, with invented characters and incidents, but however extraordinary the events of the story, I try to imbue them with a touch of believability. Since I often write about subjects outside my personal knowledge, I'm indebted to the many people who help me with research, sharing their expertise with considerable generosity. In this case, I'd like to express particular gratitude to Richard Barnett (cars), Mauro Boncampagni (Bolzano), Johnny Homer (London pubs), Sylvia Kent (female journalists), Giles Ramsay (the Gunpowder Plot and *Macbeth*), Andrew Shanks (the clergy), John Wade of *Amateur Photographer* (cameras and photography), and Liz Waight (records of deaths).

Among the many articles and books I consulted on a wide range of subjects including spiritualism and eugenics, I found particular value in Hilary Mantel's 'The Dead Are All Around Us' (*London Review of Books*, 10 May 2001) and Jonathan Freedland's 'Eugenics and the Master Race of the Left' (*Guardian*, 30 August 1997) and 'Eugenics: the Skeleton that Rattles Loudest in the Left's Closet' (*Guardian*, 17 February 2012).

I'm also grateful to my family for their continuing support, my agent James Wills, my various publishers, and of course all the readers whose expressions of enthusiasm for the Rachel Savernake mysteries are such a wonderful boost to morale.

Martin Edwards
www.martinedwardsbooks.com

About the Author

Martin Edwards has won the Edgar, Agatha, H.R.F. Keating, Macavity, Poirot and Dagger awards as well as being shortlisted for the Theakston's Prize. He is President of the Detection Club, a former Chair of the Crime Writers' Association and consultant to the British Library's bestselling crime classics series. In 2020 he was awarded the Diamond Dagger for his outstanding contribution to crime fiction. Follow Martin on Twitter and Instagram (@medwardsbooks) and Facebook (@MartinEdwardsBooks).

Rachel Savernake will return in...

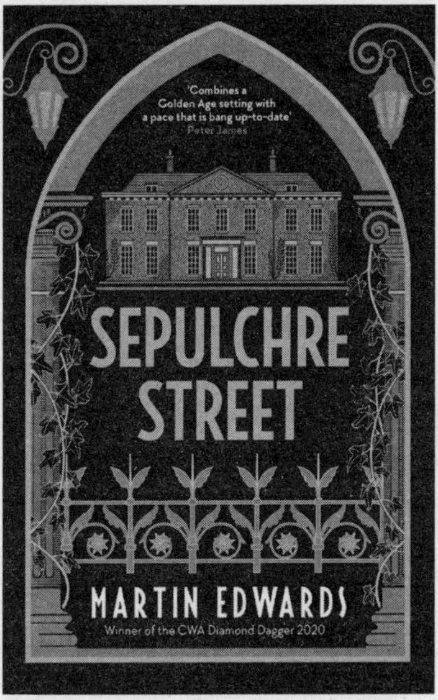

'Combines a Golden Age setting with a pace that is bang up-to-date'
Peter James
SEPULCHRE STREET
MARTIN EDWARDS
Winner of the CWA Diamond Dagger 2020

'This is my challenge for you, Rachel,'
the woman in white said.
'I want you to solve my murder.'

At renowned artist Damaris Gethin's latest exhibition, she takes to the stage set with a guillotine, the lights go out – and she executes herself.

The question is: why?

There are many clues to find for those daring enough to look...

COMING MAY 2023